# THE FIRST DIGGER BURST THROUGH THE TUNNEL WALL. . . .

A child-sized mole with four powerful limbs attacked immediately and with savage fury.

Snarling and baring his teeth, Beowulf braced himself for the digger's attack. It uncurled with amazing rapidity and hurled itself at the big scout dog. Ray brought his rifle to bear on the two, but Beowulf was too close to his attacker for him to fire. Barking loudly, Beowulf feinted and dodged the digger's claws.

Ray pressed the firing stud. The digger was flung sideways by the force of the charge. It hit the floor of the tunnel and shivered. The smell of charred flesh in his nostrils, Ray fired into the creature's midsection.

"Stay away from that damn thing, Beowulf," he commanded. "I'm not convinced it's dead."

It wasn't. . . .

*Ace Books by Kenneth Von Gunden*

STARSPAWN

The K-9 Corps Series

K-9 CORPS
K-9 CORPS: UNDER FIRE

K-9 CORPS: CRY WOLF
*(Coming in February)*

# K-9 CORPS
## UNDER FIRE

# KENNETH VON GUNDEN

ACE BOOKS, NEW YORK

This book is an Ace original edition,
and has never been previously published.

K-9 CORPS: UNDER FIRE

An Ace Book / published by arrangement with
the author

PRINTING HISTORY
Ace edition / August 1991

All rights reserved.
Copyright © 1991 by Kenneth Von Gunden.
Cover art by Jim Thiesen.
This book may not be reproduced in whole or in part,
by mimeograph or any other means, without permission.
For information address: The Berkley Publishing Group,
200 Madison Avenue, New York, New York 10016.

ISBN: 0-441-42494-5

Ace Books are published by The Berkley Publishing Group,
200 Madison Avenue, New York, New York 10016.
The name "ACE" and the "A" logo
are trademarks belonging to Charter Communications, Inc.

PRINTED IN THE UNITED STATES OF AMERICA

10 9 8 7 6 5 4 3 2 1

*This novel is for Donna—
cherished wife and partner, first reader,
and demanding wielder of a red pencil!*

Like all writers' spouses, she deserves much, much more than this meager acknowledgement because, if there's anything harder than being a writer, it's living with one.

# 1

When he first heard the ruckus, the snarling and barking, Ray Larkin thought that something had attacked the dogs. With a sinking feeling in the pit of his stomach, he soon realized the truth. His scout dogs—or, at least, two of them—were fighting again.

*Goddamnit all to hell*! he cursed.

"C'mon now, guys, break it up!" he shouted, rushing to separate the two combatants. As he had suspected, it was Maximilian again challenging Beowulf's supremacy as the leader of the pack. Both dogs were putting on elaborate displays of their impressive teeth and jaws as he pushed them apart.

"This is getting old real fast," Ray said, realizing the futility of his words even as he spoke them. The dogs were just being dogs. Maximilian was not nearly as big as Beowulf, but he was extremely smart, perhaps the most intelligent dog Ray had ever known. Max's intelligence and innate aggressiveness made him a natural leader; his youth and hormones also compelled him to constantly challenge the "alpha wolf," or leader of the pack. And Beowulf was the alpha wolf.

"Sorry, Ray," Beowulf said, "but this young whelp don't know his place."

"Maybe he does, Beowulf, maybe he does."

"Huh? What you mean, Ray?"

"Max just wasn't born to be a follower," Ray said.

Unsure what Ray was implying, Maximilian felt shame for disrupting the unity of the team again. "No, Ray, Beowulf is right. I not behaving myself."

"You think Max should be the leader?" Beowulf queried, uncertainty revealing itself in his basso profundo voice.

"Not *the* leader, Beowulf, but *a* leader."

"Huh?" said both Beowulf and Maximilian in unison.

"Max ought to be leading his own team and using his natural instincts as he was bred to do," Ray said. "He'll make a great chief." He grinned. "He better—because he's a lousy Indian."

Johnny Skerchock's head and shoulders materialized in the air in front of Ray. "Yeah, what is it?" he asked wearily, not even looking up at the holo projection floating in front of him at his end of the connection.

"Hello, Johnny," Ray said, speaking to his friend on the other side of the planet, on the other side of Talos.

"Well kiss my raggedy old butt, if it ain't Mighty Mite," Skerchock said, brightening. "How the hell are you doing, Larkin?"

"Larkin?" Ray asked dubiously. "Larkin? This is what you call the guy you shared more than one cell with, feeding the porcelain euphemism until there was nothing left to bring up?"

"Yeah, and whose fault was that . . . Ray?"

"I can't help it if my sparkling personality just happens to rub some people the wrong way."

"It was your fists that rubbed them the wrong way!" roared Skerchock.

"A mere bag o' shells," Ray scoffed.

"So what are you calling me up about?" asked Skerchock. "Not that you need a reason for my sake."

"How are you doing?" Ray asked, his manner suddenly very serious and concerned.

Skerchock's smile faded and even though he was just a holographic image floating in the air in front of him, Ray could see the pain and hurt in his friend's eyes. "Not too bad, considering." He laughed mirthlessly and rubbed his eyes with his hand. "Not too bad . . . who am I kidding? I'm doing crappy, Ray, crappy."

"I know," Ray said. "And I know how you feel, at least a little of how you feel."

"You lost two, is that right?"

"Yeah," Ray said. "Anson and Pandora. But not at the same time."

"Five, Ray. Five dogs all at once." He ticked them off the fingers of one hand. "Bernie, Harry, Ginny, Samantha, and Ishmael. All in one godawful explosion."

"You still have four left?"

"They're still puppies, Ray," Skerchock said. "They're not full-grown dogs. Not only are five of my closest friends dead, I no longer have a viable team."

"That's the real reason why I called you," Ray ventured. "What would you say to building a new team around a couple of young adults, including a new leader?"

A range of bewildered expressions passed over Skerchock's face as he digested Ray's words. "You're talking about your team?"

Ray nodded. "I'm having rivalry problems; my team's too large to work efficiently. And the situation's not fair to Beowulf, my leader, or to his challenger, Maximilian."

"Maximilian?"

"Yeah, he's a great dog, born to Mama-san out of Anson. And the three females in his litter have agreed to follow him: Clementine, Emma, and Telzey."

"Four new dogs," Skerchock said slowly, turning the idea over in his mind. "I don't know. They won't be dogs that picked me and vice versa."

"Of course they will," Ray pointed out. "You have to say yes to them, but they have to say yes to you as well before I allow them to leave."

"When can I meet them?"

"How soon can you catch a suborbital flight over here, Johnny?"

Ray and the dogs gathered in the shade of a huge red rock to have a special meeting.

"This man be comin' here soon, hah?" Mama-san asked.

"Yes," Ray said, "very soon."

"My puppies be goin' away forever."

Ray went over and held Mama-san's big head in his hands. He tilted her head up so she could look him in the eyes. "Mama-san, you always knew this day could come. Your puppies aren't puppies any longer. They're all grown up now and one of them has what it takes to be a leader. Mama-san," he emphasized,

"Maximilian will never get that chance if he stays with us; he deserves to make the most of his talent. And the others will have a better life, too."

"I know, Ray, I know," Mama-san said. "But it still hard."

"That's because you had an advantage your mother never had," Ray told her. "You watched your puppies grow up; you were taken away from your mother while you were still a little ball of fur."

"Maybe that the best way, after all," Mama-san said. "At least my heart not be breaking."

The other dogs crowded around Mama-san, licking and nudging her with obvious affection. "Please don't be sad, Mama-san," implored Grendel. "We be with you."

"Yah," agreed Frodo and Littlejohn. "We always be a team."

"Not all your puppies leavin' you," said Tajil, giving Mama-san a swipe with his big pink tongue.

That was true. Ray had told Skerchock that Maximilian and his three sisters were willing to form a new team with a new Man. Both Tajil and Gawain, for their individual reasons, were content to remain with Ray and Beowulf. Tajil had a very special bond with Ray. And, despite his enormous size, Tajil was not especially aggressive; he had no qualms about accepting Beowulf's primacy as leader. Gawain, for his part, was both loyal and more than a little slow. His thickheadedness made him unsure of the world. Gawain needed special understanding and a strong, loving hand. Neither dog had any desire to be anything more than an integral member of the team; they were content to allow Beowulf to have mastery over them.

All four dogs, feeling anguish and doubt over their proposed secession from their extended family, crowded around Ray, acting like the puppies they were not so long ago, eager for his touch, for a word of encouragement and affection from their Man.

"Oh, Ray, I not sure if'n I doin' right," whined Maximilian nervously.

"It'll be okay, you'll see." Ray scratched Max's ear.

"Maybe this Johnny guy not want us," Emma said.

"That's a possibility," Ray admitted. "And maybe you won't want to go with him, either. It's a marriage; you both have to say yes."

Feeling like an intruder, Ake joined the group. "Ray, your friend is here."

Ray took a deep breath. "Okay, Ake. Tell Johnny we'll be there in a few minutes."

Ray hugged each of the four in turn and then allowed them to overwhelm him with their rough display of love and respect. They all but knocked Ray to the ground by putting their paws on his shoulders to get closer to him.

"Okay, it's time we got started. The rest of you stay here," he commanded. "Beowulf, keep everyone back. Max and the others have to meet Johnny alone."

John Skerchock was pacing nervously by the hover vehicle that had brought him from the landing area. When he saw Ray and the four dogs approaching, he stopped and ran his fingers through his hair as if he was about to meet his date for the evening.

Motioning for the dogs to stay put for the time being, Ray embraced his old friend. "Good to see you, Johnny."

"It's good to see you, Ray."

"As you can see, I brought a couple of dogs to meet you."

"Yes. Why don't you introduce them to me?"

"Guys, come over here." When the dogs joined them, Ray said, "John, I would like you to meet Maximilian, Telzey, Emma, and Clementine."

"'Lo," the dogs chorused.

"Dogs, this is John Skerchock, the man I'm hoping might be your new leader."

"Hello, Maximilian. Hello, Telzey, Emma, and Clementine," he said formally.

"I'll leave you five alone for a little while," Ray said, turning to walk away.

As he looked back, the four dogs were tentatively working their way closer to Skerchock, surrounding him. Ray could hear their gravelly voices. He turned back, his eyes on the horizon.

There was a lump in his throat and he felt a tear run down his cheek.

"Goodbye, guys," he said softly. "Goodbye."

## II

As they waited for the shuttle craft, anxious to leave Talos behind, Ray juggled three small red balls. Ake tried not to pay attention to Ray's time-killing, but he was helpless to prevent his eyes from being drawn time and time again to the brightly colored orbs as they rose and fell in an almost hypnotic rhythm. Suddenly his hand shot out and he snatched first one and then a second of the flying balls from the air.

"Hey!" protested Ray.

"Thanks, Ake," said Littlejohn.

"You can't just grab a guy's balls . . ." Ray blurted out loudly. He stopped when everyone in the small terminal turned to stare at him.

"Grab balls," hooted Frodo. "That funny!"

Even Ray, despite himself, laughed. "Well, it isn't right, is it?"

"What's not 'right' is you making us all nuts with that routine," chided Ake. He pointed a warning finger at Ray and added, "And don't start cracking your knuckles, either!"

"Ha!" cackled Ozma. "Ake got your number even more than a wife."

"Yeah, well—"

"The shuttle to the *F.S.S. Truman* is now loading at gate number nine," a well-modulated voice announced. "To repeat: the shuttle to the *F.S.S. Truman* is now loading at gate number nine. Please have your boarding passes ready. Thank you."

"You welcome," said Tajil, rising from his position on the floor. People all around gaped as the big dogs of the scout team scrambled to their feet and gathered around their leader, Ray.

Ray looked at their faces, eager to begin this first leg of their journey toward a new assignment. He never tired of seeing the canine grins they wore when they were happy. It was a fresh start; one that would help them to get over the aching emptiness they all felt over the absence of Maximilian and the others.

"Well, guys, here goes nothing."

"Ouch," said Ake. "Don't say that."

"It's true, isn't it?" Ray said. "We're taking a leap into the dark; we don't have a thing lined up."

"Ah, Ray," insisted Ozma as Grendel helped her to groom her shiny black-and-white coat, "a first-rate dog team always gots work if it wants it."

"Sure," Ray agreed. "And if they turn it down, maybe we'll get a chance to bid on it."

At that, the big dogs all howled and good-naturedly butted Ray with their heads. The rest of the crowd in the terminal parted to allow this unpredictable group to make its way toward the waiting shuttle. "I sincerely hope we don't have to be seated near them," one woman whispered to her companion.

Hearing her remark with his canine-sharp ears, Frodo turned

and gave her a big wink. Then he smiled a crooked dog smile and trotted off after the others.

★ ★ ★

The *Truman*'s first port of call after Talos was Brigham, the Mormon planet. "They're nice folks," Ray said to Beowulf as he jogged down one of the starship's many exercise tubes with Ake and the dogs, their feet kicking up dust from the artificial soil. The tube circled the ship, with one complete circumnavigation equaling thirty kilometers. "But I don't think that's the planet for us."

"You an' Ake could each have six wives if'n you wanted 'em," Beowulf teased.

"No, thanks," Ray said. "The next port after Brigham is Hephaestus, a volcano planet. And the two planetfalls after that are New Moscow and Poseidon. With those three to choose from, we're talking real possibilities."

"Hay-fess-tus . . ." mouthed Mama-san as she ran comfortably alongside Ray. "What does Hay-fess-tus mean?"

Ray pulled on his ear. "Hephaestus was the Greek god of fire and metalworking. Kind of like the Norse god Vulcan."

"It's probably a very pleasant place," panted Ake as he tried to keep up with everyone else. "A regular paradise."

"There be jobs there?" Tajil asked.

Ray shrugged. "That I don't know." He glanced over at Ake and then back at Tajil. "But there *are* several employment agents on board the ship hiring for some of the planets we'll be visiting. If nothing works out, we have passage all the way back to Terra. But what I'm hoping is that one of these agents will offer to recruit us for a job on one of the new worlds out here in this part of the galaxy—and the likeliest candidate is Hephaestus."

"You think so?"

"Don't you? You been giving this some thought."

"Yeah, you're right," Ringgren agreed. "Nasty, brutish places can always use a good scout team. If not Hephaestus or one of the other two, there are still more new worlds waiting."

"Why don't you set up a meeting with an agent?" Ray suggested. "If he or she doesn't have anything for us, we can go on to the next one."

"Right," said Ake, as he began to drop back and to search for an exit hatch.

"I didn't mean right this minute."

"No time like the present." Ake said. "Besides, I'm a doctor—who better to know about the dangers of overexercising?"

The dogs just hooted at that.

Built in space by mainly robotic work crews, starships were huge, awkward-looking assemblages. Since they never got closer than several thousand kilometers to a planet's atmosphere, they could be as immense and unaerodynamic as their designers cared to make them. As a consequence, if you had the money, you could indulge yourself by booking a suite the size of a luxury apartment. Since they were a large contingent, and Ray felt that money was for spending, the team occupied a double suite that had all the comforts of home—if home was a palace. When Ray had dissolved his triple marriage to Mary and Taylor, their partnership had also been dissolved; as a result, Mary and Taylor's resulting buyout of his third of the "corporation" had given him more money than he'd ever had in his life. Ray invested most of it, but some of it he earmarked as "play" money. Hence, the suite.

The dogs' two favorite things were the sonic shower and the "room service" meals delivered by a little round robot on treads. When the robot arrived, one simply lifted off its semicircular top to reveal the hot food inside. Frodo and Ozma, notable chow hounds, were constantly after Ray to order snacks, despite his dislike for their penchant for eating between meals.

"This nice after that plascrete shack on Talos, huh, Ray?" queried Ozma.

"This would be nice after almost anything," Ray said.

"Aw, too soft," protested Littlejohn. "Peoples and dogs doan need all this. Give me fresh air any day."

"Like on Chiron?" Ray said.

"Yeah," Beowulf said. "That was good time." He appeared to think briefly about something and then added, " 'Cept for Pandora and Anson."

"Their dying seems so long ago . . . and just like yesterday, too," Mama-san said.

"I wonder how Runner and them Centaurs is doin'," said Gawain.

"I think they're doing fine," Ray replied. "It's the rest of the Federation I'm worried about." He rubbed his eyes and then pulled his hand down his face, his previous mood shattered by these troubling thoughts. "There are peculiar things going on back on Terra, I understand. Things involving the Judge Advocate."

"That is the machine Man?" asked Beowulf.

Ray laughed. "'The machine Man' . . . I like that. Yeah, that's the world computer that runs things. It's up to the Prime Programmers to guard access to the Judge Advocate and to maintain the fail-safe mechanisms that guarantee its incorruptibility."

Ray shook his head as if dismayed by his own innocence. "Incorruptibility, my ass! I think the Programmers have been infiltrated, seduced, or simply betrayed in some way. The Judge Advocate is turning a blind—or blinded—eye, metaphorically speaking, to too many improprieties these days for there not to be something fishy going on."

Ray shrugged. "*That's* why I think Ake is going to nail down a job on Hephaestus for us. A volcanic planet produces a rich stew of minerals, and the corporations that control most of the galaxy's wealth want to dip their buckets into the lava flows and come up with big profits."

"Money again," said Frodo.

"Yes, money again," agreed Ray.

"Just bits of plastic!" snorted Frodo. It came out as "blastic."

"Oh, no," corrected Ray. "It's more than that—it's power."

## III

Ray didn't know how many bars there were on the *Truman*—dozens, probably, he thought—but there were only two or three that were frequented by spacers and rougher elements. "Hymie's" was one of the chosen few and a plethora of the nastiest-looking squareheads Ray had ever seen made it their favorite watering hole.

"I want my mommy!" said Ake as they slid into a booth near the rear of the bar, with Beowulf taking up a position on the floor near Ray.

"I *have* been in nicer joints," agreed Ray. Feeling his own wrist, he asked Ake, "Did you remember to wear your needle gun?"

"You bet your ass I did!"

"Kenna getcha somethin'?" asked a mechanical, a servibot, appearing out of the blue haze as if it had followed a rescue beacon to their table. The servibot was configured to look like an old-fashioned waitress.

"A white wine, please," said Ake. The servibot looked at him curiously but said nothing.

"I'll have a Beefeater martini, very dry, on the rocks with olives," said Ray. Glancing at Beowulf's eager face, he asked, "Can I order something for my dog?"

The servibot tilted "her" head to point at a large, fur-covered patron at a nearby booth. "We don't discriminate," it said to Ray. "So what'll it be?" it asked the big dog.

"A bitcher of Old Yeller Ale," Beowulf replied. "Can ya bring it in a large bowl?"

"He has problems saying 'P,'" Ray explained.

The servibot just nodded and said, "Honey, you can have it in a glass slipper as far I'm concerned."

"Speaking of women . . ." Ray said slowly.

"Yes?"

"We've got just a week or ten days until we hit Hephaestus. If—that's a big 'if,' I know—if we end up getting a job there that means I have only a week or so to 'walk the dog.'"

"Huh?" said Beowulf.

"A dazzler like yourself," said Ake, ignoring Beowulf's puzzlement, "should have no trouble in that department."

"Oh," said Beowulf, catching on. "Sexing."

"I've always depended upon the kindness of strangers."

"That or pity," joked Ake.

"The drinks!" Beowulf said happily as their pseudo-waitress returned with their order.

As Ray ordered a second round, his eyes fell on a squat, rounded man with a shaved skull who entered the bar and swept the room with his eyes. "Let me guess," he said to Ake. "That's our man."

"You got it. His name's Winston."

"Winston? Winston what?"

"Just Winston," replied Ake, waving to the agent when he looked their way. A big smile on his face, Ake muttered to Ray through clenched teeth, "Be nice for a change."

"Good day, gentlemen," said the barrel-shaped agent as he pulled up an empty chair to sit across the bar table from Ray and Ake. Ray eyed him carefully. He looked like a flesh-colored sack overfilled with potatoes.

Winston glanced at Beowulf with interest. "Must that . . . that animal be here?" Beowulf, studiously ignoring him, swiped a pink tongue the size of a throw rug across his muzzle to make sure he didn't miss a drop of beer.

"Yes, he must," said Ray.

The man shrugged and said, "If the bar allows such things, it is of no consequence to me." He leaned forward expectantly. "You have come to talk business?"

"Maybe," said Ake. "Have you?"

The man spread his hands and smiled. "I am prepared to discuss several possible arrangements."

"Good," said Ray. "Let's get to it."

The rotund little man smiled even broader. "Excellent. As you know, we will soon be reaching the fire planet of Hephaestus. Hephaestus is no one's idea of a vacation destination." Here he revealed gleaming white teeth. "But that is of no account. As a young, volcanic planet Hephaestus is a cornucopia of mineral riches, and that makes it attractive in anyone's eyes." Ray softly whistled to himself. *Cornucopia*, he thought. *Old Winston has been increasing his word power. I wouldn't have thought he'd know a word not to be found in the holofunnies.*

Ake frowned. "Isn't that where that new gem is coming from? The one that is, for all intents and purposes, identical in atomic structure with Rostoff rubies?"

The squat man nodded. "Yes."

"What is Rostoff rue-bees?" asked Beowulf.

Ignoring the bald agent's hostile glance at the big scout dog (*He's going to pay us extra for that*, Ray thought), Ray said, "They're not really Terran rubies, of course. They're gemstones which amplify psi energies and make hyperspace jumps safer because of the increased abilities the stones give 'scrapers, the men and women who clean the hulls of ships transiting hyperspace. A single one-carat stone can easily go for a hundred thousand credits. Until their discovery on Hephaestus, they could only be found on a single planet near the galactic rim."

"If we can get back to business," said the bald man somewhat testily.

"Got a hot date waiting?" Ray asked.

With a "Please shut up" glance at Ray, Ake smoothly said, "Yes, business. Just what sort of assignment are you offering?"

"The rubies have to be mined, of course," said the bald man, "and they're so fragile and valuable that machines are out of the question—the work must be done by humans."

"Miners?"

"Yes. Prisoners, actually. Extremely hardcore cases—men and women found guilty of committing the most horrendous crimes against humanity."

"I can see where such perfidy would trouble such a fine, upstanding citizen of the Federation like yourself," Ray said dryly.

Ignoring his partner's sarcasm, Ake asked, "So our job is to guard the miners while they work? The prisoners, that is?"

"Yes and no. You must guard them, I suppose—that's why a dog team is needed—but your primary mission is to protect them."

"From what?"

"Hephaestus is home to numerous alien lifeforms. The one that directly concerns the mining operations is a form of vaguely molelike predators called "diggers." They have an annoying propensity for bursting from the walls of the mines to harass and attack the miners with their powerful claws. They are vicious and mindless, but they can easily be handled by scout teams."

"I see," said Ake. "And how long is the contract for?"

"There is a one-Terran-year minimum. The contract is open-ended but it may be terminated at any time after the first year by either party."

"And our employers are the mining companies?"

"Yes, but you will of course also be working indirectly for the Federation itself, since the miners are prisoners."

"Wonderful," said Ray.

"That arrangement does not suit you?" asked the agent.

"It suits us . . . if the money is right," Ake responded when Ray remained silent. "Why don't you put a figure on the table?"

After a moment's hesitation, the corpulent agent pulled a piece of paper from inside his jacket and placed it in front of Ray and Ake. Ray glanced at the figure written on it, looked at Ake, and raised an eyebrow. *Not bad*, he told himself. *But not as much as it might be*.

"Yes, this seems quite generous," Ake said to the agent, who beamed a wide smile. "Unfortunately, we have substantial overhead costs and require more." As the smile faded from the agent's face, Ake added, "The additional money is also for all the stuff you're *not* telling us."

"But that's the best I can do!" sputtered the agent.

"Of course it is," said Ake as if he were speaking to a small, slow child. "Now why don't you pull out that second piece of paper in your coat and we'll discuss the figure on *it*." He thought for a second and then added, "Better yet, go directly to the third paper—no point in endless bargaining."

"And what if I have no second or third offer?"

"Then you *might* get lucky and sign up another team for this assignment at that price," said Ake. "Of course, we're almost to Hephaestus, and with a second-rate team that works for second-rate money you'll be getting what you pay for."

"Heh, heh," chuckled Beowulf so softly that only Ray heard him.

The agent reached out, picked up the piece of paper lying on the bar table and stuffed it into his coat pocket. He began to pull out another piece of paper, thought better of it, and stuffed it back into his pocket. Then he pulled out a third piece of paper, unfolded it, and laid it face down on the table.

Ake picked it up as if picking up a hand of cards. He turned it over and, without looking at it himself, peered at Ray. Ray glanced at the figures on the paper for a moment, then looked at Ake and nodded.

"You've got a deal," Ake said, "provided all the dozens of ancillary details can be satisfactorily worked out. I should think we'd be to the point of signing the retinal contracts within forty-eight hours."

The fireplug-shaped agent looked at them with increased respect. "What was your previous posting, before Talos, if I may ask?"

Ray rubbed Beowulf's shaggy head. "Chiron."

"Chiron?" the agent gasped. "Then you are the ones who brought down the General!"

Sagging back in his chair, which snuggled up against him, the agent volunteered, "You know, not all the prisoners on Hephaestus are common—or uncommon—criminals. There are some political prisoners as well."

"Yes . . . ?" queried Ake.

"Make sure you do only what is detailed in your contract—there are many Federation officials who might wish to see that you stay on Hephaestus permanently."

Beowulf bared his teeth warningly.

"Another thing," the agent said, looking at Beowulf. "You'll be working with a scout cat team."

# 2

What saved Ray's life, he later realized, was the fact that Tajil was a terrible snorer. Not only that, but the big red dog often had pursuit dreams: He would suddenly yelp and his legs would kick spastically as he chased rabbits, antelope, or other prey through his dreams, always just a step or two behind them but never gaining.

Tajil snorted loudly and Ray, who'd been sliding into sleep, turned over and floated back up toward full consciousness. As he opened one eye, something flashed in the semidark, semilighted bedroom of the young woman he'd bedded.

It was a knife.

"Jesus H. Christ!" Ray shouted, twisting away from the quiver blade's downward arc. The knife sliced diagonally down the width of his bare back, its vibrating blade penetrating perhaps eight-tenths of a centimeter—enough to draw a scarlet line in his white flesh, but not enough to do serious harm.

As Ray tumbled from the null-grav mattress, Tajil, now fully awake, acted swiftly and almost totally instinctively. Leaping up from his resting place at the foot of the bed, the big dog instantly closed the space between himself and the attacker intent upon harming his Man.

"No!" screamed the woman as she whirled to meet Tajil's charge. She flung up her arms in a vain attempt to ward off the dog's single-minded response to her assault upon Ray; it was a pathetically inadequate reaction.

"No, Taddy!" shouted Ray as well, but it was too late. Even before the words had left Ray's mouth, Tajil had torn open the young woman's throat. She collapsed on the floor, blood streaming from her neck.

For a long, terrible second, dog and man stood staring at each other, the breath rasping in and out of their throats as the horror of the scene enveloped them. Hiding the revulsion he felt when he looked at the ruined body of the young woman he'd so recently made love to, Ray stared at Tajil with both pity and gratitude in his eyes. Taddy had saved his life, but at a cost: The psychological damage caused by the killing, necessary as it may have been, would have to be undone by counseling.

Actually, Ray realized, it was he himself who would bear the brunt of any "psychological damage." Since the dissolution of his triple marriage to Mary and Taylor, he'd only fitfully been involved with other women. This temporary union, as hasty and as apparently physically oriented as it might have appeared on the surface to a disinterested onlooker, had meant a lot to Ray. It meant warmth, the sharing of intimacy, and the sort of sexual *frisson* that a man experiences with any woman, even one he has never slept with. The companionship Ray shared with the dogs and Ake, and it was considerable, was something completely different.

"Karen." He said her name aloud and was surprised to discover that doing so caused something inside of him, something very fragile, to snap. He began to cry. The tears weren't just for Karen or for himself; they were for Mary and Taylor.

"Ray . . . ?"

"Come here, Taddy," he ordered.

He wrapped his arms around Taddy's barrel chest, burying his face in the big dog's neck. Ray pulled back and looked Taddy square in the face. "Thank you, Taddy. You did what you had to do." He coughed self-consciously, almost apologetically, and added, "My tears are really about something else. They're nothing to do with you." He scratched Taddy behind an ear. "You saved my life, big guy. Thank you."

"I took a life, Ray."

"Yes, you did."

"But I saved your life."

"Yes."

Sometime later, Ray sat staring vacantly at the unbroken white line delineating the spot where the slain woman had lain, the outline of her body mute testimony to her violent end. "We're still transmitting and receiving information through the subspace channels," Carlos Vargas, the starship's security chief, told Ray, "but it appears more and more likely that you were the intended victim of an assassination attempt."

Ray looked up, pain and sorrow radiating from his eyes. It took a moment for the man's words to penetrate the shroud of sadness and despair that enveloped him. Ake, who was standing by his friend both figuratively and literally, slowly said, "An assassination attempt?"

"In addition to the information we have been able to uncover concerning this young woman," Vargas said, pausing to add parenthetically, "her name, by the way, was Marruth Cindar—we also found this in her purse." He held out a small holopix.

"What is it?" Ray asked.

"Here. Take a look."

Ray took the holo from Vargas. "It's me."

"Yes," the security chief said. "She also deposited ten thousand credits in the ship's bank." He stared down at the seated Ray. "Marruth Cindar . . . was that the name she used?"

"No," Ray said. "She called herself Karen."

"Karen . . . ?"

"We didn't get to last names," Ray said. "At least not to hers."

"Any idea why a paid assassin would be after you, Citizen Larkin?"

"I . . . ah . . ." Ray glanced at Ake, who almost imperceptibly shook his head in warning. "No, not really," he finished.

Vargas fingered his small pencil mustache, having observed Ake's gesture. "I see. Well, you'd better be careful from now on."

"Yes," agreed Ray.

"I understand you are leaving the ship at Hephaestus?"

"That's correct."

"Good. See that you do."

After he left the two of them alone, Ake said, "It seems Winston was right. There are a lot of people who would like to see you dead for what you did on Chiron, for bringing down the General and embarrassing the Cadre."

Ray thought about that and realized it was true. "And their reach even extends out here."

Ake smiled grimly. "I should think that there are more people who would like to stick a quiver blade between your ribs out here than back on Terra." When Ray raised an eyebrow, he continued,

"Colonizing Chiron would have meant a lot of jobs, a lot of government money with the promise of enough pork to make an awful lot of folks rich. And then along comes a busybody anthropologist named Ray Larkin to piss on everybody's potato patch."

"I guess you're right."

"You know I'm right," Ake said.

★ ★ ★

"How Taddy doin'?" Grendel asked Littlejohn.

"Not bad, considerin'," Littlejohn replied.

"Considerin'?"

"Considerin' what he done," the big male said. "He killed a human woman. That a hard thing to get over."

"It not help that we be goin' down to the new job in three days," said Ozma. "Taddy could use more time to get better in his head."

"What that woman, the doctor, tell him?" Grendel queried.

"Doan know," Littlejohn said. "Taddy not talkin'."

"We can help him more," said Ozma. "We can stop mopin' 'bout him killin' a human and praise him more for savin' life of our Man."

"Ozma right," said Littlejohn. "Taddy is a hero; let's make sure we tell him that more."

Ray also made it a point to tell Taddy that he was a hero. Twice a day he took the big red dog for an hour-long sojourn in the immense environmental chamber that occupied a whole ship's deck. The two of them walked through computer-generated holos which mimicked their birth planets with astonishing fidelity. In the early morning they walked Ray's native Terra, across fields and meadows eerily similar to those he'd roamed with Taddy's predecessor—the first Tajil, Ray's boyhood pet. The afternoon stroll was across the plains of Chiron, where Tajil had been born and where he had lived his entire life before the assignment which took them to Talos.

"Will Tajil be all right?" Ake asked Ray. "He must be in a terrible state."

"Taddy *is* in a terrible mental state, that's true," Ray said. "But dogs are not all *that* conditioned against violence against humans as is popularly supposed."

"What are you talking about?" Ake asked, not quite believing

Ray's words. The sanction against the dogs committing violence against humans was one of the foundations of their use and acceptance in human society. The thought of huge, intelligent, genetically mutated dogs walking crowded city streets was palatable only if the public knew and understood that they were essentially incapable of harming human beings. A scout dog could kill a person in seconds.

"Think about it," Ray said. "Dogs are used in a lot of situations where they might have to injure or kill human beings. Hell, just look around at all the uses scout dog teams are put to and you'll realize that they have to have the ability to respond quickly and violently. They *have* to be able to defend themselves and their human leader."

"But then why—"

"Ake, do you think people would be as accepting of dogs all around them if they knew this conditioned bias against violence to humans was more window dressing than reality?"

"But you *are* spending a small fortune renting the environmental chamber to help reassure Taddy . . . why would you do that if he doesn't need the counseling?"

"I never said he doesn't need the counseling," Ray said. "Taddy *is* upset that he's had to kill a human. Besides," he added, "the dogs believe that 'deep conditioning' story even more than the average Joe does. You've been with us long enough to know how trusting and childlike they are. Since they believe themselves conditioned against harming humans, the idea that they aren't never crosses their minds. At the same time, since there really is no actual conditioning, it doesn't get in the way of what they have to do when the situation warrants it—like the assassination attempt on me."

"Sonofabitch!"

Ray grinned and put out a hand, patting Ake on the knee. "As long as I'm being frank, I have to tell you: There's no Santa Claus, either."

# II

When the klaxon's blare announced the imminency of their final hyperspace jump, the one that would bring them within a few million kilometers of Hephaestus, Ake gulped and sank back into his couch.

"You really hate this, don't you?" Ray asked, observing Ake's agitated state.

"Yeah," conceded Ake. "It's my second least favorite thing in the universe."

"What's number one, then?"

"My least favorite thing is itself coming up and at me all too quickly: the shuttle craft journey down to the surface of Hephaestus."

"Oh, no," argued Tajil, much of his good humor restored. "Shuttle rides is fun!"

"You dogs think *everything* is fun," Ake said.

"Everything *is* fun," insisted Ozma.

"What's fun about a hyperspace jump?" interrogated Ake. He didn't really want to talk about the subject, but he found that, paradoxically, discussing it took his mind off it. Or, at least, took his active and pessimistic imagination out of the equation.

"Oohh," sighed Ozma, "I like the way my insides tickle."

"I like the way you feel—just for a second—that you falling," chipped in Frodo.

"I'm sorry I asked," moaned Ake, turning a light shade of green.

"Me, I like the way—"

"Ah, thanks, Mama-san," Ake interrupted, "but I think I've heard enough."

"Oh, really?" Ray asked maliciously. "You don't want to hear how the jump sends an electrical surge through my nervous system, making me feel as if every neuron in my body is firing at the same time?"

Ake blinked at him dispassionately. "Someday—maybe not for years and years—but someday, Ray, I'm gonna be there when you're least expecting it—maybe the middle of the night—and I'm gonna get you for that! Sweet will be my revenge."

That made Beowulf laugh his deep, throaty canine laugh. Ray and Littlejohn joined in and then all the others—even Ake.

The ship jumped.

"Shit!" Ake swore.

★ ★ ★

Ray and Ake stared at Hephaestus in the viewer, a deceptively mild-looking planet hanging motionless in the star-speckled void. "They say it's the devil's summer home," Ray said softly, "but it sure doesn't look like hell when you see it this way."

"Whatever it's like," Ake said, "it'll be our home for the next twelve to eighteen months."

" 'Nother new world," said Sinbad. "Wonder what it be like down there."

"Doan matter," replied Tajil. "Whatever it be like, Ray take care of us."

" 'Course he will," said Mama-san to her son as if he had said it with even a shred of doubt or questioning in his voice. "He is Ray, he is the Man." Mama-san looked at Beowulf, lying comfortably on his side, his big tongue lolling from his mouth. "Beowulf, I think it is time for the saying of the Law."

"Yeah, the Law," agreed Gawain. "Say the Law."

"Okay," said Beowulf amiably as he heaved himself to his feet and took a commanding stance. The others arranged themselves in a semicircle around him.

"What is the Law?" asked Beowulf.

*"To place duty above self, honor above life."*

"What is the Law?"

*"To allow harm to come to no Man, to protect Man and his possessions."*

"What is the Law?"

*"To stand by Man's side—as dogs will always stand. Together, Man and dog."*

★ ★ ★

Ray realized this was to be no ordinary assignment only gradually. The biggest giveaway was the fact that no one taking the flight down to the planet's surface was allowed in the waiting area until the passengers the shuttle had carried up to the ship from Hephaestus had disembarked.

The second ominous portent was the number of passengers heading down to the planet: Besides themselves, they numbered exactly five. There was a black-robed Programmer, not a Prime Programmer, of course, but nevertheless one who appeared to carry some authority. There seemed to be something different about the Programmer's robes, though. Ray shrugged.

The others included a beefy and red-faced man whom they took to be a miner, one of the civilian supervisors. And then there were two members of the Cadre and their prisoner, a sullen-faced woman whose not unattractive features were rent by an ugly scar which bisected her face. For some reason the Programmer took an inordinate interest in the prisoner. Not that she intended to be obvious about it, but Ray could see her glancing covertly at the manacled prisoner. *Oh, well, none of my business.*

The flight itself was relatively uneventful, much to Ake's relief. He had gulped when the shuttle uncoupled from the *Truman* and "fell" away from the huge starship. Whenever the whine of the Daae-Fujiwara negative gravity engines changed pitch, however slightly, Ake gripped the armrests of his seat so tightly that the skin over his knuckles was a bloodless white. "It be okay, Ake," Mama-san consoled him.

"Yah, we with you," said Frodo, leaning into Ake.

"Thanks, Mama-san. Thanks, Frodo."

When the two Cadre soldiers threw the team a glance that was half disdain, half smirk, Ray returned the sentiment by not so subtly rubbing his nose with the middle finger of his right hand. Beowulf and Littlejohn, enjoying the gesture of defiance and dismissal, guffawed—as did the manacled prisoner, who soon regretted her outburst when one of the soldiers planted an elbow in her rib cage.

"And you were once a doctor for these slimeballs?" Ray asked, keeping his voice low.

"I was young and stupid," Ake replied, equally low. "So shoot me."

Nodding almost imperceptibly in the direction of the Cadre duo and their prisoner, Ray said, "I'm sure they'd be glad to do the job—especially if they knew your background."

"Let's not tell them then, eh?" Then, suddenly, to Ake's surprise and delight, he was aware that they had begun the process of landing. Before he had time to regain his fear of flying, they were down and the shuttle was slowly being lowered into the underground hangar. When the dogs made ready to disembark, Ray said, "Hold it a minute. Let's be polite and allow our friends the privilege of getting off first."

"That good idea, Ray," Beowulf agreed.

After the others had exited, Ray unstrapped himself, stood up and stretched, and said, "Okay, it's our turn now."

As Ray paused in the hatchway, Ake grasped his elbow and said, "I take it we're to be a team with no history . . . at least while we're on Hephaestus."

"That's right," Ray said. "There are a lot of military and other Federation personnel on this planet and, as you yourself pointed out, we're not exactly in their pantheon of heroes: Ray and Ake, destroyers of the Cadre camp on Chiron, thwarters of the General's megalomaniacal plans."

"I guess the attempt on your life on the *Truman* ought to tell us something."

"You got it, buddy," said Ray. "Now let's go."

The Larkin-Ringgren team strode purposefully through the terminal. As a new planet, and one without much human population—just over five hundred souls, Ray noted to himself—Hephaestus promised to lack almost all those amenities of civilization which so quickly move from consideration as luxuries to being the bare necessities of life. As if to fulfill that rough promise, Ray observed, they had to travel the whole one and a half kilometers between the landing area and the terminal on foot; there was no people mover, not even a small vehicle to carry them—that was reserved for the cargo alone.

"I feel at home already," Ake said dryly.

"We're not even on the surface yet," said Ray. "Give Hephaestus a chance to win your heart. Of course," he added, giving Ake a sly sideways glance, "I don't know why we ever left Talos. I was so happy there."

"Remember," Ake said evenly, "it'll be some night when you least expect it; there'll be a knock on your door, you'll open it, and some stranger will shoot you in the balls and then say, 'That's from Ake Ringgren.' "

"Not funny, you two!" fumed Grendel.

"*Au contraire*," said Ray, "*au contraire*."

# III

By the time they reached the terminal, such as it was, the other passengers, as Ray had hoped, had already departed. The main room was spacious and surprisingly nicely furnished, yet it did not entirely avoid the almost inevitable sterility of such common areas. Still, the walls glowed with warm gold and rust colors, and the carpeting was a rich earth tone. The new arrivals paid little attention to the decor, however.

"Since we're the only ones left," said Ray, "I suppose that squarehead across the room is waiting for us."

"Will you stop that! Let's at least *try* to make a good impression."

"You probably called your teachers 'sir' and 'ma'am.' "

"Be good, here he comes," cautioned Ake.

"Good afternoon, Citizens," the solidly built man said, extending his hand. "I'm Theo Kodlich, director of mining operations for the Hephaestus Syndicate. The Syndicate runs the mines for a consortium of Federation-licensed companies."

"Ray Larkin," said Ray, accepting the man's outstretched hand. Kodlich's grasp was firm and warm. Ray, who put much stock in another's handshake, was immediately impressed. Kodlich was tall, nearly two meters; and had long brown hair riven with strands of white. His features were not especially anything—neither remarkable nor forgettable—with only his piercing gray eyes standing out.

"Ake Ringgren," said Ake, taking the man's hand in turn.

"Allow me to welcome you to Hephaestus."

"Thank you," Ake said.

"And this is your team," Kodlich said, stating it as a fact, not a question. "Would you be so kind as to introduce me to them as well?"

Again the man impressed Ray. *He's probably just being politically savvy*, Ray thought, *more than expressing a genuine interest in my mutts.* "Well," Ray began, "this is Beowulf, and Mama-san, Littlejohn, Ozma, Frodo, Sinbad, Tajil, Grendel, and Gawain."

"I'm pleased to meet you all," Kodlich said as if he truly meant it. The dogs wagged their tails and grinned their peculiar canine grins, accepting his hospitality graciously.

"I guess we might as well get unloaded and settled in," Ake said.

"Of course," Kodlich said. "Please follow me. We'll take a truck to your quarters; most of your things will probably already be there."

"Not if the ground crew here is like almost every place else," laughed Ray.

Kodlich smiled a mysterious smile. "Oh, I think you'll soon discover that Hephaestus is not like any other place you've ever known."

As Kodlich turned to lead them toward the lift tubes, Ake just looked at Ray and shrugged his shoulders. *Once more unto the breach, dear friends,* Ray thought, *once more.*

The minute they stepped outside, the heat and humidity hit them with a one-two punch. "A free sauna bath," Ray observed.

"Hey, look at that," Ake said, pointing at the two cones of the volcano that loomed over them. "Is that normal, for a volcano to have two cones?"

"No," Kodlich answered. "But it's not unheard of, either. What *is* a bit different is that one lava chimney is blocked off and inactive while lava is present in the other."

Kodlich had an all-terrain vehicle, a truck with actual wheels, waiting for them. The dogs piled into the open-air bed of the cargo area while Ray and Ake opened the doors and slid in beside their guide.

"It's just thirty-five or forty klicks to the main compound from here," Kodlich explained, "but it's rough country, so fasten your seat belts—not even these balloon tires can completely smooth out the bumps." Kodlich pressed his thumb to the starter sensor and the engine began to make a high-pitched yet almost imperceptible whine. "You'd expect the 'road' to be native gravel of some type, but the jungle here, near the equator, is so voracious and alive that it constantly pokes up through the stones. Consequently, we've stripped the topsoil away and laid down plascrete chips." He shook his head as if in admiration for the jungle's tenacity. "It doesn't help all that much—we've got to burn the vines and other vegetation back every week or so anyway. We're always joking that you can actually see the jungle growing after a rainstorm."

"Rain much?" asked Ray.

"Three or four times a day."

"Is it always this hot?" Ake inquired.

"At this level, yes," Kodlich told him. "But higher up on the mountain slopes, the temperature falls off enough to make it bearable."

"Thank God."

"Of course, we're not going all that far up the mountain. The mines aren't really located on the slopes of the volcano so much as at its broad base."

As the truck bumped and lurched over the plascrete highway, the dogs lined up along the side panels in the rear and thrust their heads out into the breeze, their ears blowing in the air stream. "Hah!" said Beowulf. "Rides is fun."

"Yah," someone else agreed. "Lots of fun."

"Lookit," said Tajil, "I never see'd a bush that big!"

"That's a tree," Littlejohn explained. "You never see'd a tree before."

"'*Course* Tajil see'd a tree before!" said Gawain indignantly. "And me, too—on Chiron."

"You call them little stubby things on Chiron trees?" laughed Frodo. "Them's not trees."

"That's what I said," reiterated Littlejohn. "The pups never see'd a tree before." Having been born on the windswept prairies and plains of the Centaur planet, where they'd spent almost their entire lives, the puppies had never been exposed to anything remotely like the tall, sun-seeking trees of the rain forest.

"We not know much 'bout trees or other things," admitted Tajil. "That's what uncles and aunts is for—to teach us new things." Mama-san swelled with pride, but kept her feelings to herself: *My two little ones—though they not so little anymore—is so smart!*

"Doan be counting on us'ns too much," cautioned Frodo. "We bin around the block, but we also ain't had no 'signments on jungle worlds."

"No we ain't," admitted Littlejohn, "but when we lived in Brazil while Ray went to school, there was jungles around."

"Yah," agreed Ozma. "We *lived* near jungle."

"Not the same thing," Frodo insisted. "Not 'signment."

"Ah, who cares?" said Sinbad. "We learn jungle ways soon enuff, I bet!"

"We better," Beowulf said, " 'cause ignorance is deadly."

"Then Gawain most dangerous thing around!" said Tajil, chortling at his own joke.

The other dogs joined in the laughter, even Gawain, who looked a bit puzzled by all the hilarity. Soon, however, the dogs grew engrossed in sensing their new world: They sniffed and tasted the air, their black and brown noses wrinkling.

"Smells like something died," Gawain said.

"That be jungle smell," Ozma said. "Is dead leaves and plants and grass and stuff. Rain makes it rot."

"Not raining," said Gawain.

"It probably rains here coupla times a day," explained Ozma patiently. "This is called rain forest, I think."

"I thought it was jungle," Gawain said.

"Same thing," said Ozma.

"Yah," said Sinbad. "Rain forest. Lots of animals lives in a rain forest. There be lots of fun for us here, I think."

"Yes, there be bunches of animals here," agreed Beowulf. "Mebbe too many."

★ ★ ★

After they'd gone twenty or twenty-five kilometers, the vehicle began ascending a slight upgrade. "We're moving up the base of the double-coned volcano we saw from the landing site," Kodlich explained. He saw the look on their faces and added, "Like I said, one cone is dormant and the other one's pretty quiet. Well . . . it's about as quiet as volcanoes go on Hephaestus."

"How reassuring," Ray said.

"It's a volatile planet all right," Kodlich said. "But if it weren't for all this volcanic activity, we wouldn't find it so economically rewarding."

"It's not just the rubies, then?" Ake asked.

"Oh, no. They're the most precious result of the mining, but the lava flows here are rich in many other minerals as well."

"You been here long?" Ray asked.

"Fourteen months. I'm due to rotate out in another four."

"Then what?"

"Well, after my leave, I may come back or I may put in for another posting." He pulled a handkerchief from his shirt pocket and wiped it across his face. "The money's quite good—can't beat it, actually. But I'm ready for a cooler climate, someplace where the jungle rot doesn't get everything." He looked distastefully at a clear spray-on bandage on the back of his left hand. "You get so much as a paper cut and you've got to be very careful or it'll fester." He gestured ahead. "The saving grace is that the mining camp is a couple of klicks up the side of this volcano. It's still hot and humid but it's nothing like on the floor of the rain forest."

"I really enjoy seeing green again," Ray said. "And I don't find the heat all that annoying. Ake here doesn't care for it as much, though."

"Ake Ringgren and Ray Larkin," said Kodlich thoughtfully. "I got a cryptic letter from headquarters about you folks. You two guys possess a dangerous kind of fame, don't you?"

"Moro shit! Does everyone know who the fork we are?"

"Well, after the story first broke, the Federation put the lid on information coming from Chiron. After the initial wave of news reports from the planet, the facts were harder to come by."

"Sure," said Ray sourly. "We've probably had our faces plastered across hist-holos; kids are trading three holos of us for one of Ronald Reagan."

"Ronald Reagan?"

"It helps to be a fan of 20th-century trivia to understand

everything Ray says," explained Ake helpfully. "Reagan was president of the United States of America during World War I."

"I see. Well, fortunately for you, the garrison guarding the mines and the prison miners is mostly regular army. There are a few Cadre people coming and going, but they're never here for long and they're not in charge.

"I've only heard rumors about what happened on Chiron," Kodlich continued. When Ake began to say something, Kodlich shook his head, silencing him. "I'm sure you had your reasons for what you did, as did the General and the Cadre—everyone usually does. But frankly I don't care one way or another. My job is getting the rubies and the other goodies out. Since you're here to help, it's to my advantage to see that nobody bothers you. Hell, that may even be the official attitude! As far as the Triumvirate and their military pit bulls are concerned, money and power are more important than settling old scores." He smiled grimly. "Of course, that may not hold for the Cadre hardcases and anyone who may have known the General or someone in the Cadre camp you fellows wiped out."

"We didn't—"

"I said I didn't care what happened. Just keep my supervisory personnel and the miners safe from the diggers."

Ray looked at Ake and raised his eyebrows. What the big man had said made sense; he only hoped he was correct—that no one really gave a shit about "ancient history." To Kodlich he said, "We appreciate your honesty . . . *and* your attitude toward our assignment. We'll try to do our best."

"That's all I ask." Kodlich then said, "You must be good, real good, if you did all they say you did."

"Don't believe everything you see on the news," Ray said.

"There wasn't much about Chiron on the news; I'm talking about the scuttlebutt."

"Let's just say that if half as much happens to us on Hephaestus as went down on Chiron, we'll have our hands full."

"Then here's to a quiet tour," Kodlich proposed.

"Hey, not *that* quiet!"

# 3

Kodlich had no sooner killed the truck's engine than several heavily armed soldiers came out to inspect them. "This *is* a penal colony as well as a mining operation," Kodlich told them out of the side of his mouth. "Get used to being challenged."

When Ray lowered the back panel of the truck, the dogs scrambled out and looked around with keen interest. "Stay with us for now," Ray cautioned them.

"Okay, Ray," Beowulf answered.

The mining site consisted of a dozen or so structures built on what looked like a natural plateau. It was only when Ray observed the unnatural smoothness and perfectly level terrain that he realized it had been sliced out of the sleeping volcano's side by industrial lasers. One of the larger structures was a sinister-looking plascrete building with little more than narrow vertical slits for windows. Ray quickly theorized that it housed the convict miners when he saw the shimmer of a low-power force field and bales of archaic barbed wire. *Stone, wood, or brick*, Ray thought, *you can always tell a prison*.

The other structures included various nondescript buildings, the largest of which was a blocky edifice fronted by the three-star symbol of the Triumvirate and another design which Ray could not place but which he was sure represented the mining consortium; it was clearly the main administrative building. Ray watched as someone maneuvered a small hover-loader into one of the smaller structures. Ray could see that many of the smaller buildings were simply vehicle storage sheds, where the floaters and other work vehicles were kept when not in use.

Kodlich saw what Ray was staring at and said, "The jungle would devour even our machinery if we didn't keep it at bay. We have hover vehicles, of course, but things like the truck we came in are easier to maintain with our small staff."

"How does the jungle eat machines?" asked a perplexed Ake.

"The plascrete, the molecular steel, and the plasteel are impervious, of course," Kodlich told him, "but the bacteria and other microscopic organisms that abound here think that we brought in the lubricants and other organic liquids just for them to feast on. They even find a large percentage of the synthetics, the hoses and other connectors, to their liking."

"Sounds grand," grumped Ake.

"I doubt we'd be here if it weren't for the mines," Kodlich said.

"Us neither," joked Littlejohn, wagging his tail.

"Yah, we ready to work," said Gawain.

"Yah!" chorused the rest of the dogs enthusiastically.

"I guess I'd better show you to your quarters, then," Kodlich said. "I can introduce you to the commandant and my first engineer and the others after you've unpacked and settled in."

"Sounds good," Ray said. "Lead on."

"Your building is a half-klick down this way," Kodlich said, leading them away from the main camp. "We've found through experience that our scout teams prefer a modicum of privacy, what little is possible in a situation like this."

Both Ray and Beowulf noticed that while the surface was still level, clearly part of the massive clearing effort that had created the plateau, the jungle, even at this height, had reclaimed much of the area. What had probably been a road not long ago was now reduced to a path. It was a path which led to their new home for the next twelve to eighteen months or so.

As they walked along the path, their ears were assaulted by a cacophonous chorus of bird calls, insect noises, and the shrieks, growls, and alarms of the native animals. The puppies, Tajil and Gawain, had never heard the sounds of such abundant life. While not wanting to appear timid, they nonetheless cast their eyes about nervously.

"I forgot what a jungle in full voice sounds like," Ray said. "Is it always this noisy?"

"It's much worse on the jungle floor," Kodlich told him. "Up here, there are fewer lifeforms. Don't worry. You'll soon get so used to it that silence will sound strange." They rounded a bend and came upon a low, rambling plascrete building. It was bright orange. "Ah, here we are—your new home." If first impressions counted for anything, the ramshackle building didn't promise much.

"Jeez!" said Frodo.

"Ditto," Ray agreed. "So that's it?"

"We're not big on appearances down here," Kodlich said. "It's not a bad place, really. You'll find that the outside belies the number of creature comforts inside."

"You go ahead, Ray," Ake said. "I'll just go back to the van and then ride the shuttle up to the *Truman*."

"I thought you didn't like the shuttle?"

"Did I give you that impression? Gracious me."

"C'mon," Ray said, striding toward the door, "you'll probably love it."

"Yeah, sure," said Ake dubiously.

Kodlich unlocked the door and pressed the entry square. The door swung rather than hissed open. "Quaint," Ake said.

"The hostile native bacteria mean that the doors, the outer doors at least, open manually," said Kodlich.

"Here goes nothing," Ray said, stepping boldly inside.

Ake shaded his eyes and tried to peer into the dark interior. "So? What's the verdict?"

Ray reappeared in the doorway. "Is it too late to catch the shuttle?"

★ ★ ★

Ray, Ake, and the dogs spent the rest of the morning getting settled into their new residence. Less than an hour after they arrived, their belongings were delivered to them and they were able to unpack and begin to make their new surroundings into a home.

As they emptied out their trunks, Ray couldn't help feeling that they weren't alone. Was their new home bugged?

"Yowl!" exclaimed Grendel, leaping almost a meter into the air.

"What is it?" Ray asked, reaching for an energy pistol.

Something long and green slithered across the floor, clearly as eager to get away from Grendel as she was to distance herself from it. "It look kinda like a snake with legs," said Sinbad.

"No. More like long mossy twig with legs," opined Beowulf. "If you open door, Ray, it probably go out," the big dog added casually. Ray did as Beowulf suggested and the creature took advantage of the proffered escape route and made a hasty exit, its claws clicking on the floor.

"Ha, ha," Ray laughed nervously.

"I think that us dogs ought check out this place for more visitors, Ray," Beowulf said. "Mebbe be some that not be so anxious to get away."

"I think that's an excellent idea, Beowulf," Ray agreed. "And Ake and I will seal up any cracks we find."

"If that thing got in through a crack, it was one helluva crack," Ake said.

In an hour's time, the dogs having found no other unwanted co-inhabitants, they had made their new home secure against more intruders, at least for the time being. The kitchen cupboard yielded a patching compound that did indeed provide an effective seal. "Actually, this place isn't that bad," Ake said, flopping onto the large dilapidated sofa that had come with the living room, just one of the many pieces of furniture that the previous tenants had left behind. None of it was Ake's "style," but he could live with it.

"Maybe it's all just a ploy," Ray said. "We bitch and moan and complain about this dump, and then they show us to our *real* quarters. The idea being that after this place *anything* would seem like the Taj Mahal."

"Anything other than this *is* the Taj Mahal," responded Ake. "Anyway, it's a nice fantasy."

"Ah, you guys!" chided Ozma. "This place not bad at all." She considered that for a moment then added, "At least, could be a lot worse." She walked to a large plush chair in the corner, climbed up, circled several times, and then plopped down.

Ray looked around and then said, "Oh, sure, Ozma, you're right. With a little work . . . well, a lot of work . . . we can make this dump into a decent hovel. After all, our immediate predecessors lived here."

*Really*, Ray told himself, *it isn't bad, considering the circumstances*. The front door opened into a long entry hallway. Immediately to the left was an archway into the large and spacious living room. Although the building looked low from outside, the ceilings were admirably high. There were no windows, it was true, but there were mounting brackets for whatever holoscenics one wanted to display. Holoscenics—multidimensional and constantly moving, unless one chose a static vista like a deep-space view—allowed even the meanest home or apartment to possess a stunning and incredibly lifelike view.

The huge living area led directly into a large, comfortable-looking study with a roaring fireplace that turned out, on closer inspection, to be a holoscenic. The study gave way to a modest dining room that led into a fully equipped kitchen. There was a laundry and utilities room just off the kitchen. Both the study and the dining room also opened into the hallway.

The rooms off the right side of the hallway included a lab and work area, and two master bedrooms with a shared bath between them. The last doorway down the hall opened into a smaller hallway that accessed another full bathroom, and four smaller rooms which could be used as bedrooms (each had a small closet) or for any purpose one desired.

All in all, Ray reflected, the accommodations were generous and undeniably better than the plascrete shack they had lived in on Talos. The place may have looked like horse hockey from the outside, but the interior was startlingly homey.

And, certainly, once inside with the doors closed, it was deceptively easy to forget where you were. Not only did the powerful central air conditioning keep the outside heat and humidity at bay, the lack of windows also allowed a person to imagine he was living anywhere in the galaxy but Hephaestus. Ray intended, however, to slowly increase the temperature setting as he and the dogs and Ake became acclimated to the outside conditions. He believed the gradual increase would make transitions between the inside and the outside less dramatic and intrusive. *Besides*, Ray told himself, *we're living on a jungle planet; it makes no sense to pretend otherwise*. He wouldn't raise the indoor temperature too much, though—they *would* be spending a lot of time in the mines, where the underground temperature would be both constant and much lower than the outside air.

"Hey, these coupla rooms not bad," Mama-san said as the dogs meandered through the four smaller bedrooms.

"Well, they're yours," Ray said.

"We doan need all four," Beowulf said.

"You sure?"

"Yah. Two be 'nuff for us'ns."

Ray checked back with the dogs later. "Are you all settled in yet?" he asked Beowulf.

"Sure," Beowulf replied. "What we got to worry 'bout anyway?"

"I was just thinking that myself."

"Are the dogs doing okay?" Ake asked, joining Ray and Beowulf.

"Sure," Ray answered, throwing Beowulf a wink. "What have they got to worry about anyway?"

After everyone else except Beowulf had gone to bed, Ray programmed the hol-vee to reach deep into its memory and come up with a recording of an old television show from the 1900s.

"*Have Gun, Will Travel*," said Ray when Beowulf asked him what the title of the show was. "You've never seen this one."

As the opening credits rolled and an offscreen singer sang the theme song, Beowulf wrinkled his nose and asked, "'A knight without armor in a savage land' . . . what that mean?"

"Sh-h-h, just watch," Ray said. "I know you like Western shows and this is a great one . . . even if it is technically primitive."

"Hope it better than that one where the guy lives on Jackson beans," said Beowulf.

"That's 'jacks and queens,'" Ray said, sighing. The dogs liked lots of action—gunplay and violence. The series with the Maverick brothers was way too talky for Beowulf.

Halfway through the twenty-two-minute episode, Ray looked over at Beowulf's face. The big dog was completely engrossed in the old melodrama. *Who says you need color, holographic images, and surround sound*? Ray mused to himself.

# II

Bright and early the next morning, and still under the influence of the old West, Ray decided that a little "look-see," as he put it, was in order. He told the dogs that he wouldn't be comfortable until they'd taken a brief inspection tour of the jungle immediately surrounding their quarters. With Ake and the whole team in tow, Ray scrutinized the jungle with a much more discerning eye than he had on their journey in.

"Expecting trouble?" Ake asked, continuing to rub sunscreen into his skin wherever it was not covered by clothing.

"No," Ray replied. "I don't know what I'm expecting." He wiped a glaze of perspiration from his forehead with the back of his hand. "I didn't study the information on Hephaestus in the *Truman*'s memory banks as closely as I should have. I *do* know that the gravity is slightly higher than Terran-standard, that the days are longer in terms of hours of daylight, and that this planet teems with life." He shrugged. "But that's all basic stuff; I really didn't do my homework."

"I wouldn't feel too guilty about that," Ake said. "I wasn't able to dig out very much myself. To tell you the truth, I don't think either the Federation or the mining syndicate have permitted much information about this planet to be released."

"So there could be nasty creatures here, eh?" asked Littlejohn, speaking up from his position beside Beowulf.

"Nothing a well-trained scout dog team can't handle," said Ray. "Besides, I think Kodlich would have said something if there was anything too dangerous around."

"*Now* who believes in the tooth fairy?" asked Ake. "I've seen your reaction to this guy, Ray—you trust him. Don't."

"Yeah, you're right, but it's a bitch having to think the worst of everyone you meet."

"Maybe. But it sure as hell helps one to stay alive."

"Sure does!" agreed a high-pitched voice from the jungle.

"What was that?" asked Littlejohn as Ray and Ake unslung their weapons.

"What was that?" echoed the odd voice.

"I got a bad feeling about this," moaned Ake.

"Good!" said the voice.

They scanned the luxuriant foliage anxiously, Ray and Ake fingering the safeties on their energy rifles. The dogs' eyes, more attuned to slight movements, were the first to locate the source of the high-pitched, oddly feminine voice.

"There," said Beowulf.

"Where?" Ray asked.

"*There*," Beowulf repeated, nodding toward a vine-choked tree. Slowly, Ray made out a small form languorously stretched out on a branch, its weight making the slender limb sway ever so gently in the almost nonexistent breeze.

"I see it," Ake said excitedly. "It looks like a . . . a cat!"

"Men are *so-o-o-o* perceptive," the cat said mildly, blinking its intensely blue eyes.

"Yah, it's one o' them damn smart-mouthed scout cats," Beowulf said.

"And dogs, especially male dogs, are right up there with their human leaders," the cat said.

"What are you doing in that tree?" Ray asked, ignoring the feline's provocations.

"Watching you."

"Watching us?"

"It's fortunate I'm not one of the native predators, isn't it?" the cat asked rhetorically. "I'd have had you for lunch since no one noticed me up here. And I'm not even green," the cat added, referring to her Siamese coloring.

"We can't all be cats," Ray said through gritted teeth.

"Pity."

"I'm good at climbin' trees, Ray," said Frodo. "Let me teach this cat a lesson she—"

Ray shook his head. "I know how you feel, Frodo, but we're going to be working with her team. We've got to learn to get along with each other."

"So sensible . . . for a human male," the cat said. "There's hope for this partnership yet."

"Do you have a name?" Ake asked the haughty Siamese.

"I am called Penelope."

"Benelope," several of the dogs repeated.

"Not 'Benelope,' *P*enelope."

"They have trouble saying 'P,'" Ray explained, regretting it instantly as Beowulf shot him a look that said, "Don't reveal anything about the team to an outsider."

"Have you tried speech lessons?" Penelope said. Before Ray could answer, she rose, stretched, and then ran out to the end of the limb and leapt gracefully onto a branch of a nearby tree and disappeared into the foliage.

"*That* was a scout cat?" Ake asked.

"Yep, that was a scout cat," Ray confirmed. "Ingratiating creatures, aren't they?"

"Boy, I like to . . ." began Tajil.

"They're our partners in the mines, Taddy," Ray said. "Fantasize about rolling them around in your jaws but don't do more than that."

"We know," said Beowulf. Then the big dog faced Ray. "You know what Benelope said that really burned my butt?"

"What?"

"That we not know she there. She right—this an alien jungle and we gots to be more alert."

"I agree, Beowulf," Ray said. "If you really want to irritate someone, hit him with the truth. Yeah, she knew how to rub our rhubarb the wrong way, all right."

"Doan worry, Ray," said Taddy. "We be aware of *everything* from now on."

"Let's go," said Ray, putting up his rifle.

As the team continued their examination of the area around their camp, their senses questioning every sound and movement, Ray decided that the rain forest, even this high up the base of the quiescent volcano, was a wondrous place. And the view! He could easily see out over the canopy of trees for ten or fifteen kilometers. Dark smudges on the horizon betrayed the presence of other more active volcanoes.

"Some world, isn't it?" Ake said, noticing Ray staring across the expanse of green and yellow.

"I'll say," Ray agreed. "I can't wait to go exploring. But that's another day," he sighed. "For now, let's head over to the main compound. I want to look them over and vice versa."

With the mine site finally in view, the group fell silent. The silence seemed more profound than it should be, Ray thought. And then it came to him: the jungle. "The jungle," he said.

"Yeah?" said Ake.

"Notice how quiet it is?"

"Yah," Beowulf said. "Humans and their machines scare animals."

"I think you're right, Beowulf," Ray said.

"C'mon already," Ake said.

As they approached the compound, the main headquarters building where Kodlich and the other civilians ran things for the mining consortium loomed before them. It was smaller than both the building that housed the soldiers who guarded the prisoners and the prison itself. Ray could see the giveaway shimmer of a force field surrounding both the prison and the soldiers' barracks building.

The prison building dominated the compound. Its studied ugliness repelled even the dogs, not known for their architectural sophistication. "Why humans got to make such awful places?" asked Grendel.

"I don't know," Ray said. "I suppose it's so you know they're awful places. It's authority proclaiming its power to punish."

## K-9 CORPS: UNDER FIRE

"Jes' lookin' at that place is punishment enuff," Grendel said. The other dogs agreed with the persnickety Grendel's pronouncement.

"Yeah, well, we have a job to do and it doesn't involve liking the architecture of the Federation or its policies," Ake said grimly.

"Good thing," said Grendel.

"Take a look at the administration building," Ray instructed Ake.

"Okay, so?"

"Now look at the one where the solders are quartered."

"Okay."

"Notice anything?"

"No," said Ake, a bit of irritation in his voice; he hated playing these guessing games with Ray. "Well, wait a minute . . . the military's is bigger, a lot bigger."

"Let's try not to forget who really controls this place," Ray said. "The corporations may run things behind the scenes, they may buy and sell the Cadre and Federation officials, but guns beat everything." He nodded at the army building. "And right over there are the guns on this planet."

"I don't get it," Ake said.

"What do you mean you don't—"

"No, no, not that," Ake said. "I get what you just said. What I don't understand is why there are so many Federation regulars here. To guard the prisoner-miners? A more common ratio of prisoners to guards is ten to one, not four to one. So I repeat, I don't get it."

"Somethin' stink," said Beowulf.

"Yeah," Ray agreed. "There's something more going on here than we've been told about so far."

"Let's go talk to your buddy Kodlich," Ake said.

"Good idea," Ray agreed.

They skirted the edge of the hundred-meter-square landing field and approached the dazzling administration building. Like all the buildings in the compound, it was covered with a highly reflective material to better ward off the burning rays of Hephaestus's sun.

"Five will get you ten that it's freezing inside," Ake said to Ray.

"Hey, what's the point of air conditioning if you don't use it?"

"The moment of truth," Ray said as the door swung open. A blast of icy air hit them the moment they were inside.

"Bingo," Ake said gleefully.

"Br-r-r-r," said Sinbad. "'Frigerator!"

Ray walked down a tiled hallway and stuck his head inside the first open doorway he came to. "Hello?" The room appeared to be empty.

"You must be the new scout dog team," said a voice from behind Ray. A handsome black woman of indeterminate age strode down the hall toward them. "Theo told us to expect you sometime this afternoon."

Ray stepped back out of the doorway to join the team in greeting her. The dogs were already surrounding her and sniffing at her. "Forgive the dogs' behavior," Ray apologized. "They're . . . ah . . . just being dogs."

"Of course," she said with a smile. "Let me introduce myself—I'm Sari Fodoor, assistant director of mining operations of Hephaestus."

"Pleased to meet you, Citizen Fodoor," Ray said. "I'm Ray Larkin, this is my associate Ake Ringgren, and this is Beowulf, the head of our team."

"I'm so pleased to meet you," she said simply. She reached toward Beowulf's head, then paused. "May I?"

"Yah," said Beowulf.

Sari Fodoor scratched the big dog behind his ears. Giving Ray an intent look, she added, "I rather imagine one of the reasons you're here is to study the K'a-nii, is that not so?"

"The . . . Kay-nee?" Ray asked, puzzled.

"Yes, the indigenous intelligent lifeform. The—"

"That will be all, Ms. Fodoor," said Theo Kodlich, gliding up to the group.

"Yes, sir," she replied formally, hearing the cutting edge of authority in his voice. "It was nice meeting you," she said to the team, shooting Kodlich an indecipherable look before leaving.

Ray guessed that she and Kodlich had unofficial as well as official "relations," and that she was letting him know that she was acceding to his surface authority for the moment—but that she would have a less accommodating response in private.

When she had left, Kodlich said, "Gentlemen, it's good to see you again. I trust that you found your new quarters satisfactory?"

"Piss on that," said Ray. "What's this about a sentient native life form called the 'Kay-nee'?"

"The K'a-nii? I suppose you'd better come into my office."

# III

"Let's talk," Ray said simply.

"Yes, the K'a-nii."

"Your assistant director, this Sari Fodoor, said that they are intelligent creatures," said Ake. "Is that correct?"

"Yes, I'm afraid it is," Kodlich admitted. When both of the others tried to speak, he held up a hand and added, "We are not involved in any form of xenocide. Our only interest on Hephaestus is its mineral wealth, not its lifeforms. We want nothing from the K'a-nii and they are content to leave us alone and go about their business—whatever it may be."

Ake frowned. "Your last comment . . . please explain."

Kodlich sighed and ran a hand through his long brown hair. "The K'a-nii are warm-blooded reptiles. That much we know—and that is just about all we know. As you are both aware, a number of the sentient races we have chanced upon are surprisingly—even shockingly—humanlike in their mental processes. Humans have no monopoly on what we call Aristotelian logic. The same is true for mathematically based reasoning." He looked at Ray and said, "The Chiron Centaurs you studied fall into this category, I believe."

When Ray said nothing, Kodlich continued. "Then there are aliens who define the word alien, whose ways of thinking and relating to the universe seem beyond our understanding—like the Rhoehli of Tarddin and the Womatt of Boradin; they are truly *alien* in all meanings of the word. And, finally, there are aliens who can be communicated with and understood—but only up to a point. I think this is where the K'a-nii can be placed."

Kodlich drew his forefinger down the side of his mouth and added, "Of course, no one on Hephaestus has really tried to communicate with them to any degree. That's not what we're here for."

Ake looked at Ray and then turned his gaze back to Kodlich. "The General lost his position and took his own life over a situation not unlike this. How can the Judge Advocate allow this to happen?"

"Are you serious?" said Kodlich incredulously. "Surely it's apparent that the Judge Advocate is no longer a factor. Something has happened back on Terra, something damned big. Whatever revolution or realignment of power has occurred, the Federation now allows . . ." He stopped and reconsidered. "No, more than that, it *encourages* the exploitation of resource-rich planets like Hephaestus, regardless of their lifeform status."

He looked at them scornfully. "While you two spent a couple of years on Chiron playing footsie with the Centaurs, things changed. The hands-off policy concerning planets with intelligent lifeforms is ancient history."

"I admit it's true that you're not telling us anything we haven't already figured out," Ray said.

A light glowed on Kodlich's desk and he keyed it impatiently. "Yes?"

"The First Engineer is here, Director Kodlich," Sari Fodoor announced.

"Fine. Send him in, please, Ms. Fodoor."

The door hissed open and a tall, thin oriental man with a shock of black hair strode into the room wiping his hands on a cloth, presumably in anticipation of the inescapable handshaking routine required of introductions. Ray and Ake stood up and Beowulf watched them with a yawn.

"First Engineer Tien Tsuji," Kodlich said formally even though Fodoor had already used the man's title. "I'd like you to meet the leaders of our new scout dog team: Ray Larkin and Ake Ringgren."

"Pleased to meet you," said Tsuji, shoving the grimy cloth into a back pocket of his slightly soiled work trousers and extending his hand. His grasp was warm and firm, and Ray immediately categorized him as a technocrat, a man who lived his life juggling the disparities between the worlds of the theoretical—numbers, formulas, paradigms, and probabilities—and the tangible, a real world of physical objects and things stubbornly ignorant of the way they were *supposed* to respond to human intervention and manipulation.

In short, Tsuji was a typical engineer.

"We're pleased to make your acquaintance," said Ake.

"Tien is one of the best mining engineers in this part of the galaxy," Kodlich said as he motioned for everyone to take a seat. When the First Engineer raised his eyebrows, Kodlich laughed and added, "Hell, he's the best there is, period."

After Ray threw a meaningful look in Ake's direction and shrugged his shoulders ever so slightly, Tien said to him, "Regarding oneself as the best may seem a bit egotistical to some, but I've always found that if you believe you are the best, then you perform like the best."

*Very good*, Ray thought in admiration, *very good*. "I completely agree with you, First Engineer Tsuji. I would be lying if I said that I believed there exists a better scout dog team leader than myself."

"Good," replied Tsuji. "This job demands one hundred percent. I fully expect you to keep my supervisory personnel and the miners safe from injury."

"We'll do what's necessary," said Ake mildly, somewhat bemused by this sudden male display of self-importance that Ray and Tsuji were indulging in. Ake felt uncomfortable with announcements of self-worth.

"If all goes well," said Kodlich, "you will have very little contact with the First Engineer. Should you need to see him often, that will be bad for us all. That will mean that we've got problems. And I don't like problems."

"Understood," said Ray.

"That's good," Tsuji said. "This is an unusual operation, unlike any other type of mining performed today."

"How's that?" asked Ake.

"Normally, we use the available technology, which has made mining almost one hundred percent automated. Most mining operations use fusion torches, drilling machines with the ability to vaporize rock and pump plasmas around. A fusion torch can move through rock like a fish through water. But here, as at any ruby extraction site, we operate like something out of a hist-holo, virtually moving the rock and soil by hand." Tsuji frowned. "And, of course, we also use 'slave labor,' prison chain gangs; it is all too much."

"Are the rubies really that priceless and delicate?"

"Yes . . . and no." Tsuji made a fist. "With one this size, you could buy a whole planet. And, no, they're not *that* fragile, but would you want to be the one to take the blame for fracturing a perfect specimen? One which, if it was successfully cut, could yield enough stones for two dozen starships?"

"So you're very careful," said Ray, with atypical understatement.

"Very careful." Tsuji then removed a small holo projector from the pocket of his trousers and set it up on Kodlich's desk. Kodlich looked a little miffed that Tsuji did this without so much as a "by your leave," but contained his annoyance.

"I will show you the layout of our current tunnel," Tsuji said as a cross-section of the inactive core of the volcano leapt into existence in the air above the desk. "As you can see . . ."

★ ★ ★

When the light on Kodlich's desk again commanded his attention, he pressed something and his door hissed open. Ray and Ake turned expectantly.

"Is the mutts in there?" said in a high-pitched voice, carrying into the room.

Ray smiled at Ake. "Sounds like those making-friends-wherever-they-go cats again," he said as their new associates, the cat scout team, entered.

"With your permission, Theo, I'll be going," said Tsuji. Without waiting for a response, he got up and walked out. He nodded curtly at the new arrivals but said nothing to them.

An olive-skinned and intense-looking young woman whose profile was marked by a nose with a slight but obvious bump in it—an amazing thing in a time when cosmetic surgery was so simple and inexpensive, Ray considered—led five felines into the room. She cast a disinterested look at Ray and Ake before walking up to Kodlich's desk and saying, "Hello, Theo."

"Hello, Maria," Kodlich said. He rose, as did Ray and Ake. The dogs sat silently, observing the young woman and her cats.

"So this is the new dog team?"

Ray didn't like the almost dismissive way she said that. "Actually, we're just tourists here to see the sights. Are you our new guide?"

Saying nothing, the woman slowly raised the stick she held in her right hand and pointed it at the floor in front of Ake. When nothing happened, she shifted its focus to Ray. Moving as if it was alive, it twisted in her hand and the tip pointed directly at Ray's chest.

"Impressive, most impressive," she said. "The first one—nothing. But this one has the power in him. Hypatia?"

One of the five Siamese came forward and leapt into her arms. Slowly the cat reached out a paw toward Ray. When Ray did not pull back, the feline tentatively touched his shoulder with her paw. "Oww-w-w!" She drew back as if burned.

"Hypatia?"

"Pain. Hate. Fear. Death. Guilt." The cat jumped down and rejoined her compatriots.

Ray looked into the young woman's brown eyes. "The last woman I got close to met a violent end," he said in response to the question he saw there. He smiled a wickedly innocent smile.

"Ah . . . yes," began Kodlich nervously. "I think I'd better make the introductions now."

"Please—before it's too late," said Ake, unsure what he'd just witnessed.

"Gentlemen, and dogs, this is Maria Valdez, the head of one of the finest cat scout teams in existence."

"The finest cat team," said Penelope.

"Ah, puss lips knows the First Engineer well," Ray said to Ake.

Ignoring Ray's comment, Kodlich continued. "And these are her cats: Bastet, the leader; Marisol; Penelope; Hypatia; and Sibella."

Ray looked at Ake, who nodded. Together, Ray and Ake removed their caps and bowed, holding them in front of them. "Off-lee pleased to meet you," Ray said on behalf of them both.

"Heh, heh." This from Beowulf.

As stern a front as Maria Valdez intended to project, she almost allowed a smile to make its way to her lips; she was successful in suppressing the urge, but not, at least to Ray's eyes, the subconscious good will behind it. *Damn!* he thought. *This Maria might turn out to be a human being after all. A scout cat leader . . . who'd have thunk it?*

Kodlich continued. "Maria, I'd like to introduce you to Ray Larkin, the dog team leader, and his partner Ake Ringgren, a skilled physician. As for the dogs, Beowulf is the leader and Littlejohn is his second-in-command. The others include: Mamasan, Ozma, Grendel, Frodo, Sinbad, Tajil, and Gawain."

"I am very pleased to meet you," Maria Valdez said. "Or should I say I am 'off-lee' pleased to meet you?"

"Only if you mean it." Ray stepped forward to take her proffered hand and half squeeze, half shake it. She boldly returned his frank stare of appraisal, tilting her head so that her tightly curled black hair framed her head perfectly.

"Okay, okay," said Ake. "Let's break cleanly." As Maria let go of Ray's hand, Ake took her hand lightly in his and raised it to his lips. He kissed the air just above the back of her hand. "*Enchanté.*"

"Oh-h-h, Old Earth French!" commented Sibella. "I get all runny inside when someone speaks French."

"I'd like to make her all runny on the outside," muttered Frodo, *sotto voce*.

"Well, now that you've all been introduced," suggested Kodlich, "perhaps we can get this mine back on schedule. Without a scout dog team to work with the cats and the others, we've been limited in what we can produce. I hope that's behind us now."

"Why don't the cats and I go on ahead and meet the three of you there?" suggested Maria Valdez. "We've had the grand tour already."

"Certainly, Maria."

"Then it's goodbye for now, gentlemen."

"Goodbye," said Ray.

"Goodbye," said Ake.

"Good riddance," muttered Littlejohn.

# 4

"Jeez!" Ray exclaimed. "I never knew mine tunnels were so big."

"The lasers, fusion torches, and particle-disrupters are so efficient that it takes but a little extra energy expenditure to carve out a more accommodating space than was possible centuries ago," Tsuji explained. "People watch old sinnys and hist-holos about Terran coal mining and believe that's what mineral extraction is like today."

Ray scratched his head. "I thought you told us that the mining techniques you're using *are* antiquated?"

"The actual gemstone extraction, yes," conceded Tsuji, "but not the gross mechanics of boring the tunnels. We aren't wholly in Pickens' time."

"Dickens," said Ray absently.

Tsuji shot him a look but said nothing.

"Ugh, this creepy," Mama-san said.

In addition to the self-contained, fusion-powered lights that were spaced every ten meters or so along the tunnel walls, the tunnel's ceiling glowed with the biologically generated luminescence provided by algae especially bred for conditions like those found in the mine.

"Not creepy, neat!" Tajil said, his head swiveling around as if mounted on a gimbal as he stared in awe at the gently pulsating carpet of light that lit their way.

"I noticed the drop in the temperature when we entered," Ray said, "but I'd have imagined that it would have been more dramatic." He thought for a moment. "It doesn't feel colder than seventeen or eighteen degrees Celsius."

"On a normal, less volcanically active planet you'd be correct," Tsuji replied. "But Hephaestus's mantle is both hot and ever in motion; the geothermal effects are all too apparent underground, even inside an inactive volcano."

"Sorry I mentioned it," Ray said, glancing at the floor of the tunnel as if he could see the rivers of molten rock that coursed far below them.

After the two guards at the mine's entrance had passed them through, they'd encountered no one as they gradually made their way down the almost imperceptible decline. The near total silence was broken by an ever louder beeping that proved to be coming from a mine car slowly ascending from the depths. The mine car rolled on four fat balloon tires that bulged even more from the weight of the rocks and other waste it was bearing up to the surface. As the car's sensors registered them, it slowed even more and began to announce in a feminine voice: "Please watch your step. Mine car number 7-B is coming through."

They parted to allow the barely moving mine car to pass through their midst. "Thank you for your cooperation," 7-B said cheerfully. "It has been nine point three four days since a lost-time accident. Safety and efficiency are everyone's concern."

"You see now why we don't consider the extra tunnel space to be wasted," Tsuji said.

"Yeah," said Ray, "but do we have to hear all that blather every time a mine car passes us?"

Tsuji shook his head. "7-B didn't recognize you because you're new. After the mine cars encounter you a few times, they'll merely beep warningly unless you fail to get out of their way; in that case, they'll stop and again address you directly."

"Is mine car female?" Beowulf asked.

Tsuji smiled at Beowulf's question. "No, but most of the guards are male, so a female voice is psychologically more attention-getting."

"Sure," said Sinbad. "Ozma's voice can make Littlejohn jump plenty quick, you bet." The other dogs guffawed at that, since Littlejohn and Ozma were notorious sweethearts.

Tsuji watched as the mine car disappeared in the distance and added, "Of course, the cars recognize Maria Valdez and her cats as females and use a male voice for them."

After they had walked an indeterminate distance, the tunnel bifurcated and Tsuji led them down the branch that bore to the right.

"This is fun, but are we going to get there soon?" Ake asked.

"We're just about to one of the extraction sites," Tsuji replied. As if to support his words, a trickle of sound reached them: implements slicing into soil and voices speaking deliberately and without emotion. They "bottomed out" and rounded a gentle curve. The first person they saw was a guard.

The soldier touched his cap at the sight of Tsuji. Since Tsuji was a civilian and, presumably, had no real power over the man, Ray guessed that the guard's response was probably both automatic and no more than a formality he was ordered to observe by his superiors.

"I'm wondering why we're really needed," Ray said. "The guards are armed; it seems to me they should be able to handle the diggers."

"The soldiers have orders to see that the prisoners do their work and that they don't escape," Tsuji said. "Apart from that, they couldn't care less if the diggers slice and dice them and have 'em on toast." *And if such an occurrence wouldn't interfere with his precious mining,* Ray mused, *Tsuji wouldn't give a rat's ass about the prisoners, either.*

As they passed the first guard, several more came into view. Ray, the dogs, and Ake also got their first look at the prisoner-miners: six men and three women clad in olive-drab work jumpers. Their uniforms included work gloves and heavy, plasteel-tipped boots. Where they were not covered by respirator masks, their faces were grimy and coated with dust, despite a small barrel-shaped filtration device that removed as many of the particles swirling in the air as it could.

Ake was puzzled by the sight of the squat filter. "Why bother with an air filter since the miners wear individual respirators?"

"The dogs." Tsuji gestured toward Beowulf and the others. "They can't do their job in a mask—they're effectively muzzled." He shifted from one foot to another. "And since the cats outright refused to wear them, we saw no real reason why anyone except the miners themselves really needed them."

Beowulf's face clouded. "Them cats again."

"The crotch sniffers is here," a Siamese voice reverberated down the mine tunnel.

Ray smiled at Beowulf. "Yes, them darn cats again." From further down the tunnel came the cats, sauntering as if they were strolling down Luna Avenue in Boswash on a Sunday afternoon.

The cat called Sibella rubbed up against Tajil and said, "Nice place for a funeral, huh?"

"Yours?" Tajil asked hopefully.

"Tsk, tsk," said Sibella, swishing her tail from side to side coyly as she walked away. "A bad attitude."

Ray smiled encouragingly at Maria Valdez. "Don't worry, it'll take some time but soon both teams will be fast friends. C'mon over tonight after work and we'll have a little wine and some mouse heads and cheese on crackers. We'll get real."

Maria Valdez just shook her head. "If I enter 'obnoxious' on my dictionary cube, does a holo of you appear?"

Ray punched Ake lightly on the shoulder. "She likes me."

★ ★ ★

Although Maria Valdez and her cats didn't actually protect the prisoners physically, they were indispensable to their safety. The scout cats' genetic alterations were superficially similar to the changes wrought in scout dogs. Skilled feline geneticists induced and manipulated mutations in the cats' genes. While the dogs were bred for size, speech, and intelligence, the cats were imbued only with the latter two abilities. Although they were larger than unaltered domestic cats, scout cats rarely weighed more than seven to ten kilos. The cats' smaller brains put them at a disadvantage when compared to the size of the canine brains, but there were compensations.

Even with all the advances in genetic reconstruction, there were occasional random results. One of the first unexpected traits to emerge was telepathy. Doctors Feng and Rothschild, working with a Siamese cat named Neko-Chan, charted feline DNA which proved to be linked to psychic powers, especially telepathy. Within a short period of time, this useful new trait was isolated and emphasized.

Scout cats were usually but not always Siamese. Like Neko-Chan, Siamese cats had a higher potential for telepathy. The telepathic trait that made the cats so valuable was nearly one hundred percent among themselves and with their specially chosen human leader.

The human leader was always a woman with highly developed

psychic powers herself. The pairing of a human leader with a scout cat team was a delicate and careful process. The choice was necessarily mutual and unanimous; neither a leader nor a team could be imposed upon the other since they became as one over time. Just as Ray and other scout dog team leaders were usually dedicated loners uncomfortable with all but their team, most cat scout leaders were also solitary types. It was a description which might be vehemently denied by a young woman surrounded by a half-dozen loyal and dedicated feline friends.

The cats' telepathic powers were less evident with other humans and animals. These other beings, lacking all but rudimentary psi powers themselves, could be *sensed* by the cats, if not merged with mentally. This lack of empathy was more pronounced with alien minds, but the cats possessed the ability to sense "auras" if the creatures projecting them were within a limited range. This was the cats' special value to the miners; once a "digger" approached to within ten meters or so, the cats were able to detect its primitive but distinctive mental pattern and alert the dogs to an impending attack.

Maria Valdez had a special talent as well. Using a "dowsing rod," she was able to locate the formations containing Rostoff rubies. ESPers used the psychic enhancing qualities of the stones to help them clean the hulls of starships transiting the utter emptiness and non-being of hyperspace; the rubies' special powers to amplify psychic powers naturally did the same for Maria's talents. It would be untrue to suggest that the stones literally "called out" to her, but she and two of her cats could sense them beneath their blanket of soil and rock. Maria could not explain this special talent to someone lacking it. The best analogy she could use was to compare it to an average person's sense of hearing: You can hear sounds coming around objects or emanating from beneath the floor or above the ceiling. It's a sensory skill; it doesn't seem special or mystical.

It was, however, secret. She was not about to tell the scout dog team about this particular talent.

## II

"Colonel Natasha Bukovsky," Kodlich said, "I have the honor of introducing you to Ray Larkin, the leader of our new scout dog team, his associate Ake Ringgren, and Beowulf." Kodlich clearly didn't believe it was necessary to explain who Beowulf was.

"Colonel Bukovsky," said Ray and Ake together.

" 'Lo," said Beowulf.

"Pleased to meet you, Citizen Larkin, Citizen Ringgren and . . . ah . . . Beowulf," Bukovsky said disinterestedly. Ray noted that she made no attempt to do anything as civil as shake their hands.

Colonel Bukovsky stood stiffly at attention, her face set in an official and officious expression which betrayed nothing of what might be going behind it. *A tough cookie,* he told himself. Ray also noted that the woman's uniform was impeccably tailored and correct to the smallest detail; there was nothing missing nor was there anything extraneous. *By the book,* Ray thought. *She'll carry out every order perfectly, but I'll bet anything she lacks the imagination to speculate about tomorrow's weather.*

"You have been to the mine already?" After asking her question, Bukovsky glanced at something on her desk top, as if to underscore that she was interrupting her work for this intrusion, however necessary it might be.

"Yes," responded Kodlich. "They have also met Citizen Valdez and her scout cat team."

"Good." She raised her eyes slowly, allowing them to sweep Ray from his boots to the top of his head. The intensity of her unblinking gaze left Ray feeling as if he was being particle-scanned. Ake got the same treatment but for a shorter period of time.

Kodlich coughed uncomfortably and shifted his weight from one leg to another. Oblivious to the discomfort she was inducing—*Or is that her intention?* Ray wondered—Bukovsky again looked down at the doc-cubes lying on her desk. Clearly, she was reading their dossier. "Please sit down," she said absently.

As the commandant's eyes darted across the projection she was studying, Ray continued his evaluation of her. Her forehead was shaved except for a credit-sized oval from which an eight-centimeter-long thatch of auburn hair erupted just off center, as was the current custom. On one side of her head her hair, cut short, was carefully layered. The hair on the other side was half again as long. Ray found it a peculiar style that failed to flatter all but the most handsome women who felt compelled by fashion to wear it. Such a hairstyle would have defeated a more traditional beauty than Natasha Bukovsky.

Bukovsky's high cheekbones and the angular planes of her long face betrayed her Slavic heritage. Her emerald eyes were her most striking feature, apart from her wide shoulders and sleek, muscular build. She was probably shorter than she first appeared; her uniform and her air of command combined to make her seem larger and more imposing. Ray wouldn't have considered her his "type," but he guessed that many men would find Natasha Bukovsky and her austerity attractive. In the way that men coolly analyze women, Ray conceded that she would "do." It was not her appearance that Ray found off-putting, but her position and her probable value system.

Bukovsky looked up to see Ray's frank appraisal of her appearance. "Tell me, Citizen Larkin, do I look like what you expected me to look?"

"More or less."

"Humph." She turned her gaze on Ringgren. "And you, Citizen Ringgren, I understand that you are a doctor. Is that not so?"

"That's correct," Ake said.

Bukovsky looked down again at the glowing text projected by the cube in front of her. "It does not say here where your assignment previous to Talos was."

"Oh, really?" asked Ray innocently. He leaned over her desk and peered at the upside down doc-cubes as if to read their files.

Seeing where he was looking, Bukovsky carefully placed an inactivated cube over the projection and asked, "Would you care to tell me where you previously served?"

Ake looked at Ray, who rubbed the place on his finger where he had worn the General's ring. Ake nodded almost imperceptibly and said, "I'm afraid that's classified information."

"We do a *lot* of top secret work for the Federation," offered Ray helpfully.

Bukovsky leaned back in her straight-backed chair and bridged her fingers. Clearly, she didn't believe them; just as clearly, there was nothing much she could do about it. Ray had told Ake that he didn't see any harm in admitting that their last assignment was on Talos; Ake agreed but countered that giving out *any* unnecessary information concerning Chiron might be unwise.

Ray found it difficult to believe that Bukovsky didn't know who they were. If Kodlich, a civilian, had been permitted minimal access to the information by his syndicate—and had "read between the lines" for the rest, as he had put it—why not Bukovsky? A logical but shocking explanation suddenly occurred to Ray. *They don't trust her! It's that goddamn military mind!*

*Because she WAS a protégée of the disgraced General, she's been cut out of the information loop.*

Shifting gears, Bukovsky turned to Beowulf, whom she'd ignored up to this point. "Tell me, Beowulf," she asked in as friendly a fashion as she could, "did you enjoy your last assignment previous to Talos?"

"Oh, yes!"

"And where were you?"

"On a planet."

"I see."

Ray glanced sideways at Ake and winked.

"What sort of work did you do?" Colonel Bukovsky persisted.

"Scout dog work," Beowulf replied proudly.

"How novel," Bukovsky said. She recognized the futility of pursuing this line of questioning any further.

"Well, I know you're busy, Commandant Bukovsky," Kodlich said briskly. "So, if it's all right with you we'll leave you to your many important duties." He started to rise.

"Just a moment, please." Kodlich reluctantly settled back. Bukovsky gave Ray and Ake a long, hard look. "We run an efficient, orderly, and profitable operation here. If you want to get along with me you'll do your job well." Her eyes narrowed. "If you screw up, however, I'll have your balls on a platter. Is that understood?"

"We read you loud and clear, Colonel Bukovsky."

They rose and walked to the door. "One other thing . . ." They stopped and stood expectantly. "You are to protect the prisoners, but don't fraternize with them. They are not ordinary convicts; they include political troublemakers. To talk to them is to join them. Do I make myself clear?"

"Abundantly," Ray replied.

"Good. Goodbye, Citizens."

"G'bye!" Beowulf said for all four of them.

As the door hissed shut behind them, Ray took Kodlich by the arm and said, "That went well, don't you think?"

# III

The jungle was alive with sound and color; the visual and aural impact was almost more than mere sensory organs could encompass. Things that resembled Terran monkeys—and things that didn't resemble them one iota—swung through the trees, chattering and shrieking in a never-ending symphony of dissonance. Flying insects the size of the *Truman* zigzagged past, their buzzing as loud as any earthly cataract. After the eerie and tomblike quietude of the tunnels, Ray found the contrast refreshing, a welcome tonic to the grimness of the mines.

The air was also wonderful. It wasn't at all like Terran air—*Of course*, Ray thought, *that's probably a blessing*—nor was it like the thin, metallic-tasting air of Talos. It was thick and almost palpable; it smelled of vegetation and of hot, burnt rock. Ray decided there was nothing to compare it to; it was something special.

This sojourn in the jungle, away from the grimness of the mining and prison compound, was marvelously restorative, Ray thought. After their meeting with the coldly professional Colonel Bukovsky, Ray needed this communion with the natural world. The rain forest was as dangerous as the camp, but its threats were straightforward and honest, not sneaky and hidden.

"Beowulf, don't let anyone wander off too far," Ray commanded, his flared nostrils imbibing the heavy rain forest air like a drunkard guzzling draughts of beer. *God, I love it!*

"You heard Ray," Beowulf said. "Try to stay together or close to each other; no solo excursions."

"Yah, yah," the other dogs said, eager to plunge into the teeming foliage.

Ray made one of his many simple gestures that he used to communicate nonverbally with the dogs and they whooped and dashed off to explore on their own. All, that is, except for Beowulf and Littlejohn, who insisted on staying with Ray and Ake to act as bodyguards.

"I know a few already, but you'll have to teach me more of your hand signals," Ake said.

"Later," Ray said distractedly, acting like a man whose eyes are gazing at his lover.

"I didn't mean this minute."

Ray, who'd been staring intently into the rain forest, turned his attention back to Ake and said, "Right. I'm sorry, Ake, I wasn't really paying attention. Forgive me."

"Mary once told me she knew an old expression that fit you perfectly: 'You can take the boy out of the country, but you can't take the country out of the boy.'"

Ray smiled. "I do love it so. Just think, the rain forest covers most of this planet. Don't you want to know what's in it?"

"Sure," Ake replied. "But not knowing won't kill me, either."

As they paused to glance around the small clearing they suddenly found themselves in, something small and furry and looking rather like a hare as drawn by a committee that included Salvador Dalí and Hieronymus Bosch burst from the luxuriant undergrowth followed closely by one of the dogs. The pursuee and pursuer negotiated a zigzag pattern in front of them and plunged back into the jungle on the other side of the clearing.

"Was that Ozma?" Ake asked.

"No, it was Frodo," Beowulf said.

"I thought so."

"Ray?"

"Yeah, Littlejohn?"

"What's that?"

Ray looked in the direction Littlejohn was indicating. Roughly one hundred meters away, a slender figure stood watching them. It was motionless for several moments; then it retreated and melted back into the jungle.

"Was that . . . ?" began Ake.

"Yep. I'd say we just ran into our first K'a-nii."

★ ★ ★

Maria Valdez and her cats lived in a structure much like the one which housed Ray, Ake, and the dogs. The only obvious difference from the outside was the color, which was an electric blue rather than the more vivid orange the men and dogs enjoyed. For this visit, Ray and Ake brought only Beowulf with them. The other dogs had complained about being left out but soon got over it.

"Hey, she has a door bell," Ray observed as they approached the front door. "Why don't we have a door bell?"

"We do, Mr. Observant," replied Ake, pressing the glowing panel.

"We do?"

"Trust me."

The door swung open and Maria looked out with interest. "Why, goodness, it's the new neighbors. What brings you out to these parts?"

"Just thought we'd drop by to say howdy and to introduce ourselves to you and the young-uns," Ray said, nodding toward the cats who were congregating behind Maria.

Ake was surprised that Maria was good-humored enough to

play along with Ray's "Aw, shucks" cowpoke routine. It helped that Westerns had suddenly and for no apparent reason made a comeback on the hol-vee, especially back on Terra. Otherwise, he doubted if Maria would have gotten Ray's drift. *Drift? Now I'm thinking that way!*

"May we come in, ma'am?" Ray asked.

"Only if we drop this ridiculous routine," Maria told him.

"Amen," seconded Ake.

"Sure thing, Miss Kitty," Ray couldn't resist tacking on. Since Maria didn't know a thing about 20th-century television Westerns, she took Ray's words at face value.

"Ouch," she said. "No awful puns, either!"

"Let's go on in, Festus."

"Humor him," said Ake. "We can't get his medication out here."

The house was laid out much the same as their own dwelling. Maria led them directly into the large living room and asked them to please have a seat. Ray and Ake plopped themselves down on a large and comfortable sofa whose very plushiness and firmness mocked the sorry condition of a similar one in their own living room. Actually, Ray considered, the whole living room mocked and shamed their place.

Ray took in the colorful oriental carpet; the soft, indirect lighting; the hard to get cuddle chairs; the expensive-looking end tables and other bric-a-brac. Whistling slowly through his teeth, Ray said, "What you've done here is truly amazing, Maria. This is a revelation."

"An embarrassing revelation," Ake said ruefully. "Now we see what can be done with our place."

Marisol, conscious of the fact that Maria had warned the cats to try to behave themselves when their guests arrived, just said, "Scout dogs is big animals and that wears out furniture real fast."

Ray was less astonished by the insightfulness of Marisol's comment than by the civil way she presented it. "That's certainly true . . . ah, Marisol," he said gratefully to the slender Siamese.

Beowulf didn't care for this turn of events. "What you mean we wear out furniture?"

"Beowulf," said Ray, "you and the other guys *are* very big dogs and you like to lounge on the chairs and sofas as much as Ake and I do." He smiled at Beowulf to make sure the dog didn't mistake what he was saying. "You are my leader, my number one—but you *are* a load, Beowulf. It's no big deal, but it's the truth."

"Besides," added Ake, "the real truth of the matter is that while you guys accelerate the deterioration of the furniture, Ray and I have shit for taste." He swept his eyes around the carefully thought-out design and execution of the room and added, "This reflects a lot of hard work and planning."

"Sometimes I wonder why I bother. I rarely have visitors, so it's mostly for my own satisfaction."

"How *did* you get so many beautiful furnishings?" Ray queried.

Maria shrugged, tossing her curly black hair. "Every time a starship makes a connection with us, it brings something else I've ordered. You'd be surprised how quickly things accumulate even with only a few flights a year."

"We should try doing that," Ray said to Ake.

"Oh, sure," Ake said. "We get around more than Martian flu. We'd no sooner get things just the way we wanted them before we'd have to move on."

"We're always moving on in our professions. It doesn't mean a person can't have nice things," Maria said. "Anyway, what can I get you two to drink?" When Beowulf gave her a baleful stare, she amended, "You three to drink?"

When Ake had his white wine, Ray his bourbon and water, and Beowulf his bowl of beer, Maria leaned back with her own gin and tonic and waited for them to bring up the reason for their visit. Knowing men and dogs as well as she did, Maria assumed they hadn't come by just to exchange pleasantries.

"Are you sure there are no listening devices secreted away somewhere in here?" Ake asked.

"I'm sure," Maria said. She picked up her stick and held it out in front of her. "With this, I can quickly ascertain whether or not something foreign has been planted here."

"You can sense a bug?" Ray asked.

"Yes."

"That's a nice talent to have." Ray stared at the stick she grasped. "Is the power in that wand?"

"It's not a 'wand.' What do you think—that I'm a witch?" When Ray just smiled enigmatically, she said, "The power is in me—and in you, as I've already said. And, as for the bugs, try it—I think you'll discover that you can sense them if you concentrate."

"Ray hasn't concentrated since grad school," Ake told her.

Ignoring them both, Ray just snorted. "Humph. You know what power I'd really like to possess?"

"No."

"The power to get people to talk about the K'a-nii. So far, neither the mining consortium nor the military seem to have any great interest in adding to the store of knowledge about them." Ray looked at Maria strangely. "What I really find incomprehensible, however, is how little interest you seem to take in an intelligent alien species."

"The K'a-nii *are* intelligent," Maria admitted to Ray, "but they are also stolid and impenetrable. Since they are not warlike and are content to leave us alone, we are equally content to leave them alone."

"That's nuts!" burst out Ray. "We haven't come across all that many sentient races in the galaxy so far; each one is a chance to learn important things."

"You haven't got unlimited time to spend studying them—and it would take weeks, months, maybe even years, to get to a point where you had even a rudimentary understanding of them and their customs."

"How can you know that if you haven't tried communicating with them yourself?"

"Mark Van Aalst, your immediate predecessor, was also determined to understand the K'a-nii."

Ray's eyes widened; this was interesting information. "Yes?"

"Don't get excited," she said. "In the time he could spend going to the closest village, he found out virtually nothing. It was a waste of time, and when Bukovsky discovered he was beginning to neglect his duties here she had the consortium buy out his contract."

"He learned *nothing* at all about them? I find it hard to believe that."

Maria shot Ray an exasperated look. "They are *alien*! They're not humans in funny makeup; they don't think like we do." She softened slightly and added, "Mark said once that he had discovered something interesting about them, something he thought might demolish our assumptions about reality and the nature of what surrounds us."

A delicious shiver of premonition ran up Ray's spine. As offhandedly as he could, he asked, "Did he ever tell you what this was?"

"No."

So much for his anticipatory goosebumps.

Exasperated, Ray kept up his questioning, refusing to give up. Ake joined Ray in putting pressure on Maria. As a result of their persistence Maria volunteered that the K'a-niian Ray and Ake had seen was probably from a village located further down the sleeping volcano's broad lower slopes, nearer to the canopy provided by the rain forest's trees yet still above the dangerous jungle floor.

"I'm just guessing that is where he came from, of course," she said. "As I told you, they're a blank holo to us. I called them a 'tribe' but there's no way of knowing if that's how they view themselves. They may be an extended family; a loose alignment of several families; or a formally ordered social group ruled by custom and taboo."

"I'd put my money on the latter, since that's how most primitive societies construct themselves," Ray had said.

Maria just shook her head and threw up her hands as if Ray were a little child stubbornly demanding to stay up to see Santa Claus come out of the fireplace holoscenic. "There you go again. They are not humanlike in any way, shape, or form; don't start thinking that you can understand them."

"Miss Kitty, I can figure out any sentient lifeform's patterns."

"We'll see."

When Ray attempted to pump Maria for still more information he ran into a stone wall; she had told him all she was going to tell him about the K'a-nii. *At least for now*, Ray thought, sipping his drink and making plans.

# 5

Through a break in the trees and foliage Ray could see a few structures that looked like huts constructed of mud and vegetable matter. Lacking the technology and the means to produce the massive energy needed to carve out a suitable living area on the broad shoulders of the volcano as the humans had done, the K'a-nii eschewed brute force and coexisted with their surroundings. As a result, their village followed the curves and bumps at the mountain's base rather than attempting to overpower them.

*Well*, Ray decided, *it's put up or shut up time*.

Careful to make sure he moved slowly yet openly, Ray approached the village. When he was about fifty meters away, he found a fallen tree trunk to sit on. He picked up a good-sized stick and struck the side of the trunk several times with it to scare away any unwanted inhabitants. Something hairy, with eight or nine legs scurried away. *It's a good thing I don't suffer from arachnophobia*, Ray thought. He settled in, half facing the K'a-nii camp, half facing the jungle. "See how unthreatening I am, fellas," he said softly as if he were speaking to the encampment's inhabitants.

At first Ray wondered if they *had* seen him, since nothing happened. Then he realized how stupid that was. A K'a-niian had probably observed his every movement since he'd set foot outside his house. "Me Tarzan, you poor dumb natives," he chided himself, calling up memories of Edgar Rice Burroughs's jungle hero. It had always amazed Ray—and it was a good anthropological/social example of self-indulgent fantasy/racist thinking—that the outsider Tarzan supposedly knew and understood the jungle better than the natives.

"C'mon, dickhead," he chided himself. "Don't make the mistake of thinking that these characters are intellectually inferior just because their technology is simpler."

Ray considered the distance that separated him from the K'a-nii village and decided that he'd better keep his monologues internal. *After all, I don't know how good their hearing is. They might even understand Federation-standard English. Fudge, there's no telling what they may have picked up from Van Aalst or the first survey team.*

That was a lesson Ray had learned the hard way about people or creatures about which you knew nothing: Since you have no way of knowing what they can or cannot do, you must assume that they can do anything and everything. Ray swatted a multilegged something crawling on his neck and increased the intensity of his ultrasonic repeller. It seemed a dubious proposition that the K'a-nii were so intelligent or such excellent mimics that during their brief exposure to an alien language they had learned to understand the meaning of the words. Yet it remained a possibility; Ray had no intention of underestimating the K'a-nii, no matter how primitive they might appear on the surface.

And so Ray spent several hours sitting all but motionless on the fallen tree, watching the activities of the K'a-nii village while the wildlife and the K'a-nii observed him in return. Although he was unwilling to betray too obvious an interest in their doings, Ray still managed to observe how social they seemed to be. They had extensive sibilant exchanges which could only be speech, they touched one another with great frequency, and they moved about in groups. *Hey, that's right*, Ray considered, *I haven't seen a single K'a-niian by himself . . . or herself.*

The small buttonlike thing on Ray's shirt was really a holocorder. It was faithfully documenting every sight and sound. It was Ray's intention, after several such sessions, to set before the base computer the task of interpreting and translating the K'a-niian language. *No matter how alien they are*, he theorized, *there's still a universal core of experience—food, sex, relationships, shelter, the environment—that is amenable to interpretation and understanding.* He shrugged. *Of course, I might just be kidding myself about that, especially the sex part.* One of the only things thought to be known for certain about the K'a-nii was that they seemed not to have any discernible sexes. *Boy, wouldn't that make life a lot easier!*

It suddenly struck Ray that he'd seen no children. As far as he could tell, the K'a-nii were all roughly the same size. *That's odd*, he thought. *Well, maybe not. Maybe they're taboo and live elsewhere.*

Ray made a point of conspicuously standing up and stretching his stiff muscles. He'd shown himself enough for one day. Thinking again of Tarzan, he said softly, "Eventually, I'll win over the 'Chief,' but the 'Witch Doctor' will remain suspicious and later his jealousy of my 'white magic' will lead him to try to have me sacrificed to the volcano god." The ridiculous pop-culture scenario made him laugh out loud.

## II

*Beep, beep, beep.*

"Mine car number 5-C is coming through. Please watch your step. I repeat, mine car number 5-C is coming through."

"Good morning, mine car number 5-C," Ray said.

"Good morning, Citizen . . . Larkin."

"And how are things in the salt mines today?"

"Salt mines?" asked the car, its logic circuits analyzing Ray's words and failing to deduce a correct meaning. "This is a gemstone extraction site; there is no salt in the mine."

"Just joking, number 5-C," Ray said. "I know how much you rubber-treaded little devils like a good joke."

"Yes, sir. Er . . . no, sir. Er . . . good day, sir. Watch out please, mine car number 5-C is coming through."

As the heavily laden car passed through the dogs, Ray said loudly to Beowulf, "I hope that number 5-C doesn't encounter that swarm of synthetics-eating beetles."

The little mine car halted momentarily, tentatively rotated back toward Ray and the dogs, and then straightened out and sped away. It moved quickly up the tunnel, muttering to itself: "There ARE no beetles. This is NOT a salt mine. There ARE no beetles."

"What a maroon!" Ray marvelled.

Beowulf watched it disappear into the gloom and cocked his head quizzically at Ray. "Ray, why you tease that little mine car?"

"Don't anthropomorphize 5-C too much, Beowulf. It's just a piece of machinery. Besides . . ." He leaned down until his mouth was beside the big dog's left ear. "I like to prove to myself that it'll be a long time before robots are good enough to replace old-fashioned, carbon-based bioplasmic organisms produced by unskilled laborers."

"Huh?"

"You and I, dog breath, you and I."

"Ha, ha," laughed Gawain, who had overheard Ray's last comment. "Ray call you dog breath!"

Beowulf shook his big furry head. "Mebbe some dogs be replaced by robotics easier'n you think, Ray."

"You might be right, Beowulf," Ray agreed.

"I guess if machines can't do our job, then they can't do the cats' job, neither," Beowulf said as they continued down the mine tunnel.

"That's correct."

"So it makes sense that we work with the pussfaces, eh?" Ray had to laugh at that since it came out "buss-faces."

"They have the telepathy, Beowulf."

"What that mean?" Gawain asked, puzzled by the unfamiliar term.

"They can 'read' minds, more or less," Ray explained. "At least they can sense other sentient creatures' emotions and they can tell when an intruder is in the area."

"Oh."

"They are still butt bumps," opined Littlejohn.

"Oh, no," said a high-pitched voice dripping with sarcasm. "They saying bad things about us. I crushed to pieces." Penelope slowly sashayed up the tunnel, her tail held high and flicking back and forth.

"Speakin' of pussfaces," said Littlejohn.

"Maria is waiting for you," Penelope said. "If we know the diggers is coming and you not there to help, it not do much good."

"I got you," Ray said. "C'mon, guys, let's hustle into position."

"Why only five of us, Ray?" Beowulf asked.

"There's only five cats," Ray responded. "And I've decided I want a morning shift and an afternoon shift. It'll keep you guys from getting bored on the routine days."

"There not be any routine days," Penelope told him.

Ray shrugged. *I certainly hope so*, he fervently wished, *I certainly hope so*.

Ray passed by the three guards armed with their stumpy energy rifles. The three, two men and a woman, were at least a hundred meters from the prisoner-miners they were guarding. Since there was but one way out of the mine shaft, unless you were a digger, the three soldiers saw no need to actually hover over their charges; they weren't going anywhere. Besides, mining operations attracted diggers, and if the diggers sliced up the prisoners first, the guards would have plenty of time to prepare for their attack.

"Ah, the great man finally cometh," Maria said when she saw Ray approaching.

"I wouldn't put it that way myself." Ray then held out his right hand, which was balled into a fist as if it contained something, turned it palm side up, and slowly uncurled his fingers to reveal . . . nothing. "I wish I had brought an apple for the first day of classes, Miss Valdez, I surely do."

"Good. I like that you're thinking of it in that way—this *is* the first day of classes. Pay attention and you pass; fail to learn the lessons and you're dead."

"Jiminy, Miz Valdez, I's plenty scared now!"

"You know, you aren't that much different from Mark Van Aalst, the dog leader you replaced. What is it with you rutters? Are you all cases of arrested development or what?"

Ray smiled. Rutters was the most recent slang word for men. Ray made popping noises with his lips. "The dogs absolutely cannot do that," he said, "just cannot." Then he added, "Yeah, I didn't get enough oxygen in the womb."

"I'm serious. This is dangerous work. The diggers aren't playing around. If one can, it'll disembowel you quicker than you can say eviscerate."

"Hmm-m-m. So, tell me—what's a routine contact like?"

"Rutters," sighed Maria. "Since you haven't encountered one yet, you have no way of knowing there's no such thing as a 'routine' contact with a digger."

"I already told him that," said Penelope proudly.

"She did," Ray confirmed. "Give her a catnip ball as a reward."

"Ray, I wouldn't—" Maria Valdez put a hand to her head, her fingers touching her temple as if a sharp pain had just begun to pulse there.

"Uh-oh," said Penelope nervously.

"Digger coming!" Marisol shouted at the top of her small voice.

"Just one?" Maria asked, unshouldering her energy rifle and slipping the safety off.

"More," Marisol said. "I think two."

Maria now sensed them. "I agree, but where?"

Marisol's tail went up and then pointed at a section of the tunnel wall as the prisoners put down their tools and ran for the protection of the dogs. "There," she said. "Any second now. They real close."

"Digger coming here, too!" shouted Bastet, further down the tunnel.

"Jeezus!" Ray muttered, his fingers dancing nervously on his energy rifle's plastic stock. "Dogs, be ready."

"Well, you got your wish, Ray," Maria Valdez said. "I hope you're satisfied."

"I gotta break my cherry sometime. Better sooner than later."

It seemed to Ray that in the split-second before the first digger burst from the tunnel wall that the area bulged out warningly. But it all happened so fast Ray wasn't sure that it wasn't simply his imagination playing tricks on his eyes. The digger exploded out into the tunnel as if a giant hand had thrust it through the soil like an ice pick through cardboard. Ray thought that the digger was vaguely reminiscent of a child-sized mole with four powerful limbs tipped by molecular-steel-sharp claws. The creature attacked immediately and with savage fury.

Beowulf, as he'd been trained to do, allowed Littlejohn and Sinbad to take on the first digger and barked orders to the other two dogs. " 'Member, there's two more comin'," he told them. "Grendel and Gawain, you take second and—"

Digger number two burst from the mine tunnel just a meter from where the first had appeared. As ordered, Gawain and Grendel directed their attention to this new intruder. By default, that left Beowulf and Ray to handle the third digger when it appeared from the opposite wall. As they turned to meet the threat, the digger exploded out into the tunnel, curled itself into a tight ball, and began rolling toward Beowulf.

Snarling and baring his teeth, Beowulf braced himself for the digger's attack. It uncurled with amazing rapidity and hurled itself at the big scout dog. Ray brought his rifle to bear on the two, but Beowulf was too close to his attacker for him to fire. Barking loudly, Beowulf feinted and dodged the digger's claws as it pressed a furious attack.

"Sonofabitch!" Ray swore. "This is getting me nowhere fast!"

Unable to draw a bead on the digger that didn't quickly end up with Beowulf in his sights, Ray held his energy rifle out before him, walked toward the two combatants, and shoved the weapon up against the digger's side. He pressed the firing stud. The energy rifle's usual snapping and crackling electrical sound, was muffled, as was the weapon's flash of light.

The result, however, was instantaneous. The digger was flung sideways by the force of the charge. It hit the floor of the tunnel and shivered. The smell of charred flesh in his nostrils, Ray fired into the creature's midsection. The digger made a keening, regretful sound and stopped moving. As focused as he was on what was going on in front of him, a part of Ray's mind made note of the flash of Maria's energy rifle behind him.

"Stay away from that damn thing, Beowulf," Ray commanded. "I'm not convinced it's dead."

It wasn't.

The digger suddenly rolled over and leapt up, clearly determined to rend Ray from end to end. Beowulf met its charge and, twisting in the air like a ballet dancer, clamped down on the back of its all but nonexistent neck and bit down hard. Blood gushed freely as the muscles in Beowulf's neck bulged and his jaws were forced closer and closer. The digger stopped struggling and hung limply from Beowulf's jaws. The big dog opened his mouth and allowed the body to fall to the tunnel floor.

Ray turned to see that one of the other two diggers lay dead, its flesh mangled and wisps of smoke rising from its short brown fur. Ray saw all that in an instant because he quickly turned his attention to the surviving digger confronting the other four dogs. While normally they were berserkers, this digger was not attacking. It seemed content to cower against one of the walls, its claws waving slowly in the air in front of it. It was a standoff.

Ray made a hand motion and the dogs backed off. "We've done our duty," Ray said to Maria Valdez. "Let's let it go."

"As far as we know," Valdez said, "they aren't very intelligent and they aren't social, but . . ." She pumped four bolts of energy into the digger. The first pinioned it against the tunnel wall, and the other three pummeled it like invisible fists. The ragged remains slid down to the floor.

"Jesus H. Nixon!" Ray whistled softly. "You are one tough ESPer, lady."

Maria Valdez shouldered her still-warm energy rifle. "I'd advise you not to forget that, Citizen Larkin."

"Hey, you can call me Herr Doktor Larkin," he said to her retreating back. When Ray saw she was checking the condition of her cats, he decided that it behooved him to do the same with his dogs.

"Roll call," he said loudly. "Beowulf?"

"I okay."

"Sinbad?"

"I okay, too."

"Littlejohn?"

"No problems, Ray."

"Gawain?"

"Coupla scratches, but me be fine."

"I'll check you out and put some salve on those cuts in a minute, Gawain. How about you, Grendel?"

"Same. I gots a coupla cuts, too." Grendel shook her head and added disdainfully, "The mosquitoes on this planet prob'ly give you worse bites than these little scratches."

"That may be, but even minor wounds can fester and become infected quickly in this humidity." He looked at the others. "So don't hold anything back from me, understand?"

"Yah, Ray," they chorused.

Maria Valdez returned. "Everything all right with your cats?" Ray asked her.

"No problems."

"And the prisoners?"

"Everyone's fine." She looked at him out of the corner of her eye. "And why not? It was just a routine contact."

"Add my words to a few potatoes and a vegetable and I'll eat them for supper tonight."

"I don't believe it—the big tough man admitting he was wrong?"

Remembering an old sinny called *Little Caesar*, Ray said in his best Edward G. Robinson voice, "I ain't so tough."

"Should I know who you just 'did'?"

"Not if'n you don't know real old sinnys," Beowulf informed her. "*Real* old."

"Yeah, thanks, Beowulf," Ray said.

"Did I miss anything?" inquired Sibella.

Gawain, still unused to the cats' sarcasm, said, "Miss anything? Jeez, we knocked the heck outa some claw things! It was fun."

Sibella paused in front of Gawain. "You did! You killed some bad monsters? Oh-h-h, you so big and masculine!" She stood up on her hind legs until she could reach Gawain's muzzle. She planted a big kiss right on his muzzle.

Surprised and confused, Gawain backed away and sat down. "Ugh-h-h!" he said, wiping the back of one big paw across his mouth. "Cat germs—I'm poisoned!"

The other four dogs found this tremendously amusing. Ray, however, got a gleam in his eye. He positioned himself squarely in front of Maria Valdez. "My turn," he said, closing his eyes.

"Okay," said Maria. She picked up Sibella, who obligingly gave him a perfunctory kiss. Frowning, he opened his eyes.

"Oh, no, don't tell me that . . ."

"Hm-m-m, Ray kiss better than Gawain; Ray gots lips."

# III

Although quadrupedal, like so much of the life on Terranlike planets, the diggers didn't really resemble a Terran lifeform. Their four tiny, vestigial eyes were essentially useless; diggers found their way around via some kind of sonar. Their foreheads bulged, betraying the fact that—like whales and dolphins—the dome was where they processed the returning echoes from their almost inaudible high-pitched squeaks.

"Boy, is that ugly," said Mama-san about the digger corpse Ray was preparing to dissect.

"And stink, too," added Frodo.

"It might say the same of you," said Ray. "About being ugly, that is. And we could all use a good hosing down."

"I must admit *I* never would have thought of using the kitchen table to dissect a large, smelly, dirt-grubbing animal," Ake said.

"I haven't had time to set up any of my equipment in a more suitable area," Ray explained.

"Sure, and you wouldn't want to mess up your nice clean lab, would you?"

"Why you bring this thing back, Ray?" Beowulf asked.

"Thanks, Beowulf," said Ake. "You saved me the bother of asking that myself."

Ray considered the question. "No reason. I'm just curious to see the inner workings of a native of this soil pimple."

"The guards let you take it?"

"The bodies are put in the mine cars and dumped outside for

disposal anyway," Ray explained. "After that they don't care what happens to them. Why should they?"

" 'That which is not mandated is illegal,' " Ake said ominously, quoting the basic tenet of a short-lived Fascist regime on one of the colony worlds.

"You're such a wienie!" Ray said.

"A live wienie."

"Doan talk food," implored Sinbad. "It make me hungry."

"This should cure that," Ray said, making an incision the length of the digger's abdomen with the laser scalpel. Two quick cross incisions allowed Ray to pull back the flaps of skin and reveal the digger's internal organs.

"What are you looking for?"

"Anything. But I especially want to know how it feeds itself without having an observable mouth. And I . . . Mohammed's bones! Look at this."

"Look at what?" Ake asked, holding his nose.

Ray carefully folded the digger's leathery hide back into place. "Notice this grouping of small openings on its chest and the patch of rubbery bare skin beneath it?"

"Yeah."

"Well, inside"—here Ray peeled back the skin over the chest and abdomen again—"we can see that those holes apparently exude a viscous liquid from this gland." He pointed to a fist-sized sac which resembled a human kidney.

"What's the liquid?"

"Acid, I think." Ray poked a metal probe into the center of the mass; immediately a chalky white substance oozed out. The end of the probe was missing, smoke rising from the ragged stem. "Yeah, it's acid all right; that or something not much different."

Ray moved his attention lower to an odd-shaped organ he assumed was the creature's digestive system. "Once the acid or whatever it is has dissolved whatever it is it's meant to dissolve—small worms or grubs, basic one-celled animals, vegetable life-forms in the soil, or something else—the resulting soupy liquid is absorbed through that layer of leathery yet permeable skin." Ray looked up. "At least I *think* so. I'm no scientist."

"You're doing fine so far."

"These other organs are interesting, as well," Ray said, probing delicately with a long pair of tongs. "Let's see what else we can find."

"Why is that organ there moving?" Ake asked nervously. He

pointed at a jellylike substance that was minutely, but definitely, quivering. His attention elsewhere, Ray nonetheless recognized the sound coming from several of the dogs as a low moaning.

"That's odd," Ray agreed. "Maybe it's a reaction to—"

"Jeezus!!"

There was a blur of motion as three or four shapes exploded from the digger's body cavity. Instinctively, Ray turned his face away. In an instant, something was clinging to the side of his face, a small suckered tentacle curving around his ear like the earpiece of an old-fashioned pair of eyeglasses.

Ray shouted something incoherent, his hand scrabbling to get a purchase on the unwelcome intruder; it tightened its grip. "Get it off, get it off!" Ray shouted. He fell over backwards onto the floor and struck his head hard.

Mama-san acted quickly and with no hesitation. She stood over Ray, clamped her jaws down on the starfish shape and wrenched it from Ray before it could insinuate one of its limbs into his ear canal. Growling like a hyena with a piece of meat in her jaws, Mama-san shook her head from side to side to rend the thing's pulpy body.

The other dogs and Ake had their own distractions to worry about. The remaining three lifeforms to erupt from the digger's body went in three different directions. Sinbad levitated almost straight up into the air as one of the starfish things scurried between his legs. They moved so quickly that it was almost impossible to follow them.

"There it goes!" Grendel shouted as one of the three things went under the table and out the other side, its tiny form little more than a blur.

Ake, reacting not thinking, pointed his index finger at the tiny target and contracted a muscle in his wrist to fire his needle gun. A small ceramic shard just missed the star thing, hitting the floor behind it. Ake "walked" a stream of projectiles toward the tiny fugitive until they caught it and imploded into its plump flesh.

"You got it!"

Meanwhile, with a final snap of her head, Mama-san flung away the first parasite, the one that had attacked Ray. It smacked the wall hard, clinging there like a lump of moist bread dough, and then slid down, leaving a slimy trail of clear liquid ooze.

"Here!" Tajil and Grendel cornered and savaged the other two escapees. Like Mama-san, they crunched the little bodies and then hurled them against the wall.

It took them a second or two to realize it was all over.

"Is everybody okay?" Ake asked.

When everyone but Ray had replied, Ake kneeled beside his diminutive partner, still lying on the floor. For Ray to be unresponsive for so long was unlike him. "What about you, Ray?"

Ray seemed dazed, like someone waking from a dream. He put his hand to his ear and then looked up at Ake. "Oh, hello, Ake." His eyes moving erratically, he asked, "What happened?"

"You had an accident." Ake put his hand underneath Ray's head and felt warm, sticky blood congealing at the base of his skull. "A worse one than I first thought."

"My ear is bleeding," Ray said wonderingly, looking at the blood on his fingertips. Then he pulled questioningly at his earlobe. "Hey, my little 'hangy down' part is still there."

"Ray hurt bad?" Beowulf asked, the concern in his voice obvious to the other dogs.

"I don't know. At the very least, he almost surely has a concussion," Ake replied. "He may have fractured his skull when he struck his head on the floor."

Ake looked at the concerned dog faces anxiously watching their friend and leader. He had to give them something to do. "Sinbad and Gawain, you drag the digger's body outside and throw it down the volcano's slope. I want Grendel, Frodo, and Mama-san to put three of our four visitors into the household disintegrator. Littlejohn, you put the remaining one in a specimen containment cube."

"What you gonna do?" Grendel asked.

"I'm going to get Ray to the infirmary," Ake said. "It's time I began pulling my weight on this assignment and one way to do that is to start acting like the doctor I was trained to be." He pointed a finger at Ozma and Tajil and ordered, "Keep an eye on Ray until I can get the null-grav gurney ready. He's not to move a muscle."

"What if he tries to get up?" Tajil asked.

"You guys aren't toy terriers—put your paws on his chest and hold him down."

"Gotcha," Ozma said.

Ake, perspiring heavily despite the air conditioning, hurried into one of the two rooms the dogs had given up. While Ray had pretty much taken over the second for himself, Ake had stashed his own equipment in this one. Opening one of his trunks by pressing his palm against the sensor, he quickly sifted through his medical cubes. Finding the one he was looking for, Ake popped it into a small reader that transferred the hundred megabytes of information into an external.

With medicine as sophisticated and ever-changing as it had become over the centuries, it was both pointless and unnecessary to attend medical school for more than two years. After eighteen months or so, most students had mastered the basics and needed only to have their education augmented by an external medical memory insert. Each doctor's "black bag" of medical cubes was updated annually, guaranteeing that no doctor ever need be ignorant of the latest technological breakthroughs.

The reader chimed. With his external now loaded with brain injury information, Ake popped it out of the reader and felt for the entry point on his skull. He pulled back a small flap of skin and gently eased the tiny external into place. A series of internal commands quickly keyed the welcome flow of information into his brain.

*I'm more than me now*, Ake thought, savoring the delicious feeling of immensity of self that the external gave him. He felt enlarged, his brain bursting with knowledge. *I'm not just Ake Ringgren now, I'm Ake Ringgren-Plus*.

"Ake, you ready yet?" Sinbad asked, sticking his shaggy head through the open doorway.

"Yes," he said, rising. "Let's get Ray to the infirmary right away."

"Good," said Sinbad seriously. "He is our Man."

The dogs stayed by Ray's side while he slept a deep sleep induced by a mild electromagnetic current passing through his brain. Tubes in his nostrils, Ray floated inside a clear plastic cylinder. The wires and tubes that hung from him made him look like a giant balloon tethered to the ground by ropes. Ray himself would have remarked that he resembled a toothbrush in its clear plastic container. Of course, no one would have known what his archaic usage meant, there being no tooth decay and no need for toothbrushes.

Ake told the dogs that Ray's injuries were not serious, but the team took turns watching over their leader and friend. They would not be whole again until Ray himself was made whole.

"I hate hospitals," Littlejohn opined.

"Me, too," seconded Beowulf.

"I'd say 'Me three,' " said Mama-san wryly, "but this gotta stop somewhere."

When Tajil sighed a massive canine sigh, Beowulf said to him, "Doan worry, Taddy, Ray tougher'n any three of us put together. He be all right."

"I know, but . . ."

"But what, youngster?"

"But this like it always gonna be?" Taddy got a look of intense concentration on his face as he searched for the words to articulate his concern, to adequately express his feelings. "I mean, we hardly bin on this planet and already we bin 'tacked by diggers and stuff, and Ray almost killed. I wanna know—it always be like this?"

" 'Fraid so, Taddy," Beowulf said.

"But—"

"Taddy," said Mama-san gravely, "we does dangerous stuff. We are dogs. We a dog team with a Man to guide us. That's what we are and what we do." She smiled a crooked canine smile at her son. "That's what we *like* to do."

"I wouldn't have it any other way," said Beowulf.

" 'Sides," added Littlejohn, "neither would our Man."

Ray, floating unconscious in his plastic tube, could not possibly have heard what the dogs said. Yet there was the barest hint of a smile on his face.

# 6

"Come on, guys, this is the last day you'll have to put up with me in charge," Ake said as they started down the long tunnel to the extraction site. "Ray will be back soon."

"Ake," Beowulf asked seriously, "if'n anything happened to Ray, would you be our Man?"

Ake stopped dead in his tracks and considered. He respected the dogs too much to give them an automatic and unthinking response. He saw them staring into his eyes with concern . . . but also with love and a certain amount of regard.

"Yes," he said finally. "Yes, I'd be your Man . . . if you'd have me." When they first met, Ake had considered Ray's love for the dogs to be a little queer, but now he better understood the special bonding that takes place between man and dog.

"You the greatest!" said Gawain, coming over to lick Ake's hand with his big pink tongue.

"Yah, Ake is okay!" said Mama-san.

"Hey, hey!" Ake said in mock exasperation. "Cut out the sponge bath routine, okay."

"Ake, I gots another question," said Beowulf.

"Who do you guys think I am, the oracle of Delphi?"

Beowulf frowned. "No, I don't think you is any or-rackle, whatever that is, but the cat lady and that Hi-bat-sha cat said that Ray gots the 'power.' What that mean, 'xackly?"

## K-9 CORPS: UNDER FIRE 73

Ake scuffed at the dirt floor of the mine shaft with the toe of his work boot as he considered Beowulf's question.

"Ake?"

"I'm thinking." He recalled the incident Beowulf mentioned. Finally, he said, "At the time I wasn't sure what happened—and I'm not sure now, for that matter—but Maria and the cats are ESPers; they're psychic. I think Hypatia and Maria sense that Ray also has some psychic abilities. If he does, they're probably raw and undeveloped, but they're there nonetheless."

"Ray?" asked Ozma with such credulity in her voice that Ake had to laugh.

"What's so difficult to accept about that?" Ake asked. "That's probably one of the reasons Ray makes such a good scout dog team leader. And you guys probably have a smidgen of those special talents as well."

"Geez, imagine that," marveled Gawain. "We can read minds."

"Yah," cackled Frodo, "and yours is a short read."

Being much bigger than Frodo, Gawain gave the other dog a good-natured shove and a warning nip on the flank. "Read this, hairball!"

"Enough of this badinage," Ake said. "It's time we hied ourselves through this mudball's innards to the work site."

With Ray in the infirmary, Ake was pulling both shifts, so he was becoming accustomed to the journey's signposts: the sudden transition from heat and humidity to cooler yet still dank air that grew progressively warmer, the sounding stillness of the air after the cacophonous roar of the rain forest, the claustrophobic feeling one got from being surrounded by rock and soil, and the occasional slithering sound that underscored the fact that they were down a hole in the ground where unseen things lived. Ake suddenly remembered an old holo that showed thousands of Arakkian death's head beetles pouring out of a crack in the soil like black blood from a deep gash.

Ake shivered despite the growing warmth. *I'm giving myself the willies*, he laughed. *Booga, booga*.

The deeper down the team penetrated, the warmer and wetter it got. "That constant drip, drip, drip is annoying, isn't it?" Ake said. He had kidded Ray about loving the jungle, but he had to admit he'd take the jungle over being entombed underground any day.

"At least the water not cold," Ozma said.

"You're right," agreed Ake as a heavy drop almost hit him in the eye. "The volcano even warms the water pipes."

"Here come the mutts," Penelope announced to the rest of the cats.

"Why, it's Penelope the pussface," Ake said, forever securing a place in the dogs' hearts.

"Ray's rubbed off on you, I see," Maria Valdez said, her hands on her hips. She made a fetching picture, with her halo of curly black hair framing her face and her deep brown eyes complementing her light olive complexion. She was wearing tan work trousers and a light blue shirt with a multitude of pockets. Although the trousers were baggy, the shirt conformed to every curve and line of her torso. The dogs didn't notice this, but Ake did.

"Good morning, Citizen Valdez," he said as blandly as he could.

"It's been nearly a week now," she said. "Why don't we act like regular people and call each other by our first names?"

"Sure, Maria."

*It has been a week*, Ake marveled. He again took in Maria's compact, small-breasted figure and told himself that *Whoever said familiarity breeds contempt must never have been thrown in close contact with a member of the opposite sex . . . a very good-looking member of the opposite sex.*

"So how's Ray doing?"

"I'm going over to sign him out of the infirmary after this shift is ended," Ake said. "He's fine. He only hit his head, after all."

"You rutters," she said, shaking her head. "Bastet, let's go," Maria said to her feline leader.

As the Bastet and the other cats—Marisol, Penelope, Hypatia, and Sibella—moved into position, Ake said, "Unlike Ray, I'm looking forward to a uneventful shift."

"You no fun," said Beowulf.

"Aren't you and the rest of your team feeling the strain?" Ake asked Maria.

"Strain?"

"Your team pulls double shifts and you were already in place when we got off the *Truman* to begin our tour," Ake explained, looking for signs of fatigue in the young scout cat leader's face. Hephaestus's gravity was just a tad higher than the Terran standard of one gee, but that little bit extra was more than enough to grind you down if you were doing anything involving physical effort.

"Our mental abilities encompass much more than such mundane, if commercially exploitable, talents such as 'reading' auras," Maria explained. She gave him a sideways, evaluative glance. "If you wish, I can teach you a very relaxing form of . . . of, oh, let's just call it 'meditation.'"

"Does it work?" Ake asked, stifling a yawn.

"You're the one flashing your pearlies, not I."

"Sure," said Ake. "When Ray's back I'll look you up."

"Whenever."

The "white noise" of the ubiquitous filtration device that tried heroically to keep air free of swirling particles of dust reminded Ake that he and the dogs had a duty to perform. Still, when they weren't actively performing it—i.e., warding off digger attacks—Ake had more than enough time to observe the activity of the prisoner-miners.

Work units averaged six to twelve members and one or two civilian supervisors. Today's crew was on the high side with ten workers single-mindedly imposing themselves on the mine wall. Ake's subconscious mind noted, without bothering to pass the word along to his conscious mind, that half of the miners on this day were women. Had he paused to consider the unusually high ratio of women to men, perhaps he would have pondered its significance—a significance that would not become apparent until later.

When the goal was precious gems, as it was today in this particular shaft, one of several that branched off from the main shaft like the fingers of a glove, the miners essentially worked by hand. The Rostoff rubies were as delicate as they were unimaginably rare and precious. An automatic digging machine, a laser borer, or almost anything mechanical or lacking "touch," could severely damage or even destroy the valuable rubies.

Ray and Ake had been astounded to discover that the tools the miners worked with were not only handmade by the other prisoners but also carved from real wood. It wasn't as if they had to import timber to Hephaestus, Ake realized, but still . . . to make wooden implements. It boggled the mind!

As he watched the prisoner-miners patiently hacking at the compacted soil and rock with their rudimentary tools, Ake thought that he might be seeing what mining was like hundreds of years earlier. *No, that's not entirely true*, he thought. *It's really a blending of the old and the new*. Although the miners dug out cubic-meter sections of tunnel wall with their wooden tools, they carefully bored laser holes around the selected area to loosen it.

Only then did they attack the small section with their wooden picks and shovels.

"It's really something to see, isn't it?" Ake said to Maria.

She smiled patiently. "Yes . . . at first. We've been here long enough that we don't really think all that much about the process any more." That made sense, Ake thought. It was probably like watching the same holodrama over and over until you could recite the lines along with the computer-generated actors.

When the miners had dug out enough soil to make it worthwhile, they transferred it to a machine which vibrated just enough to loosen the dirt and separate the soil from the rocks and any valuable ore; it was a venerable mining technique dating from ancient times. Not everything was so delicate and gentle with the fruits of the miners' labors: a conveyer belt carried unwanted rocks into the maw of a massive rock crusher. Ake made a mental note to keep his distance from that monster.

Ake watched the miners patiently eroding the tunnel wall centimeter by centimeter. They were conscientious sheep busy turning grass into wool under the watchful eyes of their shepherds. *And we shepherds have our guardians, too*, Ake thought, glancing at the bored soldiers.

Watching the ten prisoners—five men and five women—work, Ake saw one of them lift her mask and wipe the grime from her face with a colored square of cloth that she pulled from a hip pocket. Her mask back in place, the woman returned to her backbreaking work.

Ake's chest felt tight and for a moment he couldn't breathe. He gasped and placed his hand on his chest; he felt faint.

Noticing his distress, Maria asked, "Ake, what's the matter?"

"I . . . ah, I . . ."

"Are you ill?"

As if mimicking the prisoner's actions, Ake wiped his face with a cloth. He knelt, putting his head between his legs. Looking up, he said, "I'm sorry, but it's just that I've had a great shock."

"What is it?"

"That prisoner over there," Ake said hoarsely. Somehow he had the presence of mind not to point.

"Yes?"

"I know her."

## II

Ray dreamed.

Ray was in a long tube; a corridor, actually. He looked down and saw that his feet were moving, carrying him down the corridor. The end, as represented by a blank, featureless door, was fast approaching. Ray turned to look over his shoulder and screamed silently at what he saw behind him. It was death and destruction. Men and odd-shaped horses lay dying. A tall man with a shaved skull looked queerly at Ray and said, "Beware the ring of fire." Then he put a gun to his head and pulled the trigger. Ray turned away in disgust.

The door. It hissed open and Ray was in the white sterility of a delivery room. A woman dressed in black was giving birth to a child. The doctors delivered the infant into the world and then placed him on a red blanket. Police came and roughly pulled the woman to her feet, clapped her in wrist restraints, and led her away.

"I'm dreaming," Ray said.

"Of course you are," the woman said to him on her way out. "That part's easy. The hard part is figuring out what it all means."

As Ray considered that, the child was picked up by a strong-looking woman and placed in a room filled with dozens of other babies. Seeing Ray finally, the woman—the nurse?—put her finger to her lips and said, "Sh-h-h." She left the room.

Ray watched in wonder as the infants began to grow. The newborn developed, in a matter of minutes, into Ake Ringgren. The other children also grew, but not to adult height. After they reached about one and a third meters they stopped growing. Compared to Ake's milky white complexion, their skin seemed red and cracked. He knew if he could touch them that they'd feel rough and hard, not soft and silky the way children normally felt.

Something agitated these strange children and they began to point angrily at Ake. Ake, his face a mask of bewilderment, turned to face Ray and said, "Don't let them take me swimming, Ray. You know I can't swim like they can. Please, Ray."

The angry children, gibbering and gesturing violently, surrounded Ake and bore him off. "Ray! Ray!" he called. Ray tried to move but found he was rooted to the floor; his legs refused to budge. "Ray! I can't swim!"

A hand tapped Ray on the shoulder. He whirled to find himself staring into the empty eye sockets of Ake's birth mother. "Let him drown, Ray, or you'll die, too. Don't go after him."

Ray was suddenly alone. The room began to contract until there was almost no space left. The walls came closer and he closed his eyes in anticipation of being crushed to death.

Nothing happened.

*It doesn't matter, I'm dead anyway. No*, he considered, *that's not what this nightmare means—I* will *be dead if I don't allow Ake to drown.*

★ ★ ★

The first question Ray asked when he awakened in the infirmary wasn't, "Am I all right?" It was, "What in the name of Vlad the Impaler *were* those things?" He decided not to mention his disturbing dream; at least not for a while.

"You mean those things that came out of the digger's body cavity?" Ake asked.

"No, the tiny points of light in the sky after the sun has gone down," Ray said. "*Of course* I mean those slimy bastards from the digger's body! If I was a cartoon character, there'd be a giant exclamation point in a word balloon above my head!"

"Don't excite yourself."

"So you gonna tell me or not?"

"According to Maria, they're parasites. Up to a half-dozen of them can successfully infest a digger's body without harming their host."

"Disgusting things."

"Hey, ever seen the inside of your body?"

"Not lately."

"Well, don't be so quick to judge."

Ray frowned. "Did they appoint you their defense lawyer or something? Why are you so eager to defend them? One almost climbed into my skull through my ear, you know."

"Life is life," Ake shrugged. "It's not evil, it just *is*."

"I guess so," said Ray dubiously. "I don't think I'll be performing any digger autopsies for a while, I must admit."

"Good idea."

Ray gingerly touched the back of his head. "What was it? A concussion?"

"Your skull had a hairline fracture as well," Ake told him. "Since it was a head injury we knew there was no danger. It's not as if it was some vital part of your anatomy, you know?"

"Thanks, Dr. Zorba," said Ray, certain that Ake wouldn't be able to place his reference to the ancient tee-vee series about a neurosurgeon and his kindly old mentor.

"Ha," said Ake, jabbing a finger at him. "I got that one: Dr.

Zorba was a Greek guy who danced on the beach in a sinny, right?"

Ray looked at Beowulf, tapped the side of his head, and asked, "Which twin has the brain damage, eh?"

Ray shared his room with two other patients, both of them military personnel. Also committed to the infirmary for relatively minor ailments, the two soldiers tried their damnedest to ignore both Beowulf's presence and Ray and Ake's conversation. Whatever they could hear was less a matter of eavesdropping than simply being unavoidably present and within earshot. Ray spouted a lot of his pop culture nonsense for their benefit, pleased as punch at how confused they must be.

Ray picked up a drink bladder from beside his null-grav hospital bed, stuck the tip into his mouth, and squeezed. "Hey, this is water!"

"You were expecting maybe bourbon?"

"At least they could have given me that rocket juice that Captain Trimble drinks while he's saving the universe. Anything but water."

"Bitch, bitch, bitch."

Ignoring Ake, Ray said, "Hello, Beowulf."

" 'Lo, Ray."

"How is everyone?"

"Okay," the big dog said.

"Anything exciting happen while I was in la-la land?"

"Nope."

"Good. That's what I want to hear."

Ake coughed for attention. "Well, Beowulf's not entirely correct, Ray. Nothing 'exciting' happened, *per se*, but there's been a new development."

"Oh, yeah? What, pray tell?"

Ake glanced at the two soldiers who were both pretending with all of their might that they were engrossed in the reading cubes in front of them. "Not now," he said. "When you get out of here."

"Am I healthy enough to leave?"

"Yes."

"Right answer."

# III

Ray and Ake once again had the rain forest around them to shield them from any prying eyes or ears. While the two men talked, the dogs joyfully plunged in and out of the vegetation, unmindful of the heat and humidity that made humans as limp as dishcloths. Only Beowulf remained at Ray's side.

"So what's your big news, White Man?"

Ake looked thoughtfully down his thin nose at Ray. "I recognized one of the prisoners when I was in the mine the other day."

"You know one of the prisoners?" Ray asked wonderingly. "What are the odds against that?" He scratched the vigilant Beowulf behind one ear. "Who was he?"

"Not he, she," Ake said. "And you know her, too."

"She?"

"Ray, it was Thane Wyda."

Ray later decided that this was one of the few times in his life that he actually involuntarily performed one of the clichés of the holodramas—his jaw dropped and his mouth gaped open. He promptly shut it when something iridescent attempted to fly in.

"Are you serious? Thane Wyda? Thane Wyda!" Ray was numb. Thane Wyda was more than just a Prime Programmer, she was in the upper echelons of power, one of the chosen few on Terra who personally tended to the Judge Advocate.

"There's no chance you were mistaken?" Ray asked, hoping against hope that Ake might say yes.

"Ray, she personally picked me to be a sleeper; she was the PP who maneuvered to get me onto Chiron with the Cadre. There are a lot of people I might be mistaken about, but she's not one of them."

"I 'member her from the Centaur world," Beowulf put in helpfully. That was not literally true; Beowulf and Ray had really only met the stern Wyda via subspace holo linkups.

"Let's assume then that you're right," Ray conceded. "If you are, what does that mean?"

Ake swatted away a few bugs that seemed undeterred by the ultrasonic repelling device he wore. He sighed heavily. "It means that the situation back on Terra is even more screwed up than we dared to imagine."

"I dare imagine a lot."

"Let's say that the current members of the Triumvirate wanted to circumvent the oversight capabilities of the Judge Advocate, okay?"

"Okay," agreed Ray, playing along.

"One of the more efficient ways to do that is to control the flow of information *into* the Judge Advocate. How better to do that than to control the Prime Programmers?"

"I'm with you so far," Ray said. "Keep going."

"But the leaders of the Prime Programmers, stubborn and with an unfortunate—from the Triumvirate's point of view—tendency to take seriously their vows of honesty and service, get in the way. They nix this attempted power play."

"Yeah!" Ray said, getting excited. "They refuse to have anything to do with suborning the Judge Advocate's watchdog position, so the Triumvirate simply has them secretly arrested and replaced by their own handpicked stooges."

"Bingo!"

Their triumphant smiles faded as the enormity of the consequences of the scenario they'd just constructed slowly sank in.

"Yeah, bingo," Ray said dispiritedly.

Ray turned to Beowulf. "Let's give the guys another ten minutes or so to run and play and then we'll head back home."

★ ★ ★

Ray and Ake had ushered Maria and her cats into their humble abode with a mixture of pride and trepidation. They had been so embarrassed by the contrast between her place and theirs that they had devoted a lot of time to "cleaning up." They honestly believed that they had worked wonders. In truth, given the sorry state the place was in *before* they dedicated themselves to whipping it into shape, their labors had resulted in a vast improvement in the overall cleanliness of their quarters. Maria, however, had not seen the "before" version.

"What do you think?" asked Ray anxiously.

"Well . . ." Maria began. There was *no* way she was going to be honest. "It's amazing how two places can be basically the same yet look so different depending on the choice of furnishings."

Ake, with a much sharper esthetic sensibility than Ray, didn't allow the fixed smile on his face to fall even though he could clearly see through Maria's carefully chosen words. To Ake's surprise, however, he realized that Ray had also interpreted her guarded response. Maybe it was that "power" he possessed, Ake considered.

"My dad used to have a favorite expression he would dust off and bring out for occasions like this," Ray said in response to the slightly stunned look on the sensitive Hypatia's face. The other cats looked smug, as if they'd expected to find nothing less than dirt and disorder in a place lived in by male humans.

"Oh, really?"

"Yeah. He used to say, 'You can't shine shit.'"

"I'm sorry," said Maria, trying not to laugh. "It's nice. What you've done, I mean."

Gawain, however, couldn't help himself. "Can't shine shit! That really funny!"

"We tried, we really did," Ake said. "We almost burned out Chips's circuits having him vacuum and mop. Even the dogs helped as best they could."

"Chips?"

"The domestic robot."

"Oh, yes," Maria said. For some reason, she felt a pang of remorse that she hadn't given her little household robot a name.

"Well, beat the vermin off the furniture and have a seat," said Ray. "I'm gonna fix us all drinks."

The dogs were spread out all over the place, having comfortably arranged themselves as only dogs can. The cats, not wanting to miss a golden opportunity to be obnoxious, each found a dog to snuggle up to. To their credit, the dogs were a picture of forbearance. Sibella, apparently annoyed that they were not successful in getting a rise out of the dogs, climbed up on Littlejohn's broad back and, flexing her claws slightly, settled in. Littlejohn's eyes widened as if someone had just inserted a rectal probe, but he didn't flinch or move a muscle. Following Sibella's lead, Hypatia climbed atop Frodo and made herself comfortable.

"Okay," Ake said once everyone had made himself or herself comfortable. "Let's start at the beginning. You have some idea who we are, correct? I mean about who we *really* are and about our nasty past?"

"Some idea," Maria agreed. "But why don't you tell me as much as you think I need to know?"

"You need to know everything if you're to give us any advice or to help us," Ray said. He looked around at their meager surroundings and tried to remember the valuable pieces in her home. "Of course, if you believe that you have too much to lose, you can leave right now. You don't have to know anything that might get you into trouble."

Maria sipped her drink thoughtfully. "What do you think, Bastet?"

The cat stopped licking her paw and looked up. "This a crappy assignment," Bastet said. "So we lose it and gots to start over again somewhere else; so what?"

"I agree. Go ahead, Ray."

Ray explained in detail about the shroud of secrecy surrounding their mission on Chiron, about the Centaurs, about the Cadre, and about the Prime Programmers and the General.

"So the Centaurs were deemed unintelligent and further study was banned, especially any work that might reveal their true nature?" Hypatia leapt up gracefully into her lap and settled in; Frodo was not sorry to see the cat abandon him for her mistress.

"Yes," said Ake.

"The point is," Ray said, "righteousness and goodness triumphed for all of about fifteen minutes, or so it now appears. But this is real life, not a holodrama. After our momentary victory, the bad guys regained control."

Ake's face was a study in dejection. "And the fact that Thane Wyda is imprisoned here means things are worse than even we might have expected," he said.

"You say this Thane Wyda was a Prime Programmer?"

"One of the primest," said Ray, not wanting to crack wise but constitutionally unable to resist doing so.

"That explains a lot," Maria said, stroking Hypatia's silky fur. The cat purred loudly and flexed her claws in pleasure.

"That's why we came to you—for answers," explained Ray.

"When I started here, almost a year ago now, the ratio of male to female prisoners was nearly three to one," Maria said, staring at the floor. "It has slowly evolved over the past twelve months to something approaching equality in representation." She lifted her eyes to Ray's face. "Instead of two hundred and twenty-five men to seventy-five women, there must be one hundred and fifty each by now." Her steady gaze implied she expected a reaction.

"Yeah?" asked Ray. His mind raced furiously. *What am I supposed to put together?*

Even Beowulf, engrossed in his bowl, looked up, beer dripping from his muzzle.

Maria cocked her head at Ray. "Aren't most Prime Programmers women?"

"Jesus H. Nixon!" exploded Ray.

Maria dug her fingers a little roughly into Hypatia's fur and the cat looked up crossly. "There's not a lot that would put me firmly on the side of a couple of smartass rutters, but this is one of them."

Ake settled back against the sofa cushions. "Shit," he said softly.

When Ray raised a questioning eyebrow, Ake explained, "I'm going to have to find a way to speak to Thane Wyda."

Beowulf put his paws over his head and sighed in canine resignation.

# 7

Ake found himself unable to resist tweaking the military stolidity of the sentries guarding the mine entrance. As he exited today, he said to them, "I'm going to be gone for a little while, fellas, so don't let anyone in while I'm away, okay?" As usual, they made no reply.

"You gettin' as bad as Ray, and that sayin' somethin'!" Ozma told him as they walked toward the compound.

*That's true*, Ake thought, *I am getting as bad as Ray. He's rubbing off on me*.

They hadn't gotten very far when they heard a loud *WHOOMP* from the prison building off to their right. A brilliant flash of light and a bright yellow flame shot from several of the narrow vertical slots that served as windows. A bilious mixture of black smoke and dust vented into the air from the shattered windows.

"Lookit that!" shouted Frodo excitedly. "Lookit that!"

"What happened?" asked Ozma.

"Somethin' blew up," Gawain said.

"No kiddin', Einstein," Tajil said.

"Let's see what's going on," Ake said.

The team approached the transparent force field surrounding the compound that housed the prison and the barracks building. The field shimmered like summer air and the dogs could hear a slight keening sound beyond the upper range of human ears.

A heavily armed soldier approached the perimeter of the force field where they stood gawking like tourists. "Stay back," he ordered Ake and the dogs, brandishing his weapon. Ake noted how young he was and how much his hands shook. This probably was the first emergency he'd ever confronted. The troops stationed here were an odd mixture of seasoned veterans and first-tour virgins.

"I'm Ake Ringgren," Ake told him, laying his energy rifle on the ground and turning around to demonstrate that he was now unarmed. "I'm a doctor and I've put down my weapon." *The needle gun doesn't really count*, Ake thought.

"You're a doctor?" the soldier said dubiously, glancing at the dogs at Ake's side.

"Yes."

"Go around to the main gate," the soldier ordered him, activating his communicator. "I'm gonna report that you're here; maybe they can use you."

"Go find Ray," Ake ordered Ozma and Gawain. "Tell him what has happened."

"Okay." Ozma and Gawain turned and trotted briskly away, their tails waving in the air.

The compound was as alive with soldiers and activity as Ake and the three dogs with him had ever witnessed. Tajil, Frodo, and Mama-san watched in wonder as the well-trained soldiers rushed to their battle stations.

"Looks like ant hill," commented Tajil.

"That's a good analogy," Ake said. "At first glance an ant hill appears to be nothing but a lot of unrelated milling around, but every ant has a specific job to do."

"Hold it right there, Citizen," a soldier standing guard outside the main entry point ordered. "Make the dogs sit," he added.

Using one of the hand signals Ray had taught him, Ake gestured and the three dogs obediently hunkered down on their haunches. "Hey, it works," Ake said.

"Huh?"

Before the soldier could say anything else, he apparently got a communication on the receiver implanted just behind his ear. He pressed a finger against his ear in the same way that Ake had seen so many of his Cadre comrades do when they had received messages.

"Yes, sir," the guard said. He turned around and asked the four others just inside the gate if they'd gotten the word as well; they had. "Then let him in," the guard said.

"Wait here," Ake told the three dogs.

"I was 'fraid he was gonna say that," sighed Frodo.

★ ★ ★

Ray's most recent foray to the outer limits of the K'a-nii village had provided him with several hours of marvelously detailed visual and aural recordings. Even so, the base computer was not having much success rendering their sibilant exchanges into comprehensible speech.

"It *is* language, isn't it?" Ray asked the computer, speaking to it via the interface in his work room. Physically, the computer was housed in the administration building.

"Of course it is," the computer replied in that maddeningly mellow voice it affected.

"What about . . ." Here Ray made a half-strangled, half-hissing sound. "Doesn't that mean food?"

"It seems to at certain times," the computer conceded. "However, at other times and in different circumstances it may also mean fecal matter or moon."

"Then we're getting nowhere fast."

"A fascinating concept: getting nowhere fast," the computer mused.

"I'm not interested in discussing philosophy with you," Ray said, mildly annoyed. "Just linguistics. Or are you unable to help me?"

When the computer did not reply, Ray said, "Well?"

"Well, what?" the computer retorted. "I'm capable of many things, but I cannot perform magic."

"Meaning what?"

The computer, which was often cheeky, decided to explain patiently. "I am an incredibly cross-programmed and knowledge-encompassing entity. However, I have one serious limitation in a situation such as this. Just as man is supposed to have been conceived in the image of his creator, I have been conceived in the image of man."

"You don't look a thing like me," Ray said.

"Not man's physical image," the computer said, "but his mental image. I would be a poor instrument if I were not founded upon the functioning of the human brain; humans made me, hence

I think substantially like humans think—not like a totally alien mentality."

"So you're telling me that you're having difficulty figuring out the K'a-niian speech because their minds are different?"

"With some reservations, yes."

"What do you mean, 'With some reservations'?"

"You have set before me a formidable task; very formidable. This does not mean, however, that it is impossible."

"Where does that leave me?"

"I need a much larger baseline. You must continue to record the alien's speech patterns," the computer said. "I am confident that with enough information, I will eventually be able to formulate at least a rudimentary dictionary."

"Pardon me if I don't hold my breath."

The visual recordings had at least allowed Ray to study the K'a-nii anatomy. They were short, shorter even than Ray. *Can't be much more than one hundred and thirty centimeters tall, most of them. Maybe they'll be afraid of me, someone who's such a giant*, Ray mused. *Yeah, right.* Their torsos made up most of their body length, unlike humans where it is the length of one's legs that makes him or her either tall or short.

Ray thought it interesting, and possibly revealing—no pun intended—that they didn't wear clothing, just assorted straps and leather harnesses. That fitted in neatly with their lack of obvious sexual characteristics. The purpose of human clothing was to both hide and highlight the physical differences between the sexes; to modestly remove body parts from sight and, paradoxically, to boldly proclaim their existence.

The K'a-niis' legs seemed to sprout on either side of their trunk rather than descending from it as humans' did. Similarly, their two arms were relatively short; presumably, it was a matter of ancestry. The arms of human beings were their heritage from an early primate who had lived in the trees and who needed long arms to swing from branch to branch. Where Ray's arms weren't that much shy of reaching to his knees, the K'a-nii were lucky if their slender arms reached below their waist.

Ray also studied their hands and feet, since intelligent beings manipulated the physical world around them with their digits. The K'a-niis' feet were padded and their four blunt toes sported formidable nails; their five-fingered hands were more delicate, with smaller nails. The different number of toes and fingers was an anomaly, but not unknown. Most alien creatures so far encountered followed the rule of equivalency and possessed an equal number of fingers and toes—if they had fingers and toes.

With a short tail thrown in for good measure, the K'a-niis' physical appearance was a cross between an upright Kokomo dragon lizard and an impossibly large salamander. *Not unlike how we might have turned out if the dinosaurs hadn't become extinct, giving way to tiny mammals grubbing in the dirt*, Ray realized. Then he laughed, since "what if" theorizing had always seemed like a waste of time to him. "Yeah," he said, "and if the Spanish Armada had not been destroyed by a storm, we'd be two-meter-tall intelligent Spanish-speaking dinosaurs!" He giggled at his preposterous scenario.

"Well," said the computer, "then maybe it would be easier to decipher the aliens' speech if you were descended from dinosaurs, too."

Ray had forgotten that the damned computer was still listening. "Sí, Señor," he said.

Ray stared at the images floating in the air in front of him. He seemed so close to the answers, yet still so far away. Their faces were what made the K'a-nii seem so promising. They had little folds of skin for ears, their noses weren't much more than two small holes, and their mouths were filled with the sort of carnivore teeth that could give a person nightmares. But it was their eyes that dominated their faces. Ray thought he could see the intelligence they possessed shining out of their large eyes. As black as space, with bright red wedge-shaped pupils, the K'a-niis' eyes came equipped with two eyelids. The outer one was thick and scaly, the inner one was a nictitating membrane which functioned to keep the eye moist. Since the inner eyelids were transparent, Ray assumed that the K'a-nii could see through them while they protected the sensitive eyes from the elements.

Ray believed that the K'a-niis' eyes were more than merely reptilian. To him they were the eyes of creatures which looked out on their world with understanding. Maybe he was wrong, but he did not think so.

Ray snapped off the holo projector with a weary sigh. Even though the computer had so far failed to give any help in deciphering their language, Ray knew it was time to take the next step. He had to go into the village. He didn't think that would be a problem. What *would* be a problem was getting Maria to agree to allow one of the cats to go with him.

Having once been a member of a military organization himself, Ake appreciated the order and discipline the Federation regulars displayed as he was escorted inside the prison grounds. *She might be a hardass*, Ake noted, *but Bukovsky's a competent commander*.

Access to the prison building was by retinal scan only; there was no fast and easy palm-print admittance here. A major drawback to the high security imposed on the prison was that it made for slow-motion responses in time of emergencies since there seemed no way to short-circuit the process. Things took as long as they took and that was that. Once Ake was logged in as a visitor, the massive molecular steel door slowly swung open. Ake shivered involuntarily; prisons had a way of making him feel vulnerable. The thought of that twenty-five-centimeter-thick door closing him in forever was chilling. Each journey into a prison made him sympathize just a little with the inmates, no matter what crimes they might have committed.

The guards inside the door body-scanned him once again. He was "clean," the needle gun strapped to his wrist having already been confiscated at the main gate by a guard who had clucked disapprovingly at Ake's indiscretion.

The prison even came equipped with stairwells in addition to lift and drop tubes of varying dimensions. It was a terrible waste of space, but in times of trouble, like now, the tubes were shut down and access to each floor was possible only by taking the steps. Ake looked longingly at the entrance to the lift tubes, but the soldiers barring access seemed in no mood to allow any exceptions. Ake just sighed; he enjoyed physical exercise about as much as sticking spikes into his eyes. As he huffed and puffed his way up to the infirmary floor, Ake was frankly amazed at the lengths the buildings had gone to for the sake of security. Even more amazing was the fact that Bukovsky's troops so completely followed the game plan.

Ake recognized the middle-aged sergeant who oversaw his admission to the prison's hospital floor from his previous visits to the infirmary. Although the man couldn't be older than his mid-forties, Ake guessed that the sergeant was one of the oldest non-commissioned soldiers he'd ever encountered. The Federation had no use for a military that wasn't young and reckless.

"Afternoon, Sergeant Hildebrand."

The Sergeant nodded and touched his cap. "Doctor Ringgren."

"Doctor Ringgren, Sergeant?" Hildebrand had never addressed him by his formal title before. "Why so official?"

"'Cause you're here on official business—to be a doctor."

"That must have been a brutal explosion if Doctors Carpenter, Jayanthi, and Ramos need my help."

The sergeant stared at him, his round face troubled. It seemed he wanted to say something but was holding himself back. One of the younger men by his side was less reticent. "There's a rumor that one or two of the docs were killed by the blast."

"That'll be enough, Corporal Chang," the sergeant said.

"Is that true?" Ake asked.

Stony-faced, Sergeant Hildebrand would just say, "There's a lot of wild talk circulating. I wouldn't put any stock in it if I were you, Dr. Ringgren." He pierced the young soldier who'd spoke with a steely gaze and said, "It's against orders to spread rumors, Corporal Chang."

"Yes, Sergeant." Chang swallowed, his Adam's apple bobbing.

"I can tell you that Captain Ramos was not in the prison at the time of the incident," the sergeant said. He turned to the two soldiers flanking him and said, "Corporal Chang and Corporal Malinsky, escort Dr. Ringgren to the infirmary."

Ake had expected a scene of frenzied activity: first-aid personnel and orderlies rushing about, calls for blood, calls for instruments and emergency procedures. There was some of that, certainly, but not as much as Ake imagined there would be. All that may have occurred in the first minutes after the explosion and fire, but he observed little evidence of it now.

"Here's where it happened, Doc," Corporal Chang said, indicating the main operating theater. The doors were blown off and there was a strong smell of smoke and something which Ake took to be the residue of the explosive. The inside of the operating room was in shambles. The delicate equipment, once all gleaming glass and plasteel, was shattered, smashed, or reduced to shards. The warm and humid outside air had already infiltrated and occupied the now-windowless room.

"There's nothing I or anyone can do here; let's move on."

Ake was taken to Operating Theater Number Two. Again, there was less panic and turmoil than he expected to find. The easy explanation for that was that apparently everyone in the main operating room had been killed outright. Of course, Ake didn't know for sure that anyone had been in the operating room, but

Chang's slip about one or two doctors having been killed was probably what had happened. Seeing the carnage, Ake had little difficulty believing that no one inside the operating room could have survived the explosion. The few injuries belonged to people who hadn't been in the immediate blast area, those who had been struck by shards of flying plastic or by rubble.

Unlike a "real" hospital in a major population center, the infirmary's beds were relatively unoccupied. For greater security, the infirmary had a whole floor of the prison to itself. There weren't many people roaming the halls who did not have a duty chip authorizing them to be there.

An orderly dressed in blue hospital fatigues brought Ake a bag containing the necessary medical equipment, saying, "I got it from Dr. Jayanthi's office."

"Hand it over, then," Ake said. "I've got injured to tend to." He opened Jayanthi's bag and got to work. Ake had seen much worse injuries than these superficial wounds. They didn't require a great deal of expertise, and, indeed, the orderly did much of the taping and bandaging himself.

Having dealt with the immediate situation, Ake stretched and asked, "What happened?"

The orderly shrugged helplessly. "All we know is that Doctor Carpenter and Doctor Jayanthi were performing a scheduled exploratory operation on a female patient." He looked at a clipboard. "The patient was a newly arrived prisoner named Marte Kales."

"Newly arrived?"

"She came in on the last shuttle." Ake swallowed hard, aware that this Kales must have been the female prisoner they'd shared the shuttle with on the flight down from the *Truman*.

"You said they were performing an exploratory operation? Why? What were they looking for?" Ake asked.

"The only people who know that were in the operating room," said one of the male nurses. He had helped Ake attend to Ray during Ray's stay in the infirmary. Ake looked at the five white sheets. "Yeah," the orderly said, "and they're all dead now."

## II

"What is it, Beowulf?"

The big dog's nose wrinkled as he sampled the air. "Smells like one o' them kay-nees."

Moving slowly and quietly, Ray parted the vegetation in front of him. Through the leaves he could see a K'a-nii staring intently into the treetops.

"What he doin'?" Beowulf whispered.

"I don't know, Beowulf," Ray said, following the K'a-nii's line of sight.

"There!" said Beowulf.

"Yeah, I see it," Ray said.

The K'a-nii was watching a small, monkeylike creature cavorting through the trees. It withdrew something from a belt at its waist.

"A blow gun," Ray said.

The K'a-nii carefully inserted a dart into the hollow tube and raised the blow gun to its mouth. Ray and Beowulf were too far away to see the K'a-nii's cheeks inflate, but it lowered the tube, apparently having propelled the dart at its target.

"Watch," Ray commanded Beowulf.

Sure enough, in a few moments the tiny lemurlike thing toppled drunkenly from the limb it clung to and fell to the jungle floor near the K'a-nii. The K'a-nii picked up the fallen prey and casually bit its throat with its own formidable teeth. Ray would have been more than a little surprised, given those impressive teeth, if the K'a-nii had not been first-rate predators. The K'a-nii lived up to their anatomy by being highly efficient hunters and meat eaters.

"Didn't use a knife," Ray told Beowulf. "That's probably the traditional way of dispatching your victim."

"What now?" asked Beowulf.

"You go back to the house."

"And you?"

"I'm going to follow this guy to their village."

*Well, here goes nothing*, Ray thought as he slowly made his way into the K'a-nii village. Ray wasn't sure what he had been hoping to happen, but he'd been expecting something, some reaction from the inhabitants.

No one paid him the slightest mind. No, that wasn't exactly true. They did seem to be aware of him. They glanced at him as they passed in much the same way a human pedestrian might look down and see a small coin lying in the street. They noticed him—how could they fail not to?—but they *took no notice of* him.

*Jeez, I did bathe today*, Ray thought. That was more than could be said for the K'a-nii who passed by. *Whew! They're kinda ripe,*

Ray observed, his nose wrinkling. He had a sudden thought: *Perhaps they depend heavily on scent; maybe I'm not really registering because I don't possess a noticeable odor. That could be*, he allowed. *Hell, I'm just guessing*, he told himself. *It could be just about anything.*

Like that of some Terran reptiles, the K'a-nii sense of smell appeared to be in the roof of the mouth. Ray noticed that they periodically sampled the air with their long, slender tongues. A K'a-nii's tongue would slither out and flick left-right, left-right, and then withdraw back into its mouth where the molecules of air would be tasted. The tip of the tongue wasn't forked; instead, it looked remarkably like a small pitchfork with its tripartite construction. While the anthrobiologist in Ray found this all fascinating, his parochial human being half simply shivered and went "Ugh!" The reptile/mammal antagonism went back a long, long way. *I wonder if that's what's behind everyone's reluctance to want to learn more about them?*

Feeling shunned, Ray made the best of the situation and took advantage of his hosts' disinterest to approach one of the dwellings. Constructed of mud and sticks, it looked remarkably like an African hut. *Hm-m-m, wonder how they keep the mud from dissolving in all the rain? Maybe I can ask Tsuji; he's an engineer.* He scratched his head thoughtfully. *Bricks used to be made from clay and straw, didn't they? Seems to me they held up pretty good in the rain. Must be the same principle.*

He sensed someone watching him. He turned slowly and saw two K'a-nii gravely observing his actions. "Hi, there, how ya doin'?" He smiled broadly, even as he considered that a smile might mean "I hate you and would like nothing better than to see you dead, you sonofabitch." In reality, it probably meant nothing. Ray wasn't sure the K'a-nii *could* smile. Of course, if this village was any indication, what did they have to smile about?

One of the two K'a-nii pointed a finger at the hut—*Well, that gesture seems to mean the same thing*, Ray thought—and produced an amazing variety of sounds. The alien's speech was a mixture of guttural utterances and soft, sibilant hissing sounds. Ray had no idea what the K'a-niian was saying. He did move away from the dwelling, however.

Ray pointed in the general direction of the camp. "I have a place, actually. But, if I want a vacation home, I'll keep you in mind. Maybe we could work out a time-sharing deal, okay?"

The second K'a-niian said something, touched his forearm with one of his taloned fingers, and abruptly turned away.

"Yeah, a touch to the forearm to you, too," Ray said . . . but softly and with no real bite to the words.

As the two K'a-nii walked away, Ray had to laugh at the preposterousness of his situation. "I don't know one goddamn word of their language. I don't know whether they're male, female, or hermaphrodite. I don't know forking diddlysquat about these guys! What the hell am I doing here?" Ray's last words were for the benefit of the small recording device he wore on his lapel. He decided he'd have to do some editing before he fed the information to the computer. No sense giving the computer the satisfaction of seeing him struggle. He knew that computer was really emotionless, but it was programmed to act as if it wasn't.

Ray approached the communal fire in the center of the twenty-seven-hut village—this was not an estimate; he had carefully counted each structure. A number of K'a-nii had begun congregating there, and Ray wanted to see what was up. "Ah, meal time," he said when he saw two villagers carrying a spit toward the fire. Several of the small lemurlike creatures similar to the one he'd seen earlier, freshly killed and skinned, were impaled on the spit and placed over the fire, about a meter or so from the hot coals.

The K'a-nii gestured and jabbered among themselves as they watched the meat cooking. *It's not as if they're stolid, close-mouthed types*, Ray had to admit. They seemed to be relatively animated and social beings. Ray hunkered down to wait and see what would happen when the food was ready.

One of the K'a-nii finally took a stone knife and tested the meat. Apparently it met his requirements. He cupped his hands around his mouth and uttered a series of short barking sounds. Immediately, half the K'a-nii present left and were replaced by an equal number of newcomers. The nine K'a-nii then removed the meat from the fire, placed it on a bed of broad leaves, and began to cut off hunks small enough to push into their mouths with their slender fingers. After the first K'a-nii had eaten its fill, it (he/she?) jumped up and down several times and then stood absolutely motionless, like a statue, with its hands on its head. The others ignored it and finished eating, using both hands to stuff the cooked flesh into their mouths as if they hadn't eaten in days.

"Weird," Ray whispered. "Very weird." So far, he had to

admit, Maria was proving prophetic; the K'a-nii were definitely truly *alien*.

Then something extraordinary happened. One of the eight K'a-nii remaining by the fire rose and walked directly to where Ray was kneeling. Ray stood up, unsure what was happening. The K'a-nii held out a piece of meat toward Ray. Ray got the idea that it wasn't offering the food to him, just displaying it very clearly. After it was sure Ray had looked at what it was holding, the K'a-nii hefted the cooked meat in its hand and deliberately enunciated, "Kasso-liss-ahh."

Then it walked away.

★ ★ ★

"So why have you come to me with this ridiculous request, Dr. Ringgren?"

Ake pulled on his earlobe and thought, *All of a sudden I'm Dr. Ringgren to everyone.* "Is it ridiculous to want to understand what happened in Operating Room One this morning . . . Director Kodlich?" *I can use formal titles, too*! "There was an explosion of indeterminate origin. There is also the possibility the blast was premature. What if it had happened in one of the mine tunnels . . . or more ominously for us all, near an ammunition cache?"

"I take your point," Kodlich said. "But now what? What makes you think I have any influence with Colonel Bukovsky?"

"I believe you have more than you realize . . . or are willing to admit."

"How so?"

"Bukovsky's in a double bind here. Certainly, she's under orders to enforce strict military discipline and retain control of your mining operation. On the other hand, she must allow you a certain measure of independence if you're to meet your quotas. If something is going on which might interfere with the flow of the rubies, I believe she's obligated to share that information with you if you make an issue of it. Face it, Theo, you've got the power to make her shake in her boots, not vice versa. She can't afford to fuck up this posting and you both know it."

Kodlich ran his hands through his thick brown hair. "Goddamn you to hell and back," he said. "Why do you have to be right all the time?"

"It's a curse," said Ake, fully meaning it.

"Where's your partner?"

"He's . . . ah, doing a little sightseeing, I believe."

"Oh, no—don't tell me! He's sniffing around the K'a-nii, isn't he?" When Ake didn't respond, he repeated, "Well, isn't he?"

"I thought you said not to tell you."

★ ★ ★

When Ray got back to the house, he found Ozma and Gawain patiently waiting for him. "What's up, guys?"

"There bin a 'plosion at the prison," said Gawain.

"We see'd it when we come out the mine with Ake," Ozma explained.

"An explosion! Was anyone hurt or killed?"

All Ozma could say was, "Doan know, Ray."

"Where's Ake now?"

"He stayed to help since he a doctor."

"I better get down there right away," Ray said. He looked at the two dogs, considering. "You two stay here for now and guard the fort, okay?"

"Okay, Ray," Gawain said forlornly. "We never gets to have any fun."

Ray picked up his energy rifle and hefted it thoughtfully. "I wonder if I should take this along."

"It couldn't hurt," suggested Ozma.

"I think you're right," agreed Ray, making up his mind. He swung the rifle over his shoulder and strode toward the door. He paused there long enough to say, "You can watch my wrestling holos, but no *Captain Trimble*; I'm the only galactic hero in this house."

"Yes, Ray," Ozma said, but he was gone.

# 8

"I wish Ake would get here already," Ray said. "Bukovsky isn't going to see us until he does."

Maria glanced at Theo Kodlich and then over her shoulder as if to reassure herself that there wasn't someone else behind her. "Am I a holoscenic? Wasn't I here twenty minutes ago when the Colonel's aide told us that himself?"

Ray cracked every knuckle on his left hand. When he saw the looks of disapproval on the others' faces, he said, "Hey, at least I don't bite my nails."

"We don't have to *hear* you if you bite your nails," Maria said, nervously twisting a strand of her already curly black hair around a finger.

"So why don't you stop playing with your hair?" Ray told her.

"Would you two please knock it off?" Kodlich said. "I'm sure Ake will be here as soon as he can get away from his new duties in the infirmary."

"That tells us at least one of the military doctors has been killed or severely wounded," Ray said. He glanced at Bukovsky's aide, guarding access to her inner sanctum and probably recording their every word.

"You think so?" Maria asked.

"Ake is a damn fine doctor," Ray said. "So, of all his skills, the one that is most likely to be in demand in an emergency is his medical training."

"You forget my incredible tap-dancing abilities," Ake said, striding into the room confidently.

Ray smiled to himself at the change in his partner's demeanor; clearly, Ake had been involved in treating patients. There was something about being a doctor that gave a man or a woman the glow of self-confidence.

"Are you going to tell us what's going on, Ake?" implored Kodlich.

"Let's go see Bukovsky," was Ake's reply.

"Lieutenant?" Kodlich said, addressing Bukovsky's aide.

The lieutenant disappeared into Bukovsky's inner office, only to pop out again almost immediately. "You may go in now."

When everyone had entered and the lieutenant had keyed the door to hiss shut, Colonel Bukovsky said, "I suppose you'd all better take a seat."

After they found chairs and settled in, Kodlich said, "You know why we are here, of course."

"Yes, I do," replied Bukovsky. "For the briefest period of time I imagined that I could keep what happened in the prison infirmary a secret from those outside the compound." She laughed mirthlessly. "If nothing else, that shows my unbounded optimism."

"What exactly did happen?" Kodlich continued. "What was the cause of the explosion?"

"Why don't you ask Dr. Ringgren?"

"Because we're asking you, Colonel," Ray said. "You said it yourself—it's hard to keep certain things secret around here, so why not come clean with us? Sure, Ake has a pretty good idea about what happened, but you *know*."

Bukovsky leaned back in her chair, put a finger to the side of her mouth, and pierced Ray with a laserbeam stare. Just when everyone thought that Ray had pushed the wrong buttons, the Colonel dropped her hand and said, "You're right, of course, Citizen Larkin. I need the cooperation of everyone in this room if this command is to be successful. Given how much you already know, or suspect, further secrecy would be pointless, perhaps even counterproductive." Bukovsky smiled and the others decided they preferred her sterner look.

*A nice speech*, Ray thought. *Taking it into account, I'd say we have a fifty-fifty chance of hearing the truth from Bukovsky. Not the whole truth, of course, but it'll be a start.*

# K-9 CORPS: UNDER FIRE

"So the explosion was caused by an implant?" said Ake. "It was a bomb?"

"To the best of my knowledge, yes. Dr. Ramos has told me that the medical staff was suspicious of this new prisoner from the beginning. A series of scans revealed nothing. Rather, they revealed very little. Dr. Jayanthi was troubled by his inability to account for a small dark line running the length of one of this Kales woman's ribs. Apparently there was nothing especially noteworthy about this anomaly except for one thing." Bukovsky paused; like any good storyteller, she knew how to whet her listeners' appetites for more.

"Yes? Please go on," said Maria.

That was all Bukovsky was waiting for. "The line was absolutely straight, even where the rib itself was slightly curved. Whatever it was, it was artificial, not natural."

"You're telling us that something was placed inside this prisoner's rib by a surgeon?" asked Ray.

"There seems to be no other explanation."

"And what was placed inside the rib was an explosive implant," Ake said. It was a statement, not a question. Ake found the whole topic a bit unsettling; he was remembering his own implant which would have detonated if his mission on Chiron had failed. He had succeeded, of course, and the implant had been removed.

Bukovsky nodded. "Again, there seems to be no other reasonable explanation."

"All right, I'm easy, I'll bite," said Ray. "The woman was carrying an explosive implant, a bomb. If we accept that, the next issue then becomes 'why'?"

Bukovsky looked at them all, one at a time. She seemed to be sizing them up, evaluating how much she dared reveal to them. "There are several possibilities, each of them with its own level of plausibility. Sorting them out may take time."

Ray looked at Ake, who just shrugged in response. *What the hell*, Ray thought. *If I'm gonna get blown up, I want to know who's doing it and why.* "It wouldn't have anything to do with the unusually high number of female prisoners, would it?"

Everyone in the room was absolutely still, as if Ray had committed a social *faux pas* like loudly passing gas at a dinner party.

"Does this fact hold any special significance for you?" asked Bukovsky finally.

"Only if these women are members of the Order of Programmers."

Bukovsky's response was instantaneous and totally unexpected: She laughed. Her laughter was genuine, Ray decided, but it was also hollow.

"May I ask the colonel what she finds so funny in Citizen Larkin's response?" asked Kodlich.

"The intelligence reports I have been privy to for the last two years have been severely censored, with information like this withheld from me," Bukovsky said. "Yet the supposedly well-guarded secrets my superiors are unwilling to trust me with seem to be common knowledge. Even mere Federation contract workers are able to deduce them on their own." She daubed at her eyes. "Forgive me if I find that hilarious."

*Piss on that*, thought Ray. *That "mere" toasts my buns!*

"It's true, then?" said Kodlich. "The new prisoners are mostly Prime Programmers?"

"Yes, it's true," Bukovsky confirmed. "Technically speaking, though, they are *former* Prime Programmers; they have been arrested and convicted of crimes against the Federation."

"Baloney," Ray said. "Crimes against the Triumvirate is more like it."

"So they're being imprisoned for not rolling over onto their backs and spreading wide!" Maria said hotly.

"I find that comment to be quite vulgar," Bukovsky said sourly.

"But not untrue?"

"No, not untrue," the commandant conceded.

"So the Prime Programmers are responsible for the bomb?" asked Kodlich.

"Yes," said Bukovsky simply.

"We pretty much got this far on our own," said Ake, glancing at Ray and Maria. "But we wanted our suspicions confirmed."

"And are you happy that they have been?" demanded Bukovsky.

"Not especially," Ray said. "But now we know what to expect."

That interested the colonel. "And what is it that you expect?"

"More attempts."

Bukovsky nodded knowingly. "Yes, that is why I have ordered the planet sealed until further notice." She placed her hands flat on the top of her desk and leaned forward. "We will not accept any more prisoners; the population must not be further contaminated."

"Sealing the planet means nobody new can infiltrate," Kodlich said. "I suppose that's a wise precaution against new threats, but what about the prisoners already here? A lot of them have arrived in the past six months."

"That's why there must be no contact between the prisoners and anyone else save for their guards." Bukovsky stared at Ake and added, "This means you in particular, Dr. Ringgren. You will necessarily have a certain amount of contact with sick or injured prisoners since you are assuming some of Doctors Rayanthi and Carpenter's medical duties inside the prison. Treat the prisoners, but do not speak with them."

"You don't trust Ake?" asked Maria.

Colonel Bukovsky didn't answer for a long time. Finally she said, "It's not so much that I don't trust Dr. Ringgren as I don't trust any of you."

"Oh, we know that," said Ray matter-of-factly. "I assume that's why you're not telling us the whole truth."

## II

Standing on the edge of a precipice overlooking the jungle and watching the sun falling toward the horizon might not be the best possible use of one's time, Ray thought, but it had to be up there in the top ten. He returned to the small clearing where Ake had built a fire. Since the wood was not especially dry, the fire tended to smoke more than Ake initially wanted. But then he realized that the smoke kept away a good proportion of the droning insects eager to dine on them.

"What did these bloodsuckers do for sustenance before we got here?" wondered Ake as he threw another piece of wood on the fire. Sparks flew up like a thousand fireflies.

"They waited," said Ray. "Their shamans predicted the coming of the Promised Ones—impossibly large creatures filled to the skin with delicious fluids." Ray swatted something away. "Oh, the faithless and poor in spirit scoffed, but the believers kept their faith and continued depositing their eggs in shit. Generations of maggots reached adulthood without the coming of the Millennium. And then one day a great fire from the sky heralded the coming of the Juicy Ones. The Prophecies were fulfilled."

"Geez," said Gawain in awe. "That was wonderful!"

"It was, wasn't it?"

"Doan encourage him," Beowulf told Gawain. "He can talk like that for hours."

"And we don't have hours," Ake said with a wide, theatrical yawn. "I gotta be in the infirmary in the morning, so I have to get my beauty rest." He yawned again. The first one had been for effect, but it triggered a small series of genuine yawns. Both Grendel and Littlejohn followed Ake's lead.

"Stop that, Ake, it catching," Beowulf said.

"Yeah, it *is* contagious," Ray agreed, fighting back a yawn of his own. "And it isn't even dark yet, for Pete's sake." Then he cocked his head as if he heard something in the jungle.

"Somethin' there?" asked Beowulf. "I don't hear nuthin'."

"I thought I . . . I *sensed* something or someone watching us," Ray said.

"The K'a-nii?"

"Yes . . . ah, no."

"Well, which is it?" Ake asked.

"It's the oddest thing," Ray said. "It *feels* like one of the K'a-nii is out there, watching everything we do, and yet . . ." He shivered. "And yet something's different. It feels like a K'a-nii and yet it doesn't."

"We gonna tell ghost stories?" asked Gawain eagerly, his tail wagging.

Ray shook his head. "Never mind. It must be my imagination."

"What's your reaction to our meeting with the estimable Commandant Bukovsky?" Ake finally asked, poking the fire with a long branch and causing more sparks to fill the air.

"I don't know," Ray admitted. "It's clear that she told us just enough of the truth as she could get away with, hoping that we don't discover what she's leaving out."

"So you told her," said Ake. "Just what do you think she's trying to keep from us?"

"Could be anything. I've been away from Terra for a long time and I have no sense of what the atmosphere is like back there. We've been cynically assuming all the while that everyone's going along with the Triumvirate's power play. What if that's not the case? What if there's unrest—riots, martial law, work stoppages? There could even be an active resistance, an underground."

"If there is, then the Prime Programmers—the real Prime Programmers—are almost certainly up to their necks in it."

"That's probably true."

Ake shivered as night came down like a black curtain being

lowered. "I've never seen it get dark so fast anywhere as it does on this planet," Ake said. The stars began to appear, almost like small bulbs being turned on randomly.

"It's not cold," observed Ray. "So why are you shivering?"

"Everything. This whole deal stinks. And the more I discover how much I don't know, the more fearful I become." Ake looked into his friend's face. "I'm even beginning to doubt the wisdom of revealing my background to Maria."

"You mean about us being on Chiron?"

"Hell, no! I mean about being a sleeper for the Prime Programmers. That's the sort of thing that, if it gets out, I can spend the rest of my life—which might not be a very long period—denying and everyone will say, 'Sure, you used to be a deep-cover agent, but now you're just a plain and simple partner in a scout dog team. Spying for the Prime Programmers is behind you. Uh-huh!' Jeezus, Ray, I *know* I'm not working for Thane Wyda and her people any longer, and even I would have a hard time swallowing that story!"

"What we do now?" asked Beowulf.

"Good question," said Ray. He turned and looked down the slope of the volcano, unable to really see anything in the pure, primeval darkness. "I'm going to spend every free moment with the K'a-nii."

Ake was astonished. "Now? Now, with all that's going on in the compound?"

"Especially with all that's going on in the compound."

"Wanna tell us why?"

Ray looked pained, as if unwilling to voice a sincere if suspect belief.

"You remember what Maria said, about me having the 'power'?"

"Yeah."

"Well, I just know, I *sense*, that they know something that can help us if only we can uncover it." Ray shrugged helplessly. "That's it; I have nothing more solid to go on than that."

"Ray usually right 'bout these things," Mama-san said.

"I'm not going to argue the point," said a reluctant Ake.

"What about you?"

"I still have the same plan," Ake said. "I have to find a way to speak to Thane Wyda."

"If you're caught, Bukovsky will roast both of us over a fire like this one," Ray said. "Especially after what you said about no one believing you're not still working for the Prime Programmers."

"I know."

## III

The K'a-nii accepted Ray, and even the dogs and Ake when they tagged along with him, as part of the scenery. They also even accepted Hypatia—certainly a lot more easily than Maria had accepted Ray's suggestion that one of her cats accompany him on his next few forays into the K'a-nii camp.

"Look," he'd told Maria. "You say I've got this 'power,' right? Well, maybe I do. But there's no denying that Hypatia's telepathic senses are keener than any I might have. She could be a big help to me. Ake went with me twice, but he's got too many new duties these days to do it again."

"I don't want to lose any of my cats to the K'a-nii."

"I won't let them eat her, if that's what's worrying you."

"You thick-headed boob. It's not that, it's . . . it's . . . Ah, what the hell." She threw up her hands in exasperation. "Maybe if Hypatia goes with you she'll keep you from making some outrageous error in judgment. If she wants to go—which I doubt—you can take her along. But only if she wants to go."

Full of Siamese curiosity, Hypatia wanted to tag along all right. That surprised the heck out of Maria, but she grudgingly gave her permission for Hypatia to accompany Ray.

As Ray watched the K'a-niis' movements and attempted to derive useful data from what he observed, it seemed that Hypatia had little to offer him until he could make a more meaningful connection with them.

While they themselves retained their mystery, their alienness, what they did was becoming less alien to him and more and more like a comprehensible lifestyle. As he had theorized, they had certain necessary bodily functions; these he could understand on the simplest and most uncomplicated level merely by watching the K'a-nii as they performed them.

Eating was a obvious example. Understanding the rituals and the routines surrounding the clear and unequivocal act of eating was still beyond his ability, however. Eating the flesh of a small mammal was one thing, but did the K'a-nii who performed this act do so simply because he or she was hungry? To honor an ancestor? Because it was a gift from another individual in a socially inferior or superior position? Because it was what one ate when the stars were in their current position? Ray simply didn't know the answers to any of these questions. And Hypatia was getting only vague readings from the aliens.

It wasn't as if Ray was making *no* progress, however. Already he knew the names of a third of the K'a-nii in the camp. A third. That figure made him pause. *A third?* he mused. *A third . . . things in threes?* He glanced swiftly around the village. *There are twenty-seven huts, aren't there? That number is divisible by three.* While he could not remember every instance, it suddenly struck Ray that a number of elements in the K'a-nii culture appeared in threes or were divisible by three. *Damn, they'd be easy pickings for a Neo-Christian missionary, wouldn't they?*

With Hypatia hugging his shoulder like an organ grinder's monkey, Ray walked over to where Beowulf and Littlejohn were having an animated conversation. They broke off their discussion when he joined them, and looked at Hypatia with ill-disguised antagonism. Hypatia loved it; not as much as the smart-mouthed Penelope would have loved it, but she loved it nonetheless.

"How's it going?" Ray asked. "Anyone approach you or attempt to interact with either of you in any way?"

"No, Ray," Beowulf said.

"Yah," agreed Littlejohn. "Nuthin' change there."

"Odd, isn't it?" Ray asked. "I wonder why they're so uninterested in you guys?"

"Mebbe they got their own pack," suggested Beowulf helpfully.

"Huh?"

"You our Man. Mebbe they see that. We don't count; you the leader of the pack."

Ray brightened at that. "Hey, that's a good observation. I'll try to test it when I get a chance."

"And, course, a little fur ball on your shoulder prob'ly not even worth considerin'," Beowulf added, unwilling to pass up a chance to take a shot at a cat.

Before Hypatia could say anything in response, Littlejohn said, "Uh, Ray."

"Yes, Littlejohn?"

"Here comes one of them lizard guys."

"Ray," one of the K'a-nii said to him—or at least it was an acceptable approximation of how his name was pronounced. That was the other development that had occurred over the past several visits; they now knew and used his name.

Ray had been both surprised and halfway expecting it when one of the K'a-nii natives addressed him directly and in understandable English. Ray had the sneaking suspicion that the K'a-nii were a quick study when it came to linguistics; it wouldn't have surprised him to discover that they understood everything he said. He only wished the reverse were true.

"Gezsss?" Ray hissed, using one of the few K'a-nii words he knew. It meant yes, and if you drew it out as Ray just did you meant it as a question.

"K'a-nii K'a-yass," the K'a-nii said.

Another native came forward and stood in front of Ray. The native's tongue flicked in and out of his mouth as he remained standing in front of Ray for just a moment or two before turning away. It may not have seemed much of anything, but the surface banality was deceiving. The mere fact that the native had stood near Ray for a moment was important; they didn't do it lightly. As if to underscore that fact, the way the native had positioned himself clearly announced that he/she was not including either of the dogs in his personal aura. Since Hypatia was almost a part of Ray, it wasn't clear to him how the native viewed her.

Still, while Ray knew that the native's actions implied something, maybe something important, he really didn't understand what the ritual or gesture was supposed to mean. Nothing new there.

"K'a-nii K'a-yass?" Ray repeated slowly, more to himself than to anyone else.

"Gezsss," the first K'a-nii native said as if replying to Ray. It seemed pleased. Apparently it thought that Ray understood whatever the special usage meant. And it *was* special: Ray and the computer had precious few examples of the K'a-nii using the name of their race. Clearly, it was something significant, something important. But what?

"I gets a feeling of happiness, deep happiness," Hypatia told Ray. "That and a sense of expectation. Somethin's going to happen soon."

The K'a-nii who had stood before Ray now joined a group of nine other natives. One of them stared at Ray and then they strode off as if they had something very specific in mind.

"Guys, stay here," Ray said to the dogs. "I'll be back as soon as I can."

"Okay, Ray."

Ray picked up the little backpack/cat carrier Maria had made for him, all but stuffed Hypatia into it, slipped his arms through the loops and slung it on his back. With his cat papoose on his back, he followed the ten K'a-nii at a short distance. He assumed they wanted him along, but he was hesitant about joining them. If they all ate a plant that was poison to him, he didn't want to be considered a member of the group and be forced to go along. Whether that was a valid fear or not, Ray stayed between five and ten meters behind the others.

Since normally the K'a-nii were quite vocal, he found it interesting that they didn't speak. Trailing behind them and being bigger than they were also made Ray feel as if he were an adult scoutmaster taking his charges on a nature hike. *Tonight we'll toast marshmallows in the volcano*, he mused as he noticed that they were steadily climbing the steep slopes.

"I gettin' funny stuff from you, Ray," said Hypatia. "You must be thinkin' odd thoughts."

"Maybe I'm just getting lightheaded from the lack of oxygen, Hypatia," Ray said. He told her what he'd been thinking and she sniffed a disdainful cat sniff. The cats found Ray's sense of humor less sidesplitting than did the dogs.

Up and up they climbed. "Maybe my marshmallow idea wasn't so farfetched."

As they steadily worked their way skyward, the vegetation grew sparser and sparser. *Whatever's going on*, Ray thought, *I don't think we're following a path*. If they were on a trail, it was a rarely used one. A small fuzzy-wuzzy that the K'a-nii seemed to particularly relish as a delicacy darted out in front of them, froze, and then scurried down a hole. They barely glanced at it, their minds elsewhere. Ray looked at his watch and realized that ninety minutes had passed since they'd left the village.

Ray could hear the breath rasping in and out of the K'a-nii as the upward climb took its toll. "Good thing we all seem to be in pretty fair condition," Ray muttered to Hypatia, grateful for all the time he'd spent in the *Truman*'s jogging tubes.

Hypatia agreed. "You doin' great, Ray. The view's good, too."

Agreeing with the cat, Ray took a moment to look back and down at the jungle and then up ahead. "Piss and crackers, we're going all the way to the top!"

"I thought I was kidding about my eating a poison plant," he muttered for the benefit of the recorder on his shirt lapel as well as to Hypatia. "What if they all jump into the volcano and want company?" Then something worse occurred to him. *What if they asked me along so they can throw me in the volcano? Well*, he thought as they neared the volcano's peak, *I guess I'm going to find out real soon whether I'm just an observer or the guest of honor.*

"Damn, I wish I'd paid more attention in class the days we discussed Hawaiian volcano rituals," he said to Hypatia.

"Like you say—you don't want to be the guest of honor."

Ray was nonplussed. "How'd you know that? I was thinking it, but you cats aren't supposed to be able to actually read minds . . . not *really*."

"Don't know, Ray," replied Hypatia, as confused as Ray. "But we seem to be gettin' better at mind stuff since we bin on this planet."

Ray and Hypatia finally joined the others at the volcano's lip. Without warning the K'a-nii suddenly began jabbering and gesturing at the glowing red core that lay hundreds of meters below. Ray stepped as close to the edge as he dared and stared down. *Now what?* What happened next was so sudden and unexpected that for a moment Ray refused to believe it. Sure, he made jokes about a sacrifice to the volcano gods, but he didn't take the idea seriously.

"They not thinkin' about you or me, Ray," Hypatia informed him. "We not even in the picture. But they happy about somethin'. Someone is . . ." The cat cocked her head in a way that mimicked the way Maria so often cocked her head when she was using her psi talents. "Is . . . is growing up."

"Growing up?" asked Ray. "What the hell do you mean, 'growing up'?"

"It's not words," Hypatia explained. "It's a feeling. You gots some of the power, you try to feel them."

It was true, Ray conceded; he could sense them projecting the idea that one of their number was on the verge of a great and wonderful journey.

While Ray and Hypatia groped for meaning, the other nine K'a-nii picked up the odd man out and, after swinging him (her?) vigorously back and forth to pick up momentum, hurled him as far out and toward the middle of the volcano's throat as they could. Awestruck, Ray watched as the K'a-niian native tumbled limply through the air toward the faintly glowing lava far below. If the others' intentions were to propel the chosen one far enough out into the center so that he cleared the sides of the volcano and fell directly into the viscous lava, they were successful. Ray averted his gaze at the last second, unwilling to witness the inevitable.

He heard, or imagined he heard, a faraway popping sound as the native's body plunged into the fiery furnace of lava.

"Ohmygod!" Ray said over and over. "Ohmygod!"

"That was . . . interesting," Hypatia said. Ray sensed that her coldness was a calculated method of dealing with the psychological impact of what they'd just witnessed.

Ray slowly became aware that one of the nine remaining natives was standing beside him. "K'a-nii K'a-yass," the native said.

"They . . . The others don't seem to believe that the other one is dead," Hypatia said with wonder in her feline voice.

"Then they're fucked!" Ray said. "He's dead, all right. You don't fall into volcanic lava and live."

Hypatia stared at the native who'd spoken to them. Its eyes glittered and its mouth gaped open. The native's tongue slithered in and out of its mouth. "It's envious of the dead one."

"Maria was right," Ray said, stumbling down the slope, eager to get away from the scene of the bizarre ritual he'd just observed. "They *are* alien; too damned alien."

"Wait," said Hypatia. But it was too late: Ray was stumbling down the slope, kicking soil and cinders before him in his eagerness to escape the scene of the bizarre and alien ritual he'd just observed.

# 9

While Ray was out pretending to be Sir Richard Burton, explorer and other cultures enthusiast, Ake had the life-and-death responsibility of a physician. Actually, Ake would have hooted at that rather dramatic interpretation of his duties; in reality, they were much more mundane.

"We've got the usual assortment of cuts, scrapes, sore throats, and intestinal disorders today, Doc," announced a hulking blond orderly named Corporal Hamstedt.

"Okay, let me see their charts," Ake said, reaching out expectantly with his left hand while he cradled a steaming mug of hot black coffee in his right. He took a sip of coffee and put down the mug to look through the printouts on the clipboard Hamstedt handed him. "Seems simple enough," he said as he scanned the list quickly. He was preparing to hand the clipboard back to the orderly when something odd about the charts struck him.

"Wait a minute," Ake said. "I want to look at these again."

"Something the matter?"

"These charts contain only Federation identity numbers, no names," said Ake.

"Oh, you didn't get the word?" Hamstedt asked.

"Now what?" asked Ake wearily.

"It's a new order. Colonel Bukovsky wants the prisoner-patients identified by their Fed-Id numbers only. Didn't Captain Ramos tell you?"

"No."

Ramos and Ake had taken an instant dislike to each other's guts and soon made it a habit to avoid unnecessary contact with one another.

"Oh," said Hamstedt. He rubbed the top of his crew-cut head; it was a hairstyle coming back into vogue. Ake hated it, vaguely recalling its origin as the embodiment of Prussian military efficiency and regimentation. "Well, Captain Ramos said that the colonel doesn't want us to have anything more to do with the prisoners than is necessary to treat them."

From the odd way he looked at him, Ake guessed that Ramos had given Hamstedt orders to report any unnecessary or suspicious contact between himself and the patients. *It would make Ramos's day if he could prove I was conspiring with the Prime Programmers*, Ake thought, sipping his coffee and returning Hamstedt's stare with a bland look of innocence.

He finished his coffee and put the mug down. "Let's get started."

As Ake slowly worked his way down the row of null-grav hospital beds in the ward, he noted that the majority of the patients were women. Many of them were relatively youthful, in their mid-twenties to their mid-thirties, but a disproportionately high percentage were middle-aged. They seemed unlikely candidates for a prison planet unless they were political prisoners of the highest rank.

One of this day's few male patients was a soldier who had ventured into the jungle and stepped on one of the nastier varieties of plants. The vegetation's means of defense, an eleven-centimeter-long center spike, had pierced the sole of his footwear, gone through his foot, and emerged from the top of his boot. The chart indicated that he'd already gotten his universal-antibody booster injection. Not even Ramos could screw up something that basic.

"Some plants they got on this ball o' dirt, eh, Doc?" the young soldier asked. Just looking at his unlined face made the thirty-six-year-old Ake feel like he was a hundred years old.

"There are some wicked things in the rain forest," agreed Ake, unable to resist glancing guiltily toward Hamstedt to see if the corporal was monitoring the conversation. So far, he wasn't. That made sense since the young man was just that, a young *man*.

"Yeah," the soldier said. "Jesus and Mohammed, I never felt pain like that before and I hope I never do again."

"I realize it must get pretty boring in camp," said Ake, "but what were you doing out in the bush?"

"Butterflies."

"I beg your pardon?"

"I was looking for butterflies. Well, the closest things to Terran butterflies that this planet has to offer. A real beauty flew over my head and I wasn't watching where I was going." He looked down at the foot of the bed, where Ake had moved to change the dressing on his wound. "Do you realize how many new specimens I could return home with? I could have the honor of naming dozens of species. Heck, I could even have one named for me."

"Now I've heard it all," Ake said. "A soldier who collects butterflies."

"I wasn't always a soldier, you know," the young man said. "Before I joined up to make the galaxy safe for decent folks, I was a Star Scout and I achieved the top rank with my collection." He beamed proudly. "I was the only kid from my troop ever to be awarded five stars."

"Impressive," said Ake as if he really meant it, which he didn't; he had no idea what winning five stars represented. He sprayed a clear plastic bandage on the youngster's foot and then stepped back to admire his handiwork.

"Ha, ha—that tickles."

"Now it does," Ake said wickedly. "But just wait until it starts to itch and you can't scratch it."

Ake continued on, cleaning and bandaging, applying ointments and sprays, looking into ears and down throats. Everything was routine until he reached the last null-grav bed in the ward. The patient was an older woman. Her chart said early fifties.

"Well, I see you have a—" Ake froze.

"Hello, Ake," Thane Wyda mouthed silently.

★ ★ ★

Littlejohn nudged Beowulf with his snout. "Someone comin'," he said.

Beowulf stared up the mountain's slope in the direction Ray, Hypatia, and those strange reptiles had disappeared, anxiously watching for Ray and the mind-reading puss's return. "Where? I doan see nuthin'."

"Not up there. Over this way."

Beowulf looked in the direction Littlejohn indicated. It was true; they were getting company.

" 'Lo, Beowulf, 'lo, Littlejohn," said Frodo.

" 'Lo, Frodo," Beowulf and Littlejohn said.

With Frodo were Mama-san, Ozma, Grendel, Sinbad, Tajil, and Gawain—the rest of the team, minus Ake. Beowulf and Littlejohn stood up and shook themselves to get rid of the dust that had infiltrated their thick fur. The two dogs, especially Beowulf, made a great display of greeting the rest of the team one by one.

"This unusual," Beowulf noted. " 'Bout the only time we ever get together all in one group is at night, back at the house."

"Yah," said Sinbad. "Ake workin' at the prison today, so's we thought we come over to see how you'uns doing with the lizard people."

"Yah," agreed Ozma. She looked around. "Where Ray?"

"Him and the pussface went up the mountainside with them lizard peoples," said Littlejohn.

Grendel looked horrified. "He did! And you two didn't go with him?"

"He dint want us," Beowulf explained. "He got the cat, course, but she no help in a fight," he sniffed.

"Jeez, I hope nuthin' happen to him," said Tajil.

"We all hope that," said Beowulf. "You think I *like* seein' Ray disappearin' with these guys?"

"Hey," said Gawain. "Somethin's goin' on."

"Yah," agreed Mama-san. "They's gettin' all excited or somethin'."

It was true. The K'a-nii, usually so unconcerned about the presence of the dogs as to be insulting to the canines, were now gesturing in their direction and hissing and making those throat-clearing sounds Ray had told the dogs was their speech.

"What they gettin' all riled up over?" wondered Sinbad.

"They never see'd us all together before," said Littlejohn. "Mebbe that be it."

"Big deal," said Frodo. "There's just the nine of us."

★ ★ ★

"I can't get these supplies without authorization," Corporal Hamstedt was saying.

"*I'm* authorizing you," said Ake.

"Begging your pardon, sir," Hamstedt said with phony deference, "but you're a civilian replacement without any military rank. Captain Ramos was quite adamant about that point."

"I'll bet he was," said Ake. "And where is Captain Ramos now?"

"I think he's in the administration building seeing Colonel Bukovsky about some matter."

"So give him a call. What's the problem?"

"I'm afraid that's impossible, sir," Hamstedt insisted. "The colonel has issued strict orders that there is to be no communication between the infirmary and any other part of the compound."

"That's stupid," Ake said. "That means even the colonel can't call in if she wants to." *Shit!* Ake thought. *I called Bukovsky stupid in front of this lap dog.*

Hamstedt's eyebrows shot up. Ramos would be pleased to hear that Ringgren had insulted the colonel. "I wouldn't know about that, sir," he said with a smarmy smile.

*If I was your superior officer, I'd wipe that smile off your face quick enough*, Ake thought, balling his hands into fists which he wanted to use to smash in Hamstedt's face. *It's really Ramos whose teeth I'd like to push down his throat.*

To Hamstedt, Ake just said, "Well, then, I suppose you'd better get over to the administration building and have this request approved. I need the stuff today."

"Yes, sir."

Ake watched him go. It suddenly dawned on him that Hamstedt's departure provided him with the perfect opportunity. He glanced around. There were a few other orderlies making the rounds, but none whom he suspected of being in league with the hated Ramos. If he acted quickly . . .

Most of the other patients were sleeping, the result of the afternoon sedative they had been given. His hands shaking, Ake pushed a wheelchair over to Wyda's bed and said in as normal a voice as he could muster, "Well, number 1699–366Q–T1232, I see you're responding well to the treatment. But I think I want to take you over to the allergy lab for a few tests. Please get into the chair."

Wyda's eyes widened, but she did as Ake suggested.

"That's good," Ake said, wheeling her out of the ward and down the hall. He used his thumb to key open a door marked "Allergy Lab" and he hurried them inside a small and especially cheerless room, even for a hospital.

"Can we talk?" asked Wyda as soon as the door hissed shut.

Ake activated the locking mechanism and turned around to face her. "I certainly hope so. That's why I brought you in here."

★ ★ ★

"Here comes Ray now," Littlejohn said.

"Jeez, he doan look so good," Ozma said, shocked by Ray's appearance.

Having half stumbled, half run down the mountainside, Ray was a mess. He'd fallen several times, scratching his face and opening several long gashes on the palms of his hands. After he took his first header, Hypatia decided she'd be better off on foot instead of riding in the homemade cat transporter.

Muddy rivulets streamed down Ray's face, the result of his heavy perspiration mixing freely with the volcanic dust that coated his face and clothes. Seeing the dogs, he suddenly felt ashamed of the picture he knew he presented.

"Hi, guys."

"Ray, you all right?" Beowulf asked.

"I've been better, but I'm basically okay."

Hypatia couldn't resist piping in with, "Yes, I'm fine, too. No problems. Thanks for your concern."

The dogs ignored her. "We gotta get you back to the house," Beowulf told Ray.

"In a minute," Ray said. He was bent over, hands on knees, gasping for breath. "Damn, I never want to see anything like that again."

"What happened?" asked Mama-san. "Them kay-nees try to 'tack you?"

"It wasn't that," answered Ray, still breathless. "One of them took a dive into the volcano." He shook his head grimly. "I guess he couldn't swim." As soon he said that, Ray got the oddest look on his face; it was as if he was remembering something—or trying to.

"A kay-nee jumped into the volcano?" asked Tajil. "He killed hisself?"

"It—he—had help, actually," Ray clarified. "The others threw him in but he seemed to be expecting it. He didn't resist."

"Why they do that?" wondered Beowulf.

"I don't know, Beowulf, I just don't know."

"Yes, you do," countered Hypatia. "We both know—sort of."

"What she mean?" asked Tajil.

Ray looked at Hypatia and then at Tajil. "The others didn't

project any sense of . . . of killing him," he said finally, groping for the words. "It was as if they were doing him a favor."

"We gonna take you back now," said Beowulf authoritatively. "Littlejohn and me take turns carrying you," the big dog said. "I be first."

For once, Ray put up no argument. "Sounds good to me." Then, feeling foolish for his behavior in front of the Siamese, Ray asked, "Do you wish a piggyback ride, Hypatia?"

"No thanks," Hypatia said with a swish of her tail. "I can walk."

As Ray climbed on Beowulf's back, one of the K'a-nii approached. "What he want, I wonder?" asked Frodo.

The K'a-nii looked at Ray, hopped up and down in place, and hissed something. Then he turned away and rejoined the others by the fire they were rebuilding.

"I'll repeat what I said to Hypatia earlier," Ray said slowly. "Maybe Maria's right. Maybe they are too weird to ever understand."

"You just tired and discouraged," Mama-san told him. "You figger them out, you wait and see."

"I hope so, Mama-san, I hope—" Ray stopped and cocked his head. "What's that?"

"What's what?" Beowulf asked, twisting his head around and looking back toward Ray.

"Did any of you hear anything? Is there another native close by?"

The dogs looked puzzled. "I dint hear nuthin', Ray," said Tajil.

"Me neither," added Frodo. None of the other dogs had heard anything, either.

Hypatia's tail twitched, but the Siamese said nothing.

"C'mon," said Ray. "Out with it, Hypatia."

Her deep blue eyes bored directly into Ray's blue-gray eyes as if daring him to contradict what she was about to say. "He not dead, is he, Ray?"

"Of course he's dead," Ray said, prepared to contest her words with special vehemence. Then his chest fell as he expelled a breath of air and admitted, "I thought he was dead, but I don't know now."

## II

"I guess I don't have to ask how things are going, do I, Prime Programmer?" Ake said.

"That depends, Ake," Thane Wyda said. "The fact of my

imprisonment here is obvious, but there are other things which have been set into motion which will drastically alter the situation."

"And what are they?" asked Ake with obvious interest.

Wyda looked at him disdainfully. "And why should I trust you enough to tell you anything? You appear to me in the guise of an employee of the mining consortium—in other words, as an employee of the Triumvirate. If you haven't noticed," she said dryly, "the Programmers loyal to the integrity of the Federation are not on the best of terms with the Triumvirate right now."

"I don't know what I can say or do to convince you that I'm *not* an agent of the Triumvirate," said Ake, shrugging and putting up his hands helplessly. "If Bukovsky and her people discover that I know you, that I worked for you, and that I've contacted you here, they're going to think I'm still working for the Prime Programmers. Ray and I took this job for the money. We didn't know what was going on. Besides, this isn't the Federation or the Judge Advocate I once worked for."

"And what *is* going on?"

Ake shook his head. "Oh, no, you don't—that's *my* question."

Wyda considered him gravely. "You were one of my best people, one of the best sleepers I ever had. I would like to believe that you still espouse the ideals of the old Federation, the Federation I served for so long." She sighed. "I would very much like to trust you . . . but can I?"

"That's the problem with having been a first-rate secret agent," Ake said. "The more convincing you sound, the less people want to accept you at face value."

"Can you blame me for my caution?"

"Hell, no," Ake said. His eyes narrowed and he leaned forward. "So don't tell me your big secrets, just let me in on the little ones. Ray and I want to help, we really do."

Thane Wyda said nothing for a long time. Finally, she held out her hand. "Take my hand, Ake." Ake did as she said. "I will tell you what I can, but there is a price."

"I'll pay it, whatever it is."

"Don't be so anxious to agree," Wyda remonstrated him. "Wait until you hear what it is."

"Go ahead."

"Remember the explosive implant that you carried?"

"Yes." Already Ake didn't like where this was going.

"I'm sorry to have to tell you this, but it was never removed."

Ake looked stunned. Then he laughed. "Whew . . . you had me going there for a moment. Don't joke about something like that."

"Do I look like I'm joking?"

"But . . . but . . . the operation," Ake sputtered. "I remember the operation."

Wyda shook her head. "The implant was in place for so long and was so biologically inert that your body completely accepted it. Your cells intermixed with it so thoroughly that the surgeons decided not to make the attempt to remove it."

Ake looked down at himself, feeling betrayed by his own body. "It's still in me?" Ake recalled being told that his implant was an especially powerful one.

"Yes." She paused a second and then proceeded. "There's something else."

Ake licked his lips. "There's more?"

"I'm afraid so," Wyda said apologetically. "You see, I can trigger it any time I choose to."

"Jesus, Mary, and Joseph!"

"I can tell you everything now," Wyda said. "You're working for me and the Order again."

★   ★   ★

When they arrived back at the house, Ray was disappointed that Ake was not there. "That's actually for the best, I think," Ray told the dogs after some consideration. "I don't mind you guys seeing me like this, but it would be a little embarrassing for Ake to observe what has happened to me."

The dogs looked at each other, proud that Ray—the Man—felt as close to them as his words proved him to be; he not only loved them, he *trusted* them.

"You gonna get cleaned up?" Gawain asked.

"No," said Frodo scornfully. "Ray gonna roll around in the dirt!"

"Don't fight," Ray said wearily.

"You heard Ray," Beowulf said, asserting his authority firmly yet quietly.

"Thanks, Beowulf," Ray said as he began stripping off his outer garments. He noticed that Ozma, following him down the hall, picked up each item of clothing as he let it fall. "Just take everything to the disposal unit and toss it in please, Ozma. I never want to see those clothes again."

When he was naked, Ray went into the bathroom, turned the shower on full force, and stepped into the middle of the stream of water. He increased the intensity of the flow until the droplets stung his skin. Then he regulated the temperature, turning the heat up so high that clouds of steam escaped the shower stall. Ray lathered up and then scrubbed himself from head to foot, attempting to scrub away the events of the afternoon. When he felt clean and whole again, he slowly rotated the dial from red to blue. The cold water now closed the pores that had opened to the hot. The effect was bracing and he began to feel like a human being again.

Once out of the shower, Ray put a healing salve on his scrapes and cuts and decided that his quick patch job would have to do until he got Ake to look him over. He slipped into a terrycloth robe, poured himself a stiff bourbon and water with lots of ice, and sat down by the computer interface.

"It's time binary brain and I had a little talk," Ray explained to the dogs.

"Don't let it be a smartmouth with you, Ray," said Mama-san. Like all the dogs, Mama-san did not approve of the computer's unwarranted familiarity with Ray.

The dogs believed the unseen computer thought it was better than Ray and they had difficulty with a machine that put itself above their master. Ray mostly ignored the computer's jibes at him; he realized that thinking machines were incapable of making the neurological quantum jumps from one energy state to another that were the basis for real insights. This meant that they could never duplicate human creativity. Ray permitted the computer to twit him over his lack of inability to crunch enormous amounts of information, because that was really the only advantage the machine had over him.

"The computer thinks fast," conceded Beowulf, "faster'n any human or dog, but it really doan *know* anything, not the way humans and dogs knows stuff."

"Yeah," said Gawain. "It 'sposed to be smart, but it doan know its hole from an ass in the ground."

"That's not *exactly* how the quote goes, Gawain," Ray said, laughing. "But I appreciate your support. The computer has been getting a bit a cheeky for a machine that hasn't been much help to me so far."

Ray sipped his drink and opened the link with the computer. "Good afternoon, Ray," the computer said pleasantly. "I trust that your most recent trip to the K'a-niian village has been productive."

Ray connected the holocorder to the computer's input terminals and said, "It was certainly eventful. That much I can say." He keyed a control and the images and sounds flowed into the computer. The computer took a long time assimilating the information. That is, it was a long time for the computer—a few seconds.

"This is most . . . interesting," it said finally.

"Ain't it?" Ray put his glass down and leaned forward. "There's a lot of material to be gone over in today's recording, but first I'm interested to see if you can make any sense of what that last native said to me before I . . . before I left the village."

The computer's response was instantaneous. "That's easy, Ray. The native used a very simple combination of two basic nouns."

"Yeah?"

"The native said to you, 'hand-foot.'"

"Hand-foot?" Ray repeated. "You're sure about that?"

"I will admit to having unforeseen difficulty making sense of their rather unusual language, but the words for their basic body parts are no challenge. Understanding the synergistic meaning of the combination of those two simple words is where the problem of interpretation lies, not in the straightforward presentation of the words themselves."

"How come his brain don't blow up?" asked Littlejohn.

"Sh-h-h, I'm thinking," said Ray, pressing the cool surface of the glass against his forehead.

"Sorry, Ray."

"Never mind," Ray said, looking at the big dog. "Tell me, Littlejohn, if I say 'break'"—here Ray pronounced the word very deliberately and paused before adding—"'fast,' what does that mean to you? How do you make sense of it?"

"Break-fast?" Littlejohn asked. "It mean . . . ah . . . Well, 'break' means smash somethin'. 'Fast' means break it quickly."

Ray looked at Tajil. "Put the two words together, Taddy."

"Break fast," Taddy said, puzzled.

"Faster."

"Break fast. Break fast. Break fast . . . Oh! *Breakfast!*"

"Yeah," said Ray. "Breakfast. The meal you eat first thing in the morning. You 'break the fast' you endured while you slept."

"What you gettin' at, Ray?" asked Beowulf.

"The meaning of words rarely exists just in their literal

meaning, but what the combination has come to stand for. No little kid recognizes the literalness of break-fast, but he understands that 'breakfast' means cereal and milk or eggs and bacon."

"So hand-foot mean somethin' more than hand-foot?" asked Beowulf.

"That's right," Ray said. "But what?"

"I have sixteen possibilities," offered the computer. "Each has a plausibility rating of between five and forty percent."

"So what's the meaning that comes in at forty percent?" asked Ray.

"Nine."

"Huh?"

"A K'a-nii has five digits on each hand and four on each foot. The total is nine, so 'hand-foot' means 'nine.'"

# III

With Beowulf in attendance but waiting outside the dispensary door, Ray submitted to Ake's ministrations. Ake shot Ray full of antibodies, cleaned and bandaged his minor scrapes and cuts, and pronounced him nearly as good as new. "I'm glad I didn't see what you looked like before you cleaned yourself up," Ake told him.

"Yeah, I was a mess," Ray conceded. "With the torn clothes, the dirt and the grime, and the blood, I looked a fright."

Sitting on the edge of the examining table, Ray swung his legs back and forth. Ake just looked at him in amusement, aware that Ray's agitation meant he was bursting with news he wanted to deliver.

Ake grabbed his friend's legs, holding them still, and said, "I know, Ray. I have news, too."

"Are you almost finished up here?"

"I have a few duties to complete, but not much," Ake told him. "Go on outside and I'll meet you by the main checkpoint."

Ray slid off the examining table. "Okay."

"Ake comin'?" asked Beowulf when the door hissed open and Ray walked out.

"In a little while. We're gonna meet him outside."

"Okay," Beowulf said amiably. Then he asked, "Ake say you okay?"

"Never better," Ray replied. "I'll be ready to hit the mine bright and early next morning."

"Hunnh," snorted Beowulf. "We sure not doin' much of our real work."

"Bukovsky's slowed everything down, including the mining operations," Ray told Beowulf. "She's not going to allow any freighters to land until she's sure she's got things under control."

"She *got* things under control?"

"No, I don't think she has. I think that's what Ake is itching to tell me, Beowulf," Ray explained.

"Don't you think we should have Maria here?" Ray asked Ake as they walked back and forth at the edge of the jungle near their house.

"Maybe later," Ake said. "But for now, I got too much dangerous information to pass on."

"Dangerous?"

"Yeah—to me!"

"So shoot."

"I don't know where to begin," Ake said, wiping his brow.

"The beginning?" offered Gawain helpfully.

Beowulf cringed. "Gawain, go join the others," he said. "Sorry, Ake."

"Hey, he's right," Ake said. "Except there is no natural beginning." He plunged in anyway. "Things are deteriorating on Terra, Ray. By subverting the Judge Advocate's mediating influence, the Triumvirate has made a naked grab for absolute control of the Federation. And a lot of people, not just the Programmers, aren't willing to let that happen without a fight. Terra is close to civil war. Most of the news coming offplanet during the past ten months has been censored out the whazoo or we would know more about how serious the situation there is. That's just what Wyda told me for openers."

"Wyda! When did you talk to her?" Ray asked.

"This morning," Ake said. "Now shut up and listen; it gets better and better. Ray, this place is lousy with Programmer spies and sleepers. Wyda's a very intelligent person, but I think she's overlooked one nasty possibility—the chance that some of those agents are playing a double game."

"Jeezus!"

"And that ain't all, dog boy," Ake said. "A high percentage of the Prime Programmers imprisoned on this planet are carrying explosive implants in their bodies. It seems that Marte Kales wasn't the only walking time-bomb infiltrated into the prison.

Probably half the Programmers sent here in the past twelve months can detonate the bombs inside them, taking soldiers and weapons with them."

"Some humans can blow up?" asked Beowulf.

"Including one just a meter away from you, Beowulf."

Ray looked puzzled. "What are you talking about?"

"Remember that self-destruct device I had removed after my mission on Chiron?"

"Yeah."

"It wasn't—removed, that is. It had become so much a part of me that they couldn't take it out."

Ray looked at Ake's torso with a growing sense of horror. "You . . . you got a bomb inside you still?"

"If I believe Wyda's story."

"Do you?"

Ake shrugged. "My only real option is to act as if it's true. I guess that involves playing along with Wyda's plans."

Ray considered that. "We seem to have an ongoing inability to coexist with authority, don't we?"

"I have lots more to tell you," Ake said. "But what was it you wanted to tell me?"

"Oh, nothing much," Ray said. "Just that the K'a-nii occasionally throw each other into a volcano. You know—the usual native shit."

# 10

When nothing much happened over the next few days, the tension that pervaded the compound retreated a bit and things slowly got back into a natural rhythm. More and more prisoners were allowed to resume their daily work schedules. Almost no one believed that things were truly back to normal, but everyone recognized the deleterious effects of waiting for the axe to fall. Commander Bukovsky and Director Kodlich apparently decided that the best way to face the uncertain future was to proceed with caution. So things returned to a state approaching normalcy and the mining resumed.

"What are you doing, Larkin?" Maria asked. She reconsidered her formality and said, "Ray, I mean."

"I'm just observing the miners," Ray said as he watched the eleven-member work crew hacking and poking at the soil like industrious insects.

"Yeah, why?"

"No reason, really," Ray replied. "No, that's not true. I'm looking at the women and wondering if they're Programmers. Ake said—"

Maria's snort of derision stopped Ray. "Ake said?" she said hotly. "He talks to *you*, does he? He confides in his buddy? Well, that's nice."

Ray looked at Maria's flashing eyes. She was angry that Ake

had apparently learned a great deal more about the situation than he was willing to reveal—at least to her and her cats. Not being trusted didn't go down well with Maria.

*Can't say I blame her*, Ray thought.

"Ake's told me a few things," Ray began patiently. "Things I'm not sure you *want* to know since there's little either of us can do about them." His eyes on the miners, Ray continued. "But there's more to it than that. The truth is, Ake's in danger. He's in some danger whether or not he shares with you all that he knows. However, he could be in a lot more danger if he tells you anything and you let slip what you know or if you're compelled to talk by someone wielding a nerve whip."

"But he still trusts you with his knowledge and not me."

Ray looked at her, his own eyes blazing now. "Goddamn it, Maria, I'm tired of tiptoeing around with you 'cause your feelings might get hurt! Well, too goddamn bad! You're a big girl and you'll have to take it. I'm Ake's friend and partner and I need to know what he knows. You're a lovely woman and a fine scout cat team leader, but we haven't known you all that long. This place is lousy with Federation informants and we can't risk the possibility that you're one of them. It's Ake's life on the goddamn line—and maybe yours too if you know too much!"

Bastet's back arched and she hissed at Ray, reacting instinctively to his violent tone of voice.

"Be still, Bastet!" Maria said, whirling and pointing a finger at the cat. Maria turned back and stared at Ray, her chest rising and falling.

Ray said nothing; he didn't *dare* to say anything.

Some of the fire in Maria's brown eyes ebbed and she said, "All right, you win. If my knowing what Ake and you know puts his life in danger, then I can't fault you for keeping me in the dark. I don't *like* it, but by the grace of St. Francis I'll live with it."

"Maria . . ." Bastet began tentatively.

"Bastet, I told you—"

"Diggers are coming, Maria."

"The diggers are on their way," Ray said to the miners. "Put down your tools and head back down the tunnel so you'll be between us and the soldiers."

"Where are they?" Maria asked Bastet.

"Dunno. Everywhere."

"Everywhere?"

"Yeah, all 'round us. Lots of them, Maria."

"Jeezus!" Ray exclaimed. "I sent everyone the wrong way!"

The guards, who usually kept their distance anyway, weren't in sight. They had retreated around the last bend in the tunnel; probably to smoke a happy stick or two out of everyone's sight.

*Well*, Ray thought, *They can look out for themselves; they have weapons.* "Come back, come back," he shouted at the retreating miners, his hands cupped around his mouth. He sent Grendel to retrieve them, but they had heard him and were returning, their eyes wide with fear.

"Damn it!" Maria said. "I've never sensed so many diggers at one time!" She put her hand to her head as she did when she was receiving the diggers' auras, the action suggesting someone reacting to a migraine headache.

Ray, to his surprise, also felt a strange sensation, one not unlike a balloon being inflated inside his skull. He realized immediately that he was sharing the cats' and Maria's ability to detect the diggers. He would wonder about it later. For now, he had other things to worry about.

"Mama-san, Ozma, Grendel—you three stay with the prisoners. Beowulf and Taddy, you stick with me."

"What are you going to do?" Maria asked.

Before Ray could answer, there was an outburst of firing and shouting from around the bend of the tunnel where the soldiers were. Under the crackling and hissing of energy rifles, Ray could hear the soldiers cursing. The shouts quickly turned to screams.

One of the three soldiers stumbled around the corner like an early-morning drunk weaving his way home. Ray noticed two things: He was holding his energy rifle by the barrel, dragging the butt in the dirt, and he didn't have much face left. Mercifully, he fell dead before he could reach them.

"They'll be comin' for us any second now!" Bastet said, her tail lashing the air in anticipation. The other cats were arching their spines and spitting, and the hair on the dogs' backs was rising in ragged clumps as they bared their teeth.

"Ohmygod, we're gonna be killed! We're all gonna die!" one of the prisoners shrieked. He was a fortyish man who clearly hadn't done any physical labor before being assigned to work in the Hephaestus mines. The other prisoners, especially the older women that Ray had marked as Prime Programmers, looked at the cowering man with a mixture of disdain and pity. One of them grabbed him by his work shirt and snarled, "Don't get in the way of our babysitters, Fairchild, or we'll throw you to the diggers ourselves!"

Maria saw Ray put his hand to his head, mirroring her earlier action. "Can you feel them as well?" she asked.

"Yeah."

"They've stopped. They're just around the turn of the tunnel, but they're not advancing."

"I wonder why they not rushin' us," Littlejohn said.

Sibella looked up at Maria and said, "They . . . they're waiting for something."

"What?" asked Beowulf.

The answer came quickly. "They're on both sides of the tunnel!" Maria shouted.

Two arms burst from the soil and wrapped around the man the others had called Fairchild as he cowered against the tunnel wall. "No!" he shrieked as the digger's carbon-steel-sharp claws ripped across his midsection. The upper half of his body disappeared into the tunnel wall. The bottom half remained behind and his legs fell to the mine floor, thrashing and kicking spasmodically. Ray fired several bursts into the spot where he had disappeared and then turned to face a digger emerging from the opposite wall.

Before Ray could fire, Beowulf seized the attacker's neck between his powerful jaws. Much as the other digger had pulled the ill-fated Fairchild into the soil, Beowulf pulled the digger out into the tunnel. Beowulf shook his head, working his jaws, and the digger's decapitated head fell into the dust, spraying blood.

Maria pumped five quick bursts into two diggers halfway out into the tunnel and the dogs attacked and worried those already there. One of the cats warned, "The others is coming now!"

Mama-san and Grendel were efficiently dispatching a digger when Grendel was forced back into Ray and the bump sent him sprawling. He pitched face-first into the dirt and his rifle went flying out of his grasp. He scrabbled forward on his hands and knees and flung himself onto the dead soldier's weapon. *Just in time!* Ray thought as the diggers continued to advance.

Stretched out prone, but able to prop himself up on his elbows, Ray snapped off several powerful bolts of energy at the pack of diggers that rushed around the corner of the tunnel. His shots slowed but didn't stop them.

And still they kept coming from the tunnel walls. One of the female prisoners screamed in agony as a digger slashed four long gashes down her back and then swiped his claws horizontally across her backbone and severed her spinal cord. A gray-haired woman scooped up Ray's fallen weapon, stepped up to the digger, placed the rifle against its head and blew its brains out. "Suck on that, asshole!" Armed with Ray's rifle, she now joined the battle.

The cats, aware that they could best help by not getting in the way, formed a little knot over by one of the machines. The nimble dogs kept out of the reach of the diggers while darting in whenever an opening presented itself and ripping at the bulky attackers with their teeth. The dogs' long hair proved an effective defense against the diggers' claws. Diggers futilely lashed out at the dogs expecting to rend flesh, but found only fur instead. While the dogs suffered minor cuts, the diggers were being decimated by their foes' powerful jaws.

Ray stumbled to his feet, firing as he rose. When a digger charged at him, he blasted it at point-blank range and stepped back. Something stung his cheek as the diggers' arm disappeared in a shower of blood. Undaunted, the one-armed digger swept the energy rifle from Ray's grasp and then tried to slice him from head to toe like some unfortunate victim in an old *Tom and Jerry* cartoon. Ray caught the digger's descending arm, and it took all of his strength to keep the nails from tenderizing his face. The two of them shuffled drunkenly and then toppled over.

They were moving.

"Jesus H. Christ!" Ray shouted as he realized they'd fallen onto the conveyer belt and were slowly being pulled toward the maw of the rock crusher. Still struggling to keep the digger's claw from his face, Ray managed to slide his leg over the edge of the belt and hook his foot under a metal bar. The belt's incessant motion strained Ray's leg muscles and he could feel the tendons in his calf threatening to give way against the pull. *I can't hold on much longer*, Ray thought feverishly.

Still warding off the digger's arm with his left hand, Ray let go with his right and his fingers scrabbled to find something hard. He discovered a medium-sized stone that had gotten caught between the belt and the frame. As he pulled at it, he could feel his leg cramping. The stone came free.

"I've"—smash—"had"—smash—"about"—smash—"enough"—smash—"of"—smash—"this!" Ray said through gritted teeth as he methodically bashed the digger's skull with the stone. Finally, the creature went limp. But Ray's worries weren't over yet; the belt still tugged at him.

"Beowulf!"

"I comin', Ray!"

As the belt pulled inexorably at the two of them, Ray rolled the unmoving digger off him and averted his gaze as it was carried into the clashing jaws of the rock crusher. A fountain of blood gushed out of the rock crusher's metal throat. *I don't believe this!* Ray thought as he could feel his leg and foot, made slippery by the blood, start to lose their grip. Just when Ray was about to be pulled headfirst into the rock crusher, he felt Beowulf's teeth clamp down on his foot.

Ray had never experienced such wonderful pain.

Slowly and carefully, Beowulf dragged Ray off the moving belt and dumped him unceremoniously onto the mine floor.

"Thanks, Beowulf," Ray muttered. "That would have been a crushing experience."

He hardly had time to rejoice before the air was filled with the crackling and popping of numerous energy rifle discharges. Ray raised a weary head to see a squad of soldiers advancing down the tunnel, their weapons discharging steady streams of deadly bolts of energy. Their concentrated firepower made quick work of the remaining diggers.

"Are we glad to see you!" said Maria, stepping forward, a big smile on her face.

"Put down your weapon," ordered the lieutenant leading the squad.

"But we're—"

"Put it down . . . NOW!" he barked.

"Do it, Maria," Ray told her. "Do it quickly."

Maria was reluctant to surrender the gun, but she followed Ray's lead and let her weapon fall to the mine floor. "Colonel Bukovsky will hear about this!" She said to the lieutenant. "You have no right to—"

She turned and looked where Ray was pointing. The Programmer who'd picked up Ray's rifle and joined them against the diggers was lying in a heap. One of the soldiers, probably the lieutenant himself, had blown her face off with a bolt of energy.

"What's going on?" Ray demanded.

"I suppose if you're enemies of the Federation you already know," the lieutenant said. "There is a revolt in the prison."

# ||

Since Captain Ramos and his flunkies had the honor of taking care of the sick and injured this day, Ake Ringgren found himself with a rare morning off. While Ray and some of the dogs went off to the mine, Ake slept in. Around ten, feeling decadent and liking it, Ake filled the bathtub with hot soapy water and his pipe with rich Barkovian mountain leaf. *Ten credits a pouch*, he reminded himself. *Well, I'm worth it.*

Up to his neck in the hot water, puffing on his pipe, and wiggling his toes to the music, he gazed happily at a hol-vee recording of *Götterdämmerung*. Ake loved Wagner, and this version of one of the musical giant's Ring Cycle operas achieved near perfection. The producers had gone to great pains to make this release the definitive one, synthesizing the talents of the greatest singers and musicians ever known. The voices of the computer-generated singers which "sang" each part were programmed to reproduce exactly the timbre, range, and vocal expressiveness of the finest vocal artists ever to assay the parts. The musicians were faithfully captured in the same way. And the result, rather than being an awful, artless pastiche, was a marvelous fusion of the best with the best with the best. Toscanini was even the model for the conductor.

His eyelids closed in rapture, Ake slowly became aware of someone near the tub. He cracked one eye open to see Frodo sitting on his haunches and nodding his head to the music.

"Pause, please," Ake said. The music and motion froze, the singers hanging motionless in the air at the foot of the tub. "Good morning, Frodo," Ake said. "Something I can do for you?"

"No," Frodo replied. "Jes' listenin' to the pretty music." He looked at the totally relaxed Ake and added, "I botherin' you?"

"No, Frodo," Ake told him. "I don't think you or anyone else could bother me this fine morning." He glanced at the unmoving Siegfried and Hagan and commanded, "Stop and save at this point, please." The images sparked into nothingness.

"If you and the others want to go outside," Ake told Frodo, "why don't you? I'm going to be a while since I'm in no hurry to do what I have to do—which is nothing, absolutely nothing."

"Okay, Ake," the dog said. "But Littlejohn stay with you, okay?"

"Another canine babysitter, eh?" said Ake. "Oh, well, get out of here—but don't go too far, you hear?"

He stood up, stepped from the tub, and centered himself inside the air dryer. "Kitchen, prepare Ake-11A for ten minutes from now."

As he sat eating his eggs and bacon (well, the eggs weren't

really eggs and the bacon had never been within a klick of a real pig), he realized how much tension he'd been under recently and how much this morning off really meant to him. Happy and relaxed, Ake looked heavenward and thought, *Take me now, Jesus. Take me now.*

The slice of toast smothered in raspberry jam was halfway to his mouth when the phone trilled. "Sonofabitch!"

"Let the machine answer it," suggested Littlejohn. "You not here."

"No, I can't do that," Ake said, getting up and going over to the phone.

"What is it?" he asked when Hamstedt's image appeared. He listened for a moment, then said, "Okay. Give me fifteen minutes."

"You gotta go in?" Littlejohn asked.

"Yeah," Ake told him. But then he looked at the big dog and brightened. "Stay here and then we'll all go for a walk when I'm done."

"Sure, Ake."

★ ★ ★

"What's going on this morning, Captain Ramos?" Ake asked the swarthy staff physician.

"I don't know," Ramos admitted, shocking Ake with his uncharacteristic display of honesty. "I've never seen so many prisoners here for sick call. They started coming in right after breakfast. Maybe something went wrong in the kitchen this morning."

"You mean something *different* went wrong?" asked Ake. When he was on duty he had occasionally eaten the prison food. "I always thought that the grub they served in this place was part of the punishment."

"Cruel and unusual, eh, Doc?" joked Hamstedt.

The twenty-three new patients were accompanied by six guards. Ake noticed something different about them. "Hey, the guards are carrying guns," he said to Hamstedt. "Aren't only nonlethal weapons allowed inside the prison?"

Hamstedt looked at the nearest guard. "You're right," he agreed. "I wonder what's going on."

Ake examined one middle-aged woman who was complaining of feeling dizzy and of being beset by an upset stomach. "Well, I can't find anything wrong with you," Ake told the woman.

"But I feel so weak," she replied.

"Uh-huh," Ake said dubiously and moved on. He approached one of the guards and asked, "How come you guys are armed? I thought guns were banned inside the prison."

The soldier looked disdainfully at Ake for a moment, then shrugged and said, "New orders came down this morning. Said if more than four of us were together, we could carry weapons." The soldier clutched his energy rifle tightly and said, "Now that's an order I can live with. I hate going around naked."

"Yeah, sure," said Ake, rolling his eyes.

"No, there's nothing wrong with you that I can find," Ramos was saying to one of the new admissions, a woman with mousy brown hair. Ramos saw something on her work belt. "What's that?" he demanded.

"It's my respirator," the woman replied. "I need it in the mines."

"Just as I thought," Ramos sneered. "You're not sick at all. You simply wanted a day off from working in the mines."

Something about the respirator struck Ake as odd. What if . . . ?

There was a blinding flash of light and the examination room was filled with a burning cloud of white smoke. Ake's eyes immediately began to fill with tears.

"Gas bomb!" someone shouted—stating the painfully obvious—as pandemonium broke out.

Ake dropped to the floor. He hugged the cool tiles less in search of fresh air than for safety's sake. Flashes of light from the energy rifles' muzzles lit up the white haze that masked everyone's movements. The only sounds were screams, curses, thuds, and the soft, apologetic cough of a needle gun.

Tears streaming from his eyes, Ake crawled toward a door. About halfway there, he considered. The gas was clearly not poisonous, merely disabling. By keeping close to the floor, Ake was able to get enough oxygen to breathe, no matter how ragged and painful the effort proved. Since any attempt to get out of the room might prove fatal, Ake was content to make his way to the shelter of an empty gurney and wait for the air to clear—literally and figuratively.

"Get up, Doc," a voice muffled by a respirator ordered. Ake looked up into the muzzle of an energy rifle held by one of the prisoner "patients." Ake scrambled to his feet, wiping his eyes with the sleeve of his white coat. Feeling fresh air pouring in from an open door, he maneuvered crabwise in the direction of the flow, drawn to it like a moth to a flame.

Since none of the prisoners, now in possession of the guards' weapons, even glanced toward the door, Ake surmised that they had been expecting company. As the gas was replaced by fresh air and he could again see without his vision blurring, Ake observed that four of the six soldiers had been killed during the surprise rebellion. The other two were in the process of having their hands secured behind their backs. Both Ramos and Hamstedt had their hands on top of their heads, awaiting restraint.

"I assume that the order rescinding the carrying of weapons inside the prison walls didn't come from Bukovsky," Ake asked one of the gun-toting inmates.

"Of course it didn't," she said. "Colonel Bukovsky's no fool." She looked at the two remaining soldiers, seemingly shrunken in size by their unexpected captivity, their hands bound at the wrists, and scoffed, "You can't say that of whoever received our phony transmission and accepted it without double-checking to make certain it was a valid order."

"You've got their weapons," Ake said. "Now what?"

"Now we get more."

# III

As they walked across the compound under the intense midday sun, Ray looked around carefully. He could see nothing out of the ordinary; it looked just like any other day, with no unusual or suspicious activity. If there was any uprising, it must be contained to the prison itself.

"I'm sure glad Ake didn't have to go to the infirmary today," Ray told Maria.

"I said no talking," the lieutenant said.

"Kiss my hairy butt," Ray retorted. The lieutenant let that pass. *Hey, why not?* Ray thought. *Sticks and stones and all that; he's got the guns.*

When they reached the administration building, certain that his energy pistol would be sufficient to keep his two prisoners in line, the lieutenant gave his unit orders to wait outside with the miners and the two animal teams. "Surprise me and see that nothing goes wrong," the lieutenant told them. Someone took offense at that and grumbled inaudibly. Ray chuckled to himself. *This turkey's a born leader, ain't he? His men are probably willing to follow him anywhere . . . and to take the opportunity to shove a grenade up his ass the first chance they get.*

"I assume you're taking us to see Colonel Bukovsky?" asked Maria.

"Your assumption is correct," the lieutenant said stiffly.

As they walked down a long corridor, someone was approaching from the opposite direction. It was Sari Fodoor, Kodlich's assistant director. Ray might have paid her scant attention under the circumstances but for the odd premonition he had that something unusual was about to happen. He placed a hand to his head; a dull ache had taken up residence just above his eyes.

As Fodoor came abreast of them and she was about to pass their little group, she casually lifted her arm and fired the needle gun concealed by the sleeve of her blouse at the lieutenant's head. The tiny ceramic shard struck him directly between the eyes and he started to pitch forward without uttering a sound.

(*Grab him.*)

Ray and Maria reacted instantly to Fodoor's words, catching the lieutenant's body under the arms and preventing him from collapsing in a heap. "This way," Fodoor said, keying open a door with her thumb. Ray and Maria hustled the dead man into the room—a small, empty staff room. The lights came on automatically when the body-heat sensors detected that the room was now occupied.

"Anybody see us?" Ray asked Fodoor.

"I don't think so," she said, sticking her head out and looking both ways. "We're lucky no one else was in the hallway."

Fodoor closed the door and faced them. "You two have great reflexes," she told Ray and Maria. "The way you caught him before he even started to crumple was amazing."

"I just did what you said to do," Ray replied.

"Said?" Fodoor questioned. "I never said anything."

"You said, 'Grab him.'"

She looked at him oddly. "No, I didn't."

"She said it in her mind, Ray," Maria explained. "She projected it so strongly that I picked it up. But you heard her, too." Maria gave Ray an evaluative look that made him feel strange.

As unexpected as all this was, Ray and Maria both slowly realized that they were holding up a dead body between them. Gently, as if they might cause him pain if they weren't careful, they stretched the lieutenant out on the floor and stepped away from his corpse. His eyes, wide with surprise, stared at the ceiling.

"Forgive me, Ms. Fodoor," began Ray, "but what the fork is going on here?"

"With any luck, we're about to seize control of the base," Sari Fodoor said. "I'm unclear about where exactly you two stand on all this, but I took your arrest by the military as proof that you're not on their side in all this." She smiled. "Well, 'proof' might be too strong a word. I need you to convince me that you're willing to join us if you're not already involved. And remember, I still have my needle gun."

"We'll do our best to prove to you that we're not on the Triumvirate's side," Ray said, after looking for support from Maria. "Right now, though, Ake and I are not officially or unofficially on anyone's side but our own. Maybe Maria feels differently. But who is this mysterious 'we'?"

"The Order of Programmers, obviously. But there are others unwilling to see a Federation of laws and rights replaced by a military-economic dictatorship. That includes people like me, some of the engineers, and even a few of the soldiers."

"Kodlich?"

Fodoor shook her head. "No, Theo is not the sort to get involved with anything so adventurous as a revolution."

"I think you're right about that," Ray agreed.

"Enough about me," Fodoor said. "I'm still waiting to hear why I should trust you two."

"First off," Maria said, "we're both independents. I run a scout cat team and that's where my allegiance lies. I'm sure Ray will tell you that the same is true for him and Ake. When I took this job it was with the understanding that I was working for the consortium. It's only recently become clear that the Federation—the newly and illegally elected Triumvirate, rather—is calling the shots."

Maria looked at Ray and smiled ruefully. "I don't know if it'll help my cause," she said to Fodoor, "but Ray and Ake have been reluctant to reveal to me all they know for fear I might be a Federation agent. I think that goes a ways toward demonstrating *their* stance in this, if not mine."

"A pretty speech," said Fodoor. Turning to Ray, she asked, "What do *you* believe? Is she a Federation plant?"

"I don't think so," Ray responded guardedly. "But if you're

looking for proof, I doubt I can come up with anything irrefutable."

Fodoor considered that. "You're right, of course. And, as I said, being taken into custody by the soldiers speaks well for you."

"What happens now?" Ray asked her.

"I was on my way to the subspace communicator when I saw you and your chaperone," Fodoor told them. "I have to disable the console before the colonel is able to report what's going on."

"Good," said Ray. "Anything that shoves a pie in Colonel Bukovsky's face is fine by me."

Ray manually switched off the lights, put his finger to his lips to warn the others to silence, and keyed open the door. "It looks clear," he whispered. "Let's go."

"Wait a minute." Maria reached down and pulled the lieutenant's energy pistol from his hand and tucked it into her belt. "Okay."

The subspace communicator was located two levels below ground. They took a drop tube to the first level but then had to walk down a circular plasteel staircase to the final landing. The heavier cold air had sunk to the building's lowest levels, and it made Ray shiver. He was still rubbing the bare skin on his arms as they approached the entrance to the subspace communications area. It was guarded by two sentries who seemed shocked to have visitors.

"Good day, Citizen Fodoor," one of the sentries said so tonelessly that he sounded less like a flesh-and-blood human being than the synthesized voice of a computer-generated image. "Do you have authorization to proceed further?"

The other sentry noticed the energy pistol peeking out of Maria's belt. The sight put starch in his spine. "Excuse me, Citizen, but you're going to have to remove your weapon. Please do so slowly and carefully, pulling it out and placing it on the floor with your thumb and index finger."

"What about *my* weapon?" asked Sari Fodoor.

"Huh?"

Fodoor pointed her arm at the first sentry and fired her needle gun. The ceramic shard plowed a groove through the top of his closely cropped hair. "Damn!" she said, firing a second time. The second shard blew a fine pink spray out the back of his skull. As the second sentry was about to pump a bolt of energy into Fodoor, Maria palmed the energy pistol and shot him dead.

"Sufferin' salamanders!" Ray exclaimed, admiration in his voice. "Remind me not to get uppity with either of you two *girls*." When they both turned narrowed eyes on him, Ray laughed nervously and said, "Hey, I forgot I don't have Beowulf with me to point out that I'm just kidding."

"What a rutter," said Sari Fodoor.

"Well, are we just gonna stand here until friends of theirs come by to relieve them?" Ray demanded. He took advantage of the opportunity to arm himself with one of the dead sentries' energy pistols as Maria had done earlier with the lieutenant's.

"You're right, Larkin," Fodoor said. "Let's go play with the subspace communicator."

# 11

The white-tiled communications room was brightly lit but unoccupied; most of its functions were automatic and needed no human overseers. Fodoor moved quickly to the main console and confidently began keying the glowing panels in a way that indicated she knew what she was doing.

"I take it you've been waiting for this moment for a long time," Ray said.

"You might say that," replied Fodoor, her eyes never leaving the console's glowing readout.

A deep, low-pitched hum began to fill the room. It was the sound of immense power—the raw power needed to punch a signal into subspace and across parsecs. "The energy cores buried beneath us are coming on line," Fodoor explained. "I'm going to send two subspace messages. The first will take every bit of power that I can summon up. The second is less demanding, however."

Within minutes a chime sounded. "We're at maximum capability," Fodoor explained as Maria and Ray gaped in wonder. "Here we go." Her hands flashed across the keyboard as she typed the first message. She touched a red cube and it slowly sank into the console. The massive humming sound changed pitch and then died down. "The first one's been sent," Fodoor explained. "Fortunately, we don't have to wait to fully repower for the second message; it's not traveling as far."

Again her fingers danced over the keyboard. By the time she had encrypted her second message, the red cube was almost halfway back to its original position. She glanced at it, evaluating what she saw. "Ready or not, here goes number two." Again the red cube sank into the control top in response to her touch.

"Is that it?" Maria asked. "You're done?"

"Yes."

"Then let's get out of here."

"One more thing first," Fodoor said, removing a diamond ring with an obscenely large stone from her fingers. She found a water bottle and filled a glass. Pressing the ring on either side of the gem, she popped the stone into the water.

"What the hell are you doing?" Ray asked.

"You'll see," was her enigmatic reply.

The stone seemed to absorb some of the water and swelled slightly. Fodoor took it from the glass and began working it like a small piece of clay, squeezing and molding it. Finally, Fodoor said, "I think it's ready." She opened a panel on the side of the communications console and wedged the malleable mass that the false stone had become into a cranny.

She replaced the panel and said, "Okay, let's get out of here. When that dries out it's going to create one hell of an explosion."

"Ake used to do that sort of stuff all the time when he was a sleeper for the Programmers," Ray said, shaking his head over the games some grownups played.

"Why are you going to destroy the subspace communicator?" Maria asked.

"I've got to, Maria. If I didn't, Bukovsky would use it to summon reinforcements."

"Won't silencing it be just as much of a giveaway?"

"It will arouse suspicions, sure. But there are a host of reasons for an outpost not reporting in as scheduled. The powers that be won't *know* for sure what's happened. They can suspect the worst, but they can't be certain."

By this time, they were at the spiral staircase. "Maria and I need to get our teams back before we do anything else," Ray said. "What are you planning to do next?"

"So far, no one knows I'm working for the Resistance," Sari Fodoor said. "I'm going to go see Theo and stay by his side. I might be privy to some of Bukovsky's maneuverings if she and Theo still believe that I'm part of the inner group."

"Be careful," Ray cautioned. "You're playing a dangerous game."

"What about the explosion down here?" asked Maria. "Will you be safe from it?"

"The charge I planted is a focused one meant to damage key parts of the communicator but not to destroy it beyond eventual repair. The rest of the building will be unaffected."

They took the lift tubes up to the ground-floor level and split up. Fodoor went one way, back into the building's core, while Ray and Maria walked quickly toward the exit.

"Despite what you may think, Ray," Maria began, "I'm not a heartless killer." She pulled her energy pistol out. "So, if it's all right with you, I want us to set our pistols to stun."

"I have no more desire than you to kill kids just following orders," Ray said, complying with her wishes and resetting the regulator on his weapon. "There's also less danger for our teams this way."

Brilliant sunlight greeted them when they stepped outside. Ray blessed the heat as they approached the prisoners and the two scout teams that were sitting on the ground with the soldiers hovering over them. Ray carefully shielded Maria with his body, preventing the soldiers from seeing that her energy pistol was drawn and leveled. Ozma could see Maria's drawn pistol, and she let out a small, involuntary yelp of surprise. Lacking the necessary imagination to conceive of anything going wrong, the young soldiers paid scant attention to it.

"Howdy, gents," Ray said.

"Where's the lieutenant?" one of the squad asked, leaning lazily against the side of the building.

Ray stepped sideways to reveal that Maria was holding the pistol. "Now don't do anything stupid, guys, and you might see your loved ones again," Ray said. "Put down your weapons or my friend here will fry your brains."

The soldiers did as he ordered and Ray kicked the guns away. "Good. Now lie down on your stomachs against the side of the building where you'll be hard to spot. You're going to take a little nap. You'll have a headache when you wake up, but you *will* wake up."

When they complied, Maria said "Sweet dreams," activating the firing stud and sweeping the pistol's invisible beam over them. Fearful and rigid, they went limp as the stunner knocked them unconscious. Maria began securing their wrists.

"So how are you guys and gals?" Ray asked the dogs and cats.
"We okay," said Bastet.
"Yah," said Tajil. "Saved by the cavalry."
"We've got five weapons to distribute," Ray told the still shocked prisoners. "It's part of the new guns for felons program. Anyone interested?"

## II

The Programmers who overwhelmed the soldiers didn't have to lead Ake very far, just down the corridor to one of the staff rooms at the other end of the infirmary floor. "Someone has requested your presence," they told him.

Thane Wyda looked up as Ake was brought in. "I'm pleased to see you again, Ake," the Prime Programmer said. She did look happy to see him; she also looked very tired.

"It seems as if you've got a good start on your revolt," Ake said to the Prime Programmer. All around them was the sort of ordered chaos that comes with any quasimilitary operation. That was not what caught Ake's eye. A better gauge of the newborn revolt was the fact that it looked to Ake as if all of Wyda's people were armed. Since each weapon in the hands of the former Prime Programmers represented a captured or dead soldier, he was impressed.

"Yes, it's going almost too smoothly. I get nervous when so many things go exactly as planned."

"Well, I wouldn't worry much along those lines," Ake assured her. "In my experience things have a way of going from A-plus to Z-minus so quickly it can make your head spin."

"Then I should be well prepared for that eventuality, shouldn't I?" Wyda said, gesturing at her prison garb and her surroundings. "From Prime Programmer to prisoner to revolutionary is a substantial realignment of one's life."

As she spoke, Ake could hear the occasional crackle of energy rifles and the sharp retort of at least one high-caliber slug thrower. He had bad memories of those from Chiron.

"You've obviously had the element of surprise on your side so far, but Bukovsky is no dummy and she'll hit you with everything she has as soon as she figures out what's going on."

"Yes, she will—if she can."

"Thane! Thane, I must talk to you," gasped a young woman also clad in prison fatigues, her voice high-pitched and breathless.

"Calm yourself, Kendra," Wyda said patiently. Wyda's placid exterior drained some of the nervous energy out of the younger woman. Wyda allowed her subordinate to catch her breath and compose herself while she herself turned to Ake and told him, "This is Kendra Vine, a brilliant young associate of mine on Terra. Unfortunately for her, she was loyal as well as brilliant, so she ended up here with me." She turned back to her protégée. "Now what is it you wish to tell me, Kendra?"

"We have taken the two levels below this floor and freed everyone from their cells," Vine said. "That leaves four levels to go before we can be sure we have gained control of the building."

"Things are proceeding in good order, then," Wyda said. "We should now attempt to secure the ground-floor level. This will isolate and trap the guards on the levels we've bypassed, and we can then subdue any resistance that we meet with on each floor at our leisure." When Ake raised his eyebrows at that comment, Wyda added, "Yes, Ake—I fully realize we can't allow the guards to retain control of those levels for very long." Her eyes glittered. "But if we control the building's entrance, we control the prison itself."

Wyda became aware that Kendra Vine was vibrating like a tuning fork. Better to let the youngster have her say before she exploded. "Yes, Kendra, what is it?"

"There is more, Prime Programmer Wyda," Vine told her. "Although we are freeing everyone, the others are not content to share the weapons equally."

"The others . . . ?" said Ake questioningly before he realized that she was speaking about the one hundred and fifty prisoners who were definitely *not* ex-Programmers.

Ake frowned. While the Programmers and some of the other inmates were political prisoners, not common criminals, that could not be said of all the inmates. More than a few were hardened murderers, rapists, and thugs. While it was true that Hephaestus's mines had become a key dumping site for the Triumvirate's enemies, many of the hardcore nasties who originally made up the prison population remained.

"Yes, the others. . . ." said Wyda slowly. "How many of them have been freed?"

"I'm not sure," the younger woman replied. "Perhaps twenty or thirty."

"And how many of those twenty or thirty have weapons now?"

"Nearly all of them."

Wyda did not attempt to hide her dismay. "This is troubling news."

"Shit on a stick!" Ake exclaimed, imagining the damage thirty sociopaths armed with energy rifles and pistols could do. "You mean the rest of the prison population are not only *not* with you but actually might be *against* you?"

"I'm afraid that's the case, Ake," Wyda admitted. "The truth is, we don't know what to expect of them. We hoped that once the revolt began they would join our cause." She pursed her lips. "But we could not take them into our confidence earlier because of the danger that any one of them might—" She fumbled for the correct word.

"'Squeal' is the word you're searching for, I think." He looked at her unsmiling face and added, "Well, probably not."

"Isn't that an old sinny term?" Vine asked. But both Wyda and Ake ignored her.

"These guys—and they are mostly men—would cut your throat for the fun of it," Ake told Wyda. "If they get their hands on the soldiers' weapons, forget about Bukovsky. With friends like those, you don't need any enemies."

Wyda smiled grimly while Kendra Vine looked like she was about to burst into tears. "I wish I could prove you wrong, but unfortunately, you're probably right."

"Thanks," said Ake glumly.

Wyda looked at Kendra Vine. At least she was managing to contain her excitement. "I think it best if you seek out Prime Programmer Estéban and warn her that we must be more discriminating in releasing people from their cells, Kendra. Tell her what you told me about the other prisoners and the guards' weapons and that I believe it is imperative that we restrict their access to weapons."

"Yes, Prime Programmer Wyda. Do you think Programmer Estéban will know what to do?"

"I hope so, Kendra. Now move it!"

"I'm going to say my prayers that there's enough of you with guns of your own to convince the others to give up their weapons," Ake said. "If not, those dickheads will go on a rampage that'll make the Lunaville riots look like a Sunday school picnic."

Before Wyda could answer, there were a series of small explosions from somewhere in the bowels of the building.

*Grenades?* Ake wondered. Whatever—it was a rude reminder that the battle for control of the prison was not over yet.

"Come on," shouted Wyda as she picked up two energy rifles and threw one to an astonished Ake. "Well, you're with us now, aren't you?"

"Yeah, I guess I am."

"It's about time you committed to the cause," Wyda said, leading him toward the stairwell. "Not that I ever really doubted that you would."

"You didn't leave me much choice," Ake said, thumping his chest. "But I'm with you because I want to be, not because I'm compelled to be."

"I'm touched," said Wyda, meaning for it to be taken cynically. Ake, however, could see that his allegiance *did* move her. Not that she would ever admit it.

"So where are we going?" he wanted to know.

"It sounded like it came from the ground floor."

"That's our cue, then," said Ake. "Oops, wait a minute." He went back and picked up a medical kit. "Okay, let's go."

At the landing of each level, just outside the manual doors which provided access to that floor, prisoners were stationed to make sure that the guards could not escape. *That's amusing*, Ake thought. *The "prisoners" are now the guards and the "guards" are now the prisoners.*

Giving voice to his thoughts, Ake said, "I hadn't thought of it before, Thane, but given the change in the situation here, I guess I have to call the 'prisoners' something else. They're no longer prisoners; at least, not once they get out of the prison."

"How about just calling us Programmers?" Wyda asked.

"That could work."

The first floor of the stairwell was filled with armed prisoners, mostly Programmers. There were one or two males among them, but Ake quickly ruled them out as possible troublemakers. These flabby, big-butted rutters looked more like aging bureaucrats than hardened criminals who'd take a quiver blade to their own mothers for a five-credit note. And even if they could be trusted with guns, Ake decided, they'd probably be as much help as a paper umbrella in a hailstorm.

The two men didn't even register in Thane Wyda's eyes as she sought out the Programmer in charge. "Margaret, what's the problem here?"

A big, powerful-looking woman with meaty arms, the person

Wyda had addressed as Margaret, said, "We fought our way down here as soon as we could. It wasn't quick enough, though. They'd already cycled the building's door shut and threw together a pretty good barrier constructed from desks and chairs in front of it." She blinked as a bead of sweat rolled down her forehead and into the corner of her eye. "We lost two people and took some casualties before we realized the futility of trying to advance down the corridor with them holed up at the far end. We left the dead in the hall but not their guns."

Although the woman's words were direct and unadorned, Ake could only guess at the fierce firefight that must have been waged between her people and the soldiers defending the only way in or out of the prison.

Wyda looked at the grimy, spent woman and her tired compatriots and fought back the lump in her throat. "You did well to get here so quickly and to hold the stairwell for us, Margaret," Wyda said. "No one could have done more."

"Thank you, Thane," the woman said gratefully.

"What I don't understand," Ake said to Wyda, "is why there aren't tons of reinforcements pouring in from the soldiers' barracks."

"There were only about eighty or ninety soldiers to begin with," Wyda explained. "And we must have killed or captured somewhere between fifteen to twenty-five of them by now."

"That's true," Ake conceded. "Under normal conditions at a regular prison, there wouldn't even be half as many 'guards.' Eighty or so isn't really that high a number."

"So they're content just to keep us pinned down inside the prison," the big woman said.

"Yes," agreed Wyda. "For now, at least."

Ake looked troubled. "All it takes is a call to the nearest military outpost to bring on the reinforcements," he cautioned them.

"For that you need a working subspace communicator," Wyda told him.

Ake opened his mouth to respond, closed it, and then opened it again to say, "You sabotaged the equipment!"

"Someone did . . . I hope."

When she saw her friend staring at Ake, Wyda said, "Margaret, this is Ake Ringgren. He's a doctor but he once slept with the Cadre for me. Ake, this brave old warrior is one of my dearest friends, Margaret Scoresby."

"Pleased to meet you," Ake and Scoresby said simultaneously.

"Now that that's out of the way, give Margaret one of the comlinks we took from our hosts." Ake handed over one of the hand-held units they'd brought with them.

"Damn, I could have used one of these earlier," Scoresby said.

"Things were moving quickly, weren't they?"

"Too quickly, Thane."

As he watched the normally stern Prime Programmer acting anything but officious and distant as she worked her way through Scoresby's people, patting backs and exchanging hugs, Ake decided nothing about her would ever again catch him by surprise. Then, when she knelt down to speak with two badly wounded women, Ake got a very strong feeling she was saying goodbye to them. All too soon, he would realize that was exactly what she was doing.

The first casualty Wyda spoke to was clearly just a few meters ahead of the grim reaper, Ake noted. A blue sheet covered her lower body, hiding whatever injuries she'd received. But you didn't need to be an M.D. to guess that the blood soaking the sheet was a testament to the grim nature of her wounds.

After a few minutes of quiet conversation, Wyda rose and prepared to move on. Ake stepped close to her and, indicating the dying woman, asked, "Does she need help from my little black bag?"

"She is beyond pain," Wyda told him. "She says she can feel nothing below her neck."

"Oh."

"Hello, Thane," said the second of the wounded Programmers as Wyda knelt to comfort her. "It's good to see you again." Half her face was blackened and burned. Ake almost gagged when he realized where the strong smell of charred meat that assaulted his nostrils was coming from.

"I wish I could say the same for you, Tasha," Wyda said.

"Oh, it doesn't hurt much," the burned woman said. Then she grimaced in pain. "Well, not very much."

Ake pulled something from his kit, knelt down beside the grievously injured woman and pressed a tube against the side of her throat. "That should ease the pain considerably." He smiled at her. "What's the point of being in a building with an infirmary if you don't take advantage of what's available?"

"Did that help?" asked Wyda after a moment had passed.

"It did," the woman replied. "But it's only temporary. I'm

afraid I need a more lasting painkiller." She squeezed Wyda's hand and said, "Be strong, Thane! Be strong enough to allow me to perform one last service for the Order."

"As you wish, Tasha." She squeezed the woman's hand in return.

"Margaret," Wyda said, rising from her position beside her dying friend, "please send for the null-grav gurneys and ask that Zeeta Bethune be assigned to bring them down—those and one of the many offerings we've collected."

"Offerings?" said Ake.

"Donations from the heart," explained Wyda. "Actually, from the mouth, the fingers, the toes, the jaw, and god knows from where else."

"Yeah, sure," said a puzzled Ake.

In a few minutes a beautiful young woman with a shaved skull and impossibly luminous green eyes arrived with the two null-grav gurneys in tow. The gurneys held drink bladders, small packets of high-energy snack foods, and various sandwiches, even including vegetarian offerings.

At a time when it was necessary to eat to keep up one's energy, Ake wondered if any of the Programmers would be so particular or adhere so closely to her own moral code that she'd refuse to eat a sandwich that contained meat. He looked at their determined faces and, remembering why and how they had come to be in this place, thought, *What am I, stupid? Of course one of them would refuse to eat something nonvegetarian if it violated her beliefs.*

The food and drink Ake understood. He also understood the need for the extra power cells for the energy rifles. He did not understand why there was a small black cube lying on one of the gurney's crisp white sheets.

"Thank heavens someone up there had more brains than we do," said Scoresby. "I never thought to ask for something to eat."

"Here," said Zeeta Bethune, handing the much appreciated rations to Ake to pass around. As Ake distributed the goodies like an office-party Santa Claus, Bethune picked up the black cube and gave it to Wyda. Wyda held it in her hand and stared intently at it as if she were Hamlet standing in the graveyard and contemplating the skull of "poor Yorick."

As the others voraciously dug into the food—the term "feeding frenzy" popped into Ake's mind—Wyda returned to kneel beside the two wounded Programmers. Because the first woman was now unconscious, Wyda turned to her friend and asked, "Are you ready, Tasha?"

"Yes, Thane."

"Ake, Zeeta, please bring the gurneys over here," Wyda called over her shoulder.

Ake and the young woman did as Wyda requested. Wyda keyed each gurney's controls so that it sank to about fifteen centimeters above the floor. "Good. Now help me get each of them onto her own gurney, please." Ake, asking no questions, followed Wyda's orders.

*I don't even know this sister's name*, Wyda thought as she directed the placement of the dying woman's unconscious body onto a gurney.

"Easy now," said Ake. "We don't want to unbalance it."

"Now you, Tasha," Wyda said to her friend. "Careful, be very careful with her," Wyda instructed as the three of them lifted the burned woman onto the gurney. Ake could see Wyda grimacing in sympathetic reaction to every stifled groan of pain from her old compatriot. When Tasha was carefully balanced on the gurney, Wyda rose and walked back to Scoresby.

"Okay, Margaret," Wyda said. "We're going to take out the barricade at the end of the corridor first, and then the door."

Squeezing the last jet of water from one of the bladders into her mouth and tossing it aside, Scoresby replied, "Good. We're ready to do what it takes, Thane."

Looking at Scoresby resolutely clutching her energy rifle in her meaty hands, Ake decided that if all the Programmers were as dedicated as she, Bukovsky and the others were in for an unpleasant surprise.

"Get your people into place, Margaret. I want you to lay down a heavy fire."

Scoresby's refreshed crew crawled into position and launched a withering enfilade at the soldiers' defensive line at the other end of the long corridor leading to the heavy molecular steel door that guarded the only way in or out of the prison. One of Scoresby's people was firing the old-fashioned automatic slug thrower that Ake had heard earlier. Its lead projectiles ripped and tore into the piled-up chairs and desks like angry hornets, sending splinters flying.

"I do like a machine gun—when it's on my side," Ake said to no one in particular. "It tends to get people's attention."

"Forget about that," Wyda told him. "I have something for you to do."

"Cheer helpfully?"

"Very amusing, Ake. No, I want you to take this cube and hurl it at the barricade. If it lands in the correct position, it'll blow a good-sized hole in their defenses and maybe even incapacitate some of the defenders."

"You're joking."

"This is getting tiresome, Ake. Every time I tell you something you don't wish to hear, you suggest that I am joking."

"All right. All right. I'm sorry," Ake said. He windmilled his right arm a few times to loosen it up.

"Ake."

"Yeah?"

"Don't linger out there to see the results of your throw. Just do it and get back."

"Yassir, boss." Scoresby's people increased the intensity of their fire, if that was possible, and Wyda told Ake to get ready.

"Now!"

Ake cocked his throwing arm, leaned out into the hall, and hurled the cube at the distant barricade. He quickly withdrew to the safety of the stairwell as the cube hit the floor and skittered into the front of the barricade.

After risking a quick look at his handiwork, Ake shouted in triumph. "He scores!"

Wyda pressed a small switch in her hand and the cube disappeared in a brilliant flash of light. The barricade was split asunder by the blast and almost immediately they could hear the screams of the injured. Peering through the smoke and debris, Ake could see the door.

"We've breached their defenses!" he shouted to Wyda.

"Good," said Wyda. "Now the door."

Wyda and Bethune maneuvered the first gurney to the stairwell doors. "They're shaken up," Wyda said to Scoresby, "but that won't last long. We've got to move fast. Keep them pinned down, Margaret."

As Scoresby's people again directed streams of fire at the soldiers' less and less tenable position, Wyda and Bethune manipulated the unconscious woman's null-grav gurney into the corridor and then pushed against it with all their might, aiming it for the narrow passage blown through the center of the barricade.

Bethune lingered a second longer than was necessary, impatient to see if their aim was true, and was hit in the shoulder. "Goddamn!" she screamed as Wyda grabbed her and pulled her back to the safety of the stairwell.

Ake carefully peered around the corner and down the corridor. The gurney containing the unconscious Programmer hurtled toward the opening Ake's explosive had created in the soldiers' barricade and passed through on its way to the door. Just as it cleared the barrier, someone leapt out and seized it, halting its forward motion and throwing the unconscious woman onto the floor.

"Damn!" shouted the woman with the slug thrower, unleashing a furious burst of firing that stitched a pattern up the length of the soldier's body, from his leg to his neck.

"I'm triggering the explosive," Wyda said.

"She's not close enough to the door," protested Scoresby.

"Maybe she is," replied Wyda. "Anyway, I have no choice."

Without warning a small sun blossomed at the far end of the corridor. This was followed almost immediately by a deafening roar and a steady rain of debris. Most of it was plasteel, wood, plastic, and shards and bits of metal and plasglas. Most of it . . . but not all of it. As the dust settled, Ake could see something bright and shiny lying near the doorway. It was a severed finger with a ring on it. Even from where he was, Ake recognized it by its design. It was Sergeant Hildebrand's wedding band.

"Ohmygod!" Ake said. "Oh-my-god."

They peered through the smoke and dust to see if the door had been taken out. Bursts of gunfire from that direction indicated that the blast, however powerful, hadn't killed all the well dug-in defenders.

"The door's still there," said a dejected Scoresby.

"My turn," said Wyda's friend Tasha. "I'm the last arrow in your quiver, Thane. Aim me straight and true."

"Come on, Ake," Wyda said. Together they pushed the gurney out into the corridor and propelled it on its way. It skimmed over the rubble-strewn floor like a surfboard riding the waves. It passed cleanly through the gaping hole in the defensive barrier and didn't stop until it collided with the door. The severely wounded Programmer was thrown up against the door and lay there motionless for a moment. Then Ake saw her arm move.

"She made it, she—"

Wyda pulled him back a scant second before the Programmer

triggered the explosives implanted in her body. A ball of flame shot down the corridor as the energy of the explosion erupted in all directions.

Clutching her shoulder, Zeeta Bethune stumbled into the corridor. "I can see light," she said simply.

"Now what?" Ake asked, peering out into the open plaza outside the prison entrance. "If we try to go through this door, they'll cut us to pieces."

Well-armed soldiers crouching behind jury-rigged defensive positions as hastily erected as the desk-and-chair barricade that had prevented them from reaching the door for so long had turned the plaza between the prison and the barracks building, the only other structure under the impenetrable dome of the force field, into a formidable first line of defense against those inside the prison.

The soldiers' barracks was directly across from the prison building, a mere forty meters away. A meter-high wall running the length of the front of the barracks building bristled with firing points and other defensive and offensive advantages that the freed prisoners didn't have.

Ake turned to Wyda, a frown on his face. "Now what, Glinda the Good?"

"Since you're nothing but a slimy, lying Triumvirate loyalist, we could try shooting you before you can escape," Wyda said.

"Huh?!"

# 12

"What shall we do now?" Maria asked.

"Hm-m-m," mused Ray. "That depends on what the holy heck is going on, doesn't it?" He approached one of the freed mine prisoners who was appreciatively caressing the plastic stock of an energy rifle as tenderly as if it were a lover's limb. "Say, Sparky, assuming that some of you knew about this uprising in advance, what happens next?"

"We can do nothing until the force field falls. When it does, we will join the attack on the soldiers in the barracks inside the prison compound."

"Where are the controls that maintain the force field?" asked Maria.

"Inside the soldiers' barracks."

"Even if the riot inside the prison is successful and produces a few weapons, what makes you think you're going to be able to overwhelm a barracks full of heavily armed, well-trained troops?"

"There is a plan," said one of the prisoners mysteriously.

"It better be a good one," muttered Ray.

"We're repeating ourselves, but now what?" Maria asked.

"You may come with us, if you wish."

"And where are you going?"

"To the administration building."

"Why don't you go ahead?" Ray said. "We'll catch up later, okay?"

The freed Programmers looked at each other and shrugged. "As you wish," one of them said.

Since Ake and Ray's place was the closest, Maria and the cats went with Ray to pick up Ake and the rest of the dogs.

"Hi, guys," Ray said when the dogs greeted him at the door of their house.

" 'Lo, Ray," said Littlejohn.

"Where's Ake? I have to talk to him right away."

"Ake had to go to work," Frodo told him.

"He went to the infirmary?"

"They called him 'bout ten or eleven," Frodo said.

Ray smashed his fist into his open palm. "Sonofabitch!"

"Somethin' wrong, Ray?" Littlejohn asked.

"There's been a riot in the prison," Ray told Littlejohn and the other three dogs. "If Ake's in the middle of all that . . ." His voice trailed away.

If Ake was in the middle of the uprising, anything could have happened to him, Ray realized. He could even be dead. *No, he's not dead*, Ray thought. *I don't know how I know that, but I just know Ake's still alive.*

★ ★ ★

"I don't like it," said one of the soldiers crouching behind a makeshift barrier, just fifteen meters from the prison entrance. "It's been ten minutes since they took out the door. Why don't they do something?"

"Don't be so anxious to die," the soldier's companion said. "They're just—"

The inside of the prison erupted with the sounds of a vicious firefight. Energy-bolt flashes lit up the interior and a slug-thrower was having its say. "Jesus, there must still be some resistance to those bastards," one of the soldiers said as the sounds of a furiously joined battle poured from the prison.

The troops surrounding the prison saw a soldier make it as far as the twisted ruins of the molecular-steel door before he was all but cut in half by a hail of slugs from somewhere inside. At least, that's what they thought they saw. In reality, the already dead soldier—the blood washed from his face and dressed in a passably intact uniform—was stood up, placed in the doorway, and shoved out amid a maelstrom of firing. Even though he was as dead as a politician's conscience, the impact of the hits he took animated his arms and legs. The effect was most convincing.

"See, Ake," said Wyda, speaking over the noise of the mock war raging around them. "That was to make the soldiers conscious that anyone coming out the door might be one of them. Now they'll hold their fire long enough to be sure who they're shooting at."

"Yeah, you're a genius, Thane," Ake said, his cracking voice betraying the terror he felt over the crazy stunt he was about to try to pull off. "Just give me the next meat puppet and let me get this over with."

Scoresby's people dragged another body over to him and draped the dead man's arm around Ake's neck. "I told him not to drink," Ake said to Scoresby. "He's just dead on his feet."

Zeeta Bethune whistled. "How can you crack jokes at a time like this?"

"It's that or drop a load in my pants," Ake said. "It's something I learned from my partner Ray."

"Positions, everyone," Wyda said. Then, looking at Ake, she asked, "Are you ready?"

"As ready as I'll ever be."

"Then go!"

With everyone around him firing his or her weapon, Ake stumbled out the gaping hole blown in the door. Supporting his wounded comrade with one arm, Ake blindly fired an energy pistol back into the smoky interior of the prison with his other hand as the dust around his feet was kicked into the air by the shooting coming from inside.

"Give him some cover!" he heard someone shout. The soldiers opened up with a withering fire designed to make those inside dive for cover as the two escapees made good their getaway.

With bullets and bolts of energy streaming past him in two directions, Ake didn't have to pretend to be frightened out of his wits. "Christ, don't let that crack about shitting my pants come true," he muttered. With impeccable—if inadvertent—timing, Ake's foot caught on something at exactly the same instant the dead soldier he was supporting took a direct hit in the back of the head. The two of them tumbled to the ground.

"Christ, he's down!" one of the soldiers shouted.

"Christ, he went down beautifully," Scoresby said in admiration. Then she aimed her rifle in Ake's direction and unleashed a volley of bolts.

A piece of plascrete flew up and struck Ake on the forehead. He put his hand to his temple and it came back bloody. "Jeezus H. Nixon!" he swore. Craning his neck to stare back at the prison doorway, he muttered under his breath, "If you hairless bastards get any closer to me, dammit, you'll convince them I'm for real by blowing my goddamn head off!"

Lying beside the body he'd carried this far, Ake looked into the dead man's unblinking stare and said, "Thanks, buddy. You did a great job, but here's where we part company."

"One of them's still alive," a voice called out as Ake scrambled to his feet and ran toward the safety of the nearest soldiers' outpost as if pursued by all the demons of hell. Firing his energy pistol as he zigzagged across the open space of the plaza, he rapidly closed the distance between himself and the refuge that beckoned to him. With a last few desperate bounds, he reached the protection of the closest position and dove headfirst over the defensive barrier.

"Fan-fucking-tastic!" one of the two soldiers there said. "You made it; you got away!"

"I'm never gonna let the plate pass me by again without putting in every credit I have on me," Ake said.

"Don't make any promises you can't keep," laughed the other soldier. "So, buddy, what's your name?"

"Ringgren. Doctor Ake Ringgren."

"That was the most heroic thing I've ever seen," said the first soldier. "I bet Colonel Bukovsky will see to it that you get what's coming to you."

"Heh, heh," laughed Ake uneasily.

# II

"Why are we going to the spaceport, Ray?" Maria asked, stroking the head of the cat she was carrying in her arms. It was Marisol, and the Siamese purred loudly.

"Ray loves surprisin' folks," Littlejohn said.

"But why the spaceport?" Maria persisted.

"You have to ask? It's to get some of that good spaceport coffee," Ray said. Taking a cue from Maria, he scratched Beowulf and Gawain behind the ears.

"I should go about this logically," Maria said. "For beginners, what's at the spaceport?"

"You tell me."

"Landing facilities, a few hover vehicles, fuel, and a couple of limited-range shuttles. That's it," Maria said.

"The shuttles just go up to and come back down from starships—freighters and passenger ships, right?" Ray said. He was enjoying this.

"Yeah, that's about all they're capable of," Maria said. She paused for a moment, thinking. "Do you think there's some way of using them against the soldiers' barracks?"

"How?" Ray asked. "Shuttles don't have any weapons as far as I know. And even if they did, the barracks building is inside the protection of the force field."

"Maria?"

"Yes, Marisol?"

"Why don't we jes' wait until Ray decides to tell us why he wants us to go to the spaceport?"

"I think you're right, Marisol," Maria said. "Well, can we at least pass by the compound to see what's going on there? Maybe we can do something for Ake."

"As long as he's inside the force field, there's nothing we can do to help him," Ray insisted.

"Mebbe not," Beowulf offered. "Mebbe not—but we can be there if there be *any* chance to help. There ain't nuthin' goin' on at the spaceport." Pronounced by dog lips, it came out as "spacebort."

"All right," conceded Ray. "If that's what everyone wants to do, we can have a look-see on our way to the spaceport."

Frodo trotted back up the partially overgrown road from down below where he'd been checking things out. " 'Lo, Ray. 'Lo, Beowulf. 'Lo, everybody."

"What's it look like down by the compound?" Ray asked, making a hand signal that sent Grendel back down the road as Frodo's replacement on the point.

"Okay," Frodo said. "But the jungle 'tween here and there is sure somethin'! It sneakin' up to the road pretty good."

"Yeah, with all this hell breaking loose," said Ray, "I have to wonder what will happen to the road if there's no one to burn back the rain forest."

"Boy, I sure would like to do some real 'splorin' in this place sometime," said Beowulf, looking up into the treetops. Several small arboreal creatures, all long arms, legs, and prehensile tails, flitted from branch to branch howling and shrieking. "We find lots of neat animals and things, I betcha!"

"Maybe we can when all this is over," Ray said. "But don't expect me to get *too* excited by the prospect of hacking my way through the saw grass and creepers, guys. I've seen too many of those old Jungle Jim sinnys to trust the jungle. If it's not lions and leopards, it's giant snakes and spiders. Then there's the crocodiles and the quicksand. Not to mention the lava—every *Jungle Jim* or *Bomba the Jungle Boy* sinny had lava flowing like Cream of Wheat."

"I guess we're in the right place for that," Maria said. "The lava flows, that is."

"You've never been to the Cream of Wheat geyser, then?"

Maria laughed. "Did they have any of those in your corny kiddie sinnys?"

"They *were* pretty corny," Ray conceded. "As a kid, I got the idea that the most common causes of death—in Africa, at least—were rock avalanches, flowing lava, and quicksand. That's what comes of watching too many jungle sinnys."

Grendel trotted back to announce, "We almost there, Ray. Doan seem to be a whole lot goin' on right now, though."

"Thank God," Maria said. "I'm a ball of sweat. My clothes weigh more than I do at this point."

"Funny what one hundred and ten percent humidity will do to you, isn't it?" Ray said.

"As fascinating as this discussion is," Ray told her, "we have more important things to attend to right now."

"Even though you won't admit it, you really are worried about Ake, aren't you?"

"What do you think?"

"He's fine, I'm sure."

Ray looked at her with a half-smile on his face. "He *is* fine," Ray told her. "He's safe and sound inside . . ." His eyes widened. "He's not in the prison—he's inside the barracks building!"

★ ★ ★

Ake sat quietly in a corner nursing a soft drink. The butt of the energy pistol he'd used in his "escape" was tucked into the waistband of his trousers. Even though it pressed on his innards, feeling it there gave him a modicum of security. The soldiers, filled with admiration for his impressive deeds in getting away from his captors, finally left him alone. For a while, he thought they'd never stop slapping him on the back and telling him what a good guy he was. All the bonhomie and warm wishes made him feel peculiar; after all, he'd gotten into the place under false pretenses and intended to do what he could to destroy it at the first opportunity that came his way.

*Being a spy is a shitty thing*, he told himself sourly. *These guys thought they were saving my life and I'm gonna repay them by doing things that may result in them ending up dead. Why do I have to get all the good jobs?*

After being helped into the soldiers' barracks by his two rescuers, Ake had seen evidence which explained why the expected counterattack on the prison was so slow in developing. There was fire and blast damage everywhere. Even more ominous were the streaks of blood on the floors that terminated in sheet-covered bodies stacked against the walls.

"Hello, Doctor."

Ake looked up. "You!"

"Yeah, me," the young butterfly collector said. "My foot's much better now, thanks to you."

"What's your name, if I may ask?" Ake queried. "You were just a number in the infirmary."

"Milo," said the young soldier. "Milo Dalitto."

"It's nice to meet you formally, Milo."

"The pleasure's all mine," Dalitto said loudly. "As a matter of fact, why don't I buy you some real rocket fuel?"

He leaned down, put his mouth close to Ake's ear, and whispered, "I think we have a mutual acquaintance in Thane Wyda." He straightened back up.

Ake was more than a little stunned. "I . . . ah . . ."

"No, don't say anything," said Dalitto loudly and heartily for the benefit of anyone listening. "I fully understand; you're a damned hero but you're already sick and tired of being told how brave and wonderful you are. Well, as I said, the drinks are on me if you want to go down to the club and have something a little stronger than that sugar water you're sucking on."

Ake nodded as if he was agreeing with Dalitto's words. He contemplated the implication of what the butterfly collector had told him. The damage Ake had seen—and which he'd been hustled past without explanation by his hosts—was clearly the work of people like Dalitto. Ake wondered if the young soldier really was a butterfly collector or if that was just a convenient way to justify frequent forays outside the camp. He remembered his own days as a sleeper in the Cadre camp on Chiron and decided it was the latter.

Ake snapped out of his reverie when he realized that Dalitto was looking at him as if expecting some kind of response. "You know, that's a good idea," Ake said finally. "I think I *could* use a real drink." He got up slowly and stretched.

"Now you're talking," Dalitto said, wrapping a long arm around him and leading him toward the door. "Let's go."

Although they passed a few well-wishers, there weren't many soldiers around to question them about their destination. *That's good*, thought Ake. *Because if anyone asks me, I have no idea where the hell we're going.*

"Would it be too much to ask where you're really taking me?" Ake inquired in as low a voice he could produce and still be heard.

"You're going to help me destroy the force field generator," Dalitto told him casually.

"Oh, that's nice," Ake replied as if Dalitto had told him they were going to an afternoon tea. "And afterwards?"

"Afterwards there's a very good chance we'll be dead."

# III

Ray gazed through his binoculars at the compound. "There's not much movement down there," he announced to the others. "I suppose most of the action is taking place inside the prison, although I can see a number of soldiers in that open area that lies between the two buildings." Then something caught his eye. "Wait a minute."

Ray touched a stud and the autofocus rotated the focus ring. "It looks like the Programmers have blown out the plasglas in the upper-story windows and are firing at the soldiers in that open area."

"May I see, please?" asked Maria politely.

"Sure." Ray handed over the binoculars.

"That's odd," Maria said.

"What's odd?" Ray asked.

Maria ignored him for the moment. "Penelope," she said, "if I adjust the focus for you, do you think you can look through these glasses and tell us what you see?"

"Sure, Maria," the cat said. She walked over to where Maria held the binoculars for her.

"What's going on?"

"The cats have incredible eyesight compared to ours," Maria explained. "And Penelope has the best eyes of any on my team."

"She gonna look through the bye-nock-lars?" asked Frodo.

"Doan be lookin' at no birdies, pussface," Littlejohn told the feline sourly.

Ignoring the dogs, the slightly cross-eyed cat looked through the glasses Maria held in place for her.

"Can you see all right?" Maria asked. "Is it clear?"

"No." Penelope looked away and shook her head as if to dismiss the blurred image that had greeted her.

Maria turned the focus ring manually. "How about now?"

Penelope put her eyes to the binoculars again. "That's better," she said. "Wow, they look so close and . . . oh-h-h!"

"What's she supposed to be seeing?" asked Ray.

"Penelope?"

"I sees men with guns firing at the soldiers from the prison windows."

"She means womens," said Beowulf irritably. "Brogrammers."

"No, I sees men," Penelope said firmly.

Maria took the binoculars away and looked through them again herself. "I didn't trust my own eyes," she said, peering at the prison. "But if Penelope sees them as well, there's no question about it."

"What that mean?" asked Tajil. "Why it important that Benelope sees mens?"

Ray sighed. "I think it means that the male prisoners, the hardcore prison population, have taken over the revolt, Taddy."

"Maybe they're working together," said Maria hopefully.

"Did you see *any* women firing at the soldiers, Penelope?" asked Ray.

The cat shook her head, her large blue eyes wide with wonder. "No, Ray."

"This situation is getting out of—" There was a flash of light and moments later the sound of an explosion radiated out to their position. "Where did that come from?" he asked.

"From the barracks," Littlejohn said.

Maria studied the compound. "Littlejohn's right."

Without warning there was a second and much more powerful explosion. The roof of the building seemed to levitate and a geyser of flame shot high into the air.

"Holy bat shit!" Ray exclaimed. "That explosion was tremendous! Look at the building, for chrissakes! It's half blown away!" Pieces of the building's reflective outer coating were kiting through the air and sending rainbow-hued flashes of light in every direction as if someone had just turned the largest snow-filled glass ball in the world upside down and shaken it.

Maria peered at the compound before putting down the binoculars and saying, "Ray, the force field just dropped away."

"That must have been the goal of the explosion," said Ray. Then he moaned and softly said, "Christ almighty, Ake was inside that building."

"Oh, no!" said Mama-san.

"Here," said Maria, handing over the binoculars.

Ray peered through them and said, "Come on, come on!" The building was enveloped by a large black cloud of smoke, dust, and debris. Slowly, it began to clear away.

"Yeah, the blast blew it to hell and gone, but I think there's more of it standing than one might expect after the intensity of that explosion," said Ray.

"Ake be alive?" Frodo asked.

"Maybe. I hope so," said Ray, putting down the glasses. "There's nothing we can do here right now. Let's head for the spaceport."

Maria put her hand on Ray's arm. "No fooling around now, Ray," she said. "I want to know why we're going to the spaceport."

"Remember that low-power message that Sari Fodoor transmitted?"

"Sure."

"Well, I think it was beamed to a spaceship not all that far away."

★ ★ ★

Ake couldn't believe how successful Dalitto's acts of sabotage had been so far. It made him nervous—then he realized that it was the exact same kind of this-is-too-good-to-be-true feeling that Wyda had confessed to experiencing. With no opposition—or even awareness on the part of the defenders as to what was happening—Dalitto had planted a shaped plastic charge in the force field generating area.

Since the charge was timed, Dalitto and Ake were then able to plant a second such charge, this time in the armory. Actually, since the armory was off limits to anyone without a freshly minted daily pass, Dalitto simply placed an inner-directed charge on the wall. Then he and Ake casually walked away, careful not to draw attention to themselves.

"How long until the first charge detonates?" Ake asked.

Dalitto looked at his watch. "About three minutes." He glanced back down the corridor toward the armory to see if anyone was following them; no one was. "And the charge we just set will go off in about four minutes."

"Four minutes?"

"Yeah," Dalitto said. "The first one should destroy the generator. If it doesn't the second surely will; it's gonna be a corker of a blast. It's a powerful plastic matrix that may take out the whole building."

"Shall I bend over and kiss my ass goodbye now?"

"Just shut up and follow me."

"Where are we going now?"

"If there's time, we can make it into one of the utility rooms on this floor. I sabotaged all but a couple of the Ivanhoes this morning and shoved the good ones in a locker I have access to."

"What's an Ivanhoe?"

"That's what we call the armored personnel battle suits. They're supposed to protect the wearer from a level alpha explosion."

"How many more like you are there?" Ake asked him.

"None. I'm an only child."

"I mean, how many members of the Resistance are there among the soldiers?"

"I really have no idea. For all I know, I may be the sole infiltrator." Ake watched a strange, wistful expression cloud Dalitto's face. "Then again, maybe there's more than I might imagine. When I bring the building down on top of us, I could be killing a lot of people fighting for the same things I'm fighting for."

*That's a sobering notion*, Ake thought. *But how does one get around the problem?*

"Here we are," said Dalitto, opening the locker by pressing his palm against its security mechanism. He pulled two of the three suits out and they struggled into them.

They helped each other to seal up and then Dalitto showed Ake how to lower the helmet's blast shield. "Do these things really work?" Ake asked, his voice tinny and mechanical-sounding on the suit's radio.

"Guess we'll have the answer to that in just about . . . Oh, Jesus!"

At that moment, certain molecular and electrochemical reactions took place within the plastic matrix explosive that Dalitto had planted in the room housing the force field generator. The force of the resulting explosion threw both Ake and Dalitto to the floor. The shaped charge had been multidirectional, so the blast's concussive effects became a shell of heat and light that expanded outward like the original Big Bang.

"That's one," said Dalitto's voice on the radio. "The next one ought—"

The directed charge that Dalitto had placed on the armory wall exploded inward, a fireball of hot gases igniting the ammunition stored there. The resulting blast—or, rather, series of smaller but almost instantaneous blasts—was even more powerful than Ake could have anticipated. The floor where the armory was located ceased to be as it was simultaneously consumed by the explosion and blown out and away. The building above and below the blast smashed together in the same way a pile of concrete blocks does when someone removes a block from the middle.

Aware that he was in the center of a maelstrom of destruction, Ake wondered if this was what it would be like to find yourself in the magma core of one of Hephaestus's volcanoes. The universe seemed to tilt and Ake realized that the floor was collapsing as the building caved in on itself. Suddenly, he felt as if he were in a drop tube; he was falling.

His senses numbed by the fury of the explosion that ravaged the building, Ake did one of the more practical things he could have done under the circumstances—he blacked out.

When Ake regained consciousness, he felt a tugging on his legs. He panicked for a split-second before he realized that he was being pulled from the rubble.

He deactivated the blast shield, but with the suit's helmet made opaque by soot and grime, Ake was unable to see his rescuers. He was glad that someone was undoing his suit's fasteners for him, since his own fingers didn't seem to be working too well. *I'm alive. I survived the blasts*, he told himself, *but that doesn't mean that I'm a hundred percent.*

It took a few seconds after his helmet came off for his blurred vision to clear. When it did, the first face that swam into focus in front of him was bearded. He remembered that the soldiers were prohibited from wearing beards. A bearded Programmer? He saw that there were three others with the bearded man. Suddenly, everything made sense to him.

"You're not Programmers, you're—"

"That's right," the bearded man said. "We're the 'others,' the nasty boys."

"Hey, this one's a soldier," said one of the others as Dalitto struggled out of his suit, revealing his uniform.

"What are you waiting for, then?"

"Jesus, no!" shouted Ake as the man put a slug thrower to Dalitto's head and pressed the firing stud. Blood spattered the inside of Dalitto's helmet.

Then the killer put his gun to Ake's head. "Should I do this guy, too?" he asked the bear-sized man with the beard.

The other man looked at Ake, pulling at his scraggly whiskers. "Lemme think on that a moment."

# 13

By the time Ray and Maria and the dogs and cats reached the vicinity of the spaceport, they knew that a shuttle landing was imminent. That is, they just knew they knew; *how* they knew was a different matter.

"It's this damn planet, isn't it?" Ray asked Maria. "I mean, I may have the 'power,' in crude form, but I've never been known for my psi abilities. Not until lately."

"Not until you were exposed to the rubies?"

"I wasn't going to say that, but I can't think of any other explanations."

When Maria gave him a look, he added, "Well, yes, I can think of lots of explanations. But none of them make as much sense as what you just said about Hephaestus and the rubies."

Ray wasn't satisfied, though. "There's still one thing I don't get," Ray told her. "You're naturally psychic and the cats are bred for their psychic powers, right?"

"Right."

"Being here has dramatically increased my little bit of natural psychic talent. For instance, I can sense that Beowulf is hungry," Ray said, glancing down at the big lionlike dog.

"You think you gots to be sigh-kick to know that?" hooted Littlejohn.

Ray ignored Littlejohn's interruption. "I didn't used to be able to 'read' him like that, even as closely bonded as we two are. But you've been here almost a year longer and you also had more ability to begin with. My question is, how come with those advantages you're not klicks ahead of me instead of just incrementally? Thoughts and feelings ought to be leaping out at you as clearly as spoken conversations."

"Maybe the planet or the stones do nothing more than help a person to reach his or her potential," Maria said. "I was closer to utilizing my abilities one hundred percent. You had further to go, so you're showing a more marked and dramatic improvement."

Ray pulled on his lower lip. "Hm-m-m. Could be." Then he made a dismissive wave and said, "Listen to me: 'Could be.' Hell, it *could* be anything! We have more pressing matters to concern ourselves about."

"Then let's assist the shuttle that we can both sense is coming to land, shall we?"

"Yes, let's."

"How many soldiers is there in the spacebort?" Beowulf asked.

"Fewer than a half-dozen, I think," said Ray. "That sound about right to you?" he asked Maria.

"I think so," she replied. "There's always four on duty. The other personnel are spaceport workers."

"You sure about that?"

"Damned sure." She prodded him in the ribs. "Come on, after what we've just been talking about, don't try to tell me you can't feel their auras."

"Yeah, I guess I can. So burn me at the stake—I'm a witch."

"That's warlock," Bastet corrected him.

"Huh?"

"A male witch is a warlock," Bastet explained.

"And a female dog is a bitch," teased Penelope, rubbing up against Ozma.

"A headless cat is dead," growled Littlejohn.

"Stop!" commanded Ray. "Time out. Peace." Then he giggled.

"We're all on the same side, remember that," admonished Maria, throwing Ray a look that said, "Really, dear, not in front of the children."

Ray found a fallen tree and sat down. Something small and yellow and all eyes chirped indignantly and skittered from the trunk. When a fifteen-centimeter-long beetlelike thing crawled from a hole in the rotting wood and opened its iridescent wings in a defensive display, Ray simply picked up a stick and sent it sailing.

"Okay," said Ray. "The spaceport's just a hop, skip, and a jump from here. Let's plan our entry." He looked into Maria's brown eyes. "When we get a little closer, Maria, the dogs and I are relying on you and your cats to pinpoint where the soldiers are. I may be getting better at sensing auras all the time, but I still do best when it involves Ake or someone else who is important to me like my dogs."

Maria's turned her head strangely. "I . . . I'm sensing something already." Her eyes widened in surprise.

"What? What is it?" Ray asked.

"Sonofabitch!"

"Don't start that again," Ray said impatiently.

"Is there room on that trunk for me?" asked Maria. "I think I need to sit down."

"So sit."

Maria plopped down heavily. Her amazed brown eyes stared into Ray's puzzled blue ones. "Maybe I'm wrong," she told him finally, "but I think the spaceport personnel, including the soldiers, want to surrender!"

★ ★ ★

Ake was more than a little relieved that the bearded man had decided that a live doctor was better than a dead one. Not that they appeared to be all that concerned about their wounded, since several of the more severely injured among them were summarily dispatched by a slug or energy bolt in the head. Ake was also helped by the fact that he was not one of the soldiers.

Given the bearded man and his companions' treatment of captured soldiers, Dalitto's fate was also kinder than it first seemed to Ake at the time. They had killed the young butterfly collector, but that was no worse than what they did to their own wounded. In contrast, several of the other soldiers the prisoners had captured were subjected to vindictive and brutally imaginative torture before they were finally killed. Ake assumed that a lot of old scores were being settled.

*Nice fucking guys I'm with*, Ake shuddered.

"How ya doin', Doc?" Ake looked up to see that his questioner was the bearded man who seemed to have assumed the mantle of leader. His name, Ake had learned, was Waldo Lynch. Ake wondered what his crime was since the others seemed terrified of him.

"Under the circumstances, I'm doing pretty good, I guess."

"Atta boy, Doc." The big man gave him a rough tap on the shoulder. "You keep your nose clean and you're gonna get out of this alive."

"Yeah?" Ake said. "That's more than I can say for you and your buddies." *Jesus, listen to me! I must have a death wish.*

"Oh, you're a brave one, eh?" said Lynch, taking Ake's words in good humor.

*And why not?* Ake thought. *He's got the guns.* "Stupid, too."

"You'll get no argument from me on that account," laughed Lynch.

"Why don't we just stick an energy pistol in this chump's ear, pull the trigger, and see what comes out the other side, Waldo?" one of the bearded man's confederates asked, his voice a nasal whine.

"Don't forget who's in charge of this breakout," said Lynch testily. The other man went white.

"Sorry, Waldo."

"Never mind that," Lynch said. "Tell the others we're heading back to the administration building."

"Sure, Waldo. Whatever you say." The man hurried off, happy to remove himself from his leader's presence to a less dangerous position.

"Tell me something—if you will," Ake said to Lynch.

"What do you want to know?"

"What happened to the rebellion in the prison?"

"Rebellion? Ha!" Lynch spat. "That's what did in your buddies, those crew-cut and shaved-head slaves of the Judge Advocate. They were too busy having themselves their little 'rebellion' to notice that the only thing the rest of us wanted was a jailbreak. They didn't catch on to the truth until it was too late."

"Couldn't those two be the same thing—a rebellion and a jailbreak?" Ake asked as he heard the crackle of an energy weapon nearby.

"Sure," agreed Lynch amiably, ignoring the firing. "And they were—until them old bitches conveniently killed off most of the soldiers for us and we got all the guns we needed." His features broke into a huge, face-spanning grin. "We said thank you very much ladies, and if you don't mind—or even if you do—step aside now and let us take over."

"I can't believe it was that easy," Ake said, thinking of the bravery and resourcefulness of Margaret Scoresby and the others.

"Hey, it wasn't," conceded Lynch. "Them was tough old squats, I'll give them that. But, as you may have noticed for yourself, we ain't the fuckin' Star Scouts, either!"

"They're not all . . ."

"Dead? No, they ain't." Lynch chuckled. "We got them locked up with Colonel Bukovsky, Kodlich, and the others. You might say that the Federation is reunified and all is forgiven. At least they're all in the same survival pod now."

"Congratulations," said Ake sourly. "What do you plan to do now?"

Lynch's good humor evaporated and a dark look crossed his face. "You figure on writing a bio-drama about me or what?" he asked. "You'll find out soon enough what our plans are without me telling you everything."

"We're ready, Waldo," said one of the others, a fireplug-shaped man who'd lost his teeth in the fighting. "We pulled out and sent back everyone we found alive." Looking like a little boy who's taken more cookies from the cookie jar than he was supposed to, the man beamed a toothless grin and added, "Well, almost everyone."

"Yeah, I heard the shots," Lynch told him. "Let's get moving."

## II

"Look," Ray told Maria, "whoever's coming down in the shuttle from this rebel ship is going to be a little trigger-happy and—"

"And you'd rather they shoot me and my cats instead of you," Maria finished for him.

"Sounds reasonable," said Frodo.

Ray gave Frodo a look. "No, it isn't that at all. You're a woman and they're probably mostly women themselves. I think if you greet them instead of me they'll be less likely to shoot first and ask questions later."

"That makes sense, Maria," said Bastet.

"Yeah, I know," Maria agreed. "That's what worries me."

That was how Ray came to stay with their "prisoners of war"—the soldiers and spaceport staff people who had surrendered themselves to Maria and him—while Maria and all but one of her cats marched off to welcome the shuttle passengers.

Ray's charges willingly trooped into one of the high-security luggage holding rooms and meekly allowed themselves to be locked in. It made a perfect cell since it had only one entrance. "As long as we have food, drink, and hygienic facilities, we'd just as soon be out of your hair until you make contact with the people on the ship," one of the staff told him.

"Yeah, it's no fun sitting around with someone holding a gun on you," one of the soldiers said.

His prisoners were so cooperative, Ray found it hard to believe that they weren't planning something. Yet his newfound ability to read their intentions revealed no thoughts of resistance or attempts to escape on their part. Still not convinced, Ray had the dogs and Marisol thoroughly check out the holding area. "It's fine, Ray," Beowulf told him. Marisol seconded that opinion.

Ray decided he had no choice but to accept that his prisoners' capitulation was genuine. *I guess it shows that support for the new and improved Federation just might be a kilometer wide and a centimeter deep*, Ray thought.

"Ray, just what the heck is goin' on?" Mama-san asked him.

"What do you mean, Mama-san?"

"I . . . I doan know what I mean, 'xactly," she confessed. "I jes' wants to know whose side we on. Are we with the good guys or not?"

"You gots to ask that question of our Man?" said Grendel, disbelief in her voice. "We on Ray's side and Ray is always on the right side."

The other dogs joined with Grendel in voicing their support for Ray. So much so, that Ray felt he had to stop them from verbally beating up on Mama-san.

"Wait a minute, guys," he said, putting up his hands. "Mama-san is asking a legitimate question. There's no ignoring the fact that what I've gotten us involved in is illegal. It's against the terms of our contract and it's sure as hell against the laws of the Federation." He looked into their concerned dog faces. "We . . . *I* . . . might be doing what I think is right, but I'm still leading us all way out on a limb."

"Them Broggramers is in jail 'cause they tried to do the right thing, ain't that so, Ray?" asked Beowulf.

"Absolutely," Ray agreed.

"Then what we's doing is right . . . but against the law?" asked Tajil.

"Against the humans' law," Beowulf said, drawing the distinction, "but not against *our* Law."

Ray nodded. "That's right, Beowulf."

"Then my question shoulda bin, what's gonna happen to us?" Mama-san said.

"That's one question I haven't an answer to," Ray said after a long pause.

"They comin'," Sinbad announced.

Maria and her team strode into the lounge area followed by three women clad in the severe and simply cut black clothing of Prime Programmers. Ray didn't need any special power to observe that they were not exactly bursting with joy and happiness.

"Prime Programmers, I'd like to introduce you to Ray Larkin, a scout dog leader and man of many talents," said Maria. "And this is his team," she added with a wave at the dogs sitting patiently on their haunches.

"Pleased to meet you," the women said stiffly.

"Ray, these are Prime Programmers Oljuba Mandela, Enni Su, and Mirani Youanmi," said Maria.

"Pleased to meet you," said Ray automatically, unable to stop gawking at Mirani Youanmi.

"Yes, Citizen Larkin," the Prime Programmer said in response to his frank stare. "We have met before—on Chiron."

"Small universe, isn't it?" Ray asked rhetorically. "Prime Programmer Wyda is already here for the reunion; glad you could make it."

"Well, we know he isn't an impostor," Programmer Youanmi said to Maria. To the others, she said, "Citizen Larkin seems to have made a career out of stepping on Triumvirate toes."

"We *could* stand here and chat about old times," said Programmer Su, "but I'd much prefer we take a seat and discuss the current situation."

"Let's do that." Ray led the way to the spaceport lounge's cuddle chairs. The Programmers sat down tentatively, clearly not comfortable with such concessions to physical well-being as were represented by the cuddle chairs. From the expressions on the women's faces, one might have thought the chairs were sending jolts of electricity through them rather than simply molding themselves to the contours of their bodies.

Maria picked up one of the steaming coffee cups that Ray had provided and said, "Well, Prime Programmers, if you wish to tell us what's going on, we're all ears."

"Let us begin by quickly reiterating what you probably already know," said Oljuba Mandela. "When all but a minority . . ." She shook her head. "No, that's not right—minority is too weak a word."

She tried again. "When all but a *handful* of the Order of Programmers resisted the newly—and illegally—constituted Triumvirate's efforts to subordinate and bypass the judicial and legal enforcement powers of the Judge Advocate, the Triumvirate ordered the Cadre and the FedSecPol to conduct wholesale arrests of Programmers and Prime Programmers on patently false charges. They—we—were then replaced by handpicked confederates who, in the guise of Programmers, carried out the Triumvirate's plans to render the Judge Advocate ineffective."

Ray nodded. "That's pretty much what my partner Ake Ringgren got from Thane Wyda."

"When the arrests began," said Enni Su, "we initiated a plan to save as many Programmers as we could. Through intermediaries, we arranged the purchase of a starship, an old freighter."

"A very old, very slow, and very small freighter," interjected Youanmi. "It has a cargo capacity of less than a million metric tons."

"Even the oldest, slowest, and smallest freighter ought to be sufficient for your needs," Ray said. "Especially if those needs involve rescuing your sister Programmers imprisoned here."

"The *Pequod* is *very* old," said Enni Su. She shook her head at a disturbing memory. "There was some unpleasantness with a Federation sentry ship off Ganymede as we were leaving the solar system and we sustained minor damage to our engines." She sighed. "Then the air exchanger needed a complete in-flight overhaul, there was a problem in hydroponics, and the computer has failed to function in a satisfactory manner."

"Meaning . . . ?" asked Ray.

"Meaning we're committed to staying in geosynchronous orbit around Hephaestus for at least a week. It may take even longer—perhaps ten days to two weeks—for us to get the *Pequod* in the sort of shape she needs to be in if we're to risk making a hyperspace jump."

"Do you really need hyperspace capability?" Maria asked.

"With it, we have a chance of staying out of the Federation's hands; without it, no chance at all," Su told them.

"We must leave as soon as the engines are repaired, even if the matter here is not resolved by then," Mandela said. "Thane and the others will understand."

"You can ferry down the people you've got on board, can't you?" Ray asked. "They should be enough to help the others defeat the troops if you've got an adequate number of weapons."

"The troops . . . ?" said Enni Su.

Prime Programmer Youanmi looked at Ray queerly. "Do you not know what has happened?"

Ray and Maria exchanged glances. "I guess not," said Ray slowly. "Suppose you tell us."

"Thane got a message through to us on her short-range norm-space communicator just before we put the ship in its stationary orbit."

"Yeah?"

"After the soldiers were defeated, the other prisoners took control of the prison. Our sisters are being held captive by these people."

Maria looked at Ray and then down at the floor. Beowulf put out a huge paw and gently touched Ray reassuringly.

"Ake . . ." Ray said softly.

★ ★ ★

Ake's wrists ached where the restraints he wore had begun to rub against his skin. *At least I can feel pain*, he thought. *A lot of people are no longer around to complain about their wrists hurting.*

A door hissed open and the prisoners—Ake had begun calling the others simply Programmers—herded in a dozen or so of the camp's more important hostages, including Colonel Bukovsky, Theo Kodlich, Sari Fodoor, Captain Ramos, and Chief Engineer Tsuji. Ake was surprised to note how glad he was to see them. He mused that there was now a third side when it came to the situation he and his Federation antagonists found themselves in. The prisoners who'd seized them were a common threat. And a possibly unifying one—for a while, at least.

"Hello, Colonel Bukovsky," Ake said.

"Hello, Ringgren," the colonel replied. "I should have expected to count you among the survivors of the recent events. You and your partner seem to have a knack for bobbing to the surface of any situation." She looked about the room. "And where is the redoubtable Citizen Larkin and his band of talking dogs?"

"I don't know," Ake replied. "I haven't seen him in about a decade—at least it *seems* that long."

One of Lynch's bully boys struck Bukovsky between the

shoulder blades with the butt of his energy rifle, knocking her to her knees. "That's enough talking," he said as an "Oohhff" escaped from her. "Sit down and stay down."

Kodlich, Fodoor, and the other captives needed no more urging. Not eager to feel a rifle butt in their backs, they did as the man ordered.

Waldo Lynch entered the room trailed by his band of toadies. Ake noted that Waldo and his sycophants, true to their coarse nature, had adorned themselves with rings, bracelets, necklaces, and other jewelry taken from their captives.

Seeing Lynch with a large star sapphire on his left ear made Ake think of Old-Earth pirates. *That's not a bad analogy,* Ake thought. *They've made a number of the survivors of the combat figuratively "walk the plank," and they act like a bunch of barbarians driven by nothing more than greed and lust. All they need is a Jolly Roger.*

"I have a question to ask you brave revolutionaries," Lynch said. "And I don't want you puttin' your heads together on it or tryin' to give me any phony information or other crap. Got that?" He took their silence as acquiescence. "Good. Now, which one of you knows how to get to the nearest K'a-nii village?"

No one spoke up. Ake considered it but then thought better of volunteering anything.

When he failed to get a response, Lynch said, "This is very childish of you." He gestured to one of his men. The man drew a quiver blade and, as calmly as someone cutting a piece of meat, slit the throat of the nearest Programmer. The woman shrieked in surprise and pain and rose to her feet. She stumbled forward a few steps, blood pouring over and between her fingers. She fell to the floor, gasping out gurgling noises, and then died.

"I repeat: Who can lead us to the nearest native village?"

*Shit!* thought Ake. Reluctantly, he raised his manacled hands and said, "I can."

"Why, it's the doc," Lynch said. "I knew there was a reason I kept the boys from adding extra holes to your head."

"We kill him now?" asked one of the criminals, a thin trail of mucus running from one of his nostrils.

Lynch walked over and put his energy pistol to the man's head and fired. The discharge caused the man's eyes to bulge out and a wisp of smoke to rise from his head. He fell over backwards. There was the smell of wet rope in the air.

"Christ!" Lynch exclaimed to one of his flunkies. "I heard of dumb before, but that moron must have been terminally stupid." He kicked the dead man with the toe of his boot. "We don't kill our guides, asshole!" he told the dead man.

"He's stupid? I take it you and the rest of your folks are graduates of New Harvard, eh?" Ake asked.

Lynch just shook his head. "Doc here thinks he's indispensable now. Well, maybe he's right; maybe we can't kill him." He struck Ake a great, sweeping blow across his face, all but knocking him off his feet. "Still, that don't mean we can't teach him some respect, does it?"

Lynch's men laughed.

"All I want is a laser scalpel and two minutes alone with you, Lynch," hissed Ake.

"Send it to Santa," said Lynch, turning away. "Round a couple of the others up to go along with us," he ordered one of the other prisoners. "Then I want us to split into two equal groups. The first stays here and keeps an eye on the ladies. Sooner or later they've got reinforcements coming. But they won't be able to do diddly while we're holding guns to their friends' heads."

"And the second group?" asked Ake.

Lynch turned back to face him. "Still writin' my life story, eh, Ringgren? The other one, the one led by yours truly, is going to tag along while you and some of your buddies here lead us to the K'a-nii camp."

"Whatever the hell for?" asked Sari Fodoor, unable to contain herself any longer.

"Why, to help us convince the K'a-nii to tell us where their race's treasure is stored, of course."

# III

Ray peered through binoculars at the administration building now occupied by the common criminals of the prison. "Boy, I dunno," he muttered.

"You don't know what?" asked Maria. "You don't know how many there are? You don't know how we're going to get in without them killing all their hostages? You don't know—"

"Yeah," interrupted Ray. "I don't know all those things and more."

"That's just great!" exclaimed Maria.

"Geez, she not got much faith in her cats and us dogs, huh?" Littlejohn said to Ray.

"I'm afraid not," Ray said. He shook his head sadly.

"Don't tell me you've got a plan," she said.

"Okay."

She looked at his big smile. "You *do*," she said, sensing his thoughts.

"Yeah, he does," agreed Marisol. "But you told him not to tell you that and so he *won't* until you laugh and tell him how cute and funny his sophomoric male humor is."

"Boy, what a crab cakes!" said Beowulf.

"If you're going to get snippy about it," said Ray, "then I won't kid around."

"Thank God," said Maria.

"Here's my plan," said Ray.

★ ★ ★

Lynch and his men took Ake and the others out a little-used entrance just before dawn. As Lynch put it, "Everyone will be sawing timber at that hour. By the time anyone notices that we're gone, we'll be at the native village."

No matter how hard he tried to come up with something, anything to mislead his captors—a plan, an idea, a false trail—Ake drew a blank. The last thing in the world he wanted to do was to lead this band of cutthroats into a peaceful K'a-nii village. But it appeared he had no choice.

"This is a wild goose chase, you know," Ake said to Lynch.

"No, I don't know that," replied Lynch.

"A treasure . . . hidden deep in the jungle," said Ake with scorn dripping from the words. "Don't you realize how crazy that sounds?"

"Maybe it does," Lynch said serenely. "But I have proof that the treasure exists."

"Proof?"

"I have a map that one of the first people to set foot on this planet made. After he got too drunk to know better, he showed it to someone in a bar." Lynch's eyes glittered. "It was one of the last things he did before I killed him."

"Jesus and Mohammed!" exclaimed Ake. "Just give me a hundred credits and drop me into any spacer bar in the galaxy and I'll come up with a dozen phony maps for you."

"That's the catch, isn't it?" asked Lynch. "You gotta know when you have your hands on a real one, don't you?"

"And what makes you think this is a real one?"

"The man who drew it didn't die right away," Lynch confided. "A nerve whip has a wonderful way of getting the truth out of a person."

"Could be he knew he wasn't coming out of that situation alive no matter what he did," argued Ake. "So he produced a nice big turd for you, all gift-wrapped and everything."

"Maybe, maybe not," said Lynch.

They reached the point man's position. Waiting patiently for them to catch up, he asked Ake, "Now which way?"

Ake raised his arm. "Down there."

"Is it far yet?" asked Lynch.

"Just another couple of klicks."

"Good."

Tattered curtains of fog hung eerily from the trees as the group approached the K'a-nii village and the jungle became alive. Their arrival was no secret to the natives, who had come out of their huts to silently observe the approach of the humans.

"These guys have any weapons?" Lynch asked Ake.

"Nothing to speak of—short spears, knives, blow guns. Certainly nothing to trouble anyone with an energy rifle."

"That's what I want to hear," said Lynch.

They halted at the edge of the village. Lynch pulled thoughtfully at the gem he wore in his left ear. "This buddy of yours who has been studying these buggers; did he send his findings to the consortium's computer?"

"Yes, I believe so."

"Good," Lynch said. "I was counting on that. That's why I brought this along." He made a 'come here' gesture and one of his flunkies approached him and gave him a small comlink. "Since I don't speak the natives' language, the computer is going to have to translate for me."

Ake stared at the comlink dumbly and then said, "Without Ray's access code, that's not going to do you any good."

"So what's the code?"

When Ake just stared stubbornly at him, Lynch sighed and said, "Okay. You pick out the person I kill first."

"Suck my dick! All right, you win," Ake said dejectedly. " 'Anson-Chiron-Pandora.' "

"You wouldn't shit me, would you, Doc?"

"Just try the goddamn code."

Lynch did. "Access to file 'K'a-nii-stroke-Larkin-stroke-Prime' is granted."

"Hey, thanks, Doc," said Lynch. "Now let's go talk to the big chief."

# 14

The floater gently set down on top of the administration building in predawn darkness already challenged by the sunrise that was inexorably making its way toward them. The hatch cracked open and the barrel of Ray's energy rifle emerged from the hatchway. He proceeded to sweep the roof with a medium beam of energy.

"No one," Ray said. Anyone there would have felt himself go numb and then would have lapsed into a state of unconsciousness, his nervous system trying to cope with the electrochemical agitation caused by the stunner's charge. Ray and Maria led their respective teams out of the floater and onto the roof.

Frodo trotted to the edge of the roof and looked down, peering into the jungle. "Hey, there somethin' goin' on down there," he said.

Ray half ran, half walked over and followed Frodo's gaze. "Where? I don't see anything."

Frodo looked again. "Geez, there *was* someone there, goin' into the jungle."

"If so, they're gone now."

"Bastet, Marisol, Penelope, Hypatia, and Sibella," Maria called softly. Then she had an idea. (*Come here, please.*)

The cats meandered over obediently and looked up into her face expectantly. (*Yes, Maria*?) asked Bastet.

"I'll speak aloud for now," said Maria as Ray joined her side.

*(The dogs will appreciate that,)* Ray directed at her. *(As for me, I'm on your wavelength . . . girls.)*

Penelope bared her fangs at him, but with access to her emotional aura, Ray knew that she wasn't really pissed off at him, just giving him a cat's good-natured version of the finger.

"What's goin on?" asked a confused Gawain.

"Oh, they is jes' talkin' to each other in their heads, I think," said Beowulf.

"Give that dog a bone," Ray said. "Yeah, like I said when we discussed my plan, this mind-reading ability is really going to help us take this building back and free the hostages. It's . . ."

Ray and Maria exchanged odd looks. Ray ran over to the edge of the roof, pulled out his binoculars, and scanned the jungle. "Sonofabitch!"

"What's goin' on?" Beowulf asked.

Maria stroked Beowulf's big shaggy head and said, "We just sensed a . . . an absence; Ake's not in the building any longer."

"That's a pisser!" said Ray angrily. "But we came here to do a job, so let's get on with it."

Ray passed a small pizeoelectric device over the lock mechanism on the door, and the door swung open invitingly. "Wow," said Gawain.

"Come on, come on," Maria said impatiently, glancing at her watch and at a small egg-shaped crystal she held in her hand. "It's gonna be full light in ten minutes." After another full minute had passed, the crystal finally did what Maria was waiting for—it glowed amber. "That's it," Maria said. "They begin their attack in exactly four minutes."

Bastet and Hypatia looked through the doorway at the stairs disappearing into the gloom. "Think it be booby-trapped?" asked Bastet. Hypatia shrugged. The two cats ran lightly down the steps. Ray, Beowulf, Frodo, and Littlejohn followed, with Maria and the rest of the cats and dogs bringing up the rear.

*(There's three of them just around the corner,)* Hypatia communicated to Ray.

*(Yeah, I sense them, too,)* Ray thought. It was odd: Ray knew he wasn't literally "seeing" out of any of the three sentries' eyes, but he nonetheless was receiving a complete mental picture of the room they were in. Ray theorized that what he was getting was a composite projection of their recent memories of their surroundings.

*(Something like that,)* Maria told him.

(*Hey, don't do that!*) Ray exclaimed. (*No unauthorized mind reading, if you please.*)

Ray positioned the dogs with hand signals, the subtle movements of his fingers not only telling them where to station themselves, but also how many guards were in the next room and where they were.

The dogs thought all this was the next thing to black magic, but they were willing to accept any advantage Ray's newfound mental powers might provide them.

(*There's only three of them; I'll take two and Beowulf can take care of the third,*) Ray told Maria.

(*The hell with that!*) said Maria, but not in time.

Energy rifle leveled, Ray stepped around the corner and unleashed two silent but lethal bolts. The first sentry just crumpled to the floor like a scarecrow held by the back of his straw-stuffed shirt and then dropped. The second man, seemingly surprised to find himself suddenly dead, still leaned against one of the walls, a coffee cup in his hand, a happy stick in his mouth—and a small black-edged hole between his eyes. The coffee cup fell to the floor and the dead man slowly started to slide down the wall as his feet skidded out from under him. Smoke streamed out of his nostrils, making him look like an angry cartoon bull.

The third man, who'd been dozing on a cot, was aroused to full consciousness less by the noise than by the whirl of activity Ray and the dogs brought to the small room. He fumbled for an energy pistol but Beowulf seized him by the throat and shook the man like a rag doll until he stopped struggling.

"Ray and Beowulf got all three of 'em!" exulted Gawain.

"Sh-h-h-h!" everyone hissed at once, making it sound like a steam pipe had just burst.

"Sorry!" said Gawain, a little less loudly but with enough volume still to make Ray wince. His fingers flashed a furious rebuke and Gawain hung his head in shame.

Ray felt Gawain's anguish and regret, but there was no room in a scout dog team for anyone's feelings when it came to completing a mission successfully.

(*Hey, boulder balls! I've got a rifle, too, you know!*) Maria "transmitted" at him furiously.

(*Okay, the next ones we'll . . .*)

They could hear the sounds of an attack: energy rifles, slug throwers, and the low-pitched *whomp* of concussion grenades. "I almost forgot," Maria said softly, glancing at her watch. "The others are mounting the frontal assault on the building now."

"Let's move it," Ray said.

★ ★ ★

The retaking of the administration building proved to be no stroll in the sun, but it was accomplished with the loss of very few lives on the part of the attacking Programmers or the Programmer hostages. The assault by the Programmers from the *Pequod* had the advantage of superior numbers.

The simultaneous attack from above by Ray, Maria, and the dogs linked the element of surprise to their enhanced psi abilities. Their "magic" enabled them to sense the location of the prisoners and to effortlessly counter their defensive moves. The prisoners who survived the scout teams' laser-quick descent from the roof later commented that it seemed as if the attackers were reading their minds. Even later they realized that was precisely what had happened.

Despite the criminals' threat to kill the hostages if attacked, it proved to be without substance. None of the surviving Programmers or base personnel were summarily executed, not a one. As Thane Wyda put it when she was freed, "When they saw that their fight was hopeless, they realized that killing us would have given our people an excuse to respond in kind. They're criminals, not idiots or fanatics; they chose life over death."

"Where is Ake?" Ray asked Wyda anxiously. "We know he's no longer in the compound." When Wyda looked at him questioningly, he added, "We sensed his absence."

"They took him with them," Wyda explained. "They also took Bukovsky and several others as well."

"Took them?" said Ray. "Where?"

"To the K'a-nii village."

"But why?" asked Maria.

Wyda shook her head hopelessly. "For the treasure of the K'a-nii."

"The treasure of the K'a-nii!" Ray exclaimed incredulously. "Their *treasure*?"

"It sounds crazy, I know," Wyda said. "But in the prison a rumor circulated about this vast treasure trove of the K'a-nii. Apparently it's supposed to consist of offerings to their gods, a generations-old tradition that has resulted in a fortune in gems beyond belief."

"It's beyond belief, all right," muttered Ray. "Offerings to the gods, eh? The fucking K'a-nii don't *have* gods as far as I've been able to tell. Who would believe such a fairy tale?"

"The murdering sons-of-bitches who took Ake and Colonel Bukovsky," said Wyda simply. Ray looked at her stern, almost "Old Testament" countenance, and decided that the leader of the prisoners, this madman Lynch, had already made a grievous error: He had allowed Wyda to live. Ray didn't doubt that the fury of her vengeance would scorch the flesh from Lynch's bones if the opportunity arose.

"She's right," said Maria. "This 'treasure of the K'a-nii' horseshit doesn't have to be true; people only have to *think* that it's true."

"Let's go," said Ray.

"You're going after them?" asked Wyda.

"What do you think?" Ray said grimly, clicking a new energy pack into place.

## II

Nothing seemed to faze Lynch, Ake thought. When it became evident that there was no "big chief" or witch doctor or shaman in charge of the K'a-nii community, Lynch simply plunged ahead as the computer did its best to translate the complex and many-layered K'a-nii speech patterns. The computer had made great progress since the early days of Ray's first visits to the village, but there was still much it didn't know about the K'a-niis' language.

No matter how hard the computer tried, no matter how many variations on the word or similar words it came up with, the K'a-nii simply could not make heads nor tails of the idea of "treasure." Finally, the computer admitted that its efforts in that area were stymied.

"Are these peckerheads really this stupid, or are they so smart they're holding out on me?" Lynch mused out loud.

"Can't you get it through your thick skull that they lack word or concept structures that either linguistically or mentally encompass the idea of a fortune?" asked Ake. "Look around you, Lynch. These people live a dirt-poor, dirt-dull life—by our standards if not their own. A heaping pile of those monkey nuts they chow down on might possibly translate into an image of wealth, but I tend to doubt it."

"Maybe this Ake guy is right," suggested one of Lynch's braver lieutenants. When a frigid look blasted him, he mumbled, "Or maybe not."

Lynch looked at his compatriot again, this time with speculation instead of icy dismissal in his eyes. "You brought it with you, didn't you?" When the man nodded, Lynch said, "Get it out."

Ake watched with great interest as Lynch's man unshouldered the pack he wore and withdrew an immense ruby from its interior. As the ruby flashed in the bright white sunlight, reflecting incarnadine rays that dazzled and delighted the onlookers, Ake heard a strange sound coming from the assembled K'a-nii.

"What are they doing?" asked Bukovsky nervously.

"I'm not sure," replied Ake.

The K'a-nii were emitting a disturbing and oddly threatening sound that Ake could only compare to the sound a feral cat makes when it sees a possible avian victim but finds its instinct to kill frustrated by circumstances. Like Terran cats, the K'a-niis' teeth chattered in a tetanic frenzy intended to rend whatever was held between them into small bits.

"Well, Lynch, it looks like you finally got their attention."

Lynch laughed nervously. "Hah, yeah, Doc. Can't argue with you on that one."

One of the K'a-nii slowly walked toward Lynch's flunky. Holding the ruby in the center of his open palm and clearly terrified that he might make a wrong move, the man looked up at his confederates like an animal held fast in a leg trap. Stunned into immobility, he stood as still as he could, but he was unable to stop himself from shaking.

The K'a-nii halted about a meter away from the man, its gaze intent upon the ruby. "Dhnass elo sahm Dorusss," the native hissed, his tongue flicking in and out of his mouth.

Lynch touched the butt of his energy pistol for reassurance and then said, "Okay, Dak, hand it over to me."

"You can have it," the man said gratefully. He handed Lynch the ruby and then backed away.

Looking at the stone in his hand, Lynch asked the comlink, "Did you make any sense of that little speech?"

"A little," the computer replied. " 'Dorusss' seems to be their word for ruby." Ake laughed to himself: Despite whatever other difficulties with the K'a-nii language the computer might have, it certainly had no problems stating the obvious.

Lynch held the ruby out toward the K'a-nii native. "Dorusss?" he asked.

"Gezsss."

Lynch didn't need the computer to translate that for him. "Now we're getting somewhere," he said. "Ask it if there is a place where there are a lot of the rubies," he told the computer. The computer translated Lynch's Federation-standard English into K'a-nii. In response, the native made a lot of hissing and clicking sounds.

"Well?"

The computer considered for a half-second, then replied, "It says there is a place—a cave, I believe—where there are many such stones."

"How many?"

"I'm not sure," the computer admitted. "But the words imply that the number is analogous to the number of bright lights in the night sky."

"The stars . . ." said Ake softly, almost to himself. He looked up, considering. In this part of the galaxy, the local clusters and systems were beyond counting when viewed from the pristine night sky of Hephaestus with the naked eye.

"Jesus!" Lynch said softly. He rolled the roseate stone in his hand, hefting it and estimating its weight to be something under half a kilogram. That was roughly . . . two thousand carats.

"What are these stones bringing these days?" Lynch asked Ake.

Ake looked at Bukovsky and then at Lynch. "Something on the order of a hundred thousand dollars a carat, I believe."

Lynch reacted as if the ruby was a hot coal and not a gemstone, almost dropping it. "That's . . . that's two hundred million credits." His eyes glittered. "As many Rostoff rubies as there are stars in the sky . . ."

"That many would tend to bring the market price down a tad, I imagine," Ake said dryly.

Lynch licked his lips and looked around the village. The assembled K'a-nii stood passively, as they had stood throughout the computer's interrogation, no longer making that unnerving sound. "Everybody . . . get ready. If you got your safety on, click it off."

"Now what?" asked Ake irritably.

"Shut up," said Lynch. He crossed the two meters separating him from Ake and crashed his fist into Ake's jaw, knocking him to the ground. Ake lay motionless, unconscious as a result of the unexpected sucker punch.

"You sonofabitch!" shouted Colonel Bukovsky. "You have about as much guts as—" In response to a gesture from Lynch, one of his men cracked Bukovsky across the back of her skull with the barrel of his rifle. She joined Ake in lying unconscious on the ground.

"I let 'em live and the whore calls me a sonofabitch," said Lynch. "That's gratitude for you."

"What now, Waldo?" one of his men asked.

"Now we grab a couple of these walking suitcases and persuade them to take us to this cave."

"What about the map?"

"It might not be enough, dickbrain!" said another. "Waldo's right—we need a coupla guides just in case the map ain't specific enough."

Lynch paused, seized by an idea. "Before we grab two of these dinks, let's have the computer ask them one last question. They might not be so eager to volunteer stuff once we've snatched a couple of them."

Lynch directed the computer to translate a query concerning the general direction the cave lay in and its distance from the village. "The native says the cave is one or two days travel to the river below and then another several days through the bush once the river is crossed," the computer told him.

"Good," said Lynch. "Now, let's snatch frog boy here and another one for insurance and hit the fuckin' trail."

Several of the K'a-nii made that strange chattering noise, unnerving everyone, but they made no attempt to resist or interfere with Lynch or his men's actions. Even the two natives the prisoners seized and then prodded with their rifles seemed unwilling to contest their kidnaping.

"Pussies," scoffed Lynch. "If they ever open up this jerkwater planet for colonization, the colonists will wipe these limp dicks out in about a month or two."

As they left the village with their unresisting hostage/guides, they could hear the remaining K'a-nii chanting something.

It was "K'a-nii K'a-yass."

"What the hell does 'Kay-nee Kay-yass' mean?" Lynch asked the computer.

"I don't know," the computer lied.

The computer didn't actually lie; its words came in response to the automatic activation of a data-defense bug Ray had hidden deep inside his K'a-nii research files.

# III

They stopped several klicks from the village and Ray pulled out his comlink.

"Whatja doin', Ray?" Tajil asked.

"I've no doubt that these BB-balled jerks have a comlink of their own, so I want to see what they may have learned from the computer. Access to my files is restricted by a code, but Ake knows what I used."

"Oh."

"Good morning, computer," Ray said.

"Good morning, Ray."

"Has access to security file 'K'a-nii-stroke-Larkin-stroke-Prime' been permitted to anyone other than myself?"

"Yes."

"They had the code, then?"

"*Please*," the computer said. "You know they did or I would not have allowed them access to the files."

"Sorry. Just double-checking," Ray said.

"Apology accepted," the computer said magnanimously.

"What use did the others make of that access?"

"They asked me to translate for them on the basis of the rough and incomplete dictionary of K'a-nii words and phrases that I have been able to compile," the computer told Ray.

"In what direction did their interest lie?"

"They wished me to ask the natives about 'treasure.' Unfortunately, there exists no exact parallel word in their language, at least none that I have discovered so far."

"Did their inquiries force you to activate any defensive shunts?"

"One."

Ray felt his insides twist. He licked his dry lips and asked, "What was the activating mechanism?"

"They asked for a translation of K'a-nii K'a-yass."

"Jesus H. Nixon!"

A guttural Siamese cry escaped from Hypatia. The other cats' fur rose involuntarily, and in her mind's eye Maria saw a solitary figure splashing into a seething cauldron of lava. She blinked and the image was gone.

Ray started to shake violently, a human violin string vibrating in sympathetic frequency to a powerful harmonic wave emanating from an irresistible source. He went rigid and started to pitch forward onto his face.

"My God, Ray!" Maria said, catching him in her arms and breaking his fall. Unable to overcome his momentum totally, she lowered him to the ground and looked around frantically as Ray convulsed. She grabbed a leather strap and thrust it between Ray's teeth to keep him from biting or swallowing his tongue. His eyes rolled back in his head and his muscles spasmed uncontrollably.

"What's goin' on?" asked a horrified Beowulf.

"I . . . I don't know," Maria said through gritted teeth.

Hypatia was also affected by the unexplained malady, but much less so than Ray. She appeared to have fallen asleep and been overcome by a realistic and disturbing nightmare that caused her to hiss and snarl in response to some unknown threat.

Suddenly, Ray went limp. For an instant, Maria thought the worst, but she could feel his chest rise and fall slowly. Cradling Ray's head in her lap, Maria gently stroked his fevered brow and said, "It's okay now, Ray. Everything's okay."

Uncertain what had triggered this alarming episode, but with an obvious starting point, Maria picked up the comlink and asked, "Computer, what does 'K'a-nii K'a-yass' mean?"

Still inhibited by the defensive shunt, the computer said blandly, "I don't know."

"K'a-nii K'a-yass," Ray said in his restless sleep. "Ake . . . K'a-nii K'a-yass."

Maria calmed herself, centered her energies and her being, and established a mental link with Ray's mind. She was drawn in instantly with such force it was as if a thousand tiny hooks had pierced her flesh and, connected to a winch deep inside Ray's mind, were irresistibly pulling her inside.

She seemed to pass through a portal of sorts and found her detached mental self projected onto the slopes of a Hephaestusian volcano. Standing in front of her, as if he was intended to be her guide, was Ray. He wore a large bell around his neck and Hypatia crouched on his right shoulder.

Seeing Maria's gaze resting on the bell, Ray spoke. "My Judas bell," he said. He pointed down the slope, behind them. "I lead and they follow." He thrust a finger in Maria's direction. "You follow as well."

Below her, further down the slope, was a strange procession consisting of two groups of ten robed and hooded figures. In the first of the groups, the ten cowled climbers of the volcano each seemed to be the same size. In the second group, one of the mysterious figures was clearly taller than the other nine.

Maria turned to find Ray already climbing the volcano slope. She hastened to catch up.

The double pilgrimage following them ended when Ray and Maria reached the lip of the volcano; they stood aside as the others arrived at the top. The ten wayfarers of the first group threw off their cloaks, and at first Maria thought they were children. In fact, she was absolutely certain that they were thin-limbed and somber-countenanced children until one of them turned to look back at her. Then, before her eyes, the figure of the child blurred and scintillated like diamond dust in a whirlwind and was transformed into a K'a-nii native. She looked at the others and saw that they too were now K'a-nii natives.

The one she'd thought was a solemn child allowed—in some indefinable way *encouraged*—the others to pick him/her/it up and to throw him out and into the throat of the volcano.

Unlike Ray's observance of the ritual, Maria intently watched as the native slowly and unresistingly tumbled through the air and into the waiting lava. The intensely hot lava vaporized the moisture in the K'a-nii's body and clouds of steam burst from the lava's surface.

Clouds of steam . . . and something else.

Something elusive, some will-o-the-wisp manifestation which was half insubstantial and half corporeal, seemed to issue from the roiling lava. Maria stared and stared until she was certain that whatever it was was now gone.

Maria looked questioningly at Ray and Hypatia—who did not return her gaze. Instead, they were staring over her shoulder.

Turning slowly, Maria could feel the hairs on her neck rise raggedly in anticipation. As she completed her revolution, she confronted an unearthly apparition. A tall, thin creature, shimmering faintly and elusively, stood evaluating her gravely. No, that wasn't right—what came from the being was a sense of fulfillment, of great happiness, of completion.

"The K'a-nii?" she asked Ray.

Ray's figure simply nodded assent.

The second group of pilgrims now decowled and Maria noted with a shock of recognition that the oddly out-of-place figure she'd observed earlier was Ake Ringgren.

As did the other nine, the K'a-nii pilgrims picked up the ritual's chosen one and prepared to hurl him into the awaiting volcano. Unlike the K'a-nii native, however, Ake both resisted their efforts and screamed for help. "Please!" he shouted. "I can't swim! Don't throw me in!"

They paid him no attention. And, like human parents lovingly putting their child to bed, threw him into the volcano.

Maria tried to turn away, but Ray said, "Watch," and she found herself unable to resist his command.

Like a heaven-seeking hawk shot out of the sky, Ake fluttered and turned all the way down. Finally, when it seemed as if he'd been tumbling toward his fate for hours, he plunged into the waiting lava.

The result was much the same as before. But with one crucial difference. No evanescent manifestation of Ake's core of being emerged from the lava.

Maria looked at Ray. "The K'a-nii are transformed, aren't they? They're released to another level of being?"

Ray nodded.

"But Ake . . . Ake's not a K'a-nii."

Again Ray nodded.

Maria looked around. "This is not real," she said. "It's some kind of dream. But it could happen, couldn't it?"

When Ray remained silent, she shrieked at him, "Answer me, goddamnit! I'm right, aren't I?"

"Gezsss," Ray said, his mouth opening impossibly wide like a snake's. A tripartite tongue slithered out at her.

Maria shrieked and backed away. She felt the soil collapse under her feet and she fell into the volcano's throat.

She didn't scream. And when the fiery lava terminated her fall, she welcomed the oblivion that it brought with it.

# 15

The realism of her fiery demise had left Maria shaken. When she finally awoke, she looked up to see Ray staring at her with concern in his eyes.

"Are you all right?" Ray asked.

"Hey, that's 'sposed to be my question," she slurred through numb lips which felt as fat as jelly rolls to her.

"Well, you went under just as I was coming out of it," Ray said, as if that explained anything.

"What happened?" Maria asked. "What happened to you and Hypatia, and then what happened to me?"

"I had a . . . a vision, I guess you could call it," said Ray. "That or a premonition."

"About Ake?"

"Gezsss," he said without realizing it, and Maria shrank back.

"What's the matter?" Ray asked, leaning toward her.

Maria did her best not to try to pull away further. "Sorry, but *my* dream, my vision, when I linked minds with you, was quite vivid as well."

"You saw the kay-nees being thrown into the volcano in your dream?" Hypatia asked, already knowing what Maria would answer.

"Yes," Maria said. "It was horrible."

"And Ake?" Maria just nodded.

"The K'a-nii don't die when they're thrown into the volcano, do they?" said Maria softly. It wasn't really a question.

"In a way they do," said Hypatia.

"The lava liberates them from their old bodies," Ray said. He cocked his head at Maria. "But you already know that, because you saw it happen—in the vision."

Maria returned Ray's evaluative glance, looking deep into his eyes, her senses telling her that he had learned something. "What is it, Ray?"

"Huh?"

"What is it you know but are reluctant to tell me?"

"It's Ake," Ray said finally. "He's been moved again."

"By whom?"

"The K'a-nii."

"The K'a-nii?" It was not the answer she expected; of course, she no longer knew what answer to expect. "Why?"

"Because the prisoners took two of the K'a-nii as hostages/guides to lead them to the K'a-nii treasure cave. Unfortunately, their leader—that crazy-like-a-fox Lynch—just happened to seize two K'a-nii intended to undergo the K'a-nii K'a-yass ritual in less than two weeks." Ray rubbed his face with his hand. "I guess they're gonna miss their date with the volcano."

"What will happen to them?" asked Maria.

"I don't know," Ray admitted. "Perhaps nothing. Perhaps they will have simply missed the first of several opportunities to be transmogrified. But the ritual itself *must* occur."

"You mean . . . ?"

"Yes," Ray said. "If the two guides are not returned in time for the fulfillment of the ceremony, their places will be taken by surrogates."

"Surrogates?"

"The K'a-nii will perform the transformation ceremony with Ake and Bukovsky. They've taken them away and hidden them somewhere in the jungle."

"But they're not natives," protested Maria, remembering the horrifying sight of Ake endlessly tumbling until he fell into the lava. "The ritual will . . ."

"Yes," Ray finished for her. "It will kill them."

"Ake told you he can't swim," said Maria softly.

"Huh? How did you know that?" asked Ray. He looked shocked, then he realized Maria wasn't referring to his original dream but to the vision she'd shared with him.

She pulled him close and kissed him. When their lips parted and she pulled back, she said, "I was part of you for a few moments, Ray—a few moments and an eternity."

Ray put a finger to his lips, wonderingly.

"Geez, Ray, who tole you all this stuff?" asked Beowulf, bewildered by the mad pace of recent events. " 'Bout Ake bein' kidnapped by the kay-nees and all?"

"Isn't it obvious?" Ray asked. "Ake did."

"Ake," said Beowulf, confused. "When this happen?"

"When I had my . . ." Ray looked embarrassed. "My 'fit.' "

If Sari Fodoor was surprised to hear that Ray and Maria already knew about Ake's abduction, she did a good job of hiding it. Instead, she acted as if their awareness of Ake's predicament was a perfectly natural thing.

"How long have they been gone?" Ray asked her.

"They must have left here about . . . oh . . . noon," Fodoor told Ray and Maria, glancing at the late-afternoon sun.

Ray flicked beads of sweat from his eyelids and stared into the jungle. "What about Ake? How did it happen?"

"The remaining K'a-nii did not move or react for a very long time after Lynch left," Fodoor said, remembering. "You know, it was the strangest thing: As I leaned over Ake and the colonel to check on their condition, I had the weirdest feeling that someone was leaning over *me* at the same time. I looked behind me, but there was no one there." She laughed uneasily. "The feeling was so . . . *peculiar*."

"It was then that the K'a-nii acted, didn't they?" asked Ray knowingly.

"Now that you mention it, yes," Fodoor agreed. "Without a word being said, they gathered around Ake and the colonel and just stared at them. It was kinda creepy; it was as if they were *willing* them to stand up."

"And that's when they took them away?" asked Maria, stroking Hypatia.

"Yeah," confirmed Fodoor. "But it wasn't like that. I mean, they didn't *take* them away—Dr. Ringgren and Colonel Bukovsky seemed to go voluntarily."

"We go after them, Ray?" Beowulf asked.

Ray shook his head. "No. We'd have a better chance of finding one specific graviton in the oceans of Cousteau."

"What *are* we gonna do?" asked Penelope, her Siamese-blue eyes wide with curiosity.

Ray glanced at the dogs—who looked back eagerly. "Beowulf thinks a little hike through the jungle would be fun. I agree."

"You mean . . . ?"

"Of course," Ray said. "I'm going after the prisoners and their K'a-nii hostages. It's the only way to free Ake."

"Him and them dogs not goin' alone, are they?" Bastet asked Maria, staring up at her leader's face with a fierce look in her eyes.

"No," Maria said. "They're not."

★ ★ ★

By mid-morning, they had covered fewer than ten klicks. "Holy jumping jackshit!" Ray exclaimed. "At this rate, we'll be lucky to get to the river before the universe stops expanding."

"Ah-h-h, we not doin' so bad," Gawain said, panting from the exertion of carrying a full pack of supplies on his broad, strong back. Only Beowulf, Frodo, and Ozma were not similarly burdened.

"I agree with Gawain," said Maria, stopping to swipe the back of her arm over her forehead. "It's a rain forest, for goodness' sake. There are no people movers, and the only trail is the one we make." Her black hair was now cut extremely short, the result of five minutes in front of a mirror with a pair of scissors; she called it her jungle cut.

"And Leonardo finds the easiest way through the grass and stuff," added Beowulf.

It was Ray who'd begun calling their K'a-nii guide Leonardo. "Why you want to call him Leonardo?" Littlejohn asked.

"In honor of the great Old-Earth artist and inventor," Ray explained. But he had a twinkle in his eye when he said it, so the dogs suspected that he really had another Leonardo in mind.

His/her/its name was not Leonardo, of course, but everyone went along with Ray's nickname for the K'a-nii native rather than attempting to use his actual name. As Frodo put it, "Sayin' his real name sounds like Ray clearin' his throat and makin' lip-fartin' noises at the same time."

Ray nodded. "Expressive primate lips do come in handy, sometimes."

Maria had laughed at Frodo's crude but accurate description of the sound. "Oh, Frodo, you're awful!"

"Not as awful as Leonardo's real name," Frodo had said.

Ray and the others waited for Leonardo to return from his foray into the jungle immediately ahead of them. The first few times he'd spoken to them, the dogs couldn't stop guffawing—unable to get Frodo's description of the native's speech patterns out of their minds.

Maria scanned the ceiling of the rain forest, barely able to see the sky through the canopy of leaves. After taking a sip of water from her canteen, she resealed it and said, "I still wish you had allowed Wyda to provide us with floaters so we could reach the other side of the river ahead of Lynch and the others. I mean, why walk *through* a jungle and to a river when you can float over them both in comfort and safety?"

"I agree that it seems foolish to hack your way through klicks and klicks of bush when there appears to be an alternative, but Leonardo and the other K'a-nii were adamantly opposed to us using any of the floaters."

"Maybe it some kind of no-no; a taboo," suggested Marisol.

"It no taboo," replied Hypatia simply.

"Oh, yeah?" said Beowulf. "How *you* know so much?"

"Yes," joined in Maria, more than a little jealous of Hypatia's new intimacy with Ray and the increased empathy both of them shared with each other and with the K'a-nii. "How do you know that about the floaters?"

"I don't know how I know," said Hypatia, clearly confused. "I just know that I know."

"Great," said Maria. Looking at Ray, she queried, "And if I ask you, I'll get the same damned frustrating response, won't I?"

"Not at all," Ray said. "Ake told me."

"Ake told you, huh?" Maria said. "Mohammed's cat, if Ake and you are so damn close, why can't he just tell you where they're holding him so we can rescue him, and the hell with Lynch and the Treasure of Ali Baba!!"

"Is that a question?" Ray said mildly. When Maria began turning purple, he said, "Ake doesn't know where he is—not exactly. Besides, I think the K'a-nii are using him to communicate to us . . . up to a point."

"Meaning?"

"Meaning they aren't going to let him tell us where he and Bukovsky are being kept, but they are willing to have him provide us with limited help."

"How Ake helpin' us, Ray?" asked Beowulf.

"For starters, he told me to accept the K'a-nii's word about trying to use the floaters. He said to do so would result in something . . ." Ray searched for the proper word. "Something, ah . . . *unpleasant* happening."

"Mebbe crashing," suggested Beowulf helpfully. "That 'bout as bad as it gets." When several faces turned to stare at him, he added, "Well, *almost* as bad as it gets."

"Are you certain, are you absolutely *sure* you're communicating with Ake?" Maria asked Ray.

"It's Ake, no doubt about it."

"Leonardo is back," Ozma informed everyone.

The K'a-nii had suddenly materialized out of the jungle, carrying his blow gun in one taloned hand and two small rodentlike things in the other. He made a weird whooping sound and then twisted his head from side to side.

"Them kay-nees is wacko," opined Tajil.

"You get no argument there," said Beowulf. The big dog watched as the native gutted one of his prizes with his stone knife and made short work of devouring his prey. That done, he approached Ray and offered him the remaining rodent.

"Thank you, Leonardo," Ray replied formally, the comlink translating for him as he accepted the proffered gift.

"What we 'sposed to do with that?" asked Littlejohn, sniffing it suspiciously.

"First," said Ray, "I'll follow Leonardo's example and gut the little rat thing with my trusty knife." He unsheathed a bush knife that made Leonardo hiss in awe and did just that. "Then I'll pop the carcass into a vac-cube until tonight—at which time I will make a great, and generally empty, show of cooking it and then pretend to eat it."

"You gonna waste good food?" asked Penelope, looking hungrily at the small rodent's eviscerated body.

"If you mousers want it, you can have it," Ray said.

"We'll take it!" said Penelope gleefully.

"So," asked Beowulf impatiently. "What the great hunter see up ahead?"

"I'll ask him," Ray said. The comlink translated Ray's query and Leonardo's response. As best the comlink was able to render the K'a-nii's reply, it seemed that the area they were heading into was more or less typical of the jungle they'd already made their way through. Leonardo had seen nothing extraordinary.

"I wonder what passes for extraordinary in these circumstances?" Ray mused.

"I'm more concerned about the comlink," Maria told him. "Is the signal from the camp going to be able to reach us when we get further and further away? We're going to have a hard time of it without the computer translating for us."

"I've done a decent job of assimilating what the computer already knows," Ray replied. "Of course, as long as we have access to the computer, it's easier to let it do all the hard work."

When Maria looked exasperated and began to open her mouth to complain that he hadn't answered her question, Ray added, "I told Sari Fodoor to have Wyda patch the camp computer through the Programmer ship in stationary orbit above us. That way they can beam the signal down to us from the ship no matter where we are."

"That's a great idea," Maria conceded. Then she stared at Ray, a broad smile flooding out to cover her entire face.

"What?"

"When we transmit back up to them, they can trace the signal and know exactly where we are at any moment!" Her smile retreated as a knowing smirk appeared on Ray's face. "You've thought of that already, haven't you?"

" 'Course he did," said Beowulf proudly.

"And what else?" asked Ray.

" 'What else . . . ?' " Maria looked at him oddly. "Oh-h-h!"

"Yeah," said Ray. "If they can pinpoint our location, they can do the same for Lynch's party."

Bastet looked from Ray's face to Maria's and back again to Ray's. "Hey-y-y," she said. "If'n they can do that, how's come we gots to follow them like this? Is it the floater thing again?"

Ray looked at Leonardo's masklike countenance and nodded. "Yes, but it's also more than that. The area of the planet that we'll be heading into across the river is *different*."

"Different?"

"Some of the ore deposits are so concentrated and massive that they can play hell with navigational systems. As I understand it, a shuttle might be immune to whatever prevents us from using the floaters, but a shuttle is also loaded to the gills with electrical gear which *isn't* immune to the screwy electromagnetic emanations present where we're going. Besides, if something were to happen to Lynch's comlink, we'd be left in the dark."

When Maria saw Hypatia give Ray a look, she asked suspiciously, "Is that really true? Is that the only reason we can't fly there?"

"Yes, everything I said is true," Ray responded, ducking as a squadron of yellow-and-black insects flew by his head in formation. "For better or worse, we're fated to follow Lynch on foot."

Ray hooked a thumb in the native's direction and said, "If it's all right with you, I'll tell Leonardo that we're ready to move out."

"Sure," said Maria. She stared at Ray's back as he followed the K'a-nii's lead. She had the damnedest feeling that while everything Ray told her *was* the truth—she could sense his honesty—he was leaving something important out. But what? That was the rub. When she surreptitiously attempted to read his mind, she came up against an impenetrable barrier. Of course, she was keeping a secret from Ray as well: She could sense that Leonardo was in possession of a very large ruby.

## II

The rain forest was an incredible place, Ray decided. It was both the most beautiful and fragile ecosystem he'd ever encountered while at the same time being as hostile and frustrating as any place could possibly be.

To speak of a jungle "floor" was to speak in misleading terms. There was nothing remotely floorlike about the saw grass and vine-choked terrain. There were stumpy plants that the dogs quickly dubbed "knife bushes" because of their sharp-edged leaves. To brush against one meant coming away with a wound as smooth and straight as a laser beam—a gash that would be as slow to heal as a small paper cut because its perfect edges wouldn't mesh well enough to begin the knitting-together process.

Creepers and other vines cluttered the rotting vegetation that carpeted the jungle, entering and erupting from the soil like rope through sailcloth or a sea serpent's long spine undulating above and below the emerald waves of the ocean.

Exotic birds of all types flitted from tree to tree, calling to mates and to members of their flocks, singing their songs of life in the air. Ray had also seen large beaked birds that he took to be the local versions of parrots and macaws. The din they produced was incredible; raucous and piercing, their cries and whistles were a constant background noise.

Beowulf saw him staring into the tree tops and said, "Them birds is sumptin', huh?" He was speaking primarily about their loud social intercourse.

"They're wonderful," Ray agreed, but mistaking the source of Beowulf's wonderment. "Their colors are from a palette unlike any I've seen before."

"Yeah," Beowulf said, unappreciative of the birds' rainbow hues because of his canine color-blindedness. "Jes' 'member what the computer said when you asked it about snakes and spiders and keep your eyes on the ground, too."

"What's Beowulf saying?" asked Maria, coming over to them.

"He was just reminding me to watch out for poisonous ground dwellers instead of oohing and ahhing about the abundant bird life."

"Even Leonardo, 'cording to that smartass computer Ray talks to through the comlink, is scared of some of the things that lives here," Beowulf reminded Maria—who just gulped.

"Yeah," Littlejohn said. "And don't forget that spider that looks like a puffball with legs and . . ."

"Ah, I think I've heard enough," said Maria, backing away. "I'm not sure I want to know about all the ways the jungle and its inhabitants can kill me, if you don't mind."

"Maria . . ." began Ray.

"Later."

"No, it's just that—"

At that moment, Maria backed into the large, twisted cobweb dangling from a branch behind her head that Ray was trying to warn her about. When Maria felt the silky substance brush against the side of her face, she screamed loudly and began beating at it with her hands. She shrieked even louder when she touched the dead bat cocooned in the sticky stuff. The cats all looked in her direction with concern in their feline faces.

Ray glanced at Beowulf and shrugged. "I tried to tell her to watch out," he said.

As Maria cursed a blue streak—"My, my," said Ray, "I never would have imagined you knew the meaning of such words, much less knew how to use them so effectively"—Leonardo hurried back to them and unleashed a torrent of sibilant hisses and tongue-twisting vowels and consonants.

"What's he saying?" Ray asked the comlink, somewhat distracted by a sudden influx of both small and large animals crashing through the undergrowth not far from them as if in full flight from a raging fire.

"This is most interesting," the computer's mild voice said from the comlink. "It seems that the native has more than one piece of news for you. First, it says there are two dead 'soft skins' not far from here."

"Soft skins?" questioned Penelope.

"I think he means there are two dead humans nearby," Maria told the cat. "Two of Lynch's gang."

"There is something else," the computer told them. "Something about . . . about . . . soldiers. Yes, the native says that there is an army coming this way."

"An army?"

"I'm extrapolating the word 'army,' " the computer admitted. "I don't think the K'a-nii language contains such a word; I chose the nearest equivalent meaning." Even as the computer spoke, the exodus of jungle creatures intensified.

Leonardo suddenly began to get the hopping jitters and said something to Ray and the comlink. "The native is quite insistent that you follow him immediately," the computer told Ray.

"Let's go, then," Ray said. "We can sort this army business out later."

Even if Leonardo hadn't led them directly to the two dead bodies, Ray was sure that the dogs would have smelled them. *Shit!* he told himself. *Even I would have smelled them!* That was saying something, because the dogs were always chiding Ray for his nearly nonexistent sense of smell. Whenever the dogs got on his back about having no sense of smell—even for a human—Ray kidded them that it was a blessing since he had to live with nine members of the Bath-of-the-Month Club.

The sources of the sickening sweet smell that permeated the air, the two dead bodies, were lying face up. A large scavenger beetle emerged from one eyeless socket—a vivid explanation of what had happened. But it wasn't the dead men's eyeless sockets that made everyone's skin crawl; it was the stupid grins on their faces.

"What killed 'em that made 'em so happy at the same time?" asked Frodo, unsure what to make of their awful rictus.

"I dunno," admitted Ray. "Let's see what Leonardo has to say about this." Through the computer, Ray asked the K'a-nii if he knew what had caused the men's deaths.

The computer absorbed Leonardo's reply and began translating for Ray. "No, that's all right," Ray told the computer. "I got most of that myself." He looked at Frodo and said, "It was a snake."

Beowulf cocked his head trying to remember something. "Was it that one that looks like a peppermint stick?"

"Yes," Ray said, and his brow furrowed as he struggled to

translate what the K'a-nii had called the brightly colored serpent. "Now I've got it," Ray said, snapping his fingers. "It's called the 'two-step snake.' "

"The two-step snake?" said Maria.

"Yah, that's it," recalled Beowulf. "It bites you and you stone cold dead before you take two steps."

"Leonardo exaggerates a lot," Ray told her. "It's probably three steps, not two."

"Oh, that's better," Maria said, pretending to wipe her brow in relief.

Leonardo said something and the computer told them that he was repeating the warning about the "army" coming in their direction.

"Ask him again *what* army he's talking about," Ray ordered the computer. The complink patiently did what Ray directed.

"Nhhgasszz," said Leonardo, pointing with his blow gun.

"Where? What?" queried Maria. "I don't see anything."

Remembering the words the computer had used, Ray again asked Leonardo for the location. "Nhhgasszz!" the native repeated firmly, again pointing in the same direction—the direction from which the flow of wildlife was coming.

"Yes, I see them!" Sibella said, her high-pitched voice filled with excitement.

"See what . . ." began Ray. "Jesus H. Disney! No wonder we didn't see them—we didn't know what we were looking for."

Maria's eyes narrowed as she peered at the jungle floor and she almost did a double-take. "Ants?" she asked.

"Annzzz," affirmed Leonardo, his tongue flicking in and out of his mouth as he mimicked Maria's pronunciation.

"Ants," repeated Frodo. "We supposed to be afraid of ants?"

"Oh, yes," Ray said softly. "Be afraid. Be very afraid."

"But little ants?"

"Look at them," Ray told the big dog. "They're pouring over that log and into that clearing like a brown river of"—he sighed, suddenly aware of the too-perfect analogy that had pushed to the surface of his mind—"lava, devouring anything organic that gets in its path."

Several more examples of the local fauna leapt and hopped past them, frantic to get out of the path of the living river of death. "Now we know what's causing the other inhabitants of the jungle to move their asses out of the area," Ray concluded.

Ray knelt down, located one of the scouts, and picked it up.

The dogs crowded around for a better look at the half-centimeter-long insect Ray cupped in the palm of his hand. "Look at this angry little devil," Ray said as the scout's mandibles clashed in furious frustration.

"That teeny bug is dangerous?" queried Ozma.

"Individually, they're not much," Ray told her. "Of course, a single snowflake isn't much either, just a tiny six-sided crystal. But a sextillion or so of them are an avalanche."

"Yah, I see what Leonardo was warning us about," said Beowulf. "If the main body of the army got between us and split us, we'd never be able to link up again. It would mean a painful death to try to cross even jus' a meter-wide column."

Wonder in her eyes, Bastet leapt into Maria's arms for reassurance. "They eat flesh?" the cat asked.

"Not if'n they can't catch it!" said Frodo, turning nervously in a circle, eager to get far away.

"Everyone keeps sayin' 'army,'" said a confused Gawain. "Why they called an army?"

"Well, they *are* pretty much the same as a human army," Ray told Gawain. "They sent out scouts to see what's ahead, they move in a coherent and organized way across the land, and they leave devastation and bare ground behind them."

Bastet, secure on Beowulf's back, looked down at the ground and said, "The scouts have found the bodies."

"Uh-oh," said Mama-san.

"Ditto," Ray said. "Let's get away from the bodies, but not too far."

"Why not?" asked Maria.

"I want to see what happens," Ray told her. "I want us all to see what happens."

Led to the corpses by the excited scouts, the river of determined reddish-brown soldiers swarmed over the bodies. At first, the bodies seemed to grow larger; then they shrank under the concentrated assault of the army's efficient mandibles. Their chitinous bodies glistening in the late afternoon sun, the ants stripped the dead men's bones bare of flesh, sinew, and cartilage in minutes. The sight was simultaneously fascinating and horrifying.

Leonardo made a half-strangled, half-throat-clearing sound and then turned and walked briskly away.

"I agree," said Ray. "Let's get the hell out of here!"

# 16

"The river is just ahead," the comlink informed them, translating Leonardo's words. Again, Ray found that he understood most of what Leonardo said without the computer's help.

"Good," said Maria, glancing at Hypatia comfortably ensconced on Ray's shoulders. The other cats were also riding instead of walking; they were perched atop less than enthusiastic dogs. The dogs may not have liked the situation, but it was necessary for efficiency's sake that they carry the cats. Hephaestus's jungle had proved an enervating obstacle course for the felines and they eagerly hitchhiked rides on the broad backs of the dogs, sitting regally on top of the food and water and other supplies the dog team carried.

"Gee," said Ray, sneaking a peek at Maria's exhausted face from the corner of his eye. "Maybe we should have taken a floater here instead of walking."

Maria's head lolled toward him. "If I weren't so tired, I'd stick my machete in a place where the sun don't shine and tell you to rotate."

Littlejohn, accustomed to Ray and Maria tossing good-natured barbs back and forth at each other, was focusing his attention elsewhere. "Hey," he said. "Why's the ground gettin' soggy?"

"It is, isn't it?" agreed Ray, kneeling and touching the rain forest's floor with his fingertips. "It must be the fact that we're so near the river."

Maria groaned. "I get it," she said. "First a swamp, then the river. Is nothing about this little trip gonna be easy?"

"If you want easy . . . Jeezus!"

In less than a single stride, Ray had moved from solid ground to an area considerably less supportive. Before he could react, he was up to his knees in a thick, viscous mixture of mud, sand, and water. Maria quickly held out her arms and Hypatia jumped from the carrier on Ray's back to the safety her mistress offered.

"Ray, what—"

"Stay back, Beowulf," Ray told his leader. "Everybody, stay back, please." He stripped off his backpack and tossed it aside.

The dogs were all barking frantically at this threat to their Man, speech forgotten for the moment.

Maria put Hypatia down and hurried over to the pack that Sinbad was carrying. Frantically digging through the contents, she finally found what she was looking for: a twenty-five-meter-long rope made of nearly unbreakable synthetic fibers.

"Hurry!" Mama-san said, watching as Maria sorted through the pack and extracted the rope.

Leonardo looked on with interest but did nothing to help.

As Ray slowly sank into the quicksand, Maria threw one end of the rope to him. "Tie that around yourself, under your arms," she ordered him.

Ray did as she directed. By the time he'd looped the rope around himself several times and made a secure knot, he was almost up to his waist in the sucking, voracious sand and mud.

Maria looked at the overhead canopy and spotted a branch which appeared substantial enough to bear Ray's weight and more. She hefted the end of the rope in her hand, calculating the distance between her and the branch, and wondering how she was ever going to get one end to loop over the branch.

Bastet, seeing where Maria was looking, ran over to her and said, "Give it to me. I can take it up the tree."

"Right," Maria readily agreed.

Maria put the end of the rope in Bastet's mouth and the cat unsheathed her claws and immediately began climbing up the tree trunk, the rope following. Leonardo made an indecipherable sound and then hit his forearm with the palm of his hand. The frustrated dogs danced around, shouting encouragement to the lithe Siamese. Bastet ascended the slender trunk of the tree, the rope held fast between her teeth like a pirate climbing up the mast of a sailing ship with a cutlass clenched between his teeth.

"I'll just wait here," Ray said as the muddy water reached his chest. He didn't feel as cheery and relaxed as his words made him sound, but he wanted to keep a stiff upper lip for the dogs' sakes.

Bastet was halfway up the tree trunk when something green and striped raised up and hissed at her. Startled, the cat lost her grip and slipped from the tree, tumbling toward the ground. Quickly, Tajil got under her and she landed on her feet on his back.

"We don't have time for this nonsense!" shouted Maria, picking up her energy rifle. She targeted the snake and blew its head off with one well-aimed bolt of energy.

"Good shot," said Ray.

Leonardo slapped his chest with both hands and hooted.

Shaken but game, Bastet climbed the tree trunk again. When she reached the designated branch without further incident, she dropped the end of the rope over it. When the weight of the rope began to pull the end back, Bastet quickly clamped onto it again with her teeth. Seeing no other recourse open in the time available to her, Bastet simply leapt over the branch, taking the rope with her.

"Catch her!" shouted Ray unnecessarily.

Maria, backed by Beowulf and Littlejohn, caught Bastet in her arms, cradling her gently.

"The rope," said Beowulf.

After Bastet spit it out, Maria pulled it tight and then tied it around Beowulf's chest. "Go," she said the instant she made sure the knot was secure.

Beowulf lunged forward, straining against the rope. For a second, it appeared as if the big dog's strength would immediately pull Ray up out of the grasp of the quicksand. It didn't. Beowulf eased back a bit and Ray, who'd at least stopped sinking, settled back into the sand and mud's embrace.

"C'mon," said Littlejohn, nudging the massive Gawain as Beowulf renewed his effort.

"Huh?"

Gawain watched Littlejohn run and leap for the taut rope where it rose from Beowulf toward the branch. Maria gasped as Littlejohn's teeth closed on the rope and he dangled there, adding his substantial weight to Beowulf's pulling ability.

"Wow!" exclaimed Gawain appreciatively.

The water and mud made rude noises and Ray began to rise

from it, albeit slowly. Following Littlejohn's lead, Gawain now got up a head of steam, leapt for the rope, and added his mass to the effort.

Gawain's one hundred and forty kilos finally made the difference, and Ray popped from the mud like a cork out of a champagne bottle.

Littlejohn and Gawain let go of the rope and dropped to the ground, halting Ray's sudden upwards motion toward the tree limb and leaving him to dangle in the air, held in place by Beowulf. Ray looked like a giant chocolate popsicle, melting in the hot jungle air, as mud dripped from his legs.

"Okay, Beowulf," Maria ordered. "Start lowering him."

When Ray was just above the quicksand again, Maria reached out, snagged him, and pulled him to solid ground.

"Thanks, everyone," Ray said. "Remind me to throw out all my old *Bomba the Jungle Boy* sinnys; I never want to see quicksand again, even in a holo."

Panting, Beowulf looked at Bastet with new eyes. "Thanks for helping our Man, Bastet," the scout dog leader said. "You pussfaces ain't such bad folks after all."

"Yah," agreed Ozma. "Thanks, Bastet."

Even Leonardo contributed a few hisses and guttural sounds to the conversation.

"What he say?" Maria asked the computer through the comlink as she removed the rope from Beowulf.

"He said to stop fooling around—the river is just ahead."

"Oh."

The rain came down in sheets and lightning lit up the momentarily darkened sky. The travelers took refuge under the limbs and broad branches of a vine-choked tree. It was the third such downpour of the day and there was nothing to do but wait it out. Since the earlier deluges had provided plenty of fresh drinking water, Ray didn't bother to get out his rain water collector, an inverted plastic tent that funneled the rain into an expandable plastic water bag.

"This tree is sure a big help," said Maria, rain streaming down her face.

"Hey," said Ray. "We're gonna get wet, that's in the cards, but we have even less of an idea where we're going in the midst of a downpour like this one. We're safer under this tree."

"If'n lightning don't hit it," whimpered Tajil.

"The chances of that happening are pretty slim, Taddy," Ray told the big red dog. "That mostly happens when you're out in the open and you take refuge under a tree that's the only tall thing around. We have a whole rain forest around us and this tree is far from being the tallest one around."

There was a flash of blue-white light and a tree not thirty meters from them was split down the length of its trunk by a bolt of lightning. The dogs flinched and began barking excitedly. Ray reconsidered his recent pronouncement. "On the other hand, I could be wrong about that business with the lightning," he allowed.

Air thick with the smell of ozone and the metallic taste of an electrical discharge reached their nostrils. As the ruined tree hissed and spit, steam coming from its exposed core, the smell of burnt wood was added to the odors produced by the lightning strike. The cats huddled fearfully around Maria, and the dogs edged in closer to Ray. Leonardo slapped his thighs gleefully and hopped up and down.

Surrounded by nine wet, cowering dogs who smelled like mildewed carpets and five bedraggled cats who looked like drowned possums, Ray remembered the recruiting holo the university had sent him extolling the fun and excitement to be had as the leader of a scout dog team. "What's wrong with this picture?" Ray said softly.

"Hunh?" asked Beowulf.

"Nothing," Ray said. "Just muttering to myself."

"The brain tumor is spreading, eh?" asked Penelope.

Instead of getting angry or defensive, the dogs just chuckled at that. *Good*, Ray thought, *Penelope's taken their minds off the thunder and lightning*.

Almost as swiftly as it had begun, the storm died down and moved on. The sun peeked down through the green ceiling of the rain forest, and the usual sounds of life and death began to override the steady drip, drip, drip of the rain water slowly trickling from the wide spoonlike leaves that had captured it for a few fleeting moments.

"Once again, peace and quiet return to Beaver Valley," intoned Ray.

Maria looked down at her drenched clothing, clinging to and outlining her womanly figure. Ray also took a long look before dropping his eyes.

"Yuck," she said, "I'm soaking wet." She glanced at Ray and

shook her head. "Well, at least the rain washed all that mud and sand off your clothes," she told him.

"Yeah, I'm ready for the spin cycle now," Ray replied. Then he noticed Leonardo standing nearby and leaned over and carefully sniffed the air around the K'a-nii. "We can thank the rain for more than just washing my clothes," Ray told Maria. "Leonardo no longer smells like five-day-old road kill."

Maria looked up at the sun, shading her eyes with her hand. "Not now," she agreed. "But give him a few hours in this heat and humidity and he'll be his old self again."

"Speakin' of smellin'," said Littlejohn, "I can smell the river. It real close now."

Ray and Maria picked up the packs, centered them on the dogs' backs, and cinched the straps tight. That done, they tugged at their handiwork to make sure everything was secure.

"Dogs ready?" asked Bastet.

"We ready," Beowulf said.

"Let's go, then," said Maria.

After a moment's thought, Maria turned to Ray and said, "I have a question."

"Yeah?"

"What are we going to do when we catch up with Lynch and his people?"

"I haven't the slightest idea."

"Oh."

When they saw the river, they all laughed ruefully. When Leonardo told them the river was just ahead, he wasn't exaggerating; they must have been within one klick of the lazy brown expanse of water when the storm hit and temporarily halted their progress.

Gawain and Tajil, who were born on Chiron and then worked their first real job on the arid planet of Talos, both gasped at the sight of the wide body of water. "Geez, how we gonna get 'cross *that*?" asked Gawain.

"Good question," Ray said.

"Thanks," said Gawain proudly.

"What does Leonardo have to say about this minor challenge?" asked Maria.

"Let's see," said Ray, getting out the comlink.

After the computer had translated Ray's query and listened to Leonardo's response, it said, "Hm-m-m. Very interesting: The native says that one way across is to swim—but it advises against that." As the computer spoke, Leonardo pointed at something in the water and made a hissing, gurgling sound.

"Lookit," said Marisol, the pupils of her intensely blue eyes narrowing to slits. "There's a big mossy log with teeth in the water."

"There's another one," Penelope said, her tail pointing.

"Yeah, I see 'em," Ray said. "They look nasty, don't they?"

"So what's the other way across?" Maria asked.

The comlink and Leonardo exchanged hisses and gurgles, and the computer replied, "The K'a'nii use the hollowed-out log boats."

"*What* hollowed-out log boats?"

"The native admits you have a point there," said the computer—continuing to maintain its practice of refusing to call their guide Leonardo. "It says the bad soft skins probably took the boats and used them to cross. After all, they did reach the river before we did."

"Well, that's just great!" said Maria. "Now what do we do?"

The computer asked Leonardo that very question and began translating the K'a'nii's response.

"The native suggests that we summon the river. . . ." The comlink suddenly went silent.

"What's the matter?" asked Maria, noticing that Ray had almost done a double-take. "Computer, please continue."

"Forgive me," said the steady voice of the computer. "The native used a term I thought was alien to them—it said it suggested that we—or it, rather—invoke the assistance of the river god."

Maria looked at Ray. "You said they didn't have gods, didn't you?"

Ray nodded. "That's why I'm not sure I agree with the computer's translation. What Leonardo said could also be translated as 'the great and powerful one who lives in the river.'" He shrugged. "There's one fast and easy way to find out, isn't there?"

"You mean ask the computer to ask Leonardo to go ahead and send for the river god?" said Bastet.

"Why don't *you* ask him to do it, Ray?" suggested Maria. "You seem to be getting pretty damn fluent in his language."

"Well, *excuse* me," Ray said sarcastically. "I'm just a quick study when it comes to languages. Not all of us can get by on our looks."

"Uh-huh," said Maria. "Now ask him."

"Okay." Ray told Leonardo that if he wished to summon this river god to take them all across, then to go ahead.

If Leonardo was surprised by Ray's sudden display of fluency, he didn't show it. Instead, he removed a very large ruby from a leather pouch that hung around his neck. It was nearly the size of the one Lynch had showed off in the K'a-niian village. Ray had "seen" that one when Ake had communicated to him just after he had become a hostage.

"That is one helluva big stone," said Maria, impressed. *Now I understand why I sensed it so strongly*, she thought.

"Let's see what he does with it," Ray said.

What Leonardo did was to find a comfortable spot on the river bank and lower himself into a sitting position. He clasped the ruby in both hands and bowed his head.

"Whoa!" said Ray.

"Yeah, I feel it, too," Maria told him.

"What *is* that?" asked Sibella.

"What's what?" asked a confused Gawain.

Ray, Maria, and the cats were "hearing" a high-pitched keening inside their heads. It seemed to emanate from Leonardo—or from the stone; it was impossible to be sure which.

Suddenly, in response, an incredibly deep, bass note resounded in their minds; it stunned them with its raw power.

"My god!" said Maria.

"No," said Ray. "Leonardo's."

## II

If Ake was not awake, neither was he asleep. Instead, he was in a sort of half-state. In some ways, this was advantageous. Ake's ability to speak any language except Federation-standard English was next to nonexistent, so even had he been fully conscious he would not have been able to communicate verbally with his captors.

Captors. Ake knew that the K'a-nii who had taken him did not think of themselves as captors nor he as a captive. Instead, they envisioned themselves as the liberators of his other self—actually, as the liberators of *one* of his other selves.

When he first became aware of his surroundings—a plain mud hut deep in the rain forest—he slowly realized that it was as an "other" observer. No, that wasn't right. He understood that although his consciousness was now largely outside his body, a part of him, perhaps the most essential part (his soul?), still remained inside his body, the instigator of the electrochemical messages that leapt from synapse to synapse each nanosecond within his brain.

*Lucky Ray*, Ake's detached consciousness thought. Ray feared for Ake because he knew that if the K'a-nii hurled him into a volcano, he would be killed. If only it were that simple.

Ake now knew that if the K'a-nii went through with the ritual of transformation, the part of him that was now only tenuously connected to his corporeal self would indeed be released from that peculiar symbiotic relationship between pure psychic energy and flesh and blood.

Unlike the K'a-nii, however, the core of his being, his unique essence, would not be the catalyst to propel him to a new and purer level of consciousness as it did the K'a-nii; instead, the separation of his two halves would leave him stranded between the planes of existence, a Flying Dutchman doomed for all eternity to seek the missing piece of his soul.

★ ★ ★

"Now I know we're not in Kansas anymore, Toto!" an awed Ray said when the massive creature that had risen to the surface of the water in response to Leonardo's summons slowly edged closer and closer to the river bank.

"Yeah," said Maria.

The creature was unlike anything Ray or Maria had ever seen. As it emerged from the languid and spent eddies of the river near the banks, the god of the river bed resembled nothing so much as some great, moss-backed mollusk, or perhaps a vast, crablike invertebrate. Since Ray could see no mouth or excretory parts, he guessed that they were located somewhere out of sight, probably on its underside.

Not surprisingly, the river god's great back resembled a portion of the river bed liberated from its usual location and brought up from the depths to face the cyclopean scrutiny of the burning sun. Here and there, fish trapped by the thing's precipitous ascent to the surface flopped miserably.

Whatever it may have been just moments before, no matter where it had come from, it now presented a more or less flat surface; it was a living raft.

Leonardo rose from his half-sitting, half-squatting position and clambered aboard as nonchalantly as a commuter boarding a null-grav taxi he'd just summoned. He rotated his head and jabbered at the others.

"He says, what are we waiting for?" Ray translated, not bothering to go through the comlink.

Maria looked at Ray and shrugged. "He's right, I guess. What *are* we waiting for if we want to get across the river?"

"We gonna ride on that thing?" asked Mama-san.

"We are unless you want to swim," Ray told her. "C'mon, Mama-san, climb on board. That goes for all of you—get a move on."

Grumbling and growling, but obeying Ray's urgings, the two teams scrambled onto the creature's glistening back. Hypatia wrinkled her black nose and said, "This thing smell like fish poop."

"Then the quicker we get on and get going, the quicker we can get off," Maria said.

"You're right," Ray agreed. He glanced at Leonardo and said, "Well, Huck honey, let's cast off 'fore the sheriff gets here."

# III

The dogs found another body about two kilometers from the river. The dead man was lying face down in the vegetation. "Ugh," Tajil said, his nose wrinkling in disgust. "He stink."

"That's for sure," Ray agreed. He carefully turned the corpse over with the toe of his boot, his rifle ready in case something nasty should emerge from underneath.

More fetid air rose from the man's bloated body. "Jesus!" Maria exclaimed, covering her nose and mouth with one hand and turning away quickly. The dead man's body was expanded by gases and his face, also swollen, was just about nonexistent, eaten away by swarming maggots and insects. Despite the bloating, he couldn't have been dead a really long time, Ray theorized, but he had no way of estimating the actual time of death.

"What killed him?" queried Marisol, looking on with interest.

Ray just shook his head slowly. "I have no idea." He looked around. "The jungle, I guess."

"Yah, that's as good an answer as any," Beowulf said, nodding his big shaggy head in agreement as a horde of treetop dwellers whooped and chattered noisily. "Sumptin' in the jungle killed him and it doan matter much what."

"Let's get out of here," said Maria. "This guy gives me the creeps."

"I agree," said Ray. "Besides, it'll be getting dark soon and we need to find a safe and secure place to spend the night."

The fire Ray and Maria built served several purposes. It allowed them to boil several liters of water to replenish the canteens, already low on rain water; it was a warning to Hephaestus's nocturnal predators to stay away; and, not least of all, it restored their psychological well-being.

If the fire posed any drawbacks, it was that it attracted an inordinate number of flying insects. Ray stopped to consider that. *What's an "inordinate number" of bugs when you're smack dab in the middle of a rain forest?* While the fire was quite efficient in drawing in unwanted airborne company, the ultrasonics that Ray and Maria wore to ward off their visitors seemed much less effective at night than they were during the day.

When Ray pointed this out to Maria, she said, "I think that's because we keep moving during the day. Heck, every bug within a kilometer must know we're here tonight."

Marisol, dozing by the fire, suddenly lifted her head and began searching the inky blackness of the night sky with her eyes, her half-dilated pupils well suited to catching what light there was.

"What is it, Marisol?" Maria asked after looking at the sky herself and seeing nothing.

"Not sure. I hear somethin', though."

"Me too," piped in Hypatia.

"And me," said Sibella. Penelope just yawned and did not condescend to join the chorus.

Ray looked at Beowulf—who said, "Yes, I hear it, Ray." Littlejohn nodded his agreement; whatever it was, it seemed too high-pitched for Maria and Ray to hear it, but not so for the animals.

Ray stood up, hands on hips, and peered futilely into the pitch blackness. Suddenly, he felt a faint gust of air cool the perspiration-soaked hair that clung to the back of his skull. He thought that odd, since there was absolutely no breeze blowing on this stifling night.

"Geez!" erupted Frodo, looking beyond Ray. "Didja see that?"

"What?" asked Ray, gazing in Frodo's direction, his attention diverted from the sky.

"Somethin' big just fly over your head, Ray." Frodo no sooner spoke than a second large shadowy shape swooped within centimeters of Ray's head; everyone but Ray saw it.

"Uh, Ray," began Maria. "Sit down."

Ray did as Maria directed, now almost afraid to look up. When he did, he finally saw what everyone else was so impressed by. "Bats . . . ?"

The air was now filled by great-winged bats, swooping and diving low over the camp to harvest the vast number of insects drawn by the fire's seductively flickering flames.

Like most people's, Ray's aversion to bats was more emotional than rational, so he forced himself to understand that they were probably harmless. Indeed, by decimating the insect rally that had commenced around and above the campfire, the bats were doing them all a huge favor.

*Uh-huh!* Ray thought. Their utility didn't mean that he had to like their presence.

Ray threw his arms over his head and slunk down beside Beowulf and Tajil, as if the proximity of the two huge dogs would discourage the bats from tearing open the top of his skull. Such fears were groundless, of course, but the rational part of Ray's mind was powerless to override his emotional response to the bats—*Slimy, dirty blood-sucking rats with wings!*

Maria just sighed and sipped some water from her canteen. "Geez, Ray, what do you think? That they're gonna get trapped in your hair or something?"

"Sure," riposted Ray. "That's easy for you to say—you barely have hair now!"

Maria smiled sweetly and sipped her water.

As the fire died down, the flames giving way to glowing embers and coals, both the insect and bat presences decreased. Thus reassured, Ray took care of other business.

Maria watched with interest as Ray got out the comlink and asked the computer to access the tracking capabilities of the Programmers' ship to pinpoint first their own location and then the location of Lynch's party. With a totally inadequate map—but a map, nonetheless—spread across his knees, Ray's finger moved across the paper's two-dee surface as he attempted to estimate where Lynch and his people were at this moment.

"Well?" asked Maria.

Ray pointed to a coordinate on the map. "The computer says we're here, which is pretty much where we should be"—he gestured over his shoulder back the way they'd come—"with the river not that far behind us. The computer also says that Lynch's position is about here." He pointed to a spot on the map.

"That doesn't seem so far," Maria said, peering down at the place where Ray put his finger.

"Yeah . . . on the map," Ray told her. He pointed at the darkened and relatively quiescent rain forest. "Unfortunately, we have to go through a jungle, not cross a centimeter of paper."

"I realize that," Maria said. "You don't have to patronize me. I'm not one of your dogs, you know."

"Oh, you're no dog," Ray agreed. "You can be a bitch at times, though."

"You bastard!" Maria tried to slap him, swinging her hand in a roundhouse arc. Ray reached up and caught her arm just before the flat of her hand would have struck the side of his face.

As he held her arm, Maria's chest rose and fell and she stared angrily into his eyes. Ray stared back and gradually the looks that passed between them changed character. Ray let go of her arm, and she pulled it back slowly.

Maria seemed to be considering something. Then she pulled her top off, flinging it aside, leaned forward, and pressed her mouth to Ray's. They kissed long and hard, and Ray felt her breasts flatten against his chest, her nipples hardening with desire. They finally broke apart long enough to come up for air.

Rising to their knees, they wrapped their arms around each other and buried their faces into the nape of each other's neck. Ray's strong fingers massaged her back.

"It's about time," Maria whispered hoarsely.

"Well, I'm goin' into battle tomorrow and who knows if I'm comin' back," Ray said. "So tonight—"

Maria pulled away slightly so she could look into his eyes again. She placed a finger on his lips and tilted her head toward the tent.

"Shut up, Ray dear. Sometimes you just don't know when to stop talking."

# 17

Ray came fully awake the instant he heard the first of the awful screams coming from the darkened rain forest. Carefully disengaging Maria's entwining arms, he slipped out of the bed roll and got into his trousers and boots.

A sudden chorus of several even louder shrieks of terror and pain reverberated through the still night air, breaking through even Maria's indifference to the conscious world. As she cracked open an eye, Beowulf was at the flap of the small tent calling, "Ray? Ray?"

"Yes, Beowulf," Ray replied, closing the fasteners on his boots. "I heard them."

"What is it?" Maria asked, still sleepy and slow. "It's not any of the dogs or cats, is it?"

"No. It's Lynch or his men; it has to be." Ray reached over and pulled open a flap. Beowulf stuck his big shaggy head inside.

"'Lo, Ray."

"Hello, Beowulf."

"That's not necessarily true, you know," the dog said.

"What's not?"

"What you said about other mens. Could be monkeys or birds—there lots of things in this jungle can make sounds like beople."

"You're right. But this time I think it was 'beople'" Ray said, gently kidding Beowulf's pronunciation. He picked up his energy rifle and checked the charge. Then he found an electric torch and said, "Let's go."

"You're not going out there?" asked Maria.

"What gives you that idea?" replied Ray. "I got dressed and picked up a torch and my gun because I'm staying here with you. *Of course* I'm going out there—I have to know who or what made that godawful racket."

"Whoever made those sounds is probably dead by now."

"Or is terribly wounded and needs to be put out of his misery," Ray said, hefting his rifle meaningfully.

Maria thought about that for a moment. "You better get going, then," she said finally. When he turned to duck down and go out through the tent flap, she added, "Be careful out there, short drink."

"I will."

Outside the tent, Ray told Beowulf to bring Littlejohn, Frodo, and Tajil. "How 'bout me?" asked Penelope.

"Okay," Ray agreed. "Jump on Frodo's back."

When Leonardo materialized out of the darkness—no one really knew where he went at night—Ray asked him if he wished to accompany them. Ray had a ulterior motive for asking the question: If Leonardo was unwilling to tag along, the K'a-nii's reluctance might make Ray reconsider calling off this hastily conceived nocturnal jaunt.

But that was not to be. "Gezsss," Leonardo said.

"All right, then," Ray replied, trapped by his own bravado.

"Wonder if'n it gonna rain," said Tajil.

"Rain?" puzzled Ray. "What makes you ask if it's going to rain, Taddy?"

"'Cause of all the lightning I seen out this way."

Ray glanced at Tajil and scratched his head. "Lightning . . . ?" Then a look of comprehension crossed his face. "I think the lightning bolts you saw, Taddy, were flashes from energy rifles."

"Oh."

The yellow-white light from Ray's torch and their deliberately noisy approach spooked everything in their path. Ray could hear small—and not so small—animals moving away from them through the vegetation. "Beowulf, don't get ahead of my torch beam," Ray ordered. "We don't know what's out and about at night."

"Yah, yah," said Beowulf impatiently.

"See how they listen to me?" Ray said conversationally to Leonardo, speaking English. "It's my voice of command."

Penelope, riding Frodo's back like a Siamese cowpoke, laughed a sly feline laugh and said, "Talkin' to him, Ray, is like talkin' to a suitcase."

Leonardo twisted his head to look at Penelope and said, clearly and distinctly, "Pussface."

Ray felt a tingle of electricity run up his spine, and Penelope arched her back involuntarily and grimaced to show her teeth. "Ouch," said Frodo as Penelope dug her claws into his back.

"Leonardo, you never fail to amaze me," Ray said softly.

"Gezsss."

"Listen, I hear something," Frodo said.

They all heard it—loud crunching and snapping noises. "That's an animal chewing bones," Penelope said, certain she recognized the sound. "At least one; mebbe more."

The torch's beam cut through the foggy near-morning air like an impossibly attenuated light saber from an old sinny—an apt description since Ray held the cylinder out in front of him as if it were a weapon and not mere illumination.

"Look," said Tajil.

The light bounced back from a half-dozen pairs of highly reflective eyes aimed in their direction. At sixty meters that was all Ray could see, so he and the dogs advanced cautiously toward whatever creatures the eyes belonged to.

Beowulf's fur began to rise in ragged clumps. "Yeah, I hear it, too," Ray said, referring to the low growling coming from the bone crunchers.

The light from the torch now revealed the source of the warning growls: fox-faced predators tearing at the bodies of four dead humans. "Looks like we found more of Lynch's men," Ray said, playing the light over the savaged bodies.

"These guys kill 'em?" asked Tajil.

"I'll put that question to Leonardo," said Ray, switching over to the sibilant K'a-niian language. He didn't bother to take the comlink out.

"Qaz," replied Leonardo.

"If you don't already know," said Ray, "that means no."

"He wasn't here—how he know?" asked Littlejohn.

"This is his home," said Ray. "Besides, I think it's fairly obvious that these guys are scavengers. I'm sure they can kill small or wounded animals, but nothing the size of a human."

"'Sides," said Beowulf, "we know they used guns 'cause Taddy saw the lightnin'."

"Yeah," Ray agreed. "Guns would have handled these beasties pretty readily. Whatever killed Lynch's men had to be something else."

"Sumptin' pretty big and tough if'n energy rifles dint kill it or them," said Frodo.

"Let's get closer," Ray said.

As they approached, the fox-faced scavengers stopped pulling and tearing at the flesh remaining on the bones and rose to their full height.

Tajil, for one, was astonished. "Geez, lookit those animals! They's on stilts!" The scavengers' legs did indeed end in one-meter-long sections that were stiltlike in their appearance.

Angry at being approached, the fox-faced animals stomped about on their stilt legs, growling and snapping at the intruders—all things intended to intimidate anyone presenting a threat to them. But when Ray and the dogs had none of it, the scavengers had no recourse but to slink away, their free meal over for the night.

Ray's small band approached the half-devoured remains. "Anything about these dead guys strike you as odd?" Ray asked.

Beowulf looked at the tracks. "They come from where we's goin'," he observed.

"Correct," Ray said. "That means they must have deserted the main party."

"Yah," agreed Beowulf. "But why?"

"That we may never know," Ray said as he stooped to pick up one of the men's energy rifles. He checked its charge—it was low, almost depleted. He threw the gun back down again.

"We go back now?" asked Frodo.

Ray looked at the sky, growing brighter by the minute. "Yeah, it'll be daylight soon and we've got to make good time on the road today."

Before they returned to camp, Ray had an idea. He got out the comlink, took its cover off, and removed the small chip that powered it and put it away. "Why you do that?" asked Beowulf.

"If Lynch is still using his comlink, he's probably starting to wonder how and why it still works so far from the mining site," Ray said. "He's no dummy. Sooner or later he'll suspect something like what we've done with the Programmers rerouting the signals, even though he doesn't know about the ship. If he figures out that *we* can locate *him*, then he'll also realize that *he* can locate *us*."

"Oh," said Beowulf.

"We have a pretty good idea where he is, and I'm getting better and better at Leonardo's language, so I see no point in letting Lynch know our position."

"Maria not gonna like you disablin' the comlink," cautioned Beowulf.

"What Maria doesn't know won't hurt her."

★ ★ ★

Maria thought it odd that they hadn't experienced more (or any, for that matter) confrontations with Hephaestus's larger animals—the counterparts to Terran grizzly bears, Amundsen snow creatures, and Chiron hidecats.

When she mentioned this to Ray, he just laughed and gestured in a circle around them. "Here's your answer—nine pretty good-sized dogs, five cats, and three two-legged folks with weapons. Wild animals aren't stupid, and they usually aren't confrontational unless surprised or provoked." Again indicating the dogs, he added, "In this heat, we're all a little ripe, but the dogs especially. Our alien scents and our noisy progress through the bush trumpet our coming; it's a wonder we see any wildlife at all."

"I guess you're right," Maria conceded. She patted the energy rifle slung across her back. "I'll still keep old faithful handy, though."

"Hey, I didn't say we're trooping through New London's Wells Gardens, either. It's always a good idea to be prepared."

"It's funny you mentioned our odor," Maria said, wrinkling her nose like a rabbit.

"I don't think it's funny at all," replied Ray. He attempted to mimic Maria's nose-wrinkling, but quit when he realized that all he was doing was bunching his features in the middle of his face.

"No, I didn't mean ha-ha funny, I meant it's kind of appropriate that that's how I'm now able to sense the rubies—I can smell them."

"You *smell* them?"

"Not literally, of course," Maria said. "But it's sort of the same thing; I just do it with my mind instead of my nose."

"Uh-huh," said Ray dubiously.

"Look, turkey, I can psychically 'smell' the rubies, and that's no shit!" Maria was half only playing at being angry and half actually steamed at Ray. "The important thing is that I'm starting to get an overwhelming sense of their presence. They're close now, damned close."

Ray glanced at Leonardo, who'd come back from his foraging ahead to stand silently by while they argued. "If anyone knows where the rubies are, assuming there really is a treasure cave, it ought to be old Leonardo here," Ray said.

"So what's the harm in asking him?" queried Maria.

"Famous last words," said Ray. Still, he turned to Leonardo and asked, "Saazzah Dorusssi essahass?"

"Gezsss."

"See," said Maria triumphantly.

But Leonardo didn't stop there. He unleashed a torrent of sibilant syllables and tongue-flicking hisses. Ray just nodded grimly as the K'a-nii native spoke.

When he finished, Maria asked, "What was that all about?"

Ray whistled for the dogs to come to him. As he unslung his energy rifle to check its charge, he said, "Leonardo had a special reason for reporting back to us: The soft skins are coming this way."

## ||

As the prisoners made their way through the rain forest's thick undergrowth, they did so with a mixture of caution and haste. They were eager to get back to their comrades at the mining site, but they also realized that they had to be on constant guard against the dangers of the jungle, which had claimed too many of them already.

Among the things that had quickly become second nature to them was the ubiquitous, droning presence of Hephaestus's voracious mosquitoes and other stinging or biting insects. So, when first one man and then another slapped at his neck, no one paid any attention to what was an everyday occurrence.

It was only when the men began to weave drunkenly that the others began to suspect that anything might be wrong. But even then their unfamiliarity with the rain forest's denizens made them think that their buddies were the victims of a new and deadly stinger, nothing more.

These judgments were, in fact, not altogether in error—the lethal sting that struck down first one and then several others was something that the criminals were ignorant of, never having seen a K'a-nii hunt treetop dwellers with its blow gun.

By the time the tired, sweaty, and grimy men realized that something was amiss, it was too late. They had walked into an ambush.

Having positioned himself on one side of the horseshoe-shaped trap, Ray carefully targeted the tall and brawny man carrying the 50mm semiautomatic slug thrower. Ray took a breath, held it, and pressed the firing stud on his energy rifle. The bolt struck the man in the chest and he fell to the ground like a poleaxed steer.

(*Now,*) Ray said, and Maria fired less than a second after his shot had felled the first of the criminals. Maria's shot burned the face off a thin blond man unlucky enough to stand out from the others because of his height and coloring; his distinctive silhouette condemned him to death.

The barrel of Ray's rifle swung back and forth as he picked targets of opportunity, squeezing off death in small packages. His thoughts were jumbled now as adrenaline pumped into his system, readying his body for possible injury, but he was thinking clearly enough to ask himself, *Where's Lynch?*

Although he had never set eyes on the leader of the criminals, Ray knew what he looked like—or at least he thought he did. He was looking for a big man with a beard—could Lynch have used a depilatory cream? Could he have been one of the dead men they'd stumbled over along the trail? With no time to pursue such questions, Ray pushed them to the back of his mind and focused his attention on the here and now.

Two of the men whirled and began to run back in the direction from which they had come. Their escape was thwarted by Littlejohn and Frodo, who burst from their hiding places in the vegetation and were on the men before they even had time to scream.

When Ray had laid out the plan of the ambush, he had first considered ordering the two dogs sealing off the escape routes to the rear to keep silent so that they would not betray their presence to the others. He had revised his thinking on the situation when he realized that the dogs' barking was an important psychological component of their effectiveness against human beings.

Simply put, the dogs' barking scared people shitless.

Maria's and Ray's initial victims were those men who kept their heads and attempted to fight back. Ray was intent upon cutting down all those actively resisting; by raising his rifle, a prisoner made himself one of Ray's principal targets, someone to be taken out immediately. If one of the escaped criminals tried to flee in fear or stood rooted to the spot, then the barrel of Ray's weapon moved on.

It was not easy for the disoriented and fearful criminals to keep their heads. While not fighters like the dogs, the cats managed to contribute to the battle by projecting images of death, destruction, and doom into the minds of the terrified convicts.

One man aimed his rifle at Ozma and was about to fire when he sensed something cold and slimy slithering up his trouser leg. His lifelong terror of snakes finally coming to fruition, the ophiophobic man screamed and attempted to shoot the snake he could feel entwining itself around his thigh. That sensation had been no less "real" than the pain he now felt from his self-inflicted wound.

Several panicked criminals attempted to burst through the closed end of the ambush loop drawn around them only to confront the powerful jaws of Beowulf and Mama-san. The other dogs encircling the criminals would suddenly appear from the jungle as if by sorcery, seize a victim, and drag him screaming back into the concealing vegetation before he or any of his comrades knew what hit him.

To Ray it seemed to last for hours; it was actually over in less than seventy seconds.

"They all dead?" asked Beowulf.

"I doan sense any of them," said Bastet, her tail lashing the air.

"Yes, they're all dead," said Maria tonelessly. As ruthless as she was, the young woman had found this savage slaughter to be dehumanizing. She had pumped bolt after bolt of energy into trapped and panicked men as casually as if she were killing vermin. And as nasty as the escaped criminals were, they were more than vermin; they were men.

Ray glanced at Maria's downcast face, sensing her pain. "The rubies are boosting my powers," he said. "I can share the anguish you feel over this."

She looked at him with brimming eyes. "It's not just that we killed them all," she explained in a halting voice. "It's that we planned it that way without even realizing it."

"What Maria mean, Ray?" asked Grendel.

Ray was about to attempt an answer when Leonardo, who was standing nearby as if eavesdropping, put away his blow gun, coughed as if he had something in his throat, and then spoke. "No prisoners," Leonardo said clearly and distinctly. The words came from Leonardo, but the voice was Ake's. Leonardo turned on his heel and went forward to take up the point again.

"Jeezus," said Ray softly. Then he told the dogs, "Leonardo—or Ake—was right. It might be fatal for us to try to take prisoners in this green hell. It's hard enough keeping ourselves alive as it is." He stared at the rifle in his hands as if he'd never seen it before. "Ah, shit!" he said finally. "Let's go search the bodies for rubies and then get the hell out of here. It stinks of death."

## III

Leonardo came back, jumping up and down, twirling around, gnashing his teeth, and otherwise making a fool of himself.

"Yeah, yeah, we know," said Ray wearily. They didn't need Leonardo to tell them that the cave was just ahead. They sensed—felt, heard, and *smelled*—the rubies.

"Ohmygod! Not again!" groaned Maria. She doubled over, and retched—or at least, her body tried to. Maria and the cats had been throwing up periodically ever since they got within a kilometer of the cave. The psychic emanations from the rubies were so strong they overwhelmed the sensitive young woman and her cats. Ray hadn't thrown up yet, though the way he felt he thought he might like to. His discomfort took the form of a massive, skull-bursting headache. His teeth ached and his eyes watered.

As they approached a vast depression in the ground, a sinkhole, Ray retained enough clarity of thought to wonder why he couldn't see vermilion shafts of light lancing up from the rubies like searchlights piercing a hazy night—that's how powerful the energy the rubies were emitting seemed to him.

Leonardo, having ceased his acrobatics, stood silently by, watching.

"Ray," gasped Maria.

"Yes?" he asked, knowing what she was about to say.

"I . . ." Maria gagged. She wiped the drool from her mouth and continued. "Ray, I can't go on. I'm sorry, but I can't get any closer."

Ray looked at the cats and decided that they were in the same sorry state as Maria. He made up his mind. "You don't have to go any further, Maria. As a matter of fact, I was just going to suggest that Frodo, Mama-san, Gawain, Sinbad, Ozma, and Grendel escort you and your team a klick or two away from this place."

"Not me!" protested Hypatia.

Ray looked down at the Siamese. She was exhibiting some of the same symptoms as Maria, but she still appeared to be less ill than the other cats. Ray dearly wanted to have her along, since she had shared his most important discoveries about the K'a-nii.

"All right," he said finally. "But only if you feel up to it." He reached down, scooped up the cat, and put her on his shoulder. "Like old times, eh?"

"Why we gots to go back with Maria and the cats?" asked Frodo.

"To keep them from harm while they're in this condition," Ray told the big dog, scratching him behind one floppy ear. "They're just pussfaces, aren't they? They need the protection of one of the best scout teams in the galaxy, don't they?"

"The *best* scout team," said Frodo—just as Ray knew he would.

"Ray . . ." began Maria.

"I know," Ray said simply. "Now, go. Get out of here."

Hopping up and down, Leonardo watched them leave. "Maria," he hissed.

"You're getting pretty good at that," observed Ray. "Maybe your people will make you the first K'a-niian ambassador to the Terran Federation."

Leonardo just stared at him, his expression unreadable. "It was just a thought," Ray said.

Beowulf, Littlejohn, and Tajil looked at him expectantly. "I guess it's up to us now, guys," Ray said.

"How you feel?" Beowulf asked.

"Remember the first corpse we found on the trail?"

"Yah."

"I feel worse."

Despite himself, Beowulf started to chuckle, his sides heaving as his deep, rumbling laugh came tumbling out.

When the other two dogs joined in, Ray said, "Hey, that's—ha, ha, ha—that's not funny!" He burst out laughing so hard he wrapped his arm around himself and tilted his head back.

"Soft skins," said Leonardo disdainfully. Then he pointed toward the sinkhole and said something in K'a-niian.

"What he say?" queried Beowulf.

"He can't go any further until the blasphemous intruder is removed," Ray translated.

"Alive or dead?" asked Littlejohn.

Ray asked Leonardo, listened to his terse reply, then said, "It doesn't matter."

"Good."

"Lookit!" whispered Beowulf excitedly, staring at the semicircular opening in the ground. "That's the cave." It looked deceptively benign.

"Oh, I hope so," Ray said, putting a finger to his left nostril and feeling something wet.

"Hey, you bleedin'!" noted Littlejohn, concern in his voice.

"Yeah," Ray replied. "The rubies are close. They're blasting my brains out with their power." He put his hand up to his shoulder and rubbed Hypatia's chest. "How you doing, mouse breath?"

"I been better, but I'll live," the cat said in her precise, little voice.

"Let's get closer," suggested Beowulf.

"Good idea."

As they approached the mouth of the cave, the fur on the dogs' backs began to rise. Tajil's lip curled back into an involuntary snarl and Hypatia dug her claws into Ray's shoulder. He was actually grateful for that; it took his mind off the supernova inside his brain. Ray eased the safety on his energy rifle to the off position, and patted the pistol tucked into his trousers to reassure himself.

"Larkin!" came a voice from inside the cave. It sounded far away. "Larkin! Answer me! Is that you, Larkin?"

Ray shrugged. What could it hurt? "Yeah, it's me, Lynch. That is, I presume I *am* speaking to Waldo Lynch."

"I used to be."

Ray swallowed hard. "You . . . used to be? Who are you now?"

"Come inside and find out."

"Ray, you can't go in there," Beowulf said urgently.

"I've got no choice," Ray replied.

"Then roll a grenade in first," the big dog suggested.

Ray gasped and clutched his head. For a moment, the flow of blood from his left nostril increased. "That's not an option," he finally blurted out when the pain subsided enough for him to speak. "The . . . ah . . . rubies might be . . . would be . . . damaged by any explosion." He looked at the rifle he'd let slip to the ground, picked it up again, and added, "Even using this is dicey; I can't injure the rubies."

"How can you injure rubies?" asked Tajil.

"You'd be surprised," said Ray. He daubed at the bright red blood trickling down to his lip. "Fuck a duck, I'm leaking ketchup by the liter!"

"I don't think the energy rifle will harm the rubies if'n Ray is careful," said Hypatia. "We know fire won't destroy them, either."

Ray really *didn't* want to destroy any of the rubies if he could help it. He realized their religious and symbolic importance to the K'a-nii—and guessed at their practical significance as well. Still, he could only glance wistfully at the *verboten* grenades. If only he could use them. Then he brightened . . . who said he couldn't use them, after all?

"Hey, Larkin—you comin' in or what?" Lynch's distant voice echoed.

"I doan like the sound of his voice," whined Tajil. "He doan sound human."

"I'm beginning to get the idea that he isn't—not anymore," Ray said as he acted to do something with his inspiration.

"Oh."

"Stay here," Ray ordered the three dogs.

"But, Ray—" protested Beowulf.

"I know, I know," Ray said wearily. "But I gotta do this myself." He twisted and looked into Hypatia's blue eyes. "That is, Hypatia and I have to do this ourselves."

"You need dogs, not a cat," snapped Littlejohn.

"No," said Ray, moving toward the cave's entrance. "I need a miracle."

# 18

Ray stopped behind an outcropping of rock just inside the entrance to allow his eyes to adjust to the gloom. Hypatia guessed why he had halted and said, (*I can be your eyes, Ray.*)

(*I know,*) he said. (*Actually, I don't need eyes at all, do I? I can sense Lynch lurking further inside. I can smell his hate and his fear,*) he told Hypatia. (*I can almost taste him.*)

"Why'd you stop, Larkin?" Lynch's voice boomed. Ray wasn't playing that game anymore and refused to respond. "Oh, that's what you're up to now, eh? Gonna give me the cold shoulder so I can't pinpoint where your voice is coming from."

Lynch laughed and Ray felt a spasm of fear twist his guts. "You don't get the picture, do you? I don't need to know where you are, Larkin. I don't fuckin' *care* where you are! Sooner or later, you got to come to me. I got your lizard friends right here beside me."

(*He's got a point,*) Ray said to Hypatia.
(*Then why is he afraid of you?*) the cat asked.
(*He is?*)
(*Yes.*)
(*Hot damn, maybe I have a chance after all!*) Ray said.

Ray had about ten seconds to think along those comforting lines before his now-adjusted eyes detected something moving further inside the cave. (*What is that?*) Ray asked Hypatia. (*You've got much better vision in the dark than I have.*)

(*Do you really wish to know?*)

Ray clutched his rifle for reassurance. (*Jeezus, is it that bad?*)

(*I think it was a spider.*)

(*You think?*)

(*It was a spider—prob'ly not a real spider, but that's what it looked like.*)

(*How big is it?*)

(*'Bout a meter from tip of one leg to another.*)

(*I'm sorry I asked.*)

"Hey, dog fucker," Lynch shouted. "What're you doin? Didja see my new friends?"

Instead of responding, Ray recalibrated his rifle to emit a tight, short burst of coherent radiation. When he detected that same slight movement again, he aimed his rifle and fired.

Something shrieked, its howls of pain sounding like a cross between the dogs' yelps when he accidentally stepped on their tails and the high-pitched screech of an Enders Planet hawk.

It also sounded pissed.

Hidden by the cave's darkness, the spiderlike thing disappeared in a blur of rapid movement as it scurried out of sight around a slight downsloping bend.

(*Ray, it—*)

(*Yeah. That nasty S.O.B. hasn't got much of a mind,*) Ray told the cat (*But I can read what little it's got.*)

Ray prepared himself and the spider thing did exactly what its tiny mind "broadcast" that it was going to do. As ready as he believed himself to be, Ray was nonetheless caught a little off-guard by the speed of the nine-legged thing's attack.

Once it was out of Ray's sight, the spider had climbed to the cave's ceiling and rapidly rushed back toward him, intending to drop on its unsuspecting prey from overhead while Ray stared at the spot where it had disappeared. Even with the advantage of being able to read its mind, Ray was shocked at how quickly the spider executed its maneuvers. He barely had time to point the energy rifle straight up and fire, almost reflexively. The little squib of energy caught the spider directly in the center of its thorax and blew the arachnidlike thing's pulpy body apart.

"Yuck!" Ray exclaimed as spider gunk rained down on him.

Hearing Ray's voice, Lynch congratulated him. "Very good, Larkin, very good. It sounds as if you made short work of one of my nine-legged friends. Now there's only fifty or sixty of them left."

# K-9 CORPS: UNDER FIRE

Even as Ray gulped, Hypatia told him, (*He's lying—hoping to scare you.*)

(*He's not doing such a bad job.*)

(*Let's find out what this bogeyman looks like,*) Hypatia said. (*What you can't see is more frightening than what you can see.*)

As Ray moved slowly and carefully down the cave's mouth, Hypatia balancing carefully atop his shoulder, he noted a faint glow. (*Hey, it's getting light.*)

As they entered the cave proper, they could see that the rubies were glowing. (*They never did that before,*) Hypatia said.

(*We never saw this many together before, either,*) Ray said. (*Maybe it's a synergistic reaction.*) He took shelter behind a large stone. At least he thought it was a stone; when he touched it, he brushed away a layer of dust. It was an immense ruby. It was flawed and therefore could never be used by starship ESPers, but it was a ruby all the same.

Even when light levels are low or inadequate, the human eye is very good at detecting movement, no matter how slight. Ray's eyes picked up swirls of activity at various locations throughout the cavern. More spider-things.

(*I think you're right,*) Ray admitted to Hypatia. (*Can't be more than eight or nine of them. We'll walk right through those babies as if they were holo projections.*) Ray paused, wetting his suddenly dry lips with his tongue. (*And by the way,*) he added, (*Tell Maria and the dogs I want a simple, nondenominational service. And not too many flowers—they make me sneeze.*)

Ignoring Ray's babblings, Hypatia said—aloud now that there was little more to be gained by remaining silent— "He's up there, up on that ledge, surrounded by those spiders and holding his two K'a-nii hostages. Can't you feel him?"

"Yeah, I feel him." Ray spat blood. His gums were bleeding. "I don't like it, but I feel him." Ray cocked his head at an odd angle; in addition to feeling Lynch, he heard a low, almost inaudible, moaning.

"You and that pussy-lovin' bitch must be pretty good," Lynch said, almost conversationally. "You were bound to run into my men as they tried to get back. You're here and they're not—which pretty much tells the story, I guess—but how'd you do it, how'd you get them before they got you?"

"How do you think, asshole? We're a team—a scout dog team. If we couldn't handle a pack of scum like your dickless wonders, we'd be a piss-poor bunch of fighters."

"Ah, sweet vanity," laughed Lynch. "Yeah, you probably are pretty good, but didn't you wonder about how few they were?"

"It crossed my mind. So?"

"The rest of them stayed here—with me."

"Bullshit! If that's the case, where are they?"

"Look above you and you'll see my loyal and trusty compatriots."

Ray did as Lynch directed. Nothing. All he could see were white cocoonlike masses that looked like bloated stomachs hanging from the roof of the cavern. It was only when he felt Hypatia's grip on him tighten that he realized what they were. They were also the source of the low moaning.

"Jeezuss!" Ray hissed, horrified.

"No, no Jesus for them," Lynch said cheerfully. "No Jesus for my very own Judas Iscariots, willing to betray me for the sake of a few gemstones." He laughed then, a cackling out-of-control laugh that sent chills up Ray's spine. "I hope my new and more trustworthy companions devour them before they die of starvation. I wouldn't want to see them suffer too much; I'm not a vindictive guy. 'Course, some of them have been impregnated with spider eggs; they'll feed the young when they're born."

Ray didn't wait to hear more. He brought the energy rifle up in one fluid motion and fired at the first target of opportunity. The rifle's short, deadly pulses fried a spider thing in its tracks. Without waiting to see what his antagonists would do, Ray leapt to his feet and ran further into the cave, skillfully working his way through the maze of watermelon-sized rubies like a champion barrel racer at a rodeo.

"On your left!" Hypatia shouted. Without looking or aiming, Ray pointed the energy rifle at the far wall and fired. The arachnid death cry was all he needed to know his aim was true. Ray stopped, crouched down behind a boulder, and then leaned out and fired straight ahead. The sizzle and pop of a spider's body announced the accuracy of his aim.

"Hey, how you doin' that?" asked Hypatia.

"The rubies," grunted Ray. "Man, do they give you the juice!" He laughed. "Give me the Hylof ESPer Potentiality Test now and I'd make the damn machine blow itself up!"

"I can really sense the spiders, too," Hypatia said. "But it's harder for me to get a fix on them than it was with the diggers—they're too close. They—"

Hypatia screamed as a spider she only sensed at the last instant appeared out of nowhere to seize her by her leg and begin dragging her away. Not able to risk using the rifle, Ray pulled the pistol from his belt and lunged for the spider thing as it backed away with its prize held between its fangs. He felt his right hand close on something wiry and bristly. It was like grabbing hold of a wire hairbrush.

"Gotcha," he shouted triumphantly. With his left hand he shoved the pistol against the spider's head and fired. The squib of energy burned a tight, circular hole in the front of the spider-thing's head, but it came out the back in a shower of blood and chocolate-syrup fluid.

The dead spider's legs collapsed and it relaxed its hold on Hypatia. Ray let go of the spider's leg, rolled over on his back, and blew the head off a spider rappelling down a silken cord from the roof of the cavern to drop on him.

"Wow!" said a shaken but still game Hypatia.

"There's more," said Ray, putting down the pistol and scooping up his rifle. He sat up, twisted to the left and fired, then twisted to the right and fired. Two more spider-things died instantaneous deaths.

(*Are you okay?*) Ray asked.

(*I'll live,*) Hypatia said, stopping her licking of the spot on her leg where the spider had seized her.

"Ohmygod, I'm hurt! The pain!" shrieked Ray, winking at Hypatia. He put the rifle to his shoulder and waited, his cheek resting on the cool stock.

Lynch leaned over the outcropping of rock where he was and risked a quick downward glance. Ray squeezed the firing stud and the squib of energy just grazed Lynch's cheek, the white-hot bolt burning a thin line in the flesh like a branding iron laid against the skin. Now it was Lynch's turn to shriek as he pulled back from the edge; unlike Ray, however, his pain was real.

"Damn!" cursed Ray. "I blew it; I had him dead to rights and I missed him!"

"Doesn't sound to me like you missed him."

"I missed *killing* the bastard," Ray said to the nitpicking cat.

"You lousy sonofabitch!" screamed Lynch. "I'll teach you to trick me like that!"

Not sure what Lynch intended, Ray readied his rifle.

"Oh, no," said Hypatia when she saw what Lynch was doing.

"How 'bout this, big shot?" asked Lynch, dangling one of the captive K'a-nii over the outcropping of rock. The K'a-nii was bound and gagged and seemed unwilling or incapable of offering any resistance. "If you try anything like that again, I'll drop this sucker on his fuckin' head."

"Let's talk," said Ray. "What do you want?"

"Put down your weapons where I can see them—both of them, the rifle *and* the pistol."

"Then what?"

"Then you come up here alone."

"And why should I do that?"

" 'Cause I'm gonna pitch these two leatherfaces to their dooms if you don't." He cackled. "I ain't no fuckin' ESPer, but the rubies is talkin' to me, too. I know you need these two alive if you want to save your friend."

"If I come up there, you'll kill me," Ray said reasonably. "If you do that, how can I save my friend, then?"

"I won't kill you, I swear it."

(*He's telling the truth,*) Hypatia said. (*At least as far as it goes.*) Ray saw where she looked: at one of the cocoons hanging like an obscenely bloated stalactite.

(*Yeah, I know.*)

"Well, gosh, Waldo, if you swear it, that's good enough for me." He got up, went out into the open, and put down the rifle and the pistol. "There you go, buddy."

"Now come up here."

It was only a five- or six-meter climb up to the ledge where Lynch was holding his two K'a-niian hostages, and Ray scaled the rocks easily. He paused at the top, allowing Lynch time to back away nervously, his hand holding a leveled energy pistol. Ray looked around, not failing to observe a few dried bloodstains clinging to the rocks and rubies.

The rubies. The little alcove Lynch had secreted himself in was filled with the most stunning collection of Rostoff rubies that Ray could imagine. The cave must have held thousands of rubies, but these were the cream of the crop; these were the perfect specimens. With what was in here a man could buy enough raw power to rule the galaxy. And what was in here was almost enough to fry Ray's brain to a crisp; he sniffed—his nose was beginning to bleed again. He also felt a trickle escape from his ear.

But if it was the rubies that first caught Ray's attention, it was Lynch's appearance that made him gape like a hick at a robot porno show. "If you don't mind the question," Ray said conversationally, "just what the hell has happened to you?"

Lynch's clothes were in tatters, his skin showing through. It was his flesh—and his face—that made Ray stare.

Lynch looked at his bare arms proudly. Ray looked also, noting the barest hint of scales—and black, bristly hairs. "I'm becoming a child of the rubies," Lynch told Ray.

"You're becoming a . . . a K'a-nii?"

Lynch smiled, and Ray could see that his teeth had mostly fallen out. "Yes . . . and no," Lynch said. "You saw my brothers of the web, the guardians of the treasure? Well, I am combining the best of both—half K'a-nii and half spider."

Ray wondered if such a thing was really possible. The rubies, in such a concentration, obviously gave one special powers. It was possible that Lynch, undeniably madder than a March hare, was inducing these bizarre changes in his own body. Clearly, he no longer wanted the gems for their monetary value.

"You're a fuckin' nutcase," Ray observed mildly.

As Ray expected, Lynch just laughed at that. "You small-thinking jerk, I will have the power!"

"What power? To scare little kids and old ladies with your half-reptilian, half-arachnid kisser? You're making yourself into a freak—a really heavy-duty *grotesque* freak."

"You shouldn't talk to me like that," Lynch said, upset by the image Ray painted with his words.

"Good to see there's a little bit of sanity left somewhere inside that pea brain of yours," said Ray.

"I told you I wouldn't kill you," Lynch said. "And I always keep my promises. But I never said anything about these two." He pointed the energy pistol at one of the two.

While Lynch was thus distracted for a moment, Ray pulled something from inside his shirt.

"Stop!" ordered Lynch. "What's that you're hiding?"

"This little thing?" Ray slowly opened his hand to reveal what he held there. "This is just an MF-40 grenade. They *do* make more powerful ones than this little feller," Ray conceded. "But he'll be enough to blow you and me and this whole cave to the center of this planet."

"But the rubies—"

"Are gonna be dust," Ray finished.

The energy pistol fell from Lynch's hand. "No, please don't."

"Now it's please, eh?" said Ray. He pressed down on the grenade with his thumb and then released the light pressure he'd applied. A tiny pin popped out and fell into the dust on the ledge.

"Oops," said Ray. "That was clumsy of me. Just five seconds to hell now."

"No!!" Lynch screamed like a wounded animal and hurled himself at Ray's feet, his fingers sweeping through the dirt and debris in search of the elusive pin. To Ray's amusement, he actually found it. Ray obligingly handed him the grenade.

Lynch fumbled with the pin and the tiny opening it had come out of, his fingers feeling fat and clumsy. He would never make it in time! He would never . . .

Suddenly he realized that more than five seconds had passed and nothing had happened. He looked at Ray, a puzzled expression on his face.

"Oh, I took the precaution of removing its explosive guts outside," Ray explained, his arm sweeping up powerfully from down around his knees. "The same time I put my bush knife in my boot."

Lynch's eyes opened wide in surprise and the blade of the knife entered under his rib cage and plunged up to its hilt in his chest. His sightless eyes still full of the wonder of his death, Lynch fell backwards, pulling himself off the blade.

Hypatia's sharp face poked up over the lip of the ledge. "What's goin' on up here?"

"Don't ask me, I just got here myself," Ray said, wiping the blade on Lynch's pants leg.

"He dead?" asked Hypatia, ever one for the obvious.

"Yep. I guess the rubies are gonna have to find a new child; maybe they can adopt." He quickly searched Lynch's tattered clothes until he found the piece of paper he was looking for. Then he strode over to the K'a-nii captives and cut them free, saying something to them in their language. If that surprised them, they didn't show it.

Ray returned the knife to its place in his boot and turned to Hypatia. "If you're up to the task of climbing back down, why don't you go get Beowulf and the others waiting outside?"

"Okay."

★ ★ ★

Once Ray had returned to the cave the rubies they'd taken from the ambushed prisoners, he piled up rocks and small boulders until he had a solid enough base to stand on. Extending his arms above his head, he carefully cut open one of the obscene spider cocoons.

One of Lynch's fellow prisoners and one-time follower of the dead madman was inside—and alive if unconscious.

As Ray pondered the best way to free the trapped man, he regained consciousness. "Don't move," Ray said. "I'll figure some way to get you out of there."

The man shook his head. "No. Please don't try." He winced in agony.

"But I can—"

Pain pulling his face taut, the man looked down at his abdomen; the skin stretched across it rippled like a blanket laid over a half-dozen active kittens. Ray looked at the undulating movement and realized what was causing it. "They've already hatched; they're eating me alive," the man said. "I'm already dead." One hand reached out and grabbed Ray's shirt, the grip powerful. "Don't let the fuckers finish it. Kill me now."

Ray turned away, as if to contemplate what to do next. Without the man seeing what he was doing, he slipped the pistol out of his waistband. He turned, put the gun to the man's forehead, and fired—all in one fluid motion. Then he contemplated the other eleven cocoons.

Hypatia had returned with the three dogs—just in time for Ray to send them away again. "Beowulf, Littlejohn, and Frodo, you three escort our guests outside," Ray told his dogs.

"What about me?" asked Hypatia.

Ray picked her up and placed her firmly atop Beowulf. There was no mistaking the firmness with which he performed the action; Hypatia didn't argue Ray's decision.

When the dogs had left, Ray wiped the blood from under his nostrils and put the energy rifle's stock to his shoulder. Picking his targets carefully, he pumped at least three short, intense bursts into each cocoon. Then he changed the weapon's setting. With the entombed humans now dead from his earlier fusillade, it took just eleven bolts of white-hot energy to cause the cocoons to burst into flame.

On his way out, he stopped and turned back, watching the cocoons burn, the infant spider things perishing in the flames. He reached up and thrust the paper he'd taken from Lynch into the flames until it began to burn. When the treasure map was almost fully engulfed, he dropped it onto the floor of the cave and watched it curl and blacken. He ground the remains into the dirt. Then he shouldered his rifle and exited.

## II

Maria got both Ray and Hypatia cleaned up when they returned from the cave. Hypatia required a little veterinary attention for the bite she had received from the spider; the poison in the arachnid's fangs was intended for native lifeforms and had only a modest neurological impact on the feline. Nonetheless, she needed several carefully measured injections to insure there would be no lasting effects.

Once the bleeding from his eyes, ears, and gums had stopped, Ray received several vitamin-loaded injections and crawled into the tent to lie down. He promptly "crashed" and didn't move a muscle for thirteen hours. Maria despaired of the passing time, but realized Ray was only following the urgent commands of his body; he needed a long, restorative rest. With nothing else to do, she slept too.

By midmorning of the third day, it was clear to Ray and Maria that they weren't going to return to the K'a-nii village in time.

Maria looked at the sun as it climbed high overhead, blessing Hephaestus with its life-giving energy. "We're not going to make it," she announced, glancing at the two K'a-nii they'd freed. "The ritual is supposed to be performed tomorrow afternoon."

Even though Ray knew she was right, he couldn't admit it; he couldn't give up hope. "It won't be easy, but maybe if we walk all night, if we keep going, we can do it."

"It gives me no pleasure to say this, believe me," Maria told him. "But saying that we can get back in time if we only try harder is bullshit—and you know it."

Ray sat down on a fallen tree. His long rest had restored his energy, but now he was slowly winding down again. "I know," he admitted. "I know that you're right." He rubbed his weary eyes with the heels of his palms, the pressure making fireworks spark and throw images against his retinas. "Christ, I'm bone tired, Maria. Aren't you? Even if there was enough time to do what I suggested, we're in no shape to even attempt it. If we try to walk through the night, we're gonna be zombies by dawn. It ain't in the cards—we're not getting back in time."

"The floaters . . . ?" Penelope asked tentatively.

"Nope, pusser. Leonardo is still adamant about them."

"How about Ake?" Maria asked.

Ray sighed. "I haven't had contact with Ake since on the way to the cave."

"Isn't there sumptin' we can do?" asked Beowulf, his tail hung low.

Ahead, a geyser erupted, sending scalding hot steam and water high into the air. Ray looked up, startled. "Sonofabitch," he murmured. "Sonofabitch!" he repeated, louder and with growing enthusiasm.

Maria, afraid to get her hopes up, cautiously asked, "What is it? What are you thinking?"

"Hephaestus is crawling with volcanoes," Ray said. "They're everywhere. Unless there's something special about the one where the K'a-nii village is, a volcano is a volcano is a volcano."

Mama-san looked puzzled. "What you talkin' 'bout, Ray?"

"These guys have a date with a volcano, right?"

"Right," agreed Maria.

"Unless it *has* to be that specific volcano, there's lots of them that fit the bill."

Maria now saw where Ray was headed. "But Ray, they can't just go up and jump into a volcano on their own accord, can they? I mean, there has to be a ritual ceremony. It takes nine K'a-nii."

"Does it?" Ray questioned. "Maybe all it takes is nine willing volunteers." He looked at the dogs and Leonardo. "I think we can come up with that many folks to help save Ake."

"That's another thing," Maria said. "What if you're right and we can do it? So what? Aren't they still going to sacrifice Ake and the colonel if we're not back in time to tell them that we've performed the ritual ourselves?"

"Let's ask Leonardo."

Ray suspected that the K'a-nii had understood much of the dialogue between himself and Maria. Whether that was true or not, Leonardo listened patiently as Ray translated his ideas into K'a-niian.

While Ray and Leonardo hissed and spit back and forth at each other, everyone else fidgeted impatiently. The dogs would lie down and then get up again and then turn away several times and lie down again. The cats groomed each other.

When Ray faced her with the first real smile on his face that she had seen there in a long time, Maria already knew the answer, but she let Ray tell her. "Leonardo says we *can* perform the ritual ourselves. As long as we show the proper respect for the ritual, and it *is* the 'growing up' time for the chosen ones, it is permitted."

"But what about Ake and Bukovsky? What about the surrogates' ritual? How will the villagers who have Ake know that we've performed the ritual ourselves?"

"I don't know," Ray said.

After observing this exchange, and perhaps understanding it, Leonardo said something else to Ray, all pops, hisses, and slick syllables. Maria saw the most sheepish expression break out on Ray's face as he listened to Leonardo's words.

"What? What'd he say?" she demanded.

"He said that the village will *know* that the ritual was performed. Don't ask me how, but they will know."

"That's not all he told you, though, is it?"

"He said if I want the other soft skins to know then I ought to speak to the voice that flies through the air and ask it to tell them what we're doing."

"The comlink!" Maria exclaimed. "Of course. Even if the K'a-nii couldn't know what we're about to do, we could get a message through via the comlink—maybe even have Leonardo himself confirm what we'd done!" Her face clouded. "But you told me the comlink wasn't working."

Ray shrugged, putting his hands out in front of himself, palms up. "A white lie. A little white lie."

"What are you talking about?" she demanded.

Beowulf grinned. "He disabled the comlink hisself. Ray dint want Lynch to get a fix on *us*."

"You bastard!" Maria said hotly.

"I can fix it," Ray said. "I just have to put back the chip I removed." When Maria continued to fume, he added, "Besides, I had an ulterior motive in not wanting a working comlink with me when I reached the cave."

"Yeah?" Maria asked dubiously.

"That cave is special. I didn't want the Programmers or anyone to get an accurate fix on its location." Ray grinned. "As a matter of fact, since Lynch and his men are lately deceased and dead men tell no tales, I'm starting to get the idea that the treasure cave of the K'a-nii was just a wild rumor that didn't pan out. I don't think there ever was such a place, do you?"

"No, I guess not." Maria looked at the cats. "You guys know about this cave?"

"No, Maria," they chorused.

"Then let's get our asses in gear," Ray said. "We've got a date with a volcano."

# 19

Ake greeted Ray and Maria by throwing his arms around both of them and hugging them to him. "Hot damn, it's good to see you two again."

"Ahem, ahem," coughed Beowulf politely.

"Sorry, Beowulf," laughed Ake. "It's good to see you all again."

Bastet nodded, endorsing Beowulf's demand for recognition. "That better. Nuthin' like being 'preciated."

"You both look well—despite being a lot leaner than I remember you."

"Tromping through a hot and humid rain forest while chowing down on that good, delicious irradiated food will do wonders for your figure," said Ray.

"Yeah, I noticed," replied Ake, taking in Maria's physique.

"Better be careful, Ake," warned Penelope. "Maria's boyfriend is watching."

"Penelope!" gasped Maria, coloring.

"*Vous?*" asked Ake, pointing at Ray.

Ray just smiled a cat-with-a-canary smile.

After shooting visual daggers at Penelope—the dogs and the other cats hooted—Maria explained, "Ray is a dear man. Out in the jungle what happened was . . . well, for a time there we needed each other." She put her hand on Ray's face, cupping one side of his visage. "Ray and I are both already in long-term relationships."

"Boy, go away for a little while and look what all you miss," marveled Ake.

"Go away!" said Ray. "Is that what you call it? Where were you?"

Ake shrugged helplessly. "Not far from here . . . I think. I'm not sure what happened to me while I was 'gone,'" he said, clearly putting verbal quotation marks around the word. "I believe that I was mostly in some kind of trance." He laughed uneasily. "Yeah, I know how stupid that must sound."

"Doesn't sound stupid to me at all," said Ray. "The more I find out about the K'a-nii, the more I discover how much I don't know. I'm not sure it's even possible for an outsider, an alien, to figure out them or their ways."

"You won't get any argument from me about that," Ake said. "But come on, fill me in on what's happened: with you, with the Programmers, with the convicts—what's the scoop?" Ray looked at Maria and dropped his head wearily.

"I think Ray's sending me a message," Maria told Ake.

"Yeah? What's the message?"

"He thinks we should get back to the compound, jump in the shower for about two hours, pour ourselves some stiff drinks, and then sit down and thrash all this out." She looked at Ray. "That about cover it?"

Ray made a circle with his thumb and index finger. "Perfect. Couldn't have said it better myself."

Ake sighed. "Okay. Let's put everything on hold until then."

"We goin' back now?" Gawain asked.

"Most egregiously so," said Ray, raising his arms to the heavens and shaking his hands. "Praise de Lawd, chillin, we's gwine home at last."

"Was that a yes?" Gawain asked Tajil.

★ ★ ★

Ray absentmindedly scratched Beowulf behind the ears as he leaned back in his cuddle chair and waited, along with everyone else, for the appearance of Thane Wyda. The meeting could not officially begin until she arrived to lead the discussion. The participants, who included Ake and Maria, were all sitting in one of the larger conference rooms inside the administration building. Most of the others, apart from Prime Programmers Mandela, Su, and Youanmi sitting ramrod stiff on straightback chairs, lounged comfortably on cuddle chairs.

Ray sipped a very dry Beefeater martini on the rocks with two olives and mused that conflicting ideologies manifested in the room might make for some heated discussion. There was Theo Kodlich, present to represent the Hephaestus Mining Syndicate; Colonel Natasha Bukovsky, representing the Federation military presence on Hephaestus; Tien Tsuji, the first engineer; and Sari Fodoor, there to speak for all the civilian personnel—her covert activities on behalf of the Revolution unknown to all but Thane Wyda and Ray and Maria. Ray was the unofficial spokesperson for the K'a-nii.

Looking slightly the worse for wear, Prime Programmer Thane Wyda made her entrance. "Please, no," she said, waving a hand when Sari Fodoor and several of the men—but neither Ray or Ake—made an effort to struggle to their feet out of the homey embrace of the cuddle chairs. Their show of respect was an attempt to recognize her supreme importance in the current situation, but Wyda saw it as mere officious obsequiousness. Wyda nonetheless took her seat at the locus of everyone's attention.

"Let's begin," Wyda said briskly, wasting no time in convening the meeting. "The *Pequod* has been repaired, and we can now safely undertake hyperspace jumps once we are out of the system."

"That's good news," Colonel Bukovsky said, and a number of people in the room looked at her as if she'd suddenly announced that she was leaving the military to join a Neo-Christian convent.

Thane Wyda smiled one of her rare smiles. "That brings us to my second order of business." Bukovsky rose and approached Wyda, and the two women embraced stiffly. There were several loud gasps of surprise. Their show of sisterhood concluded, the two women parted self-consciously and Bukovsky sat down again. Wyda then announced, "Natasha Bukovsky has decided to join the Revolution. She will be coming with us when take our leave of this wretched planet."

"Colonel Bukovsky . . . ?" Theo Kodlich asked in disbelief, his sensibilities unable to cope with this sudden revelation. Ray took a very large gulp of gin; Ake, on the other hand, seemed only mildly surprised by Wyda's words.

"I think an explanation is in order, Natasha," Wyda said, clearly relishing the bombshell she'd dropped on everyone.

All eyes turned expectantly toward Colonel Bukovsky. She cleared her throat and began by saying, "I wish to keep this short and simple." She looked at the others with a faint smile playing around her lips. "As most of you know, through the gossip and unceasing flow of rumors circulating through the base, I have not had the most distinguished career." When Kodlich made sounds of disavowal, Bukovsky fixed him with one of her patented stares and said, "Please, Theo, no more hypocrisy."

Kodlich colored, remembering the numerous times he'd gleefully recounted Bukovsky's blighted service record, and murmured, "Forgive me."

"I repeat," said Bukovsky. "I had not risen to the top in my profession—nor was I likely to even before the events of recent weeks. With the collapse of my command and the control of Hephaestus that Prime Programmer Wyda and her people have assumed, the prospects before me are grim indeed.

"Should my superiors not execute me immediately upon the landing in force upon this planet by Federation regulars and Cadre shock troops, then I face either a long period of imprisonment or—even worse—chemical-psychological 'rehabilitation.'

"I do not wish to think of myself as a turncoat," Bukovsky said sadly. "I am merely rejecting the Federation before it has a chance to reject me." She looked at Wyda, who returned her gaze with an unreadable one of her own. "You may not believe I possess many military skills, given the ease with which you took the prison and defeated my regulars—"

"It *wasn't* easy," said Ake loudly. There were a few murmurs of agreement.

"Thank you," said Bukovsky gratefully. "I humbly offer whatever such skills I may possess on behalf of the Revolution. It will feel good to fight for something I can believe in again."

She sat down to vigorous applause.

Wyda allowed a half-smile of satisfaction to cross her face. She had not only won, she had triumphed. Then she chided herself for thinking such thoughts; there would be no triumph until they were off this accursed planet and doing whatever they could to overthrow the corrupt Triumvirate.

"Prime Programmer Youanmi will now discuss the evacuation plans," Wyda announced. She looked at her colleague and asked, "We are to begin shuttling people up to the *Pequod* today, are we not?"

"That's correct, Prime Programmer Wyda," Youanmi responded. "All but a handful of mining engineers and other civilians are joining our cause—or at least leaving with us before the arrival of Cadre shock troops. Those who have elected to stay behind, especially those who continue to evince undiminished loyalty to the Triumvirate and the Federation, have been isolated and contact with them is now forbidden. The fewer opportunities they have to learn of our plans, the better our chances of evading eventual capture by Federation forces. When we leave, those remaining behind will be locked in a holding facility here inside the administration building, with access to plentiful food and water. After thirty-six hours, a timelock will release them. By that time, we will be halfway across the galaxy."

"Just where are we going?" Sari Fodoor asked.

"That information is available only on a need-to-know basis, so I'm afraid I must decline to answer your question." She shrugged. "I honestly don't know."

"Neither do I," interjected Wyda. "The ship's captain is determining the coordinates, the last of which will not be fed into the ship's computers until we leave the local system."

Programmer Youanmi had more to say, but having heard most of it before, Ray found himself dozing off despite his best efforts. It was only when Maria nudged him that he snapped back awake; Wyda was staring at him.

"Citizen Larkin has a few . . ." Wyda frowned. "Excuse me, old habits die hard. *Mister* Larkin has a few words to say about the native population, the K'a-nii. Mister Larkin?"

Ray got to his feet. "I have very few words to say indeed. Mostly, I want to inform you that the K'a-nii who live in the village nearest to this compound will be moving away, to a new village as far from here as they can get." He took a breath. "I realize—as do they—that this is no guarantee of protection from the Federation when it retakes Hephaestus. The Federation and the corporations who pull many of the strings need the Rostoff rubies; the mining will continue."

"What about these rumors about a K'a-nii cave full of fabulous treasure?" asked Chief Engineer Tsuji.

Ray shot him a look of carefully considered condescension, as if patiently hearing out the ravings of a lunatic. "There were a lot of wild and, frankly, quite unbelievable rumors about this supposed 'treasure cave,' " Ray responded. "But that's all they turned out to be—rumors and half-truths."

"There's nothing to the story of a vast storehouse of rubies, then?" Tsuji persisted.

*Bend over and we'll start a "vast storehouse" full of rubies right here and now*, Ray fumed. "No—nothing to it."

"Let's move on to other matters, shall we?" suggested Wyda in such a way that it was more an order than a question.

Ray sighed inaudibly and sat down. *Maria was right*, he thought. *She and the cats and I will have to put our heads together tonight, draw upon the energy of the rubies, and implant the idea in everyone's mind that this ruby business is all nonsense and best forgotten. By the morning, it will be like a dimly remembered dream; by the next day, it'll be gone forever.*

Wyda asked Ake to come to her makeshift command post after the meeting. When he showed up and the door hissed shut behind him, he asked, "What's this about, Prime Programmer Wyda?"

"Please—call me Thane," she said. "And have a seat."

Wyda couldn't have unnerved Ake more than with this uncharacteristic display of friendship and warmth. "Thanks," he said, sitting down. "What's this about?"

"I could not allow you to go on believing a falsehood," Wyda said.

"A falsehood?"

"Ake"—Wyda leaned forward across the desk—"you don't really have an explosive still implanted inside your body."

Ake's mouth opened. Then he shut it. "You . . . you mean that was a lie!"

"That's such a harsh word to use, Ake," Wyda replied. "Let's just say that for the good of the Order I had to have you completely on my side."

"I *was* on your side!"

Wyda nodded. "Yes, I know. My subterfuge probably wasn't necessary, but I had to be certain that I could trust you."

The shock and anger began to drain from Ake's face, to be replaced by sunnier expressions. "Hey, what am I yelling about?" he asked himself. "I should be happy—you've just told me that I'm not a walking time bomb!" His look of joy transmuted into one of calculation. "I wonder . . . ?"

"Yes?"

"I wonder if I should tell Ray right away. It'll be fun to allow him to continue sweating this out."

"I see now why your partnership works," Wyda said with a straight face. "You are the 'grownup' in the relationship."

"Huh?"

## 11

"Get it!" shouted Beowulf.

"I tryin'," panted Frodo.

The rabbitlike thing, aided by its long hind legs, was doing an excellent job of evading the dogs' jaws. At times, it would seem that one of the canines was about to overtake it and sink his or her teeth into its rear, only to have the wily little fuzzy thing do a 180-degree flip in midair and reverse direction. Then the pursuer would skid to a halt and vainly try to get back in the chase.

"That was close," deadpanned Penelope, lazing on a branch and observing the dogs' idea of fun—playing hunter and huntee.

"Yeah," yawned Marisol. "You almost got that one."

No matter. Soon the dogs would pick up the scent of another inhabitant of the rain forest and the chase would begin all over again.

"I got it this time," Mama-san said, closing in on a green-furred little beastie. Just as Mama-san was about to win the chase and claim the prize, the little fuzzball took off like it had ramjets in its behind.

Mama-san skidded to a halt. "Sumbitch!" she howled in frustration. "Those little guys can move!"

Meanwhile, Sinbad, Ozma, and Gawain were trying to dig down into the hole they'd seen something round and fat scurry down when they approached. Sinbad whined and dug furiously, his paws a blur as the dirt flew behind him like wood chips from a buzzsaw.

"Slow down, he ain't goin' anywhere . . . if'n he still in there, that is," said Ozma. "You ain't batient enuff for this kinda thing."

"I's gettin' tired watchin' all this stuff," complained Bastet. "Where these guys get all the energy?"

"Ha!" said Penelope. "You ever see them eat? If yah did, you wouldn't have to ask."

The cats were doing a good job of mocking the dogs' predatory instincts when a fluffy little ball of feathers settled on the same branch as Sibella. The proximity of the tiny bird was too much for Sibella to ignore. Her pupils grew fat with interest and she flattened herself on the branch, laying back her ears. She gathered herself and sprang. There was a flurry of fluttering and squawking and then the cat examined her prize.

"Hey, look," said Frodo, "the bussfaces finally got somethin'."

"Yah," agreed Mama-san. "Good for them."

As Ray, Ake, and Maria approached the half-empty village, the dogs and cats ranging far and wide around them, Ake said, "I suppose we'll never know exactly just what the rubies are, will we? I mean, I threw my out-of-body experiences into the pot, but we still don't have enough material to figure everything out."

"No, we don't," conceded Ray. "But that's fine as far as I'm concerned."

"Whoa!" exclaimed Ake. "Since when have you been so blasé about not getting to the bottom of a mystery?"

"Since I encountered this one," Ray said.

When he noticed Maria looking at the ground, figuratively biting her lip, Ake asked, "What do you have to say about Ray's reluctance to penetrate this enigma, Maria?"

She glanced at Ray—who looked away. "Ray doesn't want to probe too deeply into the K'a-nii secrets, Ake, because—" She glanced at Ray, who looked away. "Because he's afraid."

Ake just laughed at that . . . until he not only saw that she was serious but also saw the look on Ray's face. "She's not joking, is she?"

"No," Ray said. "I'm not exactly the most religious guy in the universe," he explained. "And the supernatural, or the unexplainable, has to jump up and bite me on the ass before I'll put any stock in it."

"Yeah?"

"Shit, Ake—it's jumping up and biting me on the ass!" He wiped beads of perspiration from his face. "If I probe any deeper, I'm gonna find things out," he said. "Things I don't think I want to know; scary things."

"Ignorance is bliss, eh?" asked Ake.

"In this case, for me, yes."

"And that's it?"

"All right, look," began Ray. "The K'a-nii and the rubies are somehow linked. The rubies *aren't* the remains of the K'a-nii who are thrown into the volcano. I mean, look, the rubies are mined. There's no doubt that they exist before the K'a-nii take their big leap.

"I *do* have a lot of theories. One of them goes that the other-dimensional K'a-nii—those ghosts, or whatever they are, released by the volcano ritual—provide the rubies special energy and power. But do they really?" He threw up his hands. "That's just *one* theory; I got a hundred more and a hundred variations on each of those. And that's as far as I want to go with it at this point."

"I'm kinda curious about the other end," said Maria.

"Huh?"

"The villagers . . . the 'adult' K'a-nii . . . where do they come from?"

"That's one mystery that could probably be solved rather quickly and mundanely if one had the time and the resources to stay and study the K'a-nii," Ray allowed. "But with the Federation sending its bully boys here . . ." His voice trailed away.

"So we're never gonna know everything?" Ake asked.

Ray shook his head. "What this incident tells me is that the universe is weirder than we ever imagined; weirder than we *can* imagine. So, no, we're never gonna know *everything*—and I, for one, am glad."


As Ray, Maria, and Ake watched the last few K'a-nii in the village leaving, one of them stopped, turned, and came back to where they stood.

"It's Leonardo," Maria said, as the native approached.

Leonardo stopped in front of Maria and put his face very close to hers, so close that he panicked her a bit by intruding into her personal space. Hardly breathing, Maria patiently allowed Leonardo to scrutinize her. Satisfied that he had seen whatever it was he was looking for, Leonardo moved on to Ake and did the same thing. Ake stared back, uncomfortable but unwilling to reveal his discomfort since Maria had braved it out.

Finally, Leonardo stopped in front of Ray. Before the K'a-nii could repeat his performance, Ray put his own face close to Leonardo's and stared. After a minute or so, longer than his close inspection of the other two, Leonardo pulled back.

"They don't have holographs," Maria said. "Maybe he's memorizing our faces; maybe that's what they do when they say goodbye to someone."

As if to show his appreciation for their submitting to his ritual, Leonardo flapped his arms against his torso and made a high-pitched whistling sound.

"I'm gonna miss you, Leonardo," Ray told the K'a-nii. "You're priceless."

"Ray," Leonardo said simply.

"Take care of yourself, scaly skin." Ray took Leonardo's hand in his and shook it. "That's a soft skins' ritual for saying goodbye," Ray told him.

Maria nudged Ake. "C'mon," she told him. "Let's go see what kind of trouble my cats and your dogs are getting into." Ake nodded and they left Ray and Leonardo together.

Leonardo watched them go with his usual blank or unreadable expression. Then he did something that shocked Ray as much as anything he'd done so far. He smiled. Or, rather, he tried to force his face into the same human expression.

The gesture moved Ray and he felt a lump in his throat. He smiled back.

Leonardo held something out. Ray looked at it, but made no effort to take it. It was a small leather pouch. "For me?" he asked.

"Gezsss."

"Shit, Leonardo, I don't have anything to give you," Ray complained.

"You gave soul-life," Leonardo said in flawless Federation-standard English. "Thank you." He looked at the pouch he'd handed to Ray and added, "Not cave." He turned on his heel and strode away, swaying from side to side in that gait peculiar to the reptilian natives.

Ray opened the rawhide strings that closed the pouch and looked inside. "Leonardo, wait."

The K'a-nii kept walking and disappeared into the rain forest.

# III

Ray punched up the hol-vee in the dogs' cabin and watched Hephaestus slowly, almost imperceptibly, dwindling in size. It was yet another world they were saying goodbye to. "Goodbye, Leonardo," Ray said softly. "Take care of yourself."

"Where we goin'?" Beowulf asked Ray. Except for Littlejohn, Ozma, and Tajil, the other dogs were sleeping.

"I don't know," Ray admitted. "They haven't told us yet."

"Oh."

"Does it matter?"

"No, guess not," admitted Beowulf. "Not as long as we together."

"Yah!" seconded Littlejohn.

"Hey!" said Tajil, "Your nose bleedin' again, Ray!"

Ray touched a finger to his nostrils. "So it is, so it is."

Beowulf got a confused look on his face. "We not on ruby planet no more, Ray—how come your nose bleed?"

Ray reached inside his shirt and pulled out the little leather pouch that Leonardo had given him; he had tied it around his neck for safekeeping. "Guess I'm gonna have to do something else with this," he said, hefting it thoughtfully in one hand.

Daubing at his nose with a handkerchief, Ray asked Beowulf, "Is that little carry-all thing you sometimes wear around *your* neck around here someplace?"

"Yah, in there," Beowulf said, pointing at one of the cases with his big shaggy head.

Ray got it out and fastened it around Beowulf's thick neck. "This is about as safe and secure a place as I can imagine for what's in this pouch," he told the dogs.

"What *is* in the pouch?" asked Littlejohn.

Ray showed the four dogs.

"Golly Geez!"

The pouch contained approximately thirty ball-bearing-sized rubies. Ray stuck his hand inside and pulled a palmful out and stared at them. He could feel the energy in them; but it was a different kind from the energy emitted by the rubies in the cave. That was as it should be, Ray noted, since Leonardo had told him that they weren't from the cave.

The dogs had an imprecise idea of the value of money, but even they realized that the rubies represented a fortune. "Them's enough to buy—" began Littlejohn.

"Yes," agreed Ray.

"You didn't let Littlejohn finish," said Ozma. "How you know what he was going to say?"

"I got the power, remember?" Ray said. "Actually, I didn't know. It's just that this pouch is enough to buy just about anything that's for sale."

Ozma gulped and stared at the rubies glowing red in Ray's hand. "We really rich?" she asked.

"We're disgustingly rich," agreed Ray. "We can do just about anything we want to with this much money—if the Federation doesn't get us." He looked around at the loyal dog-faces staring into his. "Any ideas what we should do?"

"Yah," said Beowulf.

"Oh, what?" asked Ray, his curiosity piqued.

"Get a new 'signment—a really tough one!"

"Yah!" said Tajil, excitedly. "That be fun!!"

Ray laughed, long and hard. Finally, wiping his eyes, he said, "Damn, I love you guys."

"We love you, too, Ray."

After Ray had left, Beowulf and Littlejohn got everyone up.

"What the heck goin' on?" asked a sleepy-eyed Frodo.

"We goin' to say the Law," Littlejohn told him.

"Now?"

"Yah, now."

When the eight other dogs had formed a rough circle around him, Beowulf began.

"What is the Law?" intoned Beowulf.

*"To place duty above self, honor above life."*

"What is the Law?"

*"To allow harm to come to no Man, to protect Man and his possessions."*

"What is the Law?"

*"To stand by Man's side—as dogs will always stand. Together, Man and dog."*

"Good," said Beowulf.